TABLE OF CONTENTS

AUTHORS NOTE

Thank you for deciding to start this cosmic journey with the Unbreakable Egg trilogy in one book. Originally a straightforward story about a community devastated by natural disaster, it has evolved into an investigation of the fundamental fabric of reality itself.

Follow Kavin, Dr Meena, Nnenna, Dr. Chen, Ravi, Gopal, and Elder Murali from the modest streets of Kurinji to the far reaches of the multiverse. I hope you will find yourself wondering about the nature of life, the harmony between science and spirituality, and the limitless possibilities that each of us carries.

Writing the unbreakable egg has been a journey of discovery. Like our Kurinji heroes, I found myself straying into unexplored creative territory and grappling with ideas that challenged my preconceptions about what narrative could accomplish.

Fictionally inspired by the vast revisions of quantum physics, philosophy, and the ageless human search for knowledge of our position in the universe, this story is most importantly about decision-making, friendship, and facing global uncertainties.

As you are opening the first chapter, I ask you to take adventurous and cosmic amazement with you. See the world with new eyes, challenge the nature of reality, and keep in mind that every decision you take affects the multiverse in ways we could never completely understand.

Once again, I appreciate you joining in this amazing trip to Kurinji. Your imagination and open mind to the unknown will make this adventure worthy of it all.

Until our next meeting, thank you for reading…

P.S. Watch the stars; you never know when the next unbreakable egg may show up on your road!

The Trilogy Characters:

Each of these characters played a role in the unfolding drama, contributing their unique skills, perspectives, and responsibilities to the overall story of the Unbreakable Egg trilogy.

Kavin Ogbonna: *Initially a young Kurinji village boy leader, evolved into a cosmic guardian and leader of the Kurinji cosmic explorers' team.*

Dr. Meena Modi: *Kurinji's local Veterinarian and historian who later gave way to Dr Chen in the cosmic journey.*

Dr. Amelia Chen: *A scientist invited to lead scientific research and analysis of the unbreakable egg throughout the cosmic journey.*

Ravi Thorarinsson: *Initially a farmer, becomes part of the core team in cosmic adventures.*

Gopal Green: *Initially a young, curious boy. Grows into a key member of the Kurinji heroes' team, often providing fresh perspectives.*

Elder Murali Iweka: *Wise village elder, provides guidance and ancient knowledge throughout the journey.*

Nnenna Jackson: *Joins later, possesses strong empathic abilities. Becomes crucial in understanding emotional aspects of cosmic phenomena.*

Elder Rodrigo Ogbonna: *Kavin's late father, former village elder.*

Priyanka Angelo: *One of Kavin's childhood friend.*

Samantha Asuka: *Elderly Kurinji villager with knowledge of local history.*

Mrs. Misozi Gwen: *Kurinji Museum long term volunteer, helps introduce guests to Kurinji's history.*

Mrs. Nguyen Ki: *Bakery owner represents the local Kurinji community.*

Dr. Vargas Hermiz: *Initially part of Dr. Chen's team, later becomes an antagonist.*

Professor Sophia Dickson: *Member of the scientific team studying cosmic phenomena.*

Dr. Pedro Chavez: *Another member of the scientific research team.*

Professor Mendhi Mohammed: *Contributes to the scientific research efforts.*

Professor Chukwudi Ekwueme: *Part of the team studying the multiversal phenomena.*

Dr. Anita Bolaji: *Scientist involved in the unbreakable egg cosmic research.*

Santos Kovacic: *Leader of a group attempting to steal the unbreakable cosmic egg.*

Mr. Frays Toletti: *Leader of a secret organization dealing in stolen artifacts around the Newcastle shire region.*

Sanjay Voon: *A mysterious healer/psychic from Matomara, involved in the unbreakable egg theft.*

Detective Asante Ebenezer: *Leader of the local vigilante organization protecting Kurinji.*

Edafe Manson: *Second-in-command of the vigilante group.*

Zarah Aliko: *Leader of the Stellar Ascendancy movement.*

Professor Abraham Tua: *Quantum physicist from the pacific studying the unbreakable cosmic egg.*

El Rufai Giwa: *African spiritual leader offering perspective on the unbreakable egg's role.*

The Trilogy Locations:

Each of these locations played a crucial role in the story, serving as the backdrop for key events, discoveries, and transformations throughout the Unbreakable Egg trilogy.

Kurinji:

The main setting of the story

Discovery of the unbreakable cosmic egg location

Site of the earthquake that triggers the adventure

Location of the Kurinji National Museum

Establishment of the Kurinji Centre for Harmonious Evolution

Later, home to the Kurinji Institute for Multiversal Studies

Newcastle Hills Shire:

The broader region containing Kurinji

Affected by the cosmic changes initiated in Kurinji

Kurinji National Museum:

Original home of the golden globe key

Destroyed in the earthquake

Later rebuilt and becomes a center for cosmic artifacts

Ravi Thorarinsson's Farm:

Site where the unbreakable ostrich egg (containing the cosmic egg) is found

Location of early investigations into the unbreakable egg's nature

Holy Crocodile River:

Sacred water body in Kurinji's land

Site of important events related to the unbreakable cosmic egg and crocodiles

Kurinji Town Square:

Central gathering place for community meetings and events

Location of many important discussions and decisions

Quantum Crucible:

A metaphysical space where the laws of reality can be reshaped

Site of major confrontations with the Shadow of Entropy

Bioluminescent Network:

A global energy network that develops, connecting all of Earth

Asthar Star System:

Site of a critical mission to prevent the collapse of a star

Matomara:

Neighbouring town in the Newcastle Hills Shire region, home to Sanjay Voon

Ajuorun:

Another neighbouring town in the Newcastle Hills Shire region, mentioned in historical context

Bale and Ugando:

Other neighbouring towns in the Newcastle Hills Shire area

Temporal Museum:

Temporary facility housing artifacts after the destruction of the original museum

Quantum Meditation Room:

Location where characters explore their enhanced cosmic awareness

Harmonic Resonance Chamber:

Facility for studying and manipulating cosmic energies

Multiversal Cartography Center:

Location for mapping and studying the structure of the multiverse

Cosmic Interface Nexus (CIN):

Facility housing the device for interacting with higher realms of existence

Kurinji Institute for Multiversal Studies:

Educational institution founded at the end of the trilogy

Site for teaching new generations about cosmic responsibilities

Quantum Botany Lab:

Research facility studying plants existing in multiple realities simultaneously

Multiversal Ethics Committee Headquarters:

Location where guidelines for ethical multiversal interaction are developed

BOOK I

COSMIC AWAKENING

Prologue

Within the Newcastle Hills Shire area is the ancient village of Kurinji, where the strands of history, mystery, and the human spirit entwine to form a tapestry of unmatched beauty and resilience. For millennia, this remote paradise has been evidence of the resiliency of its inhabitants, their lives tightly entwined with the pulse of the earth. Over time, the voices of ancestors resound, revealing mysteries buried deep under the ground.

Kurinji is not a typical village. Benevolent on its surface, underneath it simmers a power older than memory, one that has moulded the fate of its people for millennia. The golden globe key, a relic of immense significance lost in the aftermath of a cataclysmic earthquake, is at the core of its power; it left only shards of mythology and whispered predictions.

Four improbable heroes find their lives unexpectedly entwined as the wheel of destiny starts to revolve once again. Dr. Meena, a respected historian and veterinarian from the hamlet, finds herself at the intersection of history and the present, working to solve old riddles and guide her people forward. The very ground under Ravi's feet will give him strength; he is a modest farmer with hands smeared with dirt and a heart the size of the fields he manages. Young Gopal, full of questions and an uncompromising moral compass, will show us how even the tiniest among us could change the path of fate. Once again, Kavin will bear the responsibility of leading his tribe through turbulent waters.

Taken together, they will set out on a voyage beyond the known world. They will go through challenges that test not just their physical stamina but also the fundamental fabric of their beliefs. Deeper into the core of Kurinji's secrets, they will come to see that the depths of the human soul hold the actual key to opening the secrets of the universe, rather than any outside relic.

Their search will span millennia, integrating current understanding with ancient wisdom. Their town's comfort will give way to a realm of wonder and peril, where the boundaries between science and mysticism blur and the nature of reality itself becomes a question. The inhabitants of Kurinji will learn through their hardships and successes that the magic they yearn for—resilience, wisdom, and the pure human spirit—has always been inside them.

Dawn breaking over Kurinji prepares an epic story, coloring the heavens in shades of gold and red. The air thrums with expectation, as if the whole universe were holding its breath. In this little community, a narrative is going to develop that will test our knowledge of life, investigate the limitless possibilities of the human mind, and finally expose that the most important secrets of all lies in the uncharted areas of our own hearts rather than in the stars above.

The story of Kurinji and its inhabitants transcends a simple adventure narrative. This journey into the very core of what it means to be human explores our hopes, worries, and abilities for development and change. The golden globe key is a call not only to the people of Kurinji, but also to all those who dare to go within themselves and unleash the many opportunities latent in every human spirit as they await rediscovery.

This starts a narrative spanning millennia, beyond frontiers, and right at the centre of human existence. Those brave enough to start this epic journey of self-discovery and cosmic illumination will reveal Kurinji's secrets—and maybe the cosmos itself.

Welcome to Kurinji, where the journey within is the greatest adventure of all, and every step forward leads into the future.

Chapter 1

Little Paradise

Tucked away in the Newcastle Hills Shire, the old town of Kurinji holds great emotional appeal for many. While residents treasure it as their hereditary legacy, visitors flock to marvel at its beauty; neighbours see it as a peaceful refuge. While outsiders spread stories of a little, desolate ghost town, archaeologists treasure Kurinji as a wonderful creation of nature.

Kurinji appeals mostly because of its abundance of attractions. Travelers from all over come to the Kurinji National Museum, a treasure trove of history, as well as the Kurinji Zoo Planets, home to some of the most cherished creatures. Both residents and visitors will find a peaceful haven in the town's magnificent scenery and calm waterways.

Rich in history, Kurinji shows the marks of prehistoric warfare waged during the Stone Age utilising their popular antique armoury equipment; some of those tools are said to have been locked with the ancient golden globe key in the Kurinji National Museum. Seeking to claim their territory and establish supremacy, the native tribes of Kurinji emerged triumphant in many fights against the bigger surrounding villages of Bale, Ajuorun, Matomara, and Ugando in the Newcastle Hills shire areas. The crocodiles living in their river creeks were crucial in defending the Kurinji people, according to legend; they tore apart enemy boats trying to cross over to Kurinji and hauled the invading warriors to their watery doom. The people of Kurinji still cherish crocodiles and carefully guard their lives as if they were their own.

The morning light had barely reached the hills around Kurinji when Kavin Ogbonna, the son of the late elder Rodrigo Ogbonna, found himself before the village elders in the village town hall meeting, his heart thumping with a mix of exhilaration and fear. At just twenty-five years old, he was younger than anyone who dared to challenge the village's outdated traditions, yet his proposal carried significant weight.

"Respected elders," Kavin said, his voice calm despite his anxiety. "I am here today with ideas for our future. If we are to thrive, we must adapt to the rapidly changing world outside our village.

Elder Murali leans forward, his aged face marked with years of knowledge. Young Kavin, how would you suggest we handle this situation? Our methods have kept us going for decades.

Breathing deeply, Kavin felt the whole council staring at him. He thought his late father was a rigid conservative who had always opposed change like most of the elders of Kurinji. However, he also recalled what his mother had whispered to him on her deathbed: "The future belongs to those who are brave enough to shape it."

"I propose that we establish a learning centre," Kavin said, his voice growing increasingly assertive with each syllable. "Where our kids may learn the sciences and technology of the outside world in addition to our customs, we may welcome fresh information while also honouring our legacy. Right now, Technology is engulfing the planet.

A whisper ran through the assembly. Kavin observed that some of the expressions were filled with uncertainty, while others were clearly disapproving. Among them, however, was Elder Murali, who appeared intrigued. As the head of the Kurinji elder's council, Elder Murali had never heard of such a recommendation in his entire tenure.

While the argument continued, Kavin's attention was drawn to the antique golden globe key, which was kept in the local museum and drew many visitors. Its secrets had always captivated him, and he spent many hours reading the old books describing its ability to release the antique village armor used in past conflicts. How may he balance his urge to respect his village's customs with his insatiable curiosity about science?

Priyanka Angelo, Kavin's buddy from childhood, walked up to him later that day across the town square. "I heard about your proposal," she remarked, her eyes glittering with enthusiasm. "It's about time someone advocated development!"

Though he was grateful for her support, Kavin couldn't get rid of the picture of disappointment on some of the elderly people's faces. "It won't be easy," he acknowledged. "Change never just occurs."

Kavin felt himself pulled once again to the museum as the sun started to drop and long shadows stretched over the community. He felt the usual tug of curiosity as he stood before the golden globe key stand in the museum's protected treasures area, its surface glittering with an ethereal brightness.

"What secrets do you hold?" he said, reaching out to feel the keys' smooth glass surface. "And how might I access them without violating everything my people value?"

Kavin silently vowed in that moment, as the last of the sunlight danced through the museum windows. He would discover a means to close the distance between the earthly obligations that anchored him and the mysteries calling to him, between tradition and development. Regardless of the challenges that lie ahead, he will approach them with compassion and bravery.

The following day, the historic village of Kurinji was golden as the sun rose over the verdant hills in the Newcastle Hills Shire area. The air smelled like jasmine and freshly made sweets as vibrant flags danced in the light wind. This was the day of the yearly Kurinji Heritage Festival, which celebrated the community's rich past and aspirations for the present.

Kavin, a young man with focused eyes and a natural grin, stood in the middle of the town square, a notebook in hand, as proceedings are going on smoothly, assigning volunteers and reviewing last-minute minute. He instructed a group of neighbourhood volunteers to set up the scientific display next to the traditional crafts. crafts. "We have invited well-known local historian and veterinarian Dr. Meena as a guest speaker to show the link between our past and present."

As he worked, villagers surrounded him with inquiries and concerns. Kavin listened carefully, providing answers and comfort based on a confidence that belied his years. Elder Murali nodded graciously in the shadow of an old Banyan tree. "That boy," he said to himself, "has the makings of a real leader; I like his courage."

The festival grounds were a vivid tapestry, combining old and modern. Traditional dancers prepared their costumes right next to a display of the latest farming innovations. Centuries-old recipes combine with the metallic smell of modern devices. The Kurinji National Museum, with its timeworn stones and antique relics attesting to the village's continuing vitality, was at the centre of it all.

Kavin sees an old lady clutching an elegant locket as the festival preparations wind down, and Samantha lives two blocks away. He gets to her: Kavin enquires: "Samantha, that locket is very lovely. Does it qualify as an heirloom?

Samantha: (smiling) "Exactly, young Kav. There have been seven generations of lockets in my family. It saved the life of my historic great-grandfather during one of the historic floods."

Opening the locket, she finds a small, complex mechanism.

Samantha said, "According to legend, the Sacred Crocodiles blessed it." People believe that when a threat approaches, it becomes warmer. The museum safeguards the essence of our community, just like this locket shields our family."

As the morning went on, a crowd gathered around a small platform where local product Dr. Meena and other guest speakers were getting ready to speak. Her eyes gleamed with enthusiasm as she set up her visual aids—a strange combination of modern holographic displays and historic objects. "Welcoming, everyone!" Dr. Meena's voice floated over the area. "Today, I want to walk you around the scientific legacy of Kurinji. Though tiny, our town has been very important in helping us see the natural world."

The audience listened raptly as she spun stories of ancient astronomers and new farming methods. But none gripped them more than Little Gopal, whose wide-open amazement absorbed every word.

Gopal's hand sprang upward instantly as Dr. Meena stopped to ask questions. "dr. Meena! Are there really objects at the museum that nobody knows about? Like, actual puzzles?"
The audience burst into laughter, but Dr. Meena smiled politely. "Well, Gopal, discovering secrets is the essence of science. Indeed, there are objects in our museum that continue to captivate us. For instance, "...

Activities disrupted her path near the museum entrance. Arriving quickly, Kavin saw a group of captivated people gathered around a recently put-on show in the middle. Right in the middle was a holographic projection of this weird, spherical item.
"It's the golden globe key!" someone shouted. "I thought it was just a myth, hidden and locked under the division of protected artifacts!"

Turning to Dr. Meena, who had trailed behind him, Kavin's confusion was clear in his voice. He questioned, "What's this about?"

Before she could respond, Elder Murali's voice emerged over the din of the audience. "Ah, we decided to highlight the golden globe key as part of our exhibit at this year's festival," he continued, his worn-out face wrinkling into a grin. "Maybe it's time I told the real story of Kurinji's guardian spirit."

As Elder Murali started his story, the audience became still.

"Long ago," Elder Murali said, his voice in a regular cadence, "when Kurinji was simply a handful of huts in this valley, our people lived in peace with the earth and its wildlife." Among them were the revered crocodiles living in our rivers and streams."
Children and adults alike lean in to enthral the older man with his remarks.

"These crocodiles were not typical animals," Murali said. "They were the Kurinji guardians, blessed by the spirits of our ancestors." In times of peace, they kept our rivers clean and our fish plentiful. But they were ferocious defenders when danger loomed.

Gopal's eyes' width increased. He murmured enthusiastically to Kavin, "Did they fight bad guys?" then softly shushed him.

"During the legendary struggle of the Stone Age," Murali said, "it was the holy crocodiles that reversed the tide when the adjacent tribes of Ajuorun, Matomara, Bale, and Ugando tried to capture our territory. To preserve Kurinji's independence, they wrecked the invaders' boats and hauled fighters to watery deaths.

There was a whisper of pride among the audience. Even Dr. Meena bowed politely, appreciating this cultural legacy.

"But the crocodiles were more than just guardians," Murali remarked, his voice lowering to an almost whisper. "They were once the guardians of Kurinji's best secret—the golden globe key."
The audience remained silent, waiting for each syllable.

According to legend, the smartest and oldest crocodiles ate the key to security during one of an ancient tribe's invasions. During Kurinji's worst hour, when the need was highest, the descendant of the holy crocodile deposited the keys, exposing the secret to our forebears.

Elder Murali's eyes roamed the assembly, resting momentarily on the crucial holographic display. Some thought the key may open the fundamental fabric of reality itself. "But as the centuries passed, many disregarded the tale as simple folklore."

Dr. Meena moved forward; her scientific interest was piqued. "Elder Murali, are you suggesting that this 'key'"—she indicated to the hologram—"is more than just a historical artefact?"

When Gopal found the key, he said, "Great crocodiles! Dr. Meena, do you think we might use it to unlock the mysteries of the universe and global heroes?
Dr. Meena laughed, "One step at a time, Gopal." First, let us explore the

secrets of Kurinji.

Murali grinned eerily. "Science and folklore can entwine in ways we least expected," Dr. Meena said. Maybe the moment has come for Kurinji to rediscover the wisdom of our holy protectors."

As the elder's words faded, a strange silence descended on the gathering. For a split second, the entire air felt electrified with possibilities. Looking around, Kavin saw on the faces of his fellow people a combination of astonishment and doubt. Something historic was coming, and he couldn't shake it.

A low rumbling sounded in the distance from the stream's direction, as if in reaction to the elder's story. The people exchanged tense looks. Was that anything more than the sound of water currents over rocks?

As the celebration went on, they were unaware that the golden globe key and holy crocodiles would materialise in their generation. Under the direction of the ancient knowledge of its reptile guardians, Kurinji's destiny would soon lie in the hands of an odd collection of heroes.

Chapter 2

School Excursion

Excited pupils from Kurinji Community College gathered around Mrs. Misozi, a long-term volunteer at the museum, their eyes bright with expectation as the early light created long shadows over the courtyard of the old Kurinji National Museum. On the outing, a very young Gopal was among the students.

The chilly, silent air in the museum smelled faintly of polished wood and ancient paper. Their quiet footsteps blended with the subdued murmuring of other guests as they passed through the hallways. Under the well-placed lighting, the glass cases shone, with each artifact creating complex shadows that appeared to dance with time.

Mrs. Misozi called the children closer together with her kind smile and soft manner.

"Welcome to the Kurinji National Museum," she said, sounding rather reverent. "This building chronicles our people from ancient times to the present."

Mrs. Misozi guided the group towards the door, and the kids bent their heads to appreciate the unusual building design of the museum. With its base and lower levels built from worn stone that spoke of millennia past, and its top levels showcasing elegant lines and large glass panels reflecting the surrounding hills, the building gently combined old and modern.

Gopal stumbles in his enthusiasm as Mrs. Misozi walks the kids past an exhibition of beautiful ceramics. His hand inches away from a precious vase. The little one's gasp. Mrs. Misozi saves him in the final moments, averting disaster.

Mrs. Misozi, gasping, "Careful, Gopal! These objects cannot be replaced.

Gopal, with a wide-eyed apology, said, "Sorry, Miss Misozi. Great crocodile, I suppose history can be somewhat delicate

Like Kurinji itself, Mrs. Misozi said, "Our museum is rooted in tradition but always looking to the future."

Inside, the chilly air smelled strongly of polished wood and ancient parchment. Along the walls were display cabinets filled with meticulously preserved items that chronicled Kurinji's colourful past. Mrs. Misozi led the children around the displays, stopping to highlight certain works.

She remarked, pointing to a set of historic agricultural implements, "Here," "you can see how our ancestors cultivated the land." And over there," she remarked, gesturing to a collection of well-crafted sculptures, "are depictions of the holy crocodiles that have safeguarded our community for years."

The youngsters marvelled at their ancestors' workmanship by pressing their faces against the glass. Ever eager, Gopal asked Mrs. Misozi questions about every object. His curiosity was contagious.

Deeper inside the museum screening and inspection part, the group found Dr. Meena crouched over a desk in a corner. As she looked beneath a high-powered microscope at a tiny metallic item, her brow wrinkled in focus.

Seeing the arriving company, Dr. Meena stood up and grinned. "Ah, Mrs. Misozi! I see that you are bringing the next generation of historians.

Mrs. Misozi nodded. "Dr. Meena, would you kindly mention a little about what you're working on?"

Dr. Meena's eyes became bright. naturally! Children, this relic represents a remnant of what we consider to be an ancient astronomy tool. Although considerably older, the design of the golden globe key is somewhat similar.

She raised the piece so that it would catch the light. The surface showed odd marks, unlike any lettering the kids had seen before.

"We are still trying to interpret these marks," Dr. Meena said. "They could have hints on not only Kurinji's past, but also perhaps the nature of the golden globe key itself."

As the kids rushed around to get a closer look, a hefty wooden door at the far end of the room caught Gopal's eye. Unlike the other displays, this door stayed tightly locked without any glass or plaque to let one see its contents.

Gopal pulled on his sleeve. "Miss Misozi," he inquired, "what's in there?"

Dr. Meena and Mrs. Misozi glanced at each other before Mrs. Misozi replied. "That is quite a unique room, Gopal." Kurinji supposedly keeps his most valuable objects in this room, including the Golden Globe key itself. That is among the museum's protected areas.

"Is it possible to look inside?" Gopal asked enthusiastically.

Mrs. Misozi shook her head. "I'm afraid, no darling. We have closed the chamber for public viewing or group visits. Legend says we should only open it to public view in a time of extreme need," she explains.

Gopal stayed for a minute, staring at the door as the party started. He was about to turn away when he glimpsed a flash of something. There, etched into the wood and almost covered by darkness, was an odd symbol—a set of intersecting circles around what seemed to be a stylized crocodile.

Gopal blinked, and for a minute he could have sworn the sign flashed with a faint, golden light. Upon closer inspection, however, it was simply an ordinary carving.

Mrs. Misozi yelled, "Gopal, come along now."

Gopal felt he had just seen something significant as he rushed to rejoin the others. He had no idea, however, that Kurinji's fate would soon depend critically on this emblem and the mysteries hidden beyond that barred door.

The trip went on, but Gopal's head kept returning to the enigmatic entrance, and the emblem seemed to throb with secret significance. Stepping out into the brilliant sunshine as they left the museum, a distant rumbling emanated from the hills—a sound that would soon signal a shift in Kurinji's fortunes and set off a series of events testing the town and its protectors like never before.

Chapter 3

Earth just shifted

As Kavin walked up the street to meet Elder Murali on the opposite side, the afternoon light cast deep shadows across Kurinji's major retail district.

Kavin welcomes the neighbourhood baker and notes how delicious her fresh bread smells. He helps a group of kids secure a kite in a tree. A good-natured elderly man haggles with him over mango prices at the market square.

Upon his arrival, he found Elder Murali seated on a worn-out stone bench, his head bent in intense scrutiny as Kavin joins him. Between them lay a schematic of the settlement, neatly annotated by Kavin.

Kavin said, following a line across the map, "We need to upgrade our irrigation system." "It would at least thirty percent raise crop yields."

Elder Murali nodded gradually as; his wizened brow wrinkled in contemplation. "Progress is important, Kavin said, but we must not forget ourselves in our modernisation."

Kavin's brow wrinkled. "But surely you see the advantages, Elder? We could—"

Murali softly silenced him with a hand, thereby guiding the discussion. "Let me tell you a story, young Kavin. It's about how our museum came to be, and why Kurinji's identity is so important."

As Murali started his story, the crowded plaza appeared to vanish, replaced by vivid pictures of Kurinji's history.

Murali replied, his voice adopting a rhythmic tempo, "That was almost a century go." " Kurinji was changing rapidly; many of our young people were leaving for other communities; our elders feared we were losing touch with our heritage." New technologies are on the way riving our heritage.

Kavin imagined a younger Murali fervently appearing before a council of village elders for the preservation of Kurinji's legacy's.
"That's when your great-grandfather suggested the museum." Murali said. "He believed that by honouring our past, we could build a stronger future. It wasn't easy. Many thought it was a waste of money. But in the end, the village came together, contributing family heirlooms and working tirelessly to build that building."

Kavin nodded, starting to comprehend. "The museum is therefore a symbol of our unity, not only a gathering of old objects."

"Precisely," Murali nodded. "And at its core sits our biggest mystery—the golden globe key."

A cluster of people passed, their eager murmurs travelling to Kavin and Murali as if on cue.
"Did you hear?" asked one lady. "Mira from the bakery shop swears she saw it pulsing with a golden light when she visited yesterday! The golden globe key sometimes glows!"

Her friend snorted. "Nonsense; it's just an old relic, most likely a light trick."

A third participant said, "But what about the old tales?" "Who says the key will awaken when Kurinji needs it most?"

Elder Murali says, "You know, Kavin, there's a saying in Kurinji: 'When the key turns, the village churns.'"
Perplexed, Kavin asked, "What does that mean?"
Elder Murali says, "Some believe that significant events in Kurinji's history coincide with disturbances around the key." The last time was during the severe drought of '27. They say the key glowed for three days straight before the rains came."

As they turned away, their sounds faded, and Kavin found it difficult to reflect. As Kavin turned to face Murali, questions began to form in his mind, and the older man simply responded with an enigmatic grin.

Within the museum, a display case filled with numerous holy crocodile relics sparked a heated argument between Mrs. Misozi and Dr. Meena. "These objects are priceless cultural jewels," Mrs. Misozi said fervently. "They stand for centuries of Kurinji's spiritual relationship to the holy crocodiles."

Dr. Meena nodded as she changed her spectacles. "I don't disagree, Mrs Misozi. But consider the scientific knowledge we could acquire by more closely examining the components alone. This knowledge could tell us so much about ancient trade routes and technological capabilities."

Mrs. Misozi groaned. "And do you run the risk of hurting them in the process?" Mrs. Misozi spoke. These are more than just historical oddities, Meena. Living entities are part of our legacy.

"But if we could comprehend the technology behind them," Dr. Meena urged, "particularly the golden globe key, we may unleash secrets that could benefit not only Kurinji but the entire world!"

A deep, menacing rumbling interrupted their dispute; the floor beneath their feet shook, rattling the relics in their cases with terrible resonance.

Kavin and Elder Murali stood up in panic outside the Kurinji market square disrupted from the ground, and in the distance, they could hear the shocked shouts of the people.

The shaking stopped as quickly as it had begun, leaving Kurinji in an uncomfortable silence.

"That was what? "What?" Kavin inquired with a voice barely almost above a whisper.

Elder Murali had a sad look. "Maybe a warning." Perhaps it's a sign of things to come.
Dr. Meena and Mrs. Misozi looked anxious among the exhibits. Though the objects had returned to their natural state, something seemed odd. The atmosphere was tense, and there was a sense of anticipation.

The people went about their evening activities with a hint of anxiety as the sun started to set and sent an eerie crimson light over Kurinji. None could remove the impression that the quake was just the start—that their idyllic community teetered on the edge of a transformation that would fundamentally alter the very ground below.

They were unaware that the stories of the past would collide with the reality of the present in the coming days, revealing the true power of the golden globe key in ways none of them could have predicted.

Like every other day in Kurinji, it started with the light peeping over the verdant hills and the community gradually waking. Kavin was already awake, strolling across the still streets toward the museum to see Dr. Meena. The promise of another scorching day permeated the air, and the night-blooming flowers left a subtle jasmine aroma.

Gopal leapt up as he crossed the town square, his constant energy illuminating his face.

"Morning, Kav!" Gopal chirped. Great crocodile, where are you headed? The museum again?

Kavin nodded, glad for the boy's vitality. "Dr. Meena thinks she's found something intriguing in the artefact room. Want to come along?"

The pupils of Gopal became wider. "Good crocodiles! Really? I wouldn't miss it for the world!"

As they strolled, the earth beneath their feet shivered slightly, almost unnoticeable. They stopped and locked eyes.

"Did you feel that?" Kavin said it in a worried tone.

Gopal nodded, and his thrashing slowed somewhat. "Maybe it's just the sacred crocodiles turning over in their sleep?"

Kavin laughed and combed Gopal's hair. 'Let's hope that's all it is.'"

They carried on, with the uneasy feeling disappearing as they got to the museum. Dr. Meena, her face ablaze with intellectual enthusiasm, was waiting for them at the door.

She urged them inside: "Ah, Kavin! And young Gopal, too. Excellent. Come, you must see this."

As they entered the museum, the cold air engulfed them; the familiar smell of ancient books and polished wood stood out sharply from the rising heat outside. Dr. Meena led them to a workstation displaying a range of relics.

She remarked, pointing up a little, well-sculpted figure, "Look at this." "I think this might help one grasp the Golden Globe Key's mechanism."

The earth jerked under their feet as Dr. Meena started to explain. This time, the ground was moving; it was not confusing.

Kavin yelled, instincts driving him, "Earthquake!" Now everyone is out!

Their surroundings turned into anarchy. Exhibit cases collapsed, shattered relics hit the floor, and the museum's walls began to groan and fracture. The air smelled like dust, and glass broke everywhere.

Pulling the scared lad towards the exit, Kavin grasped Gopal's hand.

Shoving what artefacts, she could into her bag, Dr. Meena hurried to rescue what she could.

Outside, the community was in flux. Villagers fled screaming into the streets; houses trembled and broke; and the earth rolled like ocean waves. A tremendous noise permeated the air, as if the planet itself were screaming in agony.

"Great crocodiles," Gopal moaned, grabbing Kavin's arm. "What's happening to our hamlet?"

As Kavin looked around at the damage underfoot, his heart surged. The roof of the bakery had collapsed, trees had uprooted, and he could see plumes of dust rising from distant fallen buildings.

A jarring snap brought everyone back to the museum. After standing for decades, the great ancient edifice was losing its way. Its walls creased, and the ceiling crashed down with a thundering moan.

Dr. Meena held the door frame, her knuckles white, as the building around her trembled and moaned. The terrified shouts of the other visitors at the museum were mixed with the repetitive creaking of falling buildings. Dust swirled in thick, suffocating clouds, obscuring her view and shrouding the once-familiar terrain in a terrible, post-apocalyptic haze.

"No!" Dr. Meena yelled, her mask concealing pain. "All those relics—our history!"

The entire impact of what had happened began to sink in as the shaking ceased, leaving behind a terrible silence. Villagers, from whatever cover they had, came out looking pale and startled.

Elder Murali showed up with his normally cool head turned off. "Kavin," he murmured in a raspy voice. "We need to organize search and rescue teams; individuals could be in danger."

Kavin nodded and pushed aside his own anxiety to seize control. "Dr. Meena, could you look at the wounded and offer first aid? Gopal, you should be courageous. Could you assist in compiling materials?"

Kavin couldn't help but gaze worriedly at the wrecked national museum as they jumped into action. Somewhere among the ruins lay the golden globe key, along with many priceless relics. His gut told him this calamity was just the beginning of something worse.

From the well-known holy crocodile stream, a deep rumbling resounded in the distance, as if the ancient guardians of Kurinji were waking up. The village would face its toughest challenge, and the key's actual power would manifest itself in ways they never would have thought possible.

Kurinji's history will always bear the marks of this terrible day. An invisible force has just unleashed its wrath on the sleeping town; the very ground beneath their feet has trembled violently, as if possessed by an ancient, malevolent entity. The once-solid ground has fractured and heaved, sending shockwaves of terror rippling through the hearts of the unsuspecting inhabitants.

A loud rumbling tore over the peaceful streets of Kurinji, signalling the start of a dream. A quick, strong shock had shaken the ground, as if some old, evil power had grabbed the very ground beneath their feet.

The industrious local farmer Ravi Thorarinsson staggered among the rubble, his eyes wide with shock and terror. The rich farm he had worked on for years now lay in ruins, its strong walls reduced to mere rubble. He coughed, the acrid air stinging his lungs, as he desperately looked for a way out of the anarchy and save some of his animals.

Kurinji's once-vibrant streets had become a maze of rubble and broken lives as the first shock subsided. The acrid smell of smoke and dust hung heavy in the air, mixing with the metallic tang of fear and uncertainty. Other survivors emerged from the ruins, their faces etched with disbelief and despair.

United by their shared tragedy, the Kurinji people created an enduring link, a monument to the resiliency that burns brightly inside their hearts among the chaos and destruction. With relentless determination, they set about the difficult task of reconstructing their lives from the ashes.

Kavin stood there, watching the damage with a heavy heart. Around him, villagers moved in a daze, still shell-shocked from the events of the previous day. The dawn broke over Kurinji, which had permanently changed. Dust hung in the air like a shroud. The once-familiar skyline was jagged with the remains of collapsed buildings.

"Kavin!" We need to investigate the museum ruins. Dr. Meena's voice pierced through the terrible calm. She came towards him, her normally perfect look dishevelled, and heavy bags under her eyes indicated a restless night. We must uncover the key.

Kavin nodded, his face set with determination. "Build a squad. We will begin the search right away.

Gopal fell in stride with them as they headed to the museum; his youthful face was unusually austere. "Great crocodiles," he said, his catchphrase now somewhat laced with anxiety. "What if the golden globe key is broken?'

Assuring him gently, Dr. Meena said, "The key has endured for generations, Gopal. It is stronger than we could ever realise.

Kavin arranged the volunteers into search teams at the museum site, his voice firm despite the turmoil all around. The once-proud edifice was now a mass of wreckage.

"Remember," he said, "we're not only hunting for the golden globe key." "Every artifact we can recover is a preserved piece of our heritage."

A throng of people gathered as they meticulously moved trash and catalogued what they discovered. Whispers filled the bystanders.
"The key has vanished, yet the legend endures..."
"What if this were a sign? The ancient prophecies spoke of trials."

Kavin heard these whispers and felt a weight of expectation fall on his shoulders. He understood that he had to maintain the villagers' morale in the face of their terrible reality.
Suddenly, Gopal's animated voice emerged. "Kavin! Dr. Meena! Look at this!"

Hurrying there, they saw Gopal pointing to an odd imprint in the dirt next to the old museum entrance. It seemed to be a big, three-toed footprint. Dr. Meena knelt to study it; her veterinary interest was aroused despite the conditions. "This is... odd. It almost seems like—"

Elder Murali completed "An Ostrich Track" right next to them. His eyes lit up with a knowing glance. "It seems our village has an unexpected visitor."

Kavin was perplexed and wrinkled. An ostrich? But how? And why now?

Before anybody could reply, activity emerged from the far side of the ruins. Hurrying there, they saw a gathering of people pointing and shouting. A huge ostrich walked gently among the rubble, as if it belonged there. Its eyes looked to have intelligence beyond that of a typical bird, and its feathers shimmered with almost iridescent brilliance.

Great crocodiles!" Gopal spoke, his eyes beaming with amazement. "It's exactly as the myth Elder Murali told us!"

The ostrich watched them calmly, then leant its long neck to scratch at something among the debris. A collective gasp rang through the assembly as it lifted its head. Its beak hung from golden chains.

"The chain is part of the key!" Dr. Meena spoke. She sobbed. Still, where's the key itself?

As if responding, the ostrich gulped and clearly bobbled its throat. Then it turned gracefully and started to leave the ruins, heading towards the holy crocodile brook.

Kavin had a range of contradictory feelings: joy at this seeming fulfilment of a legend, anxiety about what it may imply, and a great need to act. He turned to face the assembled people, his voice booming out with power.

"Everyone, listen carefully. We have much work to do to rebuild, but this could be crucial. Dr. Meena, Elder Murali, and Gopal, please come with me. We are tracking the ostrich; the rest of you, please continue the salvage efforts and begin organizing repair teams."

Kavin couldn't shake the feeling that Kurinji, having begun after the ostrich, was about to take a historic step. Apart from upsetting the town's foundation, the earthquake awakened something old and strong.

The ostrich guided them towards the water, its deliberate step never wavering. Elder Murali talked gently and deliberately as they strolled. "In times of enormous change," he added, "the guardians of Kurinji have always appeared. We have encountered the holy crocodiles, the mysterious key gift, and now this ostrich. Our village faces its greatest trial, but we are not alone."

As they approached the stream, the ostrich halted and turned to face them. Its eyes appeared to probe Kavin, as if assessing his value. Then it entered the sea and vanished under the surface with a grace that belied its weight.

The group stood in shock, witnessing the consequences of what they had just seen seeping in. Kavin's brain raced through options and questions. The fabled bird had devoured the key. Nevertheless, he sensed that this was just the beginning.

Gopal asked, his voice barely audible in the face of such mystery: "What do we do now?"

Kavin straightened his shoulders as the weight of leadership settled more solidly on him. "We wait," he murmured, his voice full of subdued will. "We rebuild, and we also prepare: 'Kurinji will face whatever comes next together.'"

A deep rumbling from the creek sounded as they headed back towards the village, as if the revered crocodiles were waking. The new chapter in

Kurinji's historic tradition was about to start, with Kav and his companions at its centre.

These people, among the murmurs and rumours, found their lives inextricably entwined with Kurinji's developing mystery. Meena, the sole female veterinarian and historian in the town, shared Kavin's obsession with the stories and history surrounding Kurinji.
Once a rich farmer, Ravi now only shadows his former self. The earthquake claimed not only his livelihood but also his sense of security. As he struggled with the weight of his own tragedy after losing most of his farm and animals, he found himself pulled into the enigmatic web that seemed to surround Kurinji.

Then there was Gopal, a small child whose bravery belied his age. Following the disaster, he became a ray of hope, always volunteering to help others in need. His compassionate heart and unwavering spirit made him a brilliant lighthouse among the gloom that had engulfed the town.

Meena, Kavin, Elder Murali, Ravi, Gopal, and other residents soon discovered a close connection between their destinies and the essence of Kurinji's existence. The secrets buried under the rubble called to them, murmuring promises of revelation and transformation.

With each passing day, the mystery deepens, dragging them deeper into a maze of secrets and hidden knowledge. The echoes of the past are resonating in the present, pushing them forward on a path that would test their bravery, resilience, and the very boundaries of their knowledge.

Meena, Ravi, Kavin, Gopal, and elder Murali knew their lives would never be the same, as the earthquake had not only rocked the ground beneath their feet but also taken the lives of their beloved men and women, awakening something far more profound inside their hearts as the sun sank over the ruins of Kurinji, casting an eerie glow upon the shattered landscape.

The truth that awaited them promised to be as massive as the very mountains that protected their beloved town's secrets. And so, with a mix of trepidation and will, they prepared to set off on an odyssey that would untangle the mystery of Kurinji and permanently shape the course of their destinies.

Chapter 4

Awakening the age-old curse

Today, in the heart of Kurinji, it is a lovely yet hopeful morning; the weight of history hangs heavily in the air around their once apparently ordinary local national museum.

The museum's hallowed halls, once a holy haven of uncemented knowledge and rich history, have been defiled. A terrible entity had broken its holy boundaries, creeping into its very centre.

In the rubble, the relics of a once-glorious past lie. The holy objects, once revered as emblems of their Kurinji legacy, now lay strewn, their purity defiled.

Meena, the respected local veterinarian and historian, found herself mysteriously drawn to the museum in the aftermath of the catastrophe, just like other residents. Her sharp eyes, looking for hints, drew her to a gleam of gold. Among the debris was an antique key shaped like the famous golden globe key, its surface covered in mysterious patterns that seemed to dance in the wavering light. Meena groped for the key with shaking hands, her fingertips brushing across its cold metal surface as an unexplained burst of energy coursed through her veins. Long lost by the inhabitants of Kurinji, whispers of an old curse started to rise in the recesses of her brain. She pictured the key, which did not look like any other relic; it appeared to be able to open Pandora's box of incomprehensible anarchy, something she had never seen in all of her trips to museums.

Meena followed Ravi, the modest farmer whose life had been turned upside down by the earthquake's damage, as she dug more into the secrets about the key. Once content with his modest life, Ravi found himself ensnared in the web of mystery currently engulfing Kurinji. Meena and Ravi embarked on a perilous journey to unravel the mysteries surrounding the key in her palm.

Unknown to them, young Gopal, a lighthouse of purity among the shadows, had come across a secret room among the museum's wreckage. Hidden from prying eyes, a little antique box—a relic of unbounded power—hided its secrets behind an unbreakable secrecy barrier. Startled at the sight of the package, Gopal exclaimed, "Great crocodiles!" Gopal unintentionally started a series of events that would permanently change the path of Kurinji's history as his curiosity drove him closer to the box. This time, Gopal's curiosity did not drove him on; he handed over the box to the Elder Murali Council recovery team while the people kept looking for their buried relics and tending to their injured souls. This is one of the crates holding Kurinji's old battle armor. For the young Gopal, this was an amazing recovery.

Meena and Ravi quickly discovered they were not alone in their quest, as they raced against time to interpret the mysterious patterns inscribed into the key by consulting the many volumes of old cryptic signs and meanings. Long-dormant, dark forces had come alive in the shadows, their evil eyes set on the primary golden globe key and the power it promised to release. A terrible scheme spun in the shadows of silence threatened to send Kurinji into never-ending gloom.

Every step Meena and Ravi took drew them deeper into a labyrinth of treachery and dishonesty. Truths formerly considered holy broke beneath the weight of long-buried secrets; alliances changed like the sands of time. As they negotiated the perilous terrain of Kurinji's history, they came to see that the ancient curse—which now threatened to swallow them all— inextricably connected their own futures. They raced against time, their hearts thumping with awareness that Kurinji's destiny rested on Meena and Ravi. But as they got closer to the truth, they were perplexed and suddenly understood that the key had disappeared from its appointed place. On his property, Ravi had a lockable tool chest. Their hands now held no strong key to atonement. This situation left them both confused and infuriated. How could this transpire? asked Dr. Meena. Ravi in his confused self, pointed repeatedly, it was left right inside this tool chest. What has happened to this key? Meena ponders.

As the moon cast its terrible glow upon the broken remnants of Kurinji's history, Meena, Ravi, and Gopal stood at the brink of destiny, their paths crossing in a last, desperate attempt to save their beloved museum from the grasp of an ancient evil, while elder Murali and Kavin were busy tending to the wounded's needs. As the three unusual heroes set out on a journey that would challenge the very boundaries of their bravery and resiliency, the echoes of the past murmured secrets long forgotten.

Kurinji's destiny ultimately hinged on the strength of their link, forged in the furnace of hardship. Standing together against the darkness, threatening to seize their relics among the rumbles, they realized they had the ability to alter history's path.

Chapter 5

Kavin's Dream

Among the murmurs of the dusty breeze in the centre of the Kurinji hamlet stood Elder Murali, a man cloaked in a veil of knowledge and mystery. His sharp eyes, burning with a relentless will, stared far away, as if staring down into the depths of a secret. As a community leader, the weight of obligation felt like a massive mountain, threatening to crush his determination. Still, he was tenacious in the face of this major difficulty. Decades of relentless dedication to the people of Kurinji developed Murali's image as a revered elder and community leader. Everyone who knew him respected him because of his thorough awareness of the village's rich legacy and the holy customs that had kept it going for centuries. Now, as the riddle of the lost golden globe key developed, Murali felt the weight of these antiquated relics mounting. He saw that the power it had might transform not just Kurinji but also the entire fabric of life itself. They have found some relics among the ruins, but the golden globe key seems to elude them.

With a fierce resolve blazing in his eyes, Murali called his trusty council—a covert group of relentless loyalists who had always been by his side. The Kurinji cultural legacy rested in the older person's council, selected based on age groupings and charged with local community leadership.

As they assembled, the air buzzed with electrifying expectation, aware that their next project would be a perilous journey veiled in uncertainty. Driven by an insatiable need for knowledge, Elder Murali and his council set out on a dangerous journey to meet a cadre of mysterious seers, each endowed with an amazing ability to peep into the magical abyss.

In a dimly lit room in a mysterious environment, a group of hired mystics stood there, radiating mystery and curiosity. They had the elusive keys that may open the riddle hiding the most secret in the cosmos.

As they journeyed into the future, Elder Murali and his colleagues found themselves ensnared in a complex web of mystery and magic. Every meeting with a psychic appeared to expose only bits that piqued their interest and set their own souls on fire, thereby peeling back the layers of a great cosmic jigsaw.

Their hearts thumped with a combination of fear and excitement, and the air buzzed with expectation as they descended deeper into the maze of secrets. But an impenetrable barrier covered the psychics' formerly piercing clarity, casting a thick fog of mysterious images across their thoughts.

Still, their relentless will burns like a flickering candle amid the worst of darkness. One lone bird emerged from a foggy dreamscape, where ethereal images spun and whirled like phantoms. Its wings spread, and it shot across the air in a lovely arc against the horizon. With their brilliant colours, the feathers looked to have tiny threads containing the secrets of the cosmos.

Once, the images changed to reveal a secret planet buried under the tall museum building. Mysterious and intriguing, a convoluted network of tunnels splayed out like a dark web. The darkly illuminated tunnels echoed with a terrible chorus of old whispers, their ghostly voices entwining with the icy air that hung from the moist stone walls. Then they happened upon it, as if under the direction of an unseen power. Before them stood a relic, old and battered, radiating an otherworldly brightness that appeared to violate earthly rules. Elder Murali and his friends barely touched the surface of an incomprehensible cosmic mystery as they stood on its brink. They set their eyes on the horizon of this thrilling voyage for enlightenment, prepared to confront the mysterious enigmas that awaited them.

Elder Murali could feel his people's fate weighing on his shoulders as they dug farther into the centre of the cosmic riddle using the psychics. Kurinji's destiny rested on a thin line, and he understood that the solutions they were looking for within this mysterious maze might determine the course of their dear country. Every stride made the murmurs of old secrets stronger, drawing them forward into the future.

Thoughts of the catastrophe that had befallen Kurinji—the broken houses, the people lost, and the once-thriving village reduced to rubble—ran through Elder Murali's head. He understood that the secret to their atonement was the mysterious artifact throbbing with an alien force, as well as the vague visions of the psychics.

Elder Murali's mind wandered to the youthful and courageous spirits of Kurinji: Kavin, Meena, Ravi, and Gopal, as they negotiated the dangerous road. He knew they embodied their people's resilience and saw their unflinching bravery in the face of hardship. In their eyes, he saw a flutter of hope—the promise of a better future beyond the shadow of gloom.

Confused and resolved not to divulge their prior knowledge with a key they collected from the rubbles that had since vanished, Meena and Ravi are committed to helping find the lost treasured golden globe key. Murali carried a great deal of weight from leadership, yet he resisted giving up under such extreme strain. Rumours of a conflict within his council have surfaced. Two seniors had pushed him to resign after doubting his capacity to steer Kurinji out of its present problems.

With fresh will, Elder Murali pushed forward, his devoted council members at his side. They embarked on this perilous journey not for personal glory, but to save their people.

Elder Murali and his council saw this as a struggle to recover the light taken by tragedy—a fight for Kurinji's own soul. They stood together, their hearts throbbing as one, knowing their people's fate lay in their hands. They would not fail, as the love they carried for their country and people was a force stronger than any cosmic mystery.

The morning after the bird's appearance in the seer's visions, Kurinji woke up to find many spiritual and psychic signals flashing with urgency. Kavin requested a gathering at the primary rehabilitation site, just next to the former museum. The traditional festival venue now serves as a command centre for their rehabilitation activities. Villagers gathered, their resolve mixed with concern on their faces.

Kavin stood before them, his words ringing throughout the assembly. "Friends, we face unprecedented challenges; our homes have suffered damage; our museum lies in ruins; our sacred golden globe key remains missing; nonetheless, we are Kurinji, and we will persevere. Today, we continue our search."

Dr. Meena moved on, carrying a thorough map of the settlement and nearby surroundings. "We have split Kurinji into search zones; each team will be in charge of carefully looking over their designated area."

Kurinji's diverse personalities came to the fore when the villager's formed teams. Mrs. Nguyen agreed to guide a party looking around the residential neighbourhoods; the formerly famous bakery in the Kurinji core retail town is now in ruins, yet her sympathetic character always shines. "We'll not only look for the golden globe key," she continued, "but check on our neighbours', especially the elderly and those with young children."

Driven by her best effort for her community, Dr. Meena and a group of volunteers walked to the museum ruins. "We will search for any hidden chambers or objects the earthquake might have exposed using ground-penetrating radar."

Elder Murali opted to guide a small party to the holy crocodile brook; his eyes sparkled with old knowledge. "Sometimes," he said, "the road forward requires us to return to our roots."

Gopal, energy-driven, jumped from group to group, his interest aroused by every team's approach. As he watched Dr. Meena and the volunteers set up her gear, he exclaimed, "Great crocodiles!" "It feels as though we are on a real archaeological expedition!"

As the search got under way, Kavin was always on the go, organising efforts, raising spirits, and lending assistance wherever he could. He helped clean trash with one crew while keeping an eye out for any indication of the ostrich or the key, and then assisted Dr. Meena with her scans.

By noon, the hamlet was humming with activity. People were turning every stone and looking everywhere. Still, as the hours passed, irritation started to seep in. The enigmatic ostrich and the golden globe key remained elusive.

Kavin summoned the search teams back to the recovery centre as the sun started to drop and huge shadows stretched over the community. Tired and dirty faces turned to him for directions.

"We've made good progress today," he remarked, attempting to seem hopeful. "We may not have found the golden globe key, but we have begun rebuilding our village; tomorrow, we will widen our search to the nearby hills."

Gopal stayed, his youthful face wrinkled with contemplation, as the others scattered. "Kavin," he replied reluctantly. Maybe the ostrich will lead us there. "What if we're looking in the wrong places?" "What if the ostrich is the key to its discovery?"

Impressed by the youngster's idea, Kavin turned to face him and said, "You might be onto something, Gopal." What ideas are you considering?'

"Well," Gopal began, his words spilling out in enthusiasm, "the ostrich emerged just after the earthquake, maybe swallowed the key by accident while it was grazing on the rubble, and then fled into the stream. What if the ostrich wasn't just a random bird? Imagine if it were a protector, like revered crocodiles."

Kavin nodded slowly, the bits beginning to come together in his head. "You know, Gopal; I believe you may be right. Why not you and me tomorrow? I should be hunting down that ostrich.

Gopal's face suddenly lit up with the words, "Great crocodiles!" In fact? You mean as such?"

"I do," Kavin answered, grinning at the boy's energy. "Sometimes, it takes a fresh perspective to solve an ancient mystery."

The quest for the key had brought out the best in his fellow villagers, exposing abilities he hadn't realised they had. And now, with Gopal's insight, they had a new path to investigate as they parted ways for the night. Kavin couldn't help but feel a sliver of optimism.

Their journey's even more remarkable turn caught everyone off guard. Kavin and Gopal left early, their packs loaded with provisions for a day of ostrich-tracking. The following morning dawned with a cacophony of singing, nature seeming blind to the misery of the community.

Kavin said, "Remember," as they headed towards the water, "we're not simply searching for the ostrich itself. Look for anything odd, like footprints or feathers.

Gopal nodded enthusiastically, his eyes darting to the ground. "Great crocodiles," he exclaimed, projecting an air of a genuine police officer pursuing a criminal.

Elder Murali was already there, calmly meditating on a rock, when they arrived at the holy crocodile brook. He opened one eye as they came, a knowing grin on his face.

"Ah, young searchers," he replied. "I felt you would come here today. The answers you are looking for could be closer than you might believe, please continue your journey."

Kavin and Gopal looked at each other, adjusting to the older man's cryptic remarks. They started looking, with Gopal's sharp eyes seeing things Kavin could have missed.

Look! Pointing at a soft mud spot, Gopal said, "More ostrich footprints!"

Kavin knelt to study them; the new footprints stretched from the brook into the thick forest beyond. "Good eye, Gopal," he said. Let us follow them.

As they followed its course, Gopal's interest in the ostrich rose. "Do you think it might have swallowed the key, Kavin?" he said. And of all the locations, why would it come here?"

Kavin thought about the matter. According to Elder Murali's story, the ostrich has a link to the ancient key, and the holy crocodiles may be guarding it until Kurinji really needs it."

Gopal's eyes opened wider. "This is like a feathery safe deposit box." Gavin laughed at the comparison. "Something like that, maybe", Kavin added.

Their road led them deeper into the forest around Kurinji. The settlement's noises vanished behind them as the trees thickened. Gopal stopped abruptly, pointing forward.

In a little clearing stood an ostrich. Its perceptive eyes watched its brilliant feathers gently in the dappled sunshine.

"Great crocodiles," Gopal said softly, marvelling in his voice. "It's even more exquisite up close."

Kavin cautions Gopal to remain motionless by putting a hand on his shoulder. "Easy now. We want to avoid scaring it off."

The ostrich raised its head, as if weighing them. Then, astonishing them, it started to approach. The walk was royal, almost ceremonial.

Gopal saw something odd as it got close. "Kavin," he muttered, his voice muffled. "Look at its neck; is it shining?"

Kavin frowned, almost believing his eyes. Right where the ostrich's neck would be, a weak golden light appeared to pulse under the feathers.

Breathing, "The golden globe key," Kavin said, "must be responding to the key!"

The ostrich stopped a few steps away from them, bent its head slightly, then turned and started to walk away, its motions purposefully slow.

"I suppose," Gopal remarked, enthusiasm rising in his voice, "it wants us to follow it!"

Kavin nodded, his pulse pounding. "I believe you are correct. Come on but be cautious. Where is it leading us, though?

Gopal spoke of the great crocodiles as they trailed the ostrich deeper into the woods, the golden light from its neck growing brighter. The road became steeper, carrying them up into the hills above Ravi's livestock farm. "I saw the ruins of Mr. Ravi's farm; are you sure this ostrich isn't among the lost ones from his property?", Gopal asked.

At last, they surfaced on level ground. The ostrich came to a halt and faced them once more. Beyond it, a cave opening was benevolent, partly covered by vegetation and vines.

"Great crocodiles," Gopal said, his slogan now imbued with respect. "What is this space?"

Kavin, too, felt great respect when shaking his head. "I'm not sure, Gopal, but I believe we are about to learn."

The ostrich moved towards the cave entrance; its golden glow now strong enough to highlight the antique markings etched around the aperture. It turned back at them, as if beckoning their follow-through.

Kavin inhaled deeply, as fate and history seemed to weigh heavily on him. "Well, Gopal," he said, his voice calm even with his beating heart, "are you ready for an adventure?"

Gopal nodded, his countenance a combination of resolve and exhilaration. "Great crocodiles, yes! Let's solve this mystery!"

Following the ostrich into the future, Kavin couldn't help but feel as if they were about to find something that would permanently alter Kurinji. They were headed towards the cave. Though their hunt for the golden globe key had brought them here, what they would discover within was anyone's guess.

When Kavin and Gopal entered the cave after the mysterious ostrich, the air around them changed. It was colder, flavoured with an earthy aroma, and something else—something ancient and invisible. The ostrich's brilliant throat lit the way and created swirling shadows on the cave walls. "Great crocodiles," Gopal said, his voice faintly echoing. "Like in a real-time gaming scene, we're walking into another world."

Kavin nodded, his senses sharp. "Stay near, Gopal. We don't know what we might find here."

They trailed the ostrich deeper inside the cave, with the passageway eventually opening out into a large cavern. As they came in, the ostrich halted and turned to face them. The throat's brightness became stronger, softly golden, lighting up the space.
What they saw astounded them.

Nestled in a naturally occurring rock structure that resembled almost a nest, an ostrich egg sat in the middle of the chamber. But this was no typical egg. It easily matched the size of a man's skull and was beyond anything they had ever seen. Reflecting the golden light in hypnotic patterns, its shell appeared to glitter like the surface of a tranquil lake. "Great crocodiles!" Gopal uttered his catchphrase, now filled with wonder. "Did the ostrich lie there?"

Before Kavin could reply, the ostrich came forward. With its beak, it softly poked the egg; to their astonishment, the golden light from its neck appeared to flow to the egg. The shimmering became stronger, and Kavin might have momentarily sworn he saw something moving within the egg. "We have to bring Dr. Meena here," Kavin replied, his voice quiet. "This exceeds anything we have ever come across."

They heard voices from the cave entrance, as if on cue. Emerging into the room with Mrs. Nguyen and Elder Murali, Dr. Meena had a look that combined amazement and incredulity.

Startled, Kavin said, "How did you find us?"

Elder Murali grinned brilliantly. Of course, I saw both of you following the ostrich footprints, but I had to finish my meditation before I could go to Nguyen and Meena. "Remember that our sacred ancient artifacts have their own ways of communicating. They led us here." Murali said.

Dr. Meena, ever the scientist, was already walking towards the egg, her eyes ablaze with curiosity. She said, "This is extraordinary," then studied the shell closely. "I have never seen anything like it."

She started reading with a little gadget she grabbed from her knapsack. "The energy signature is off chart," she said. The egg seems, somehow, to be alive.

In this magical location, Mrs. Nguyen enhanced her sympathetic skills by closing her eyes and extending her senses. She replied gently, "I can feel something." "It's an ancient and strong presence, but it's also... young; it's difficult to describe."

As they gathered around the egg, the ostrich moved back, apparently content with its purpose. With keen eyes, it observed them waiting for their next action.

Dr. Meena kept looking and mumbled remarks as she worked. She followed a finger over the shimmering surface and said, "The shell composition is unlike anything in our records. It's harder than diamond, yet it seems to have a fluid quality to it. And these patterns..." "They are changing and developing, not only reflections."

Gopal chimed in; his wonder subordinated to curiosity. "Do you think the key is inside the egg, Dr. Meena?"

Dr. Meena stopped to reflect. "It's possible, but I'm not sure how it could be," Gopal added. The energy ratings imply that one has a strong inner force. The true mystery, however, is how it got there and what it entails."

Elder Murali came forward, his worn fingers hovering just above the egg's surface. "This is no simple relic, and clearly not one we had previously at the museum," he murmured, his voice weighted with old wisdom. "It appears like this egg is a bridge between the past and future. It contains not only our key, but also Kurinji's destiny key."

The egg pulsed with light, the shimmering becoming stronger as if in reaction to his words. For a moment, they all sensed a connection—to each other, to Kurinji, to something large and unfathomable.

Feeling the weight of accountability fall on his shoulders, Kavin said, "We have to guard this egg. If we value it, others may strive to grab it or exploit its authority.

Agreeing, Dr. Meena said, "We should relocate it to a safe spot for further investigation. Should we send it to the museum after repairs?

None of them saw a shadow separate from the cave wall while they spoke about ways to move and protect the egg. A person vanished secretly, bearing word of this discovery to those who would pay highly for such knowledge.

Each engrossed in their own thoughts on what this finding might entail, the group meticulously prepared to relocate the egg. Like a silent guardian, the ostrich trailed behind.

Kavin woke with a stronger pulse, realizing that his long ostrich chase with Gopal, the capture of this egg, and the arrival of Murali, Nguyen, and Meena were all just dreams even as it appeared real that they made their way out of the cave. He woke up, wiping his drowsy eyes, convinced that this was a real-life voyage and an honest discovery. Immediately, frustration seized him. Kavin has been sleeping poorly for several days after the events in Kurinji.

He was unaware, however, that his fantasy had some validity and might bring him closer to his cherished town's quest.

Chapter 6

Invisible Spectre

A menacing sense of mystery and anxiety permeated the streets of Kurinji districts, once peaceful. Whispers slithered into the very foundations of the wrecked homes like ghostly tendrils, leaving a path of mystery and mistrust.

Shockwaves from the earthquake rocked the once-peaceful town, leaving its people completely confused, and the golden globe key vanished from the Kurinji National Museum. An incomprehensible puzzle, seemingly defying all rational answers, abruptly disrupted their previously calm life.

Where may this priceless relic, representing Kurinji's culture, be? A tapestry of ideas emerged from the depths of conjecture as the mysterious case developed, each more fanciful and terrifying than the next.

The people of the little town were ravenous for solutions, consuming their brains in an unrelenting search for knowledge. Desperate to untangle the mystery that had come upon them, they found themselves caught in a web of uncertainty.

But within the whirlwind of anarchy, a new presence began to emerge: a dark figure watching the happenings with a menacing curiosity on the outskirts of the settlement. Under a cocoon of silence, this person seemed to walk with predatory elegance, their eyes riveted on every action of society.

The people kept desperately looking for solutions, ignoring this invisible phantom.

With every tick of the clock, the weight of unresolved questions made the air heavier. Once a quiet village tucked among undulating hills, Kurinji discovered it caught in a web of mystery.
Every citizen, once seen as a typical denizen of this perfect community, now stood covered in a cloak of mistrust; their entire existence was a riddle just waiting to be solved.

The days of polite waves and laid-back chats were long gone, replaced with quiet murmurs and furtive looks. An electric tension crackled in the air, as if the environment itself held its breath, waiting to reveal the truth.

And in the shadows, the invisible phantom kept observing, their own evil goal concealed from view, their sharp gaze directed at society. What sinister secrets did this mysterious man carry, and were they related to the golden globe key that vanished from the ground?

Unaware that this dark entity was tracking their every action, the Kurinji people yearned for solutions. This ghostly apparition prepared the groundwork for a clash that would challenge their knowledge and stretch the boundaries of what they thought was feasible.

Their frantic hunt for solutions is continuous within the whirlpool of anarchy.

Deeper into the mystery, the Kurinji dug locals started to doubt that the loss of the golden globe key was not an accident. Whispers of a secret spectre—an invisible power playing behind the scenes—started to travel. Some said that the lack of the golden globe key had set off an ancient curse long dormant. Others murmured about a dark figure, a puppet master arranging the proceedings from the shadows.

Meena, the town's respected historian and veterinarian, found herself caught in the storm. Her knowledge of Kurinji's past and sharp intuition led her to believe that a deeper, more evil reality was linked to the missing golden globe key. She pored over old books and dug into the town's neglected archives in quest of any hint that would help to clarify the mystery consuming her dear town.

Ravi, the modest farmer, and little Gopal, the courageous kid, also caught the mystery's appeal. Their paths met Meena's, Kavin's, and Murali's, and together they formed an unusual alliance resolved to discover the mysteries kept behind Kurinji's closed doors. The whole essence of their community was on the line; hence, they understood the tremendous stakes.

Meena, Ravi, Kavin, Murali, and Gopal were poised on the brink of a truth that would permanently alter their lives as the last pieces of the jigsaw came together.

Once an invisible force, the phantom, said to have come from Bale with the help of two village elders opposing Mural, now appears before them; its actual nature is now clear-cut. Antonio Sanders, the Bale Great Maffia's representative, led the charge.

Standing together against the gloom, they understood they had the ability to control their fate. Once a terrible enemy, the spectre now trembles in front of their relentless will. The two elders who supported the invader are now subject to the fury of the council's legal system.

Meena, Ravi, Kavin, Murali, and Gopal emerged from the shadows as the sun rose over the horizon, their hearts full of knowledge that they were looking for something greater than themselves, but something that the outsiders were already plotting to get hold of. Once a sign of anarchy, the hunt for the lost golden globe key now acted as a reminder of the unwavering spirit that had carried them throughout the worst of times.

Though permanently altered by the tragedies that had happened, Kurinji now stood stronger than ever, its people united against hardship. The invisible phantom has vanished, permanently damaging its eyes and covert grasp on the town. And in its place, a new chapter in Kurinji's history had started: one of optimism, resiliency, and the unquestionable ties of community.

Chapter 7

Psychic's Riddle

In the heart-stopping search for solutions to the many psychics' enigmatic messages, the council of Kurinji's revered community elders set out on a perilous journey into unknown worlds. Retrieving their communal legacy and historical Golden Globe key was no longer a straightforward search; it was a terrifying trip into the depths of spiritual battle to heal their town. As the stakes rose, the spiritual struggle consumed everyone. They're crossing the river toward Ugando to visit Sage Vidya.

The air was thick with expectation today as psychic Sage Vidya, with a dark history, teetered on the brink of life and death. She started to talk with shaky hands and a voice vibrating with an unreal force. Every word she said had a terrible resonance that made everyone who ventured to listen shudder down their spines. The barrier separating the living from the dead appeared to lift, revealing the unknowable.

Vidya's sharp eyes cut through the stress like a razor's edge. She murmured her announcement with a voice as soft as silk, bringing gasps across the room. She hid from plain sight the golden globe key, the key to opening your country's inconceivable mysteries. She instead kept it under the enigmatic shell of an ostrich egg. Look around your neighbourhood for an ostrich that is simply laying eggs.
The enigmas became more complex with every second that passed. Could a frail ostrich eggshell hide such a priceless relic? This strange spaceship carried secrets.

The room hummed with expectation as the elderly leant in closer, their eyes bright with curiosity. Vidya's vision had guided them to this remarkable discovery; now, the truth lay fatalistically near yet hidden in mystery. Cracking the riddle of the ostrich egg was imperative.

The hunt has begun now all around the village. Under the weak moonlight that seeped through the wooden wall crevices, a figure stood tall in the poorly lit temporary barn of Mr Ravi with silky feathers glistening. It was none other than an ostrich, and its royal presence suggested a relationship with the mysterious Farmer Ravi.

The townspeople softly spoke the reclusive farmer's name, long surrounded by murmurs of curiosity. Many thought he had a secret wisdom that was unique among common people. Now that this amazing bird was here, the pieces of the jigsaw began to fit together. By nature, Ravi is a brilliant farmer.

The elderly—led by Murali—creeped closer to the enigmatic nest with great caution, their pulses thumping in their chests. Like the environment itself holding its breath, an electromagnetic tension crackled in the air, waiting for the disclosure of untold truths.

Tucked within the boundaries of a once-vibrant refuge, a clutch of eggs—once full of life—now lay desecrated and damaged by an invisible evil.

Their spines shook with an ice cold, a feeling that shook their entire core. The truth emerged before them like a dark revelation. The malefactor responsible for this horrible action revealed himself as a snake with evil intentions. Its sinuous figure was curled in the darkness, concealing a terrible entity.

A snake had fallen onto the fragile ostrich egg nest. Driven by a massive appetite, it ate the innocent life within and left a terrible path of suffering and damage. Once a flourishing haven, its residents, deprived of their future, lay in ruins.

Still, among the rubble, a single egg remained nestled, and its whereabouts were unknown. Before them loomed a great mystery, beyond all reason and reasoning. The sheer enormity of the mystery shivered down people's spines and caused amazement.

With its eyes shining with ravenous avarice, the nasty snake had focused on this titan of an egg. With its mouth open, it surged forward, ready to eat its target. But destiny had other ideas. As strong as it was, the egg refused to give way to the deadly grasp of the snake. Epic-scale conflict followed, with a fight between predator and prey resolved to triumph.

The egg, untouched by the snake's deadly teeth, represented hope amidst the destruction. It was evidence of its existence's fortitude, a promise of a fresh start. Still, it also served as a warning of the risks hiding in the shadows.

The senior members of the community stood together, their will intact. They chose to keep this egg in a temporary improvised museum to investigate further with psychics, scientists, traditionalists, and any other source that would assist them in deciphering the enigma within. Little did they realise as they stood there, staring towards the horizon, that this apparently benign event would set off an incredible journey that would permanently change the very fabric of their lives.

As they travelled into the future, shadows moved menacingly about them, murmuring secrets only the darkness could hear. With their hearts pounding in their chests, every step they took was fraught with danger. The road ahead was narrow and twisted through a maze of uncertainty. Perched on the brink of an incredible journey, the seniors and the community group of recovering volunteers understood they had to be ready for anything. They realized that this was now about their survival and the destiny of Kurinji, not just the golden globe key. With their spirits intact and their determination stronger than ever, they were ready to face whatever lay ahead.

And thus a fresh story started beneath the starry sky among Kurinji Land's wreckage. Hope, bravery, and courage will abound in this next chapter. They would struggle to live and protect their last chance for their own country.

They must stay strong in their determination, even if the job of deciphering the mystery before them seems difficult. The apparently impenetrable ostrich egg, recovered from Ravi's farm, is a great enigma, with both the menace of devastation and the hope of redemption inside its shell. They had to walk cautiously, as one mistake could mean catastrophe for their dear Kurinji territory.

Even though their remarkable journey had just begun, they sensed they were on the right path. Their unity and determination would enable them to surmount any challenge and achieve victory.

Chapter 8

Broken Nest and an Unbroken Egg

r. Meena's firm hand gently cradled the mysterious egg in the dimly lit temporal museum room. The chamber appeared to be alive, seemingly aware of the secrets hidden beneath its ancient surface. Like a detective about to solve a difficult problem, Dr. Meena's eyes shone with a combination of enquiry and anxlety.

From the depths of her analytical ability, a discovery surfaced—profound and unanticipated. Suddenly enlightened, Dr. Meena's sharp mind broke through the mist of confusion to expose a startling fact hidden within the mysterious egg. She eagerly anticipated the unveiling of a mysterious metal complex, its secret nature concealed in the shadows, poised for disintegration. Mysterious as it was, the chemical had a terrible resemblance to the legendary, long-lost key.

Whispers about Dr. Meena's discovery slithered through the close-knit community, sparking explosive enthusiasm. There was much expectation; every breath seemed to hold the promise of something unique. The enchanted community was about to experience the clarity of the riddle. She chose to cooperate and examine every little aspect of the enigmatic metal complex with exacting accuracy, without skipping any ground in her unrelenting search for solutions. Anticipation permeated the air, as though the secrets she sought awaited revelation. The weight of the work fell on her, yet she stayed relentless.

With every moment bursting with exciting expectations, Kurinji's peaceful life suddenly sank into a mysterious riddle. Kurinji's people found themselves caught in a web of exciting adventures where the border between truth and illusion blurred into a tantalizing haze, and the air was filled with an addictive mix of mystery and discovery.

Rumours are now circulating that the ostrich that laid the egg had to swallow the golden globe key. Their brains whirled with questions: After the earthquake, did the ostrich swallow the key among the rubble and anarchy? Where did the ostrich meet the key? How did the key transform into an ostrich meal? When the earthquake struck, did the ostrich flee Ravi's farm?

Their curiosity piqued, and the village elders dug deeper into the riddle. Searching for any hint to help them solve the mystery before them, they pored over old books and spoke with the renowned sages of the region.

Breadcrumbs led the elderly into a maze of riddles and secret messages. They descended into the mystery's shadows, but with each stride, they grew closer. They knew the answers they were looking for were just beyond their reach, tantalizingly close yet veiled in mystery.

The improvised laboratory and museum in the town square buzzed with activity. The once-joyous meeting spot, with the enigmatic egg at its core, has become a hub of scientific research. Days of rigorous study have distorted her usually immaculate looks, as Dr. Meena now stands before a group of villagers and other researchers.

She said, pointing to a holographic display of the egg's molecular structure, that "as you can see," "the makeup of the shell is unlike anything we have seen previously. It seems to be adaptable, self-repairing substance."

While fronting the assembly, Kavin leans in for a closer inspection. "So, you are implying the shell's somehow unbreakable?"

Dr. Meena nodded, her voice tinged with both joy and anger. Indeed, so far. We have tested everything, from concentrated laser beams to diamond-tipped drills. The egg simply absorbs the energy and quickly heals itself."

A whisper passed through the assembly. With wide-open astonishment, Gopal shouted up, "Great crocodiles!" It seems alive—maybe on the brink of hatching.

"In some sense, it might be," Dr. Meena said. "The energy readings we're getting suggest some kind of internal activity, but we can't probe far enough to identify its nature."

Kavin saw Elder Murali standing in the rear of the audience, a knowing smirk on his face, as the presentation progressed, detailing failed attempts after failed attempts to break the egg's shell. He walked over to the elderly man.

"You don't seem surprised by any of this, Elder," Kavin said.

Murali giggled gently. "Young Kavin replies, 'The secrets of the cosmos frequently resist our efforts to uncover them. Maybe we should be asking other questions.

Before Kavin could delve deeper, a disturbance started around the egg. Frustrated by the lack of development, visiting scientist Dr. Peter Waters, working with Dr. Meena, tried to knock the egg with a hammer. The audience gasped as the hammer's head broke, sparing the egg.

"Enough! Dr. Meena yelled, fuelled by thin patience. "This is a fragile artifact—not a fair game of coconut!"
Kavin turned back to Elder Murali, who guided the repentant scientist away, and said, "You stated you were asking the incorrect kind of inquiries. In what sense did you mean?"

The eyes of the older man glittered. Come, let's walk together. You should hear some tales.
Elder Murali started talking as they meandered through the town, his voice assuming the steady cadence of a storyteller. "Long ago, in a world where magic flowed freely, items of great power existed." People believed these objects to be indestructible due to their connection to the fundamental fabric of reality itself, not their physical strength.
Kavin listened closely as Murali spun stories of legendary shields that could resist the attacks of gods, containers that embodied creation, and keys that might open portals between realms.

"But here's the thing, young Kavin," Murali said, pausing for impact. Force was never meant to open or shatter these things. They were protectors of great truths and abilities, guardians waiting for the right person at the right time to reveal their secrets.
Kavin's head was whirling with the ramifications of Murali's tales as they finished their circle of the hamlet and returned to the makeshift lab. Upon first seeing the egg, he perceived it as a guardian, awaiting comprehension, rather than as a puzzle to solve.

Her thoughts fixed on the riddle before her, and Dr. Meena laboured to discover the mysteries of the metal complex. She comprehended the key to unlocking the mystery of the golden globe and uncovering the hidden ostrich within its chemical structure. Driven by an insatiable need for information, she neared a breakthrough with every day that passed.

The town eagerly anticipated a discovery that would forever change Kurinji's history. Though the answers they were looking for were within reach, the road forward was dangerous and unknown.
They understood they were not alone in searching for the truth. Rumours abound that long dormant and most likely extinct dark forces had once again started to stir in the shadows, their eyes firmly fixated on the golden globe key and the power it offered. The elderly, Dr. Meena, Kavin, Young Gopal, and every other villager understood they had to act quickly as Kurinji's destiny rested on balance.

Their hearts were full of understanding that they were battling for something more than themselves, and they continued with fresh will. Though they were prepared to meet whatever obstacles lay ahead, they knew the road ahead would be long and dangerous. They were determined to uncover the truth and secure the key for Kurinji and their beloved community.

Chapter 9

A night in the Temporal Museum

Within Kurinji's remarkable temporal temporary museum, a mystery of tremendous value remained hidden; its actual relevance was lost to the public's probing eyes. The unbreakable egg was in the room. The unbreakable fortitude now conceals its brilliant beauty, a legacy of unfathomable elegance. The golden globe key, a desired ancient treasure hidden within its fragile shell, had the ability to reveal the secrets of the past.

Strengthened fortifications and a vigilante organization in the community kept the egg hidden from prying eyes.

Little did the gullible society realise that a huge treasure of unearth able value had unintentionally turned into the centre point of a terrible and evil scheme.

Stories spun like smoke in the evening air. Whispers carried on the breeze revealed a covert, hidden society engaged in a black-market trade of primarily stolen ancient relics, mostly conveyed on the wind. Those who dared to mention the name of the secret organization could only mumble it under their breath. By cover of darkness, this mysterious gang headed by Mr. Frays Toletti was said to be motivated by an unbounded, ravenous avarice.

Within the ancient corridors of the temporal museum, a covert operation burst under the ethereal light of the moon. Under the cover of darkness, Mr. Frays operatives surreptitiously entered the hallowed temporal museum halls. Their aim was clear, veiled in mystery and fascination. It was a mission of great significance—to grab the indestructible egg and release its mysterious mysteries. They primarily focus their penetrating gaze on the golden globe key inside the shell.

Shadows moved over the faces of these secret people as they huddled close. Their eyes sparkled with resolve, and their brains were preoccupied with the nuances of their exacting preparation. They waited for the unbreakable, painstakingly organizing every detail and computing every step with the highest accuracy. Their motions were as quiet as the darkness itself; they were the height of stealth.

But perhaps destiny had other ideas. The temporary museum's security measures and the members of a local vigilante organization served as an unbreakable stronghold, confronting even the cleverest of burglars. Their complex network of sensors and surveillance cameras appeared to allow them to predict any illegal intent more naturally. Those who dared to question their power shivered down their spines just because of their great presence.

As a group of committed vigilante members encircled the would-be burglars and Mr. Frays group operatives, tension was thick.

On a velvet cushion in the recently rebuilt temporary museum, a precious egg of unknown potency gleamed menacingly. Detective Asante Ebenezer, a seasoned local veteran with sharp eyes and a track record for cracking the most difficult cases, stood up as commander of the local vigilante organisation. His deep growl of voice reverberated throughout the hall.

"You considered yourself capable of outwitting us? Still, we are one step ahead. We will provide you with a lesson to share with your group so that you can try again. Kurinji's land is here; our legacy is this indestructible egg so you cannot steal it.

The broken pieces of the glass case littered the floor, serving as a terrible reminder of the bold attempted theft that had just occurred.
Under the low, ethereal glow of the improvised museum lights, the egg stood boldly, its surface glistening with an odd appeal. Captivating everyone who ventured to see it, it was the clear focal point of the great exhibition. The failed robbery left a shade of uncertainty over an already gripping story.
Another lovely day as the Kurinji temporal museum receives the sunlight. The members of the community stood in quiet contemplation, their gazes fixed on the priceless item that had come to represent ambiguity and obsession, their eyes wide with wonder.

The indestructible egg presence appears to be becoming more obvious with every second that goes by. Its glittering surface moved with the fading light, creating an unearthly impression. With a warm glow lighting their faces, the Kurinji people silently revered as day gave way to night
Once just a relic, the egg has become something considerably more significant. It had gone beyond its modest beginnings to become a powerful emblem of their unflinching strength and tenacious spirit among the unrelenting assault of difficulty.

Every day when night fell, the temporal museum started to change; the once-bustling hallways started to seem ghostly, with the odd cracking of old flooring shattering the hush.
The egg's mysterious existence seemed like a lighthouse in the night. It appeared to pulsate with an unearthly vitality, as if it held the mysteries of

the cosmos itself in its fragile shell. Those who ventured near could feel the weight of its strength, a physical force that appeared to reach out to anyone and wherever it desired and encompass them in its magical grasp.

As the witching hour drew near today, odd events started to show themselves inside the walls of the temporal museum. Long-forgotten whispers murmured down the hallways; their words were haunting but unintelligible. Shadows flicked and danced as if in a macabre waltz, with moonlight streaming through the skylights above.

The egg appeared to be conducting this phantom symphony at the centre. Its mysterious aura grew stronger with every instant that passed, driving the restless souls of the past towards it like moths to a flame. As if the egg's inexplicable force stretched and twisted the very fabric of existence, an invisible energy crackled in the air.

Asante and his vigilante gang members will never forget the encounter they had while staying alert over the temporal museum that evening. They spoke of having a presence—an invisible power apparently observing their every action. Some even claimed to have seen brief apparitions—ghostly beings that ran in and out of the shadows—whose features twisted in looks of suffering and hopelessness. We would greatly appreciate it if they shared their encounter with the elderly and other residents, Asante said.

As the first light of dawn began to cut through the darkness of the night sky, the egg's power appeared to fade. The whispering stopped, and the shadows withdrew to their hiding places once again. Once again, the temporal museum took on the role of normality, burying its mysteries securely behind its old walls.

For those members of vigilante groups who had seen the egg's nighttime manifestations, however, the memories would endure long after the sun had emerged. Deep in their hearts, they realised they had touched something very remarkable—a power without human comprehension.

And so, the indestructible egg remained silently guardian of the secrets buried beneath its mysterious shell while the inhabitants of Kurinji went about their everyday lives. It was evidence of the ongoing power of the unknown, a reminder that some forces operating in the world elude knowledge or explanation.

The egg has come to represent the Kurinji people's resilience and ability to bear hardship. It represented the hope that, no matter what obstacles were ahead, they would confront them together, united in their love for their nation and their relentless trust in the strength of the human spirit, as well as the strong communal relationships that had seen them through the darkest of times.

Chapter 10

Heist and Journey across the River

As the Asante vigilante squad stayed late, going over their previous day encounter with the egg. Chaos broke through the peaceful hallways of the temporary museum, much like its delicate glass had been broken. The startling sound of destruction now punctuates the eerie silence that once surrounded it. It felt as if something horrible had returned once again.

Before their eyes, a vision of desolation had developed. Once glorious and unspoilt, the retrieved antique relics in the improvised museum now lay in ruins, their great beauty tarnished by an invisible hand. As if the very walls murmured the secrets of the night, the air was thick with a terrible quiet. What evil power had fallen upon this revered site, mercilessly destroying its riches?

With their knowledge and keen eye for detail, the vigilante group—whose commander and second in charge, Edafe Manson—examined the surveillance tape with relentless attention. Little did he realise, however, that the video they were looking forward to would dash their dreams and send them down a confusing spiral of doubt. Their hearts sank as the pictures flashed across the screen, because the murky depths of the footage revealed only an unfathomable vacuum. The truth they yearned for remained elusive, lying in the shadow of the torturous puzzle.

Under the cover of darkness, as they were laying down their guard, a covert gathering of evil characters driven by their ravenous greed effectively acquired the much-sought-after treasure kept in the temporary museum. None of them could explain a daring theft that had occurred well into the night. An aura of mystery and peril enveloped it. The offenders had started a perilous path, their every action veiled in slyness and silence, driven with deliberate accuracy and unflinching determination. The guide was a strong local healer from the nearby town of Matomara.

Following the successful planning of the theft, the mysterious healer—covered in an air of mystery—found himself caught in the web of an unresolved riddle a day before the planned heist. He awakened from the depths of sleep gradually as the first light of the sun cut through the darkness. He found an odd sight there in his chamber, like a scenario straight from a confusing mystery. A riddle challenges all his known reasons for decorating the entrance of his chamber: several eggs placed everywhere, appearing magical overnight. He did not understand this riddle but has given his words to Mr Frays so he proceeded as planned.

Mr Frays is just one guy, driven by an insatiable need for adventure, who dares to defy the unattainable, no matter how many lives it would cost his secret organisation.

His brave operatives had gathered, their hearts ablaze with an insatiable desire for the mysterious item buried in Kurinji territory. Now they had hired a spiritual machinery to enter Kurinji's temporary museum's impenetrable sections. It was none other than Sanjay Voon, a virtuoso of the mystical world, an enigmatic sorcerer from the depths of Matomara, whose ethereal talents were known only in whispers—a mystery silhouette emerging during this effort, cloaked in an air of intrigue.

After their successful theft, Sanjay informed them that the impenetrable egg relic concealed the coveted golden globe key, rumoured to possess extraordinary powers capable of unlocking numerous doors. Only the dangerous currents of the river could carry it from Kurinji to Matomara, and then all the way to Ajuorun. The relics' mysterious power resisted climbing any hillside road so can only be transported through water. The secret to unleashing its true power in the upland—lies in a single location—the elusive Kurinji Land.

Not deterred by the menacing threats hiding in the shadows, the courageous band went forth on their sad path, their vessel cutting through the mysterious depths with a clarity like that of a razor's edge slicing through the finest silk. The calm waves of the Kurinji River silently observed their daring expedition. Its depths held untold mysteries, just waiting for exploration.

Their ferry swirled with dangerous currents, Frays and Sanjay's tired agents faced the merciless seas; each wave threatened to engulf them all. Above, a stormy storm grew, its black clouds whirling with evil, ready to strike the unlucky victims below. From the skies, floods of rain drenched the earth below. Once a calm river, now a ferocious beast, it screamed with an almost unquenchable need for death. Sanjay did not foresee this. Their boat was at the mercy of the unrelenting tempest in the middle of a dangerous storm; its weak construction could not resist nature's fierce attack. With its hull wobbling dangerously, the vessel gave way to the ruthless force of the turbulent river in a heart-stopping instant, just as it was about to pass over from Kurinji territory into Matomara. With a thundering smash, the vessel crashed and sent its terrified passengers into the merciless, swirling abyss below.

As the unfortunate vessel plunged into dangerous depths, Mr. Fray's crew's aspirations and ambitions met a merciless end. Their dreams disappeared into the sea, swallowed by the merciless waves, leaving behind a terrible mystery. Once together in their quest, the devoted agents now found themselves mercilessly split, their destinies unknown among the violent river currents.

A question lurks in ambiguity under the approaching darkness. Will the agents submit to the merciless river's unrelenting flow, or will they come out of the abyss changed and rejuvenated? What about the Kurinji treasure in their possession? The answer, hidden in the mysterious depths, determines their destiny.

Once the tempest passed, leaving a path of devastation, the once-tumultuous river slowly calmed down. Once strong and wild, its powerful currents have given way to a fresh peace. Once frenzied and turbulent, the surface of the water turned into a mirror-like expanse, reflecting the terrible quiet that had descended over the earth.

But hidden behind the calm façade was a secret story that was starting to fall apart. The daring gang of robbers, bound together by their common goal, found themselves mercilessly split among the dangerous river bottoms. Originally a ray of optimism, the ship now lay in ruins, evidence of the terrible might of the storm.

With its rich depths, the stream is well-known in old stories for having always-hungry, cunning crocodiles among other of its habitats.

Their hearts thumping with a combination of terror and will, they clung to the remains of their broken craft as they battled to survive. Like a thousand blades, the frigid waves cut their flesh and sapped their power with every instant. Still, they resisted falling into hopelessness, even in the face of hardship.

Under Sanjay's direction, several of them looked eager to negotiate the dangerous currents; their resolve was unflinching against the river's merciless wrath. Their thoughts concentrated on the one objective: survival and reaching the riverbank; with each stroke, they battled the draw of the abyss.

A survivor found himself swept ashore on an unknown riverbank as the sun started to set, giving the devastated scene an eerie hue. Weary and damaged, he fell upon the sandy coast, his chests thumping with every laboured breath.

The dead corpses of Mr. Fray's agents gathered together in the silence of the night, their hearts burdened with the weight of their agony as they confronted the fury of the river gods.

Even as their dead bodies lay there, a flutter of hope still blazes inside their master's heart, wounding their souls.

The unbreakable egg artifact, once the target of their relentless search, now appeared like a far-off dream buried within the turbulence of the tempest. Where did the indestructible egg they stole from the Kurinji temporal museum go?

And so the shattered, solitary survivor sharpened himself for the difficulties that were ahead as the moon rose high in the sky and sent its magical shine onto the devastated riverbed.

Chapter 11

Crocodile's Meal

The Kurinji's impenetrable egg teetered on the brink of an uncertain future under the eerie light of the mysterious moon, its ethereal beam throwing an unearthly shine onto the crocodile-infested stream. Its plunge into the dark sea was a dangerous dance with fate, as the evil secrets hidden there threatened to devour it whole.

With a fast, exact action, the predator's strong jaws closed to capture its unaware victim. Unknown to the sly crocodile, its ravenous appetite had brought it a fatal meeting. The sly crocodile had no idea that the naive prey it had caught was not just a meal but also a messenger of mysterious truths yet to unearth.

Kurinji's golden globe key now likely resides deep within the beast's guts, amidst the dangerous depths. It remained dormant, buried in the crocodile's turbulent depths, its secrets lost in mystery. The predator's strong and terrifying teeth were no match for the impervious shell covering its secrets.

An aura of mystery hung thick as the enormous river pushed forward, its unrelenting currents hiding the mysteries of the future. The mysterious egg set out on its dangerous journey inside the crocodile's strong gut, veiled in mystery. Nestled within the predator's stomach, the egg, a captivating enigma, concealed a multitude of enigmatic secrets awaiting discovery.

As the Kurinji peasant awaited the revelation of this remarkable phenomenon, murmurs of interest and questions floated about.

Days became nights, and nights became days as the mysterious creature's strong digestive system battled its unknown contents, which seemed to become caught within its gut.

With every passing time, the tension built in this crocodile as its digestive enzymes were unable to solve the riddle before it. Given this strong digestive system's constant attack, what could possibly survive? As the mystery grew and the suspense intensified, the response remained elusive, covered in a layer of doubt.

Though it seemed tough, the crocodile was a prisoner of its own secrets. The egg it carried was not ordinary; it was indestructible. It was a relic from a long-gone age, an object of immense power. People said the egg had the ancient golden globe key—a key so strong it may alter the path of events. The crocodile seems to have taken on the role of protector, guaranteeing its defence against anyone who would try to profit from its mysterious abilities.

This egg held the answer to a conundrum that had dogged Kurinji territory for innumerable millennia.

Once consumed, the egg appeared to have vanished forever, and the secret it held would remain forever obscured in darkness. The crocodile's jaws now controlled Kurinji Land's destiny.

Once a symbol of power and dread, the beast now offered Kurinji its final chance. Though the crocodile realised he had no option—he only wanted an egg meal—it was a hefty load to carry.

The environment surrounding Kurinji hummed with rumours of the stolen mysterious egg as the crocodile suffered in its dark room, the weight of its fate resting upon its scaly shoulders. Stories like Wildfire spark the dreams of those who long for a taste of its potency. Some warned of deadly secrets that may destroy the whole fabric of existence, while others mentioned unspoken wealth.

But within the whirlwind of conjecture and curiosity, a small number of people had started to put the pieces of the jigsaw that had vanished together.

Though the story of the predator's meal and the unusual guardian of the mysterious egg had only begun, it had already set the stage for an epic narrative full of mystery, bravery, and the strong links of destiny. Kurinji is ready to start a new chapter that will shape the next generation.

Chapter 12

Dancing with Death

For the criminals, who had set out on a mission of considerable risk, the second impenetrable theft seemed to be successful. Their aim is to pilfer and carry the most sought-after and valuable artefact in Kurinji society to their master across the river—a priceless, indestructible egg of unbelievable worth.

Their path, once filled with optimism and will, has suddenly veered. Before them came a dangerous river whose muddy waters hid secrets, like a terrible trap created by an invisible hand. As the lone survivor recovered his strength and gingerly walked towards the edge of the lake, the air became thick with expectation.

Comprising local volunteers who use their life skills as divers to avoid water mishaps across the Kurinji River, Sadly, however, the events of the preceding two weeks have troubled every resident—including the divers. Four of them learned about a boat accident from residents and decided to intervene right away. A sliver of hope burst inside the exhausted survivor.

One of the divers murmured to the others, among the worn and dishevelled assemblage of dead corpses washed ashore: "It is Sanjay, the mysterious Matomara healer, shrouded in an aura of enigma, who speared the theft at the museum," he said.

After the robbery, rumours about Mr. Frays and his machinery's remarkable powers spread like wildfire throughout Kurinji town.

The healer's sharp eyes fixed on theirs, a silent challenge glittering in their depths as the air became thick with tension. With a somewhat rebellious voice, he opened his lips and began to speak words that would unravel the mystery before them.

I am sorry about the robbery. I am not your enemy; I only gave them direction. His words sliced through the tense environment like a sharp knife. The air halted, and the accusing glances ceased abruptly as his words weighed heavily.

His words hung in the air like a cold mist, and his voice trembled with a terrible combination of dread and expectation as he gently pushed on. He said boldly, "I can help the town recover; I am certain that among these dangerous waters, one of those cunning crocodiles holds the key to solving it all," in a low voice that hardly escaped his lips.

Now, the priceless, indestructible egg sought by many had turned into the unlucky victim of the river's ravenous hunger.

The divers attentively listened, but informed Sanjay that they needed to travel to the village to hand him over to the Kurinji elders. "Do you understand the scope of what your group and you have done?" one of the divers said. "It will take the grace of the elders and other villagers to save your life before you can speak of helping us to retrieve our historical artifacts that have gone beneath the water depths." Do you know, as he said, that crocodiles abound in our rivers and creeks? Sanjay only nodded in agreement.

The river crocodiles slinked, their eyes glistening with a dark gloss. They seemed to enjoy their victim's futile attempts. The diver experienced a surge of apprehension as they contemplated the possibility that the village's relentless pursuit of the coveted treasure might now lie concealed within these formidable creatures.

The significance of the missing egg extends beyond its mere value. The marsh consumed the key, a symbol of the Kurinji legacy and a glimpse of their past. The only caretakers of these relics were the crocodiles, with their old knowledge and ravenous appetite.

Sanjay should now ask the community elders—led by Murali—for guidance on next steps.

Returning to the Kurinji community next to the temporal museum, the elder's council convened with Dr. Meena, Kavin, Gopal, Ravi, Asante, Edafe, and other residents to determine Mr. Sanjay's faith and opinions. While Asante and a few other villagers argued for a harsh penalty for Sanjay before any further action, Elder Murali advised bringing him in to help retrieve the lost egg as time is crucial. Elder Murali reminded the crowd witnessing, stressing the need for time in this context. Murali opined, "If he offered to help us get the egg, we should let him do so, and then we could talk about maybe penalising him later".

It's now time for Sanjay to explain how he can help recover their pilfered egg. As Sanjay presented his scheme to the people of Kurinji, hope began to bubble around. Once somewhat thick in the air, the hopelessness started to lift. They realized Sanjay was a spiritual man who knew the marsh's ways and its animals.

Supported by local diving volunteers, they set off on their trip into the marsh with fresh will. Though they were aware it would be risky, they were prepared to meet whatever obstacles came their way. They were on a quest to recover some of their past histories, not just a lost egg.

Driven by the moonlight and their will, they realised their trip had just started when they arrived in the riverbank. They were prepared to learn the mysteries of the marsh.

Sanjay set the pace; his steps on the unstable terrain were consistent. Their pulses thumped with a mixture of terror and expectation, and the others trailed closely behind. Around them, the marsh seems to come alive, the water rippling with concealed perils and the trees murmuring secrets.

The crocodiles made their presence known as they descended more into the river. Their eyes gleamed in the darkness; their enormous shapes hardly seen under the muddy water. The divers inhaled and tightened their hands around their rifles.

But Sanjay stayed cool, his voice consistent, as he talked to the animals in a language only, they appeared to grasp. The crocodiles seemed to listen, their gaze fixed on the mysterious healer, much to the wonder of the divers.

The mysterious healer Sanjay was resolute under the stifling cloak of hopelessness. His sharp eyes swept across the barren landscape before him, like a hawk sizing its prey. "Do not fear," he uttered, his voice resonating through the moonlit silence of the riverbanks.

Sanjay continued, "We must respect them," his words tinged with urgency. "Understand them, and then we may recover what we have lost." Sanjay realised that knowing the crocodiles would help them recover their lost, indestructible egg rather than battling them. Respect and understanding of these beings, he thought, would help them recover what they had lost. Crocodiles are well-known as Kurinji Land's assistants because of their ancient historical background.

With each stride, the group descended into the enigma's core. The air tightened and the marsh pressed in around them. But Sanjay's presence was a lighthouse in the darkness, guiding them ahead—a ray of hope.

Chapter 13

Slink into the Belly of the Beast

The community volunteer divers proceeded with great care towards the edge of the dangerous river, their bodies covered in imperceptible protective gear. An electric tension charged the environment, as if the air itself held its breath in anticipation. As the divers dropped into the muddy abyss, the water embraced them like a dark hug. Shadows moved menacingly, hiding the threats just out of view. The divers understood they were walking on the brink of the known, into unexplored land, where reason and nature appeared to bend and twist.

Sanjay's description of the unusual crocodile and its sleek, moonlit, shimmering scales piqued their interest. A monster of unparalleled speed had captured their attention, posing a true mystery. The divers knew this elusive predator might solve the riddle.

Equipped with modern underwater cameras and cutting-edge tracking systems, they set out on a dangerous search for the elusive crocodile. Their hearts were thumping on their ribcages, ready to explode from their chests, galloping like wild stallions. With each beat, adrenaline shot through their veins and energized their senses.

An aura of suspense descended over them as they crossed every meandering river, growing like an unbreakable fog covering every stride. The dark, gloomy seas muttered with hidden secrets, their undulating waves resonating with the mysterious puzzle just waiting.

Their hearts rushed within their chests; a symphony of expectation coursed through their veins. They walked carefully towards the river, its waves a turbulent maelstrom of anxiety. A wicked power, the current whirled and swirled, calling them with a terrible attraction.

With his extensive knowledge and magical skills, Sanjay devised and suggested to the divers a plan to rescue the crocodile believed to be carrying the impenetrable egg alive. Recognizing that the creature's innards held the secret to their survival, he vowed to aid them in obtaining it, thereby sparing his own life from the sins he and his team had perpetrated. Though it was their only chance, should they decide to follow his bold, risky, and unpredictable strategy? Will the golden globe key be recovered?.

With courage and will, the Kurinji divers faced the challenge. Although they realised their work was hazardous, they had no option. Their community's destiny teetered.

Like the revelation of a long-held secret, the electrifying sensation of expectancy electrified the air. Whispers of their mission announcement spread like wildfire, reaching even the darkest reaches of the town and surrounding towns, producing a wave of disquiet that sent shills sliding down the spines of anyone courageous enough to go close.

Deep in the muddy river bog, a strong predator hid itself under unknown circumstances. Hidden in the tangle of vegetation, the crocodile—a monster of unmatched power and intelligence—bided its time carefully. Its eyes gleamed with an almost ravenous desire, like those of two sharp obsidian orbs.

Knowing there was a lurking predator, the divers proceeded cautiously. Their breaths were weak and rapid, and their hearts hammered in their chests. One mistake might bring catastrophe, they understood. As they descended into the marsh, the crocodile tracked every action. It lay quiet, its body precisely hidden in the bushes, waiting for the ideal moment for attack.

Still, the divers were not easy targets for predators. They were prepared for the encounter with the formidable creature, having undergone rigorous training specifically for this occasion. They acted with a signal from their commander, Madueke Anderson, as suggested by Sanjay. Their motions were quick and exact, and their brains concentrated on the current work. Among other river dwellers, they have seen a probable crocodile.

Sensing the danger, the crocodile now roared fiercely forward. Its powerful jaws missed the first diver by a few inches. As the war for survival, man versus beast, went on, the water swirled and frothed. Still, the divers knew something. They quickly moved to capture the crocodile, dragging it within a strong net. The beast raged and writhed, its tail lashing out in a last-ditch effort at release. Still, the divers clutched tightly and firmly.

As they brought the crocodile to the surface, the healer arrived, his eyes shining with anticipation.

Sanjay provided guidance, gesturing to the animal's abdomen, leaving a trace on its form, and requesting its release back into the creek, while closely monitoring its movements. He knew the key lay in the belly of the beast and was determined to get at it, but sadly, this was not the crocodile with the unbreakable egg meal. This crocodile will guide you to the guilty person we are hunting. Once you locate the offender, this crocodile will serve as your guide; it will disappear quickly while the offender moves slowly. Their commander questioned, "Are you sure about this?" A dissatisfied expression looked at Sanjay. "Absolutely, just trust me on this one," Sanjay said.

Today, the unbreakable gg, the precise target of their search, vanished from view. It had disappeared, as if sucked down into the muddy depths of the marsh, yet it seemed to have started the trip down beneath the river.

Their hearts were heavy with their failure; they couldn't shake the feeling that their journey was far from over as they returned to the hamlet. This crocodile attention and attack towards them made them believe it was the one, but sadly it was not the beast holding their destiny.

Even though the story of the journey into the unknown and the battle in the heart of the beast had just begun, it had already set the stage for an epic narrative of mystery, bravery, and the unbreakable bonds of community.

Chapter 14

Community's Fight Against Fear

At the elder council meeting today, there was a clear feeling of urgency, as if time were running out for the elderly to save their dear community.

Murali observed that the unbreakable egg's worth and appeal are incalculable, capturing everyone's attention. But a fierce crocodile beneath the stream stood in their way, a defender of unmatched power and intelligence. Whispers of anxiety permeated the gathering of divers, their brains engulfed in the urgent question that tormented them all. How could they recover the priceless relic—the means of their redemption—from the hands of the vicious reptile sentinel without giving in? Even though Mr. Fray's gang appears to have paid the ultimate price for their actions, it's not the right time to punish them; Sanjay is currently in their custody, so it's time for their communities compensation by Sanjay if they are able to recover the stolen relic.

The ancient artifact, the golden globe key, held secrets that may change the entire fabric of the town's history itself, raising the stakes to an unthinkable height. But the crocodile, a strong beast radiating great strength and deadly danger, presented an insurmountable challenge and clouded their every action.

It required not only perfect accuracy, but also bravery to complete the intended goal by transcending the very teeth of death. Now equipped with a greater understanding of the elusive nature of the crocodile, the enigmatic kurinji divers, led by Madueke and mentored by Sanjay, embarked on a second dangerous voyage that would test their mettle to the limit.

Standing on the brink of fate, the air buzzed with a ferocious feeling of dread. Their every breath seemed to linger in the air, weighty with doubt. Their task before them had the ability to mould their whole lives—a second dangerous trip meant to test their mettle and solve the riddles afflicting the entire homeland.

They did not realize, however, that this would be the day the tides of destiny would change significantly.

The whole hamlet is waiting in the community square next to the temporary museum; everyone's eyes are focused with will and a tinge of anxiety. Though they knew the dangerous work ahead, the divers had no option. Their accomplishments determined not only their own but perhaps even the destiny of the earth. As the seconds passed, an unrelenting will flow through the diver's veins, strengthening their soul.

The divers hugged their loved ones and headed towards their dangerous path to retrieve the egg from the belly, silently nodding at Madueke. The road was hazardous, full of lethal guards and secret traps. Every step they took reflected the weight of their entire society's fate. Given his involvement in the theft that led to the current catastrophe, some are beginning to doubt the validity of the healer's claims. Madueke told them to give it a try today for Kurinji.

But Sanjay had a strategy—a bold one built on creative ability. He understood that cutting the egg from the crocodile's gut would endanger the priceless artefact within. Instead, he must guide them to become intelligent and outsmart the beast in its natural habitat and game. Crocodiles are traditionally sacred for the Kurinji tribe; the death of one is like the death of a person. Sanjay issued a warning: To access the unbreakable egg abilities, the crocodile must survive.

With a nod from Sanjay, the divers launched themselves onto the appointed riverbed. Their motions were quick and precise; they danced through them. The Madueke diver reached for the crocodile's head, staring exactly at it. In his hands, he carried a long pole—an instrument meant to save them.

The crocodile's jaws snapped, and the diver entered its mouth, wedging the pole open. The beast twisted and writhed, but the pole held firm, repulsing its lethal teeth. The other divers moved in, their hands extending well inside the crocodile's neck.

It was a charged moment, a struggle of will between man and beast. The crocodile's body was heaving as it struggled to get free, and the divers could feel its muscles straying out of control. Still, they stayed firmly committed.

Then, triumphantly crying, they defeated and vanquished the enormous crocodile, dragging it to the ground. Then Sanjay confirmed, "Yes, this is him, bending to the beast in front."

With their faces glowing with delight and relief, the town erupted in cheers as the divers headed to the village square, carrying the monster. They were now done. They had caught the crocodile bearing the secret to their atonement.

Surprisingly, the healer worked his magic by talking to the beast to relax, while watching in wonder.

Tears of happiness poured down their cheeks as the people hugged one another, relief and thanks filling their hearts. Their relationship is stronger than ever before, but now they must collect the indestructible egg. They confronted their anxieties and came out triumphant. Before the egg could be useful, the healer warned the crocodile must survive.

And so the people of Kurinji celebrated their success, their hearts full of the knowledge that they had overcome their worries and emerged stronger than ever before as the sun sank over the horizon and threw its golden glow over the ground.

Chapter 15

Veterinarian's Gambit

Now that the beast was under control, the entire town faced a lengthy road ahead. Capturing it was one thing; extracting the artifact was second; keeping the crocodile alive was third.

Amid this dire situation, struggling on ideas on how to extract the egg from the captured beast, someone unexpectedly emerged from the shadows in the town square. Renowned local veterinarian and historian Dr. Meena became an unexpected friend, well-known in the mysterious realm of reptiles. Her presence was as surprising as a breeze on a moonless night, giving the hopeless souls trapped in this web of uncertainty some hope.

Tension permeated the large community square as the gathering of impoverished elders—Kavin, Gopal, Ravi, and others—huddled together, their eyes flitting frantically from one face to another. They had tried every alternative and investigated every path, yet the answer to their problem remained far-off.

Then, however, a low, enigmatic voice disturbed the quiet. "Heed my words," Dr. Meena said, her voice almost audible over their rapid beats. "I suggest a scheme, one that is dangerous but promises to save us."

Dr. Meena was renowned for her boldness and openness to exploring uncharted territory. She had devoted years of research to reptile behaviour in their natural environment and working on historical pasts. Her expertise was unrivalled and broad. She knew she was the only one in the community who could come up with a scheme to get the indestructible egg without hurting the crocodile.

The community found themselves at a critical juncture, engulfed in despair. Dr. Meena's suggestion emerged from the shadows, forcing the elders to consider it with their backs against the wall. As they considered the fallout from their decision, whispers of doubt pervaded the atmosphere. Reluctantly, they gave in to the attraction of this enigmatic offer; their combined desperation blinded them to the possible risks that awaited.

The scheme was straightforward but bold: they would remove the impenetrable egg from the crocodile's stomach using a specially made tool and sew it back without endangering its life.

That day of reckoning had at last come. As they got ready for their bold expedition into the bowels of the beast, into unexplored territory fraught with peril, they realised they were setting off a voyage from which they may never return, and the air was heavy with expectation.

Their will grew with each passing moment. They understood they might even perish to get the egg and reveal its mysteries. Every stride Dr. Meena guided them into the swamp towards their fate resonated with bravery and will.

Ignorant of what was going to happen, the crocodile lay still in its newly built environment. Dr. Meena approached the crocodile with care and reverence, feeling wonder at this amazing creature that held such immense control over their destiny.

Under the professional guidance with her team, Dr. Meena has initiated the surgical operation. Every action was deliberate and well-considered to guarantee no injury to any of the engaged parties. Working relentlessly against time and nature itself, they sought what appeared impossible: extracting the impenetrable egg unshattered and maintaining the crocodile alive as hours moved into days and days into nights.

Dr. Meena's and his helper Peter's skilful hands worked with a consistent elegance as she inserted the specialized gadget into the crocodile's gaping mouth. Everyone was holding their breath and clearly felt tension in the air as the veterinarian worked her magic. On her brow, beads of perspiration developed, evidence of the intense strain and focus she was under.

Time seemed to stop as the gadget moved towards its aim. The crocodile's strong jaws, which could easily crush bone, were oddly calm, as if even the beast itself sensed the weight of the circumstances. As Dr. Meena navigated the perilous terrain of the crocodile's belly, her eyes closed and her concentration remained unbroken.

Then, with a strong shock, the gadget latches on to something solid. Heart pounding, Dr. Meena knew she had found some kind of metal item. "Is that not the unbreakable egg?" Meena said it in a whisper.

Her nodding in agreement that the unbreakable egg is in the beast's tummy amazed the observers. The veterinarian's gamble appeared to have paid off; one amazing lady's genius and tenacity will help to preserve the village.

As the surgical operation on the beast progressed, a subdued expectation loomed large in the air. Dr. Meena, a figure of unflinching resolve, and her committed staff captured all the attention. Their talented hands would determine the fate of their beloved town.

On the operation table, the amazing crocodile before them lay still. Its dimensions were great. Once a cause of anxiety, the iron grasp of Dr. Meena's experience held captive her strong jaws. The audience echoed whispers of anxiety, mixed with the obvious tension engulfing the scenario.

Time appeared to stop while Dr. Meena and her colleagues worked assiduously. The room was in a terrible silence, broken only by the faint hum of the medical equipment and the sporadic murmured directive. Outside, the people marvelled as Dr. Meena worked with surgical accuracy, her hands firm despite the weight of their shared hopes resting on her shoulders.

Tension permeated the room as the clock counted away. As they worked nonstop, beads of perspiration fell down their wrinkled foreheads, and their hands moved with accuracy and will. The unbreakable egg, their desired possession, had eluded them for what seemed like an eternity. At last, however, triumph was within their reach.

Dr. Meena made a final, cautious cut with her gloved fingers, reaching inside the beast's guts. The crowd gasped as she gently pulled her hand to show the shining, indestructible egg tucked gently in her palm.

The room resonated with whispers of relief mixed with the general moans of tiredness. The impenetrable egg, a mystery that had perplexed even the most seasoned professionals, was discovered. It was unquestionably beautiful; its mysteries lay within its impervious shell.

Their work was far from over, however. They discovered the egg's true value within; it merely served as a vessel. They wondered what mysteries it may have, as they meticulously cleaned and investigated it under strong lights and magnifying lenses. According to Dr. Meena, it appeared to be an egg almost ready to hatch.

Would it provide them with a means of atonement? Alternatively, would it unleash a power more terrible than they could possibly conceive? Does it still have their golden globe key?

Abruptly, they realised something terrible. Despite their success in finding the egg, a small but crucial element had disappeared. The beast, the strong crocodile, lay deadly quiet on the surgical table. As it rose and fell with each laboured breath, its chest remained immobile. As the weight of their awareness crushed their emotions, the room became quiet. Crocodile life has historically been as excellent as that of any individual living in the community. Sanjay, the healer, has informed them that the death of this crocodile would render its unbreakable egg abilities ineffective. Murali and his elder's council have taken this information into consideration, while also adhering to local customs.

Dr. Meena approached the crocodile, her expression marked with anxiety. She gently looked for any sign of life, hoping without hope that their efforts had not been in vain. But the reality became indisputable as the seconds passed.

The issue now is whether the crocodile, who watched over the priceless egg, died during surgery.

If that's the case, the people will face a flood of sorrow and despair. They had gambled everything and trusted Dr. Meena and her staff, only to experience the sourness of failure. Originally a sign of optimism, the egg now appeared to ridicule them just by virtue of its existence.

Despite her strong will, however, Dr. Meena stayed optimistic, attempting all her medical wizardry to wake the beast, and refused to let gloom overwhelm her. Her voice was firm and deliberate, and she spoke to the people with a determined glitter in her eye. "We cannot let this setback define us," she said, her words piercing the gloomy mood. "His sacrifice will not be in vain. If the crocodile dies, we must respect its legacy by devising strategies to solve the riddles of the indestructible egg and save our community."

The locals banded behind her, inspired by Dr. Meena's unflinching bravery. Though they understood the road ahead would be difficult, they were prepared to meet any obstacles head-on. They remembered that time was important; the ticking clock of destiny pushed them on.

Chapter 16

Stealthy Beast

The day after the surgical operation on the beast, its fate hung precariously on the edge of a dangerous cliff; its very existence, teetering on the brink of a dreadful feeling of approaching catastrophe, appeared to cover the entire town. If the crocodile succumbs to death's grasp, a terrible outcome veiled in mystery looms large on the horizon.

Shivers down the spines of every person who heard the healer speak echoed through the air. The healer's voice rang menacingly: "The key, a vital instrument of unknown power, shall forever be rendered useless if the beast perishes; the crocodile must not die." From quivering lips, gasps escaped as the weight of those words sank upon the assembly. Once a sign of optimism and opportunity, the golden globe key kept within an indestructible egg now looked like a portent of gloom.

The Kurinji people's hearts became a fog of discomfort; news of the crocodile remained immobile and hung in the air. Concerned whispers permeated the streets, as people felt danger lurking in the shadows. Prayers, uttered with fervour and unwavering resolve, resonated through the little streets, their cries merging and rising into the skies above.

Their expectations wobble on the brink of a cliff, barely hanging. The mystery crocodile's eyes, like unbreakable vaults, remained firmly locked, capturing everyone's attention.

Tension was high in the operation room of Dr. Meena as the much-awaited flash of insight finally arrived. Rising from the depths of its cryptic sleep, the enigmatic crocodile—covered in an impervious cocoon of silence—had finally sprung to life, but then once again had gone numb like a sudden stretch.

Only the heavy murmurs of perplexity and hopelessness broke the once-peaceful community's terrible silence. Once bound by their sense of community, the residents suddenly found themselves lost in a sea of doubt.

But within this stifling gloom, Dr. Meena appeared unconcerned about the hopelessness engulfing the people. Her pulse thumped like a drum, and she experienced a flood of fresh will. If she felt as if the weight of the world sat on her shoulders, she refused to let it break her spirit.

Dr. Meena carefully studied every sinew and scale of the strong crocodile's body, breathing softly. Her eyes darted over the terrifying body of the beast, searching for a solution.

A spark of hope flashed in her eyes suddenly. She saw a minute detail—a faint hint that may alter her path of work. She told her colleagues that maybe the crocodile was just ill.

On the second day after the operation, just as optimism was beginning to fade, something ignited Dr. Meena's fatigued spirit. A revelation hit her brain like a flashbulb. Dispersed across her mental canvas, the pieces of the jigsaw started to fit. Once evasive, the answer was now in front of her. She must carefully examine the crocodile again to ensure that everything is inside.

Once again, with extreme caution, she began another surgery with her team and gently slid her hand into the dangerous depths of the crocodile's stomach. She gingerly removed another small object, resembling a sharp surgical scissor, from the crocodile's stomach, seemingly inflicting damage on its internal organs as the air filled with tension. How did this lethal object find its way to the beast's belly?

The image that met Meena, however, really made her shudder: the beast, against all odds immediately after sewing it up, seemed to be moving merely one of its legs after all her efforts.

News whispers tore through the community, kindling a passion like wildfire. Its people started to see a sliver of hope flickering in their hearts, throwing off the gloom of hopelessness.

Dr. Meena, a renowned veterinarian and historian with native Kurinji blood coursing through her veins, painstakingly completed her last preparations for the much-anticipated awakening of the beast.

The air in the town had become thick with a disturbing silence, as if time itself had stopped in anticipation. Every person there discovered they were enmeshed in an unsettling silence; their own breathing stopped in a chorus. Meena's surgery room turned into a stage, its inhabitants' hearts thumping in their chests as they prepared themselves for the reveal of whether the beast would eventually wake. They were only characters in a thrilling drama.

Dr. Meena stood in front of a huge apparatus. Her goal weighed heavily in the air as she got ready to set out on another dangerous trip that would perhaps rouse a beast of unheard-of might. She ventured into the uncharted realm of the unfamiliar.

The historical egg, securely obtained and presented to the elders, had meanwhile become another forum for community gossipers to interact, viewed as an enigmatic item that resisted all efforts to open it. Everyone looked at the mysterious egg that had escaped them for so long, filled with expectation. Its flawless surface seems to contain the key to many secrets, with mysteries haunting them every waking minute.

With the beast still unconscious, Dr. Meena's surgery room had a tremendous sense of anticipation. And when Murali asked if the beast would come to life, the silence reverberated back with a doubtful voice. "Only time will tell," Meena said, her voice falling off and her eyes darting frantically, leaving the statement hanging in the air.

The stillness that followed was deafening; the weight of the future smothered them like a stifling blanket. Their hearts were heavy with concern, and the people could only watch and wait; their destiny rested in balance. Once a symbol of strength and mystery, the crocodile lay still, its life energy dangling on a precarious thread.

Her forehead wrinkled with concentration, and Dr. Meena kept relentlessly working. Desperate, she leafed through medical books and historical literature in search of some sign of hope against the unknown crocodile disease. Now safely in their grasp, the egg seemed to taunt them with its enigmatic presence; its secrets remained concealed behind its intact shell.

The conflict in the community became intolerable. As optimism gave way to resignation, whispers of uncertainty and hopelessness started to flow. The elders, once a lighthouse of knowledge and direction, suddenly found themselves lost; their trust in Dr. Meena's ability was erasing daily.

Dr. Meena, nevertheless, was not going to stop. Her eyes blazing with enormous will, she intensified her efforts and pushed herself almost to tiredness. She realized she was responsible for both the community's and perhaps the earth's destiny. She now believed that the crocodile, the key to unlocking the mysteries of the golden globe, and the indestructible egg were essential.

And then, just when everything seemed lost, a miracle happened. With fluttering wide eyes, the crocodile let forth a feeble but clear snarl. Their hearts were bursting with delight, and the people gazed in wonder as the beast gradually recovered its strength, its massive body rising from the table like a phoenix from the ashes.
Her cheeks contracted in relief tears, and Dr. Meena realised they had accomplished the impossible. Her relentless commitment and mastery had revived the crocodile, which had been on the verge of death. They now sought the unbreakable egg within their grasp, its secrets still hidden.

Dr. Meena understood that their road was far from over, even as the people celebrated their victory. She sensed a vitality within the impenetrable egg and its secrets, indicating that they still lay ahead, poised for discovery. For now, however, they could savour the pleasure of their triumph, confident in knowing they had surmounted the impossible. Once on the verge of oblivion, one lady's strength awoke the quiet beast and regenerated its life essence.

Although the story of the silent beast and the expected reveal had come to an end, Dr. Meena's courage and the Kurinji people's tenacity would live on for future generations.

Chapter 17

Awakening the Beast

Weeks unfolded like a never-ending chasm, everyday bursting with mystery and expectation. The mysterious egg, tightly holding its secrets, was a tantalising riddle that refused to provide even one hint or react to all the cracks the Kurinji community was looking for. An unbreakable darkness seemed to cover its fundamental essence, leaving everyone who ventured near it confused and intrigued.

The air buzzed with an electric excitement every day in the Kurinji village, as if the solution to this conundrum would open a universe of unearthly beauties. But as every second stretched into minutes, the elusive secret stayed just out of grasp, mocking and challenging everyone who tried to solve its riddle.

A tangible weight clinging to every breath in the people and, the atmosphere at the temporal Kurinji Museum—where the enigmatic key concealed in the unbreakable egg has been returned—seemed to be thickening. The very air seemed to have the secrets of a thousand mysteries, tantalisingly near yet maddeningly far.

A lethal predator had overcome the odds and emerged triumphant in the middle of death like it thrived in a dangerous forest, where peril lurks around every corner. Renowned for its razor-sharp fangs and ravenous hunger, the terrifying crocodile had defeated the most powerful of enemies, therefore demonstrating once again that it was the indisputable king of the creek. But its triumph came at a price. Its formerly strong physique is now a mere ghost of its former self as it heals from the razor cuts and sutures of Dr. Meena's team. The conflict had left it wounded and defenceless. They believed that a fierce will and a spark of rebellion remained.

Word of the crocodile's emergence spread like wildfire over the Kurinji communal neighbourhoods. Once driven by uncertainty and hopelessness, the people now felt a fresh hope. The success of the beast represented their own resiliency and a message that they too may overcome challenges.
Her eyes glittering with joy and satisfaction, Dr. Meena realised they had accomplished something rather amazing. The crocodile's waking was a triumph for both the Kurinji people and the beast itself. It was evidence of the strength that comes from unity—that which one may find in gathering courage against difficulty.

For now, however, as they celebrate their success, enjoying the emergence of the beast is an accomplishment worth cherishing. Elder Murali and his council fully understood that they had begun the path to a better future as the people danced and sang, their hearts bursting with hope and delight.
Still hidden behind the impregnable, indestructible eggshell, the key remained a mystery.

And thus, the people of Kurinji realised they had begun the journey towards a better future, as the dance of triumph carried on deep into the evening. The waking of the beast had given them the will to keep on, to boldly and determinedly meet the obstacles ahead.

With their historical crocodiles by their sides, a live tribute to their unwavering spirit, the future seemed bright, and everything seemed conceivable. The inhabitants of Kurinji were eager to welcome the difficulties that lay ahead with open arms and honest hearts; the victory dance had barely started.

Chapter 18

Bioluminescent Puzzle

Kurinji village's once-travelling visitor count has now transformed into a community of unrelenting searchers, all driven by the need to solve the unbreakable egg riddle, shrouding every inch in mystery. The once-bustling streets, full of people laughing and sellers chatting animatedly, now reflect quiet murmurs and the delicate rustle of old books. Though it was clear-cut, the metamorphosis had a special appeal that attests to the pure spirit of the Kurinji people.

But now the sun appears to be pointing out a ray of optimism that has cut through the Kurinji's gloom. Rumours about the indestructible egg recovery quickly spread, captivating the imaginations of the people and surrounding towns, and inspiring them to continue searching for solutions to extract the golden globe key from the egg.

But it was Kavin's appearance in the assembly today that appeared to rouse Kurinji's ancient communal spirit. Kavin's unquenchable curiosity was unbounded, with eyes as keen as a hawk and a mind as nimble as a cat, Kavin had an unquenchable curiosity that was immeasurable. Whispers of his name connected with the search for truth. And now, his steady eye had turned to the once-lost, enigmatic, unbreakable egg. Kavin appears to be starting from a place where people, like Gopal, Ravi, Meena, seem to have abandoned him.

Kavin's mysterious demeanour distinguished him from other Kurinji young people and enthralled the town officials. Once again absorbing every minute aspect of the indestructible egg, his sharp eye scanned the area in the dimly lit temporal museum room. As he stood there, his head a maze of many possibilities, the air was dense with expectancy. He was ready to plunge headlong into the depths of the unknown; his search was a riddle to solve.

Kavin was an exceptional leader for his age, a master of observation and deduction, and a keen eye for detail. Day after day, he would explore the depths of the temporal museum, his gaze fixed on the object of his obsession. His fixation developed, entangling his own existence in a web of mystery and discomfort with every instant that went by. A tantalising mystery, the indestructible egg appeared to be beckoning him back day after day and holding him prisoner in its strange embrace.

Time appears valuable; hence, Kavin provided himself with a chronology to solve the indestructible egg problem. He examined every minute feature and every faint nuance with a fervent, almost insane intensity. His head turned into a maze of ideas and hypotheses, each more appealing than the next. This antique relic had secrets. Whales crave to tell stories? The answers escaped him, taunting and seducing him everywhere. Upon arrival at the temporal museum, Kavin fixed his gaze on the enigmatic, unbreakable egg sitting on the table, its existence shrouded in shadow. Despite being invisible to the unaided eye, a faint light soon emerged from it, only visible under ideal circumstances. Nobody could see this brightness; it escaped all the security guards covering the temporal museum area, the trouping guests, and not anything like what the Asante vigilante gang saw.

After spending many weeks staring at the problem from another angle, Kavin was enthralled with this amazing insight. He was determined to explore the shadows of this secret relationship, driven to solve the riddle before him.

Hours stretched into days, and days into weeks, as Kavin dug deeper into the riddle before him. With unparalleled intensity, he painstakingly moved many light sources, their rays bouncing around the room and creating spooky shadows on the walls. He painstakingly evaluated every angle and intensity, as if he were a conductor arranging a symphony of light.

The truth then emerged in a flash of insight. The indestructible egg was by no means average; it was just a vehicle for life. It had a secret power and a covert life that ran against natural rules. It was a brilliant entity in and of itself—a bioluminescent organism. The bioluminescent organism electrified Kavin's senses, sending chills down his spine. What mysteries does this radiant entity conceal? Some riddles are still undiscovered. When Kavin revealed his surprise, it tore through Kurinji like a hurricane, leaving murmurs and gasps in its wake. The people were in awe as they saw Kavin's incredible find. Their hearts raced, and their eyes widened because what lay ahead would rock their small, peaceful town.

Little did they realise that the benign egg they had been so fervently striving to break open now harboured a secret much darker than they could have ever dreamed. Inside its delicate shell, benevolent was not just the Kurinji-loved golden globe Key but also a living being humming with an unknown vitality. Its entire existence violated nature's rules, engulfing them in a mist of mystery that chilled their spines.

Their quest for the golden globe key, which held the secrets to their deepest conflicts, compelled them to adopt a new approach. Rumours about the mysterious bioluminescent creature inside the unbreakable egg had reached their ears through Kavin; perhaps there was a creature beneath the shell that held the exact key they sought. This has confirmed the suspicions of Dr Meena and the encounter of the vigilante security group.

With trepidation and hope entwined, the people embarked on a perilous quest to interact with this mysterious person, should it exist. They knew convincing it to hand over its priceless load would be difficult. The stakes were high, as the key would reveal the riddles that had dogged their lives for far too long.

Chapter 19

Cosmic Riddle

I f the Kurinji people want to glimpse the live being in the unbreakable egg containing their golden globe key, they now know and are acquainted with the lighting techniques from Kavin's descriptions.

Today is a determined day to interact with the egg and personally test Kavin's findings. Under ideal lighting, the elderly council headed by Murali and Kavin approached the unbreakable egg, its luminescent shape shimmering with an unearthly brightness, while most of the people were deep in slumber. Murali leads the village elders, who are eager to hear the story and have gathered with wonder and will. They need the golden globe key, and they understand that their destiny is dependent on their ability to establish a link with this remarkable entity in the shell.

Their voices resounding throughout the still night, they started to speak as a group with bated breath. In response to their comments, the thing within the egg appeared to have moved, its glowing shape throbbing. Their pulses were thumping with anticipation; they were in awe at the sight. The Kurinji village chiefs spoke softly, their words full of regard for the creature. They begged for its aid, promising to defend it and its habitat in return if it could provide the key to secure their old armoury and guard the entire Newcastle Hills shire area. The indestructible egg seemed to have had enough of them for the day, and it stopped pulsing until it faded away and they all departed. Kavin felt like the local hero entrusted with presenting his revelation to the entire community the following day— cracking the riddle.

They had no idea that such a powerful secret would permanently link their lives and challenge their courage and fortitude from the very core. Kavin's leadership ignited a glimmer of hope in their hearts. Now veiled in greater mystery by a bioluminescent creature like a living egg, the mysterious egg contained mysteries they had missed for far too long. This search consumed every waking thought—a passion that nearly drove them insane. Now, however, they ventured to hope the answers they sought were within their reach under Kavin's direction. As they were ready to embark on a journey that would test their will, test their intelligence, and force them to the very brink of their bravery, the air hummed with anticipation. This is the way to recover their key from the live bioluminescent creature in the impeccable unbreakable egg.

Today, in front of the entire village, Kavin had the opportunity to demonstrate to everyone, just as he had shown the elders, how they could continue to communicate with the living, unbreakable egg. Unfortunately, despite his seemingly endless and futile attempts to solve the bioluminescence's pulsating puzzles, Kavin was unable to establish contact with the bioluminescent organism within the egg. The entire community was in shock, with questions looming large: What went wrong? Did the living thing pass away inside it? Was Kavin joking with us or was it just his young age that fooled him? Did the elders witness anything?

Everyone chose to go about their own pursuits in disbelief as the day ended. No one knew what went wrong, the Kurinji elders already established they witnessed it themselves when they went with Kavin the previous night. What went wrong now is the question? The confusion lingers in every villager's mind as the day goes by.

Unfortunately, the council of the elders decided to diverge from Kavin's discovery, as it seemed that the bioluminescence communication was no longer functional. Instead, they sought a different approach to unravelling the mystery surrounding the recovery of their valuable key from the unbreakable egg. Although they had seen the first signs with Kavin, it seemed that the life inside the shell chose to ignore them. This was a dead end to a once-promising investigation into the unbreakable egg riddle.

As the sun sank below the horizon, painting the sky in tones of orange and crimson, Kavin sat on a grassy hill, gazing at the village historical museum that housed the egg. His youthful shoulders felt as if the weight of the enigma that failed him was pressing down upon him; he found comfort in the peace of nature.

Seeing Kavin's thoughtful behaviour across the road on her way home, Dr. Meena—who had decided to allow herself some time away from the egg mystery—approached him with a kind smile. Quietly, "Mind if I join you?" she said.

Kavin nodded and scuffed away to make room for herself. They sat in peaceful silence for a minute, each immersed in their own thoughts "I can't help but feel like I've let everyone down," Kavin said, his voice almost audible above a whisper. "The seniors placed their trust in me; now we find ourselves back at the beginning."

On his shoulder, Dr. Meena laid a consoling hand. "Kavin, you have not disappointed anybody. At least the elder saw your initial effort;

discovering the bioluminescent creature was a milestone. For your community, it's crucial that you maintain a competitive edge. Though I paid little attention to it as I was primarily concentrating on the crocodile recovery, I discovered there was life in that egg too.

Kavin glanced up at her, hope flickering in his eyes. "Do you really think so?"

"I know so," Dr. Meena told him. "We will find a way, Kavin." With great enthusiasm, Kavin said, "We must. I must attempt to interact with the egg once again; they must provide me with the opportunity." "Yes, they need to let you investigate; we have all failed at something. Look after the earthquake, Ravi and I had possession of one ancient key artefact, but we mysteriously lost it at his house, who knows the significant of that key too". "Also, as you know recently, it felt like I failed with the crocodile surgery recovery, but no, I didn't," Dr. Meena said. Looking startled, "I see what you mean, but that wouldn't be the golden globe key," Kavin asked. "Absolutely not, I know the golden globe key, but it could be one of the ancient relics from the museum; the point is, don't go too hard on yourself, Kavin," Dr. Meena said.

Kavin and Dr. Meena felt comfort in one another's company as they sat there, seeing the sun create an amazing range of hues in the sky. Beyond years and experience, a sense of trust and understanding had developed between them.

Meanwhile, the elders council are gathered in a poorly lit hall in the middle of the hamlet beside the temporal museum, their faces furrowed with anxiety. Their last attempt to contact the bioluminescent creature under Kavin's direction had left them in dire straits.

"We cannot afford to lose hope," Elder Murali said, his voice ringing with will. "Our people rely on us to identify a solution."

But what more can we do? Another older person responded with a clearly frustrated tone. "We're no closer to getting the key, even after we have run every avenue."

"Perhaps it's time to consider alternative approaches," Dr. Meena's voice sliced through the tension. Everyone looked at her as she walked into the room with Kavin by her side. Sorry to interrupt your meeting elders, we were just around the grassy hill discussing this topic.

"What do you suggest, Dr. Meena?" Curiosity aroused; Elder Murali queried.

"We may have missed other possibilities as we have been so focused on the egg and the organism inside it," Dr. Meena said. "I think it's time we delve deeper into Kurinji's past and the legends and stories passed down through the years."

Kavin moved forward with a determined gaze. Dr. Meena is correct. Our history may include hints that might help us solve the riddle of the key and the egg.

The elders exchanged looks, a sliver of hope flickering in their worn eyes. "It's worth a try," Elder Murali said. "We cannot walk away from any stone unturned."

Kavin and Dr. Meena exchanged a knowing glance as the discussion kicked off. Though they were aware the road ahead would be difficult, they were prepared to meet it squarely. Together, they would solve Kurinji's history riddles and release the one that had engulfed their lives.

Kavin, Dr. Meena, and the village elders then embark on a journey of enquiry into the depths of their past in search of solutions, driven once more. They didn't realise that the truth they wanted would change their lives and existence.

As the days grew into weeks, Kavin and Dr. Meena spent many hours reading over old books amidst other recovered artifacts and scrolls in their temporal museum archives. Their nose smelled musty ancient paper as they looked for any reference to the egg or the bioluminescent monster within it.

The elderly also shared tales and legends passed down over the years, thereby contributing their expertise. They spoke about a period when Kurinji was a realm of enchantment and wondered where the lines separating the normal from the supernatural blurred.

One story grabbed Kavin's interest. It described a powerful relic, a key capable of revealing cosmic mysteries. Someone allegedly concealed the secret within an incredibly valuable object that embodied the very core of existence. Kavin recalled that elder Murali had once said something like this.

"Could it be an egg?" Kavin asked loudly, his heart thrashing with delight. "Could the bioluminescent creature be guarding the key?"

Dr. Meena's eyes became enlightened. "It's possible," she gasped. "But how would we persuade the creature to turn over the key?"

They delved deeper into the mythology and discovered that acquiring the key required establishing one's value, displaying a pure heart, and adopting an unselfish attitude. The monster appeared to be both a judge of character and a protector. The monster appears to interact with a select few individuals.

Equipped with this fresh understanding, Kavin and Dr. Meena presented a strategy to the elderly. They suggested a series of trials and challenges meant to test the people's mettle and establish their merit for the bioluminescent beast.

Despite their initial doubts, the elderly eventually came to terms with it. Kurinji's destiny relied on their capacity to find the key; hence, they were ready to do whatever was necessary to guarantee their existence.

The trials started from then on. Each of the demanding tasks assigned to the villagers tested their resilience, bravery, and compassion. They tackled their darkest secrets, faced their most intense anxiety, and came out stronger and more bonded than they had ever been.

Kavin and Dr. Meena were by their side throughout it all, providing direction and encouragement. Though they knew the road to the key was not easy, they felt the Kurinji people's resilience and spirit will light the path.

Chapter 20

Celebration and a Conundrum

The Kurinji people gathered around the unbreakable egg as the last trials of their many challenges came to an end, their hearts thumping with anticipation to see whether the egg would send any messages. On what appeared to be just another stunning day in Kurinji, they gathered to test the resilience of the unbreakable egg, which held their golden globe key, as part of their ongoing quest to unravel the mystery before them.

The bioluminescent beast's ethereal brilliance flooded the temporal museum woodland clearing as the Kurinji people held their collective breaths without trying. Every pulse thumping in sync as they witnessed the mysterious egg in full operation for the first time—the repository of their hopes and aspirations pulsating with an unearthly energy—the air crackled with expectation. The individual challenges and trials seemed to have worked; the unbreakable egg seemed to see everyone's heart.

As if it could feel the weight of the occasion, the bioluminescent creature inside appeared to pulse with an unearthly force.

With wide-open astonishment, Kavin walked respectfully towards the egg. His hands shook as he stretched, his fingertips barely brushing the glittering surface. Abruptly, in a blinding burst of light that was too swift for any of their eyes to process, the egg emitted a piercing sound akin to a cracking buzz. Then, with an instantaneous force and a speed comparable to light, it expelled a small amount of metal, shocking everyone present. Elder Murali, along with the other residents, found the recent events incomprehensible. Everyone held their breath as if another earthquake had just occurred, but this time, it did not affect the Kurinji ground but rather the soul of every person living there.

The key to their alleged ancestral armour, shining with the same bioluminescent light as the egg, materialized before the assembled audience, and gasps of shock rippled through them. As the weight of millennia of mystery and desire finally lifted off their shoulders, tears of delight flowed down worn-out cheeks.

The golden globe key has returned intact, as the first glimmer of energy faded with the flickering lights.

Murali and his elder's council confirmed that the expunged metal is precisely the ancient golden globe key in its entirety. The sight shocked Dr. Meena, Ravi, Kavin and the other residents.

But a fresh enigma seems to have emerged. After the picturesque show, the indestructible egg remained intact, with no opening or indication of the crack that allegedly originated the golden globe key. The indestructible egg seemed to have thrown the key out of its mysterious depths, but it remained whole, unbroken, and appeared to be somewhat alive.

Her scientific curiosity piqued, and Dr. Meena walked carefully towards the egg, staring at Kavin and the people. "This really defies all known laws of science in my experience," she said, her eyes shining with enthusiasm. "We have to investigate this phenomenon more." Ravi nodded. I cannot agree less with Meena; it is rather something else.

Kavin nodded, his head whirling with options. "This egg, the life form within... they still shape this narrative. Given our golden globe key, we cannot just ignore them now. The monster lives on, and there is a reason why it stayed impenetrable.

Elder Murali gave his beard careful strokes. "Maybe this marks the beginning of a new chapter, rather than the end of our road." Indeed, the egg has provided the solution, yet it also presents a fresh riddle for us to solve.

Dr. Meena started to sketch a schedule as the revelry carried on around them. "We have to establish a suitable research facility," she replied with a determined voice. "We will need sophisticated tools; I know a team of multidisciplinary scientists from a university where I conducted a previous study. This may transform our knowledge of physics, biology, and maybe even the essence of life itself."

Kavin's eyes shone. "And we must guard the unbreakable egg like the Golden Globe key." If information about its true nature leaks out, who knows what kind of interest it might spark?

Ravi said that he had been listening closely. "We will need the support of the entire community." This goes beyond simple science. It is about protecting our legacy and future.

As night fell, the village chiefs held an emergency meeting and resolved to secure their temporary museum further while seeking their local heroes to solve the riddle of the indestructible live egg.

They secured the golden globe key in a specially built vault in the temporal museum, but it was not their primary concern anymore. Instead, the indestructible egg, glowing with strange bioluminescence, captivated everyone's attention, begging for investigation.

With her notepad in hand, Dr. Meena stood before the egg, immediately writing notes and theories. Kavin and Ravi surrounded her, their faces set with determination. With wide-open astonishment, little Gopal stared at the egg from behind them. Unbelievably amazing, Great crocodiles, he whispered!

"What do you suppose the next development will be?" With a voice almost above a whisper, Gopal questioned.

Dr. Meena started to grin when she turned to him. "I'm not sure, Gopal," she responded. "One thing, though: we are about to start the biggest scientific journey of our lifetime. The unbroken egg is just a starting point. Who knows what additional cosmic puzzles we could find?"

They arranged the next leg of their adventure. Kurinji had ushered in a new era of scientific exploration, with the unbreakable egg serving as a cosmic puzzle awaiting resolution.

Epilogue

The inhabitants of Kurinji found themselves poised on the brink of a new age as the joyful celebrations of the golden globe key's return gently slipped into the cadence of their daily existence. Their experiences, the secrets they had cracked, and the relationships they had created in the furnace of hardship had changed them in ways they were just starting to realise.

As the sun sank below the horizon, bathing the changed Kurinji scene in warm warmth, Kavin stood on top of the hill, overlooking Ravi's temporal barn, the original location of the indestructible egg. Now securely in their hands, the golden globe key gleamed in the last of the lights, a monument to their amazing trip and the obstacles they had overcome.

The once-sleeping streets below hummed with fresh vitality as inquisitive guests and enthusiastic murmurs flooded the town. Like wildfire, the news of Kurinji's remarkable discovery had attracted people from all over the world. Each seeking to uncover the mysteries of the mysterious egg, scientists, mystics, and adventurers had gathered at the settlement.

Kavin's eyes veered to the egg itself, now kept in a specifically built vault in the middle of the town's temporal museum. Even at this distance, he could sense its force—a physical presence that seemed to pulse through the very air. The egg had produced its priceless key, but Kavin understood this was just the beginning. The relic's actual nature remained a mystery that he felt compelled to solve.

Sensing his thoughts, the egg pulsed with a faint, bioluminescent light, its surface shimmering with an exotic iridescence. Watching the fascinating show, Kavin's breath seized in his throat, and he felt both wonder and fear. The egg still carried secrets. Within its impregnable shell, what power lay latent?

He remembered the hardships they had gone through to get to this point: the earthquake that had destroyed their entire community, the crumbling of the ancient museum, the frantic search for the golden globe key, the consulted seers pointing to the ostrich egg, the heist that followed, the confrontation with one of the Kurinji's holy crocodiles, and the last, horrific trip into the heart of the tangle. Every obstacle had tried their will, creativity, and confidence in one another. The experience had made them stronger and more united in their goal.

But now, as Kurinji stood on the edge of a new age, Kavin couldn't get rid of the sense that their biggest test was still to come. The egg had selected them and pulled them into its orbit for a purpose. He felt they had a duty to find the truth, regardless of the cost, as the eyes of the world turned to his little community.

Kavin turned to find Meena and Ravi walking towards him, their features marked with the same combination of surprise and fear he sensed from the quiet crunch of feet. With their eyes fixed on the throbbing egg in the distance, they silently followed him.

"It's just beginning, isn't it?" Meena spoke, her voice barely whispering. "The key was only the beginning. Here, one discovers so much more.

Ravi nodded, his eyes focusing with purpose. "We'll be ready for it. We'll face it together; whatever happens next."

For the strong link he had created between their hardships, Kavin felt a flood of pride and love for his companions. He knew that the path ahead would be difficult, and unravelling the mysteries of the unbreakable egg would not come easily. Yet he knew they would persevere and solve this riddle.

Nestled in the town's centre, the indestructible egg pulsed with an ethereal radiance that appeared to connect with the approaching sun.

Barely six months ago, the town underwent both minor and major changes following the return of the golden globe key.
Rising above everything that had just occurred, Meena looked at Kurinji, her sharp eyes skimming the terrain she knew so well. The familiar outlines of the terrain remained, but there was something unusual in the air—a charge of promise that appeared to hum just beyond the brink of awareness. Closing her eyes, she felt the sun's warmth on her face and could almost hear the murmurs of far-off worlds.
Ravi glided with an elegance that belied his farmer's frame as he looked around Kurinji's once-priceless fields. His link to the ground had grown stronger, and as he cared for his crops, he felt the pulse of life under his feet—a rhythm that matched the bioluminescent pulse of the impenetrable egg. Every plant and every grain of earth appeared to offer a multitude of possibilities.

No more youthful, young Gopal sat cross-legged in front of the egg, his face a mask of concentration. He had demonstrated an amazing sensitivity to the changes in the egg. Now, as he pondered, little pictures of planets beyond conception flashed beneath his closed eyes.
From the shadows of the village square, Elder Murali observed these local

heroes with a worn countenance marked with equal parts of pride and worry.

Though certainly amazing, but the developments in Kurinji also caused concern. The lines separating reality were fading, and the impact of the cosmic egg became more apparent every day.

As the community came alive, Kurinji was filled with expectation. Now on display at a place of respect, the golden globe key caught the early light and seemed to glitter with inner fire. It was a lighthouse, a link between realms, a continual reminder of the road ahead, not just a relic today. Kavin felt a fresh sense of direction as the rest of the sunshine disappeared and the sky became star strewn. The egg had chosen Kurinji, and both did so for a reason. And he promised to respect that decision, as well as to guard and assist the community and its residents as they navigated the unknown seas ahead.
Kavin turned to his buddies, a little grin playing at the corners of his lips. He took a final glance at the glittering egg. "Come on," he urged, his voice full of subdued will. "We have a job to do."

Then Kavin headed down the hill with Meena and Ravi, returning to the hamlet that had evolved into the epicentre of a worldwide phenomenon. The indestructible egg kept pulsing in the distance, leading them into an unknown but exciting future—a lighthouse of mystery and promise. Kavin understood that the best adventures still lied ahead; the narrative of Kurinji and its mysterious treasure had only just started. While walking, he had a tingling feeling of expectation that they would do something special. The egg had selected them as its guardians and champions and put them on this road. And whatever challenges lay ahead, whatever mysteries the future contained, Kavin knew they would meet them head-on, armed with the power of their link and the unquenchable energy of Kurinji itself.

The planet was waiting to see what wonders and revelations the indestructible egg would produce. Kavin, Meena, Ravi, and all of Kurinji were eager to meet the challenge—to enter the future and come out changed. The cosmic egg era had begun, and with it came a new chapter in the history of their community, their country, and possibly even the planet itself.

The residents of Kurinji prepare themselves for the trip ahead with hearts full of optimism and brains humming with possibilities. The key was merely the initial clue in a cosmic puzzle that aimed to transform their understanding of themselves and their place in the universe, not the entire journey. They knew they were ready to welcome whatever lay ahead, to untangle the secrets of the unbreakable egg, and to enter a future full of adventure, risk, and unbounded promise as the glow of the egg enveloped the town in its ethereal radiance.

We are now embarking on the unbreakable egg's second journey, which will blur the boundaries between thought and matter, challenge the fundamental essence of reality, and propel our heroes deeper into the cosmic mysteries that the unbreakable egg represents. The journey was far from over; rather, it had only just started.

May Kurinji's perseverance and wisdom be your guide and may the indestructible spirit within each of us be your inspiration and strength until we meet again on the pages of the second lap adventure. The narrative goes on, with the best yet to come.

COSMIC ASCENDANT

Prologue

Deep inside the Newcastle Hills Shire region, the historic village of Kurinji throbbed with an incomprehensible force. Originally a peaceful little village tucked away among the undulating hills, it has become a cosmic lighthouse, attracting pilgrims, researchers, and seekers from all around. The unbreakable egg, with its bioluminescent core serving as a window into the cosmos' secrets, stood at the heart of this metamorphosis.

Dr Meena stood before the unbreakable egg as dawn dawned above Kurinji, throwing long shadows over the village square, her eyes reflecting its strange brilliance. Six months had passed since their golden globe key's triumphant return, but now victory felt like a precursor to the larger trip ahead. The egg had woken, revealing itself not as a simple relic but rather as a living, changing creature with the key to opening the entire fabric of creation.

Ravi arrived; his farmer's calluses now mingled with the marks of a cosmic adventurer. "It's calling to us," he remarked gently, his voice mixed with both anxiety and exhilaration. Meena nodded, the tug of the egg reverberating through her own existence.

Once cosmic consciousness tarnished his boyhood innocence, young Gopal joined them. His eyes, once wide with sheer awe, now contained depths of knowledge that contradicted his years. Staring at the throbbing egg, he said, "The boundaries are thinning." Other universes seem to be pushing against our own.

The three felt the weight of duty fall on their shoulders as the town sprang to life around them. Kavin knew such obligations well beforehand. Kurinji had evolved from their house to a hub in a vast cosmic network where the old and contemporary, the scientific and the spiritual, collided in a dance of development and exploration.

Rising from the darkness, Elder Murali's battered face mapped wisdom and compassion. "The outside world gets restless," he said in a quiet voice. "They hunt for the egg's power, not realising the delicate balance it represents."

Indeed, the world watched and waited beyond Kurinji's hills, outside their protective hug. Like wildfire, the word of the impenetrable egg sparked dreams and aspirations all around. Blinded to the cosmic ramifications of their avarice, governments, businesses, and clandestine groups all strove to assert their dominance for themselves.

Still, Kurinji was filled with optimism within this mounting conflict. In its mysterious wisdom, the egg had selected them as guardians. It promised not just information but also a revolutionary opportunity to reinvent the entire nature of humanity's interaction with the universe.

Meena, Ravi, Kavin, Gopal, and Kurinji exchanged focused looks as the sun rose higher, bathing Kurinji in golden light. They were aware that the road ahead presented both known and unanticipated difficulties. Time would again challenge the fragile equilibrium between development and heritage, between the cosmic and the earthly.

"We stand at the threshold of a new era," Meena continued, her voice consistent despite the gravity of their work. "The egg has given us glimpses of reality beyond our own, of the complex network that connects all of life. "Our path concerns the basic essence of existence itself, not just

Kurinji or even Earth."

Ravi nodded, his relationship to the ground now extended to include the heavens. "We must be the bridge between the wisdom of our ancestors and the infinite possibilities of the universe," he stated.

Gopal said, "And we must preserve the egg, not merely from those who would abuse its power, but from the repercussions of our own ignorance." His boyish face was filled with resolve. I'm still learning a tremendous deal.

As they talked, the egg's pulsations became stronger, as if its glow were reaching out to hug them. The limits of reality wavered for a minute, and they glimpsed flashes of other worlds and other possibilities that coursed about them like streams of liquid light.

Elder Murali moved forward, pride and worry gleaming in his eyes. "Remember," he continued, his voice heavy with years, "the egg's power is a responsibility to shoulder, not a tool to use." It exhorts us to grow, to widen our awareness of ourselves and our role in the magnificent fabric of life."

Meena, Ravi, Kavin, and Gopal underwent a profound transformation as the image disappeared and Kurinji reaffirmed his presence around them. They had evolved from simple people thrown into an amazing circumstance to cosmic pioneers leading the vanguard in humanity's next major step.

The indestructible egg pulsed continuously, serving as a beacon of hope and a change-heralding agent. They all understood that their best experiences were yet to come. They were at the center of it all: the lines between realms were blurring, and the essence of life itself was changing.

In the vast, unexplored domains of the universe, what obstacles lay ahead? What profound truths would they find about the nature of existence, awareness, and the connectivity of all things? Ready to start the next chapter of their remarkable journey, Meena, Ravi, Kavin, Kurinji, and Gopal went forward as the first light of this new cosmic dawn spread over their island.

Kurinji, the story of the unbreakable egg and humanity's cosmic awakening, was far from finished. The universe itself held its breath, eagerly anticipating the best chapters yet to come.

Chapter 1

Outsider's Insight

The elders gathered in serious thought as the sun rose above Kurinji and created long shadows over the village square. Despite not succumbing to defeat, their inability to engage with the bioluminescent creature within the egg had demoralized them. The impenetrable shell held their community's future, and they were determined to uncover it, which they did, but now it's a riddle.

Elder Murali spoke first, his wrinkled facial lines imprinted with wisdom. "My people, we've used all of our own expertise and resources to solve this impenetrable egg riddle; indeed, we've obtained our golden globe key, but the egg is still alive." Maybe it's time we looked outside for assistance.

Murali put up his hand as the gathering murmured disapproval. "Although we have always been self-sufficient, this riddle eludes us. We must swallow our pride for our people.

Meena, the local veterinarian and historian, seems to be the only one paying attention to inviting outside experts; she already contacted a well-known scientist, Amelia, who had collaborated with her in the past, to visit their village without the knowledge of the town council.

However, following extensive deliberation on the matter of inviting outside experts, the elders finally reached a consensus that they would invite the experts to help them. They decided to appoint Kavin as their local liaison to assist the team of scientists they plan to invite from the adjacent institution for egg research.

They applauded Meena, Ravi, Gopal, and all the other residents for their role in recovering the golden globe key from the impenetrable egg. Bringing in the outside world is a choice Kurinji would make, which would alter its life's path. Dr. Meena is glad to break from solving the unbreakable egg riddles; she had initially planned to take some time off after the crocodile's recovery. Ravi is pleased to focus once more on rebuilding his farmland. From behind, Gopal's typical youthful voice echoed: "Great Crocodiles, I finally have to sit and watch the scientists do wonders with the living thing inside that egg."

The next day, the town plaza bustled with activity under the beautiful morning light. Visitors from the neighboring university arrived, their eyes clouded with mistrust. The Kurinji people gathered. With her hands raised in a sign of peace, Dr. Amelia Chen went towards the assembly. Her voice was calm and steady. "We mean no harm," she added. "We have come to learn the secrets of the unbreakable egg."
Elder Murali moved forward; his aged face bore a lifetime of knowledge. His tone was full of mistrust. "And what makes you think you have the right to pry into the secrets of our land without our invitation?" he said.
Dr. Chen stumbled, briefly stunned by the villagers' opposition, but she said, "I have friends from your community; they trust my and my team's work." She pleaded, "Please," adding, "We only wish to help." The egg contains wisdom that would benefit all of us.
The crowd mumbled, clearly frustrated at having his team arrive while they were still planning on sending out the expert's invitation, until a little voice emerged. "Let them try," Kavin murmured, his inquisitive resolve

gleaming in his eyes. "Maybe they can unlock the egg's secrets where we have failed." Dr. Meena added, "I know Amelia and her team; we should give them a chance and see." I have previously collaborated with Amelia on a project and extended an invitation to her to see how they could assist us.

Elder Murali carefully examined their words before turning to Dr. Chen. "Very good, stranger. Despite our interest in your studies, you must not interfere with Kurinji's secrets. Tread cautiously. Our son, Kavin, must be on your team.

Dr. Chen nodded and said, "Thank you, and that's not a problem." She then signaled her staff to begin arranging their tools in the town square, while the people watched their every move with anxious eyes.

It has been two weeks since renowned biophysicist Dr. Amelia Chen showed up at Kurinji. Her group of researchers had finally finished setting up a makeshift lab on the town square, their tools in sharp contrast to the historic structures all around. Dr. Chen took the time to introduce Kavin to her team; Dr Vargas Hermiz, Professor Sophia Dickson, Dr. Pedro Chavez, Professor Mendhi Mohammed, and Professor Chukwudi Ekwueme and Dr Anita Bolaji.

In a routine check, Dr. Chen walked towards the indestructible egg with wonder and respect, as the Kurinji villagers watched the foreigners with a combination of interest and mistrust. She said, "This is unlike anything I have ever seen," adjusting her microscope. "The shell's makeup is remarkable." At a molecular level, it seems to be always changing.

Day after day, the researchers toiled nonstop, running test after test. With their daily lives now centred on the lab in the square, the residents watched with a combination of optimism and anxiety. While some welcomed the visitors, eager for their knowledge to solve the egg's riddles, others watched suspiciously, reluctant to trust strangers with the sacred relic.

One evening, as the sun sank below the horizon and painted the sky orange, a disturbance started in the lab. Dr. Chen exploded; her face was red with enthusiasm.

"We have made a breakthrough!" she said to the assembly. "The indestructible egg not only contains something but also transforms itself."

Inside is a bioluminescent creature developing at unheard-of speed.

The word quickly spread throughout Kurinji, engulfing the people in a mix of wonder and anxiety. What are the implications?

But a different difficulty surfaced as darkness fell. The forest around Kurinji showed strange lights, and tales of strangers looking for the egg started to spread. Now that Hamlet's secret was out, those who would stop at nothing to obtain the egg's power threatened them.

Elder Murali scheduled a meeting under urgent circumstances. With a stern voice, he declared, "We must protect the egg at all costs." "Our futures depend on it."

Young Kavin sat silently by the egg, his thoughts racing, while the villagers got ready for the trials ahead. He couldn't get rid of the sensation that they were lacking something vital. He believed Kurinji's history held the key to revealing the egg's mysteries; science, or force, was not the path there.

They had no idea, however, that the real test of their fortitude still lay ahead. Kurinji was poised on the brink of a metamorphosis that would redefine their perspective of the planet; the egg was more than simply a storehouse of secrets; it was a catalyst for world change.

Real-World Correlation:

Cross-cultural and Professional collaborations

The arrival of Dr. Amelia Chen and her team mirrors real-world scenarios where outside expertise's are brought in to solve local challenges using their specialist's skills.

Examples:

International aid organizations working with local communities in times of need.

Corporate consultants advising traditional businesses in times of need.

Exchange programs between universities from different countries.

Chapter 2

Deciphering an ancient Knowledge

Kurinji was in constant danger from strangers due to what it harbours; hence, there is need to tighten its security more. Meanwhile, Kavin found himself drawn to the dusty records of the hamlet as Dr. Chen and her colleagues carried out their scientific investigations. His intuition suggested that the solutions they were looking for could lie buried in Kurinji's past.

Among the ruins of the recovered library archives, Kavin found an antique manuscript in a neglected section of the village's temporal library; its pages yellowed with age. His eyes became wide as he delicately unfolded the thin sheet. The book described a fabled treasure thought to have the ability to transform reality itself—the "Unbreakable Egg of Creation." Thrilled by his find, Kavin hurried to forward the material to Dr. Chen and the elders. As they worked through the book, connections began to form. The old book stated that the bioluminescent creature, the durable shell, and the key were all related.

"According to this," Kavin said, his voice shaking with enthusiasm, "the Unbreakable Egg isn't only a receptacle for the ancient golden globe key. This living thing is always changing; it needs the golden globe key to reveal its power. The egg carries information, not a physical object. Kurinji is constantly evolving; it awaits the right question to pose.

Though she couldn't reject the connections between the old book and her own discoveries, Dr. Chen's scientific mind battled with this mystical interpretation. She considered, "But what's the right question?"

Late into the night, while they argued, odd events started to afflict the town. Village residents had vivid, shared visions of a big tree with golden leaves and light shining from it. The indestructible egg began to pulse with an alien light, visible even through its impenetrable shell.

In parallel, the invading foreigners become more audacious. Locals reported seeing shadowy individuals at the border of the Kurinji Forest; their motives were unknown but likely related to the egg. Elder Murali led the locals to set up vigilante group patrols to guard their priceless relic. During this upheaval, an unexpected guest arrived in Kurinji. At the brink of the village square stood an elderly lady from the nearby Ajuorun hamlet, her face etched with wisdom and age. She identified herself as Nnenna Jackson, a descendent of Kurinji's original colonists who had migrated to Ajuorun decades ago from their former hamlet.

Nnenna's entrance set off something in the collective memory of the village elders, who shockingly did not object to her coming, as they did when Amelia and her crew arrived. Everyone was enthralled by her accounts of Kurinji's creation and the actual form of the Unbreakable Egg. She talked about a time when people and the environment were in perfect harmony, as well as how the indestructible egg served as a link between realms. She explained that the old key the people had found was something designed to unlock an endless door to Kurinji, not just the old chemical armour they were looking to use to defend themselves.

"The egg is unbreakable because it's a gift from mother nature for Kurinji land; it isn't meant to be opened," Nnenna said, her voice bearing the weight of old knowledge. "It's intended to be understood. I'm here to help you unravel the egg's mystery.

Kavin felt a rush of exhilaration running through him as Nnenna's words sank in. The indestructible egg—a simple receptacle for the old key? No, it was much more. His thoughts focused on the ramifications—the opportunities we had all along.

"I think I know what we need to do," Kavin replied, his voice shaking with a combination of anxiety and enthusiasm. The people turned to him, their faces combined doubt with hope.

Kavin inhaled deeply and stared at the throbbing egg. "We need—"

The people held their breath in the silence that followed, waiting with bated expectation for Kavin to reveal his understanding. Kurinji's fate hung precariously, and they were certain that the enigmatic relic that had taken centre stage in their lives held the answers they sought.

Knowing that the road ahead would be full of difficulties and unknowns, Kavin sharpened his will as the anxiety grew. But with Kurinji's past weighing heavily on his shoulders, he was determined to uncover the truth, no matter the costs.

Which inquiry would reveal the egg's mysteries? And prepared for the response? As Kurinji promised to test everything they knew about their planet and their position on it, another chapter began.

Real-World Correlation:

Rediscovering an ancient wisdom

Kavin's discovery of an ancient manuscript reflects how modern society often finds value in ancient traditional knowledge.

Examples:

Traditional medicine informing modern pharmaceutical research.

Ancient agricultural techniques inspiring sustainable farming practices.

Rediscovery of forgotten languages and their cultural significance.

Chapter 3

Modern Science Meets Ancient Wisdom

Today, as Kavin's hand rested on the surface of the egg, the assembled audience lapsed into silence. The air buzzed with expectation; the weight of old knowledge mixed with modern science falling on this one moment.

Dr. Chen was standing close by, her scientific tools at hand, while Nnenna observed with eyes that seemed to span millennia. With their expressions a combination of optimism and fear, Elder Murali, Meena, Ravi, Gopal, and the other village leaders formed a protective circle.

Closing his eyes, Kavin drew on his own intuition, what he had learned from the old book, and Nnenna's lessons. His voice seemed to permeate the very fabric of existence, but it was little above a whisper when he spoke.

"We do not seek to possess you or unlock your secrets," he said. "The great, unbreakable egg of creation." Instead, we ask: How can we protect the equilibrium you stand for? Do you possess the ancestral power required to protect our society?"

Not a single thing happened for a second. Then the unbreakable egg started to pulse with a light that seemed to emanate from everywhere and nowhere at once. Slowly. Inside, swirling in patterns of amazing beauty, the bioluminescent creature grew in brightness until it was quite blinding.

The light burst suddenly, encircling everyone in front of it in a brilliant cocoon. At that moment, everyone witnessed the delicate balance of nature, the interdependence of all things, and the role humans play as stewards, not conquerors.

As the light sank away, the egg's shell began to move and alter. It changed rather than crack or break, becoming translucent like the most perfect crystal. Inside, the bioluminescent creature was majestic, throbbing with life and possibilities.

Dr. Chen's equipment went crazy, capturing information contradicting all accepted physics. She gasped, her scientific mind struggling to comprehend what she was seeing: "It's rewriting its own genetic code." "It's changing at an impossible rate—real-time adaptation to its surroundings!"

Nnenna nodded sagely. "The egg is not just a relic," she said, sounding reverently. "It is a living representation of the Earth's adaptability and evolution capacity. The 'golden globe key it handed out' was never a tangible thing for the community, but rather a tool it needed to come alive. This key gift serves as a wake-up call, reminding us of our responsibility to foster Kurinji's historical transitions.

As the ramifications of this discovery seeped in, a new sound emerged: twigs breaking and leaves ruffling. This was the moment the strangers, who had been prowling the village's margins, decided to move.

A man with a hood covering his face led a group of white-clothed guys into the area. The villagers seemed confused, everyone seemed to be asking same question. Is this Mr Frays group again? Didn't they learn their lessons yet?

"Hand over the unbreakable egg and the golden globe key; we only want these artefacts and not your science functionaries," the leader, Santos Kovacic, insisted, his voice icy and intimidating. "We will open the so-called indestructible egg in a day and extract the little live thing it is rearing; then you may keep the shell in your small-town destroyed museum, as the abilities of the artefacts belong to people who can really use them." Santos continued to chuckle. "

Elder Murali moved forward, his old figure towering in disdain. "You do not understand what you seek," he remarked with conviction. "We should shoulder this responsibility, not use it as a source of power."

As stress grew, the indestructible egg pulsed once more, its light extending to touch the invaders. They, too, momentarily lost themselves in the concept of connection. The result was instantaneous and significant. The leader's hood dropped to reveal a face transformed by knowledge and regret.

"I had no idea," Santos said, stammering and lowering his firearm. "We thought... we were so wrong."

That moment made the actual strength of the indestructible egg abundantly evident. It was a tool for understanding and transformation, rather than a weapon or a means of control. Its wisdom might change not just Kurinji but the planet as well.

The town of Kurinji found itself at the core of a significant change in human awareness as the sun started to rise on another day. The unbroken egg, now a whirling bioluminescence lighthouse, was evidence of the fine balance between development and preservation, science and spirituality, the old and the contemporary.

Around the unbreakable egg, Kavin, Dr. Chen, Nnenna, and the village elders gathered, each with their own viewpoint on the work ahead. They understood the trip was far from over. It was challenging to share this information with the world while also protecting the egg from abuse. But as they stood there, illuminated by the unbreakable egg's gentle light, they sensed optimism and direction. They anticipated a solution to the riddle of the indestructible egg, but it did not produce the desired outcome.

Kurinji was prepared for the impending changes as news of the egg's true nature began to spread. They knew that soon, scholars from around the world would visit their peaceful town. Though numerous difficulties were ahead, the future seemed bright for the first time in a long time.
The narrative of Kurinji and the Unbreakable Egg was far from finished. It was just starting. All those who came seeking knowledge, insight, and a taste of the powerful link among all living entities would write the future chapters.

Real-World Correlation:

Interdisciplinary approaches in solving problems

The merging of scientific and spiritual

perspectives of the unbreakable egg mysteries mirrors real-world trends in holistic problem-solving.

Examples:

Mind-body medicine combining Western and Eastern practices.

Environmental conservation efforts integrating scientific data with indigenous knowledge.

Technology companies employing philosophers to address ethical challenges.

Chapter 4

Global Influence

Kurinji's New Dawn places the once-quiet hamlet at the centre of a worldwide sensation, as the Unbreakable Egg's changes transcend Kurinji's boundaries and the broader Newcastle Hills shire area. Scholars, spiritual leaders, scientists, and inquisitive people from all walks of life began to flock to the little community, seeking to grasp and experience the immense knowledge the egg had to offer. Under the always-wise Murali, the village leaders confronted the enormous responsibility of controlling this flood while maintaining the dignity of their discovery. They established the Kurinji Centre for Harmonious Evolution to teach the egg's lessons in a polite and controlled manner.

Having personally seen the blending of spirituality with science, Dr. Chen chose to remain in Kurinji. She founded a modern research centre aimed at tracking the bioluminescent creature's continuous development inside the egg. Her work started to close the distance between modern technology and age-old knowledge, attracting praise and criticism equally from the scientific community.

Nnenna assumed the position of spiritual guide; her close relationship to Kurinji's past made her the ideal vehicle for the lessons of the egg. She began teaching a small number of people—including Kavin—the skill of communicating with the unbreakable cosmic egg and deciphering its ever-changing patterns.

Kurinji threw Kavin, the lad who had first discovered the true nature of the egg and the symbol of his society, into an unexpected role. Kurinji's new world included him, especially as he was naturally able to interact with and comprehend the egg. But Kavin faced difficulties combining his need for a regular existence with his duty as a translator of old knowledge.

Kurinji's shift also presented challenges. The unexpected rush of tourists taxed the village's resources and tried some long-time inhabitants' endurance. Arguments raged over how much information to share and with whom. Some were worried that information in the wrong hands would be hazardous.

These worries weren't totally baseless. Though the wonderful experience had changed the original would-be criminal group of Mr Santos, there were still some in the outside world looking to use the egg's power. The town had to be vigilant, with round-the-clock security for its valuable artifacts.

Despite all the difficulties, the unbreakable gg's existence clearly had advantages. Slowly but the information it taught started to permeate and change people's perspectives on their interactions with the environment. Once seen as fringe concepts, sustainable practices started to take hold internationally. Governments and businesses, inspired by Kurinji's rising tide of eco-consciousness, began to change their policies.

Before the gathered assembly, Dr. Chen stood with eyes ablaze with the excitement of discovery. A benevolent green fern leaf shimmered behind her on a holographic display.

"Friends," she said, her voice bursting with enthusiasm, "what we have found regarding the nature of reality is rather remarkable. "Consider using this fern leaf to help you grasp it."

We inserted the hologram into the leaf to reveal its intricate architecture. "Notice how smaller leaflets make up the entire leaf," Dr. Chen said. "Now, closely observe."

The gathering watched as the hologram zoomed in on one of the pamphlets. They were surprised that the leaflet's structure resembled a miniature replica of the full leaf.

"This pattern," Dr. Chen said, "is a fractal—that is, where the same structure repeats at various sizes. Furthermore, remarkably, we have found that reality itself conforms to this identical pattern."

Kavin slanted forward, his concentration wrinkled on his forehead. "Are you claiming the universe resembles this fern leaf?"

Dr. Chen nodded broadly with much enthusiasm. Absolutely! We've discovered that the architecture of our cosmos repeats itself throughout many layers of existence, just like the pattern of a fern repeats at ever smaller sizes.

The crew changed the hologram to display a large cosmic network of galaxies. As the hologram zoomed in, the crew observed that each galaxy cluster resembled the larger cosmic web. Further zooming in, they saw atomic structures reflecting solar systems, then solar systems mirroring the form of galaxy clusters.

From the biggest cosmic architecture to the smallest subatomic particles," Dr. Chen said, "we see the same patterns recurring. Still, it transcends that as well.

Once more, we altered the hologram to display many cosmic webs, each somewhat unique but with a general pattern.

"Every one of these denotes a different universe inside the multiverse," Dr. Chen said. Every universe is a variation of the same basic design, much like the leaflets on our fern.

Gopal's eyes grew with awe. "Great crocodile, Thus, our entire universe is just one 'leaflet' in a much larger cosmic 'fern.'"

Dr. Chen said, "Precisely." "And just as you can't fully understand the fern by looking at just one leaflet, we cannot fully understand the nature of reality by examining just our universe."

Elder Murali gave his beard careful strokes. "This fractal nature echoes ancient spiritual teachings about the conjoining of all things."

"Indeed," Dr. Chen nodded. "We never would have guessed how science and spirituality would combine. From the cosmic to the subatomic, this fractal form explains why we see parallels across all levels of life.

After listening closely, Nnenna raised a question. "And understanding the pattern at one level could give us insights into all levels if reality is fractal in nature."

"Exactly! Dr. Chen spoke with tremendous urgency." That makes our findings very important. Understanding its fractal structure helps us grasp the whole universe.

A quiet respect descended over the group as the consequences of this insight set in, a quiet respect overtook the company. They began to realize the scope of their research and its potential impact on all of knowledge.

With his determined, glistening eyes, Kavin got up. "Our future direction is therefore very evident. We must explore this fractal pattern more thoroughly to grasp its subtleties and how we may use this understanding.

Dr. Chen nodded; her expression was solemn. "Yes, but we have to exercise excellent care. Recall that in a fractal system, a little change at one level may have enormous effects on all levels. We are potential shapers of reality itself, not simply explorers.

As a continual reminder of the beautiful, complex, and linked nature of the world the group was only beginning to grasp, the holographic fern leaf spun gently as they started to talk about their next actions.

Barely six months after revealing the unbreakable egg's actual cosmic nature, something amazing happened. The egg's bioluminescent resident started to proliferate. Little, brilliant specks—each a tiny replica of the original—appeared in the water of the adjacent Kurinji River. Seeing this as evidence that the egg was ready to offer its talents more broadly, Dr. Chen and her staff were overjoyed.

After meticulously growing and investigating these "seedlings," it became evident that each one possessed a percentage of the power of the original indestructible egg, but none had eliminated any keys like the original one did. Dr Chen and her team then developed plans to introduce these new species to other countries, sharing the lessons and effects of the indestructible egg with those who couldn't travel to Kurinji.

But along with this fresh advancement came new questions and obligations. How might these seedlings fit into different environments? What unanticipated effects may they bring to fresh ecosystems? Once again, the Community was leading a careful balancing act between development and restraint.

Scientists and spiritual leaders from all over the world arrived in Kurinji, captivated by the egg's transforming potential. Renowned quantum physicist Professor Abraham Tua from the Pacific Islands found immense fascination in the egg's capacity to violate natural rules. El Rufai Giwa, a deeply spiritual African leader, expressed a different perspective on the egg's role in world peace and interconnectivity.

The Kurinji community changed once again as these fresh people blended themselves into Kurinji society, turning into a melting pot of ideas, cultures, and viewpoints. Hosting seminars, talks, and meditation retreats drawing guests from all around, the Kurinji Centre for Harmonious Evolution hummed with activity.

As a young man, Kavin discovered he was at the centre of this worldwide dialogue; his job as the main translator for the egg was more important than ever. He constantly strived to ensure the proper and careful transmission of the egg's knowledge, striking a delicate balance between upholding Kurinji's customs and embracing the insights of the outside world.

Kurinji got ready for a big party as the one-year anniversary of the indestructible egg's waking neared. The community had grown into a living monument to the power of knowledge and the ongoing wonder of nature, a beacon of hope and transformation.

And the residents of Kurinji knew their narrative was far from over, as the light rose over the horizon and warmed the changed ground. As a constant reminder of the delicate balance between development and preservation, between the old and the contemporary, the indestructible egg pulsed with the rhythms of the universe.

Still, there was an air of expectancy. Even as they got ready for the celebrations, there was an air of expectation. The indestructible egg's development showed no slowing down, and many speculated about what fresh wonders or problems the next year might provide.

Kavin often found himself standing before the egg, marvelling at the path that had brought him to this place in the still minutes before dawn as it pulsed with its strange glow. He knew, like all of Kurinji, that their story was far from over. The egg had initiated a series of events they could hardly fathom that were still in progress.

Kurinji stood ready to greet whatever the new day would bring as the first ray of sunshine slinked across the horizon, turning the heavens pink and gold. The community had grown into a living monument to the power of knowledge and the ongoing wonder of nature, a beacon of hope and transformation.

The unbreakable egg kept pulsing, its rhythms a continual reminder of the fine balance between the old and the new, between development and preservation. And in that harmony, Kurinji has once again found its rightful purpose as defenders of knowledge capable of changing the planet.

Real-World Correlation:

Global interconnectedness

The spreading influence of the Unbreakable egg's teachings reflects how ideas and movements can quickly go global in our interconnected world.

Examples:

Viral social media trends affecting global culture.

Environmental movements like Fridays for Future spreading worldwide.

Technological innovations rapidly changing industries across the globe.

Chapter 5

Global Seedlings

Kurinji had evolved from a little town into a worldwide hub of transformation as the first anniversary of the indestructible egg's emergence drew many strands of change. The next festival promised to be a gathering of ideas, spirits, and civilisations unlike anything the planet had ever seen.

The preparations were well underway. Originally a collection of little houses anchored to the dust of mother nature, the community today boasts a harmonic mix of sustainable contemporary conveniences and classic architecture. Modern water recycling technologies have collaborated with traditional rainwater collection methods.

Regarding the bioluminescent seedlings, Dr. Chen and her colleagues have greatly advanced. Each seedling appeared to adapt according to its surroundings, absorbing traits that mirrored the ecosystem it grew in. In the sub-Saharan desert, the blazing sun's intensity sparkled on one seedling, while the heartbeat of the Amazon jungle pulsed on another.

These seedlings weren't only surviving; they were flourishing, subtly but powerfully changing their surroundings. Reports surfaced, revealing not only inexplicable improvements in air and water quality but also an increase in biodiversity in areas planted with seedlings.

International students have studied Nnenna's methods to communicate with the indestructible egg and its descendants. Offering programmes that combine spirituality, science, and environmental stewardship, the Kurinji Centre for Harmonious Evolution has grown to be a revered institution.

Kavin, had become the main interpreter for the indestructible egg. His remarkable sensitivity to the egg's signals had only become better with time. Still, the weight of his accountability sometimes made him feel alone. In peaceful times, he yearned for the simpler childhood days.

A real buzz permeated the air as delegates from all over started to show up for the celebration. Scientists interacted with spiritual leaders; indigenous elders led by Murali exchanged knowledge with tech entrepreneurs; and government officials were deep in conversation with local environmental activists. Kurinji has transformed into a neutral space, setting aside long-standing rivalries in pursuit of a deeper understanding of the unbreakable egg's secret.

Kavin struggled to fall asleep the evening before the major event. Drawn to the egg, he made his way to the sanctuary housing it. Something changed as he got closer. The egg's pulsations seemed stronger and more urgent.

Setting his palm on the crystalline surface, Kavin closed his eyes and let his thoughts open. His view sent shivers down his spine. Rising oceans, changing landmasses like the one that had disappeared, the golden globe key, and severe weather patterns inundated his awareness. Along with these catastrophic pictures, however, were flashes of optimism for fresh technology, rebuilt ecosystems, and societies coexisting peacefully with the natural world.

Kavin gasped and staggered back. The unbreakable egg was a warning and call to action, not just presenting him with a potential future.

Kavin shared his vision with the village elders, Dr. Chen, and Nnenna as morning broke on the celebration day. They decided that this message needed to reach every assembled delegate.

The event started with customary Kurinji rites, but a silence descended on the gathered audience when Kavin stood forward to speak. Emphasising that the future was not fixed in stone, he passionately and urgently delivered the message of the unbreakable egg. The decisions made in the next few years will determine the course that mankind will follow.
His comments really spoke to everyone. The celebration turned into an unplanned worldwide conference. Leaders from many fields gathered to drive towards a common goal. Leaders developed ambitious plans for forestry initiatives, transitioning to renewable energy, and transforming education to incorporate the lessons of the unbreakable egg.

As a fresh future vision began to take shape, the day unfolded. Just days earlier, the egg's warning had acted as a catalyst, bringing people together in a manner that appeared unimaginable.
There was a sensation that a new chapter in human history had started as the sun sank on this historic day, bathing Kurinji in golden glory. Once a secret tourist jewel, the town is now the centre of a worldwide movement. Mother Nature once drained the land with an earthquake, but the same mother nature has restored it to an advanced contemporary society.

Still, issues persisted. Implementing the ambitious ideas would necessitate overcoming deeply embedded systems and beliefs. There were still those who merely desired to obtain the egg, others who viewed the unbreakable egg with distrust or fear, and others who aspired to harness its power for their own gain.

As the guests started to leave, the Kurinji people realised their job was far from done, taking seedlings from the stream and fresh ideas back to their homes. They had grown guardians not just of the impenetrable egg but also of a fresh perspective on humanity's role in the earth.

Standing before the unbreakable egg one more time before turning in for the evening, Kavin felt both thrilled and overwhelmed. The road forward was unknown, full of danger as well as opportunity. But as the egg pulsed reassuringly, he understood that whatever difficulties lay ahead, they would face them together—not just as a hamlet, but as a worldwide society bound by a common vision of peace and hope.

Kurinji's journey with the unbreakable Egg of Creation has transformed into humanity's daily development. As a fresh dawn approached, the planet waited to see what the next chapter would bring.

Real-World Correlation:

International cooperation

The global gathering in Kurinji mirrors real-world international summits and conferences to discuss issues, trends or discoveries.

Examples:

United Nations Climate Change Conferences.

World Economic Forum meetings.

International scientific collaborations like CERN.

Chapter 6

Quantum Surge

The whole Newcastle Hill shire area and the globe found themselves in an era of hitherto unheard-of transformation as the worldwide projects spurred by Kurinji started to take shape. Now dispersed throughout several environments, the seedlings kept developing and impacting their surroundings in ways that both delighted and perplexed researchers.

When Dr. Chen and her team found that the bioluminescent creatures had quantum characteristics, her study veered unexpectedly. The seedlings defied accepted physics principles by appearing to communicate instantly across enormous distances. This finding rocked the scientific community and offered new directions of enquiry in quantum biology.

In the meantime, Kavin's position has grown beyond that of the interpreter. He was travelling the world, visiting areas where seedlings had been planted, and guiding local populations to know and tend to their new guardians. His travels brought him personally the blessings as well as the difficulties of using the indestructible egg's knowledge on a worldwide basis.

One year after the anniversary celebration, something rather remarkable happened. Every place where the bioluminescent creatures had grown began to simultaneously produce a coordinated pulse of light from a distance. From satellite pictures, one could see a global network of brilliant spots linked by apparently inexplicable lines of light.

While the world marvelled at the original unbreakable egg, Kavin had a strong vision. It showed him a time when humans would have learned to use this network as a source of pure, limitless energy and a way of healing harmed ecosystems. The vision also included a warning, though: if abused, this ability may have terrible results.

The revelation of this worldwide network sparked new spiritual and scientific inquiries. While environmental organisations argued for caution and respect for the network's inherent function, governments and businesses rushed to grasp and maybe exploit this new phenomenon.

Along with Dr. Chen and Nnenna and other eminent village men and women, the village elders in Kurinji—led by Murali—found themselves at the centre of a mounting controversy. How could they ensure that this new discovery is used for the betterment of all life on Earth rather than its temporary exploitation?

Tensions rising, Kavin put forth a daring scheme. To supervise the research and use of the unbreakable egg bioluminescent network, he proposed establishing a worldwide council of scientists, spiritual leaders, indigenous elders, and representatives from many sectors. This council, based in Kurinji, would operate on the principles of world collaboration and openness.

The plan attracted both hope and mistrust. Many viewed it as an opportunity to develop a new global government model based on the harmony and connection the egg had taught. Others worried it would give a small number of people undue influence.

The network kept developing even as arguments raged on. Reports of naturally occurring ecosystem regeneration at network-connected sites arrived. While the contaminated water began to clean up, more rain fell on the desert areas. Through the network, it appeared that the earth itself was healing.

Throughout this global change, Kurinji remained a lighthouse of optimism and a hub of knowledge. Despite developing into a tiny metropolis, the hamlet maintained a careful equilibrium with its surroundings. It was a real-world illustration of how humans may advance technologically without sacrificing harmony with their surroundings.

Research by Dr. Chen and her team kept turning up amazing findings. She reasoned that the bioluminescent network may be a portal to other worlds, as well as a planetary occurrence. Her work generated both praise and criticism as it started to blur the boundaries between modern physics and age-old mystical ideas.

Kavin was also facing a pivotal moment. His close relationship with the original unbreakable egg had made him a worldwide sensation but also kept him far from the modest life he sometimes yearned for. During calm times, he considered his position on this new planet and his future journey.

One night, Kavin stood before the original unbreakable egg, now throbbing in unison with its worldwide network, and he had a vision more vivid than any before. He envisions a time when mankind has completely accepted its responsibility as stewards of the Earth, where technology and nature coexist, and where the lines separating science from spirituality have faded away.

However, getting to this world would require negotiating dangerous seas.

The possibility of conflict over the power of the network loomed big, as did the difficulty of conquering millennia of deeply rooted beliefs and behaviours.

Kavin knew the trip ahead would be lengthy and challenging as the vision faded. However, he also understood that mankind now had a road map, a glimpse of what might be possible if people could learn to cooperate peacefully with one another and the planet.

Rising on a fresh day in Kurinji, the sun illuminated a planet undergoing enormous change. The narrative of the unbreakable egg, and its network had evolved into the narrative of humanity's development—a story continuously under progress at every minute. As he left to face another day of difficulties and opportunities, Kavin understood that not only he and the people of Kurinji but all of mankind would write the next chapter, cooperating towards a better future.

The constant pulse of the unbreakable Egg of Creation served as a reminder of the delicate equilibrium between development and preservation, as well as the boundless possibilities waiting ahead. It appears the journey was just beginning.

Real-World Correlation:

Paradigm shifts in science

The discovery of quantum properties in the bioluminescent organism reflects real scientific breakthroughs that reshape our understanding of the world.

Examples:

Discovery of DNA structure revolutionizing biology.

Quantum mechanics transforming our understanding of physics.

Development of the internet changing global communication.

Chapter 7

Cosmic Convergence

As the bioluminescent network continued to spread its impact throughout the earth, a new phenomenon started to emerge. People from all areas of life began to document unusual, shared dreams and visions. These events were shockingly similar: echoes of ancient knowledge from the old Kurinji library archives, glimpses of sophisticated civilizations opened by a key like the original golden globe key, and clues of worlds beyond their own.

Dr. Chen began an extensive investigation, inspired by these findings. Her results were amazing. The network was somehow expanding human awareness rather than just influencing the physical environment. Whether by closeness to a seedling or by meditation techniques taught in Kurinji, people linked to the network were feeling enhanced intuition, more empathy, and sometimes even somewhat telepathic ability.

Kavin, whose relationship with the egg had always been strong, discovered his talents were expanding dramatically. He could now interact with the entire network at will, instantly receiving and forwarding data over enormous distances. However, this authority carried a lot of weight. His sleep now seemed like a luxury; the images he had were becoming more powerful and urgent.

One evening, during a worldwide meditation session run throughout the network, something rather remarkable occurred. As millions of people worldwide synchronized their thoughts with the unbreakable egg's bioluminescent pulse, a celestial gateway appeared to open.

Every participant briefly saw a shared image of a huge, linked cosmos. All linked by a cosmic network of awareness, they saw various worlds—some like Earth, others far different. It was a glimpse of a world much more intricate and lovely than anybody had dreamed of.

At Kurinji, the original egg started to transform. Its crystalline shell began to reveal the whirling, glowing creature within. It sent waves of energy throughout the global network, pulsing with an intensity never seen before.

Their bodies silhouetted against a fading world; everyone stood on the brink of reality.

The Shadow of Dr Vargas opened like a living horror before them.

It started as a pinpoint of total blackness—a place so black it appeared to absorb the whole idea of light. Transfixed in fear and wonder, the shadow started to expand, its edges whirling and swirling like ink-made storm clouds.

Dark tendrils grasped at the fabric of space-time. Where they touched, colour seemed to drain away, creating a colourless nothingness that would damage the eyes' ability to see directly. Instead of being empty, the area looked like it never existed.

Elder Murali murmured, his voice shaking, "By all that's holy." "It's consuming all."

The shadow pulsed, emitting anti-light waves that caused the people's vision to swim. The stars vanished from their final brightness, eaten by the ravenous darkness in their wake.

Trying to understand what he was seeing, Kavin squinted. Like heat waves emerging from hot asphalt, the shadow's edges appeared to glitter and dance. But rather than bending what lay behind them, they appeared to wipe everything out, leaving behind a void so great that it caused his head to spin.

"It's not just darkness," Dr. Chen replied, her voice soft with a combination of scientific curiosity and anxiety. "It's the absence of everything—light, matter, even space and time itself."

Galaxies in the Shadow's path started to distort and twist as they watched. The emptiness inexorably drew perfect spirals of stars, their shapes elongating like taffy. As reality tore apart, they could almost hear the cry of wounded space-time.

Something moved in the centre of the shadow. It was a wriggling mass of non-existence, a contradiction given shape. Looking at it was like seeing the back of one's skull—the mind couldn't comprehend what the eyes saw.

Nnenna gasped as her sympathetic senses overflowed with emotion. With her voice barely above a whisper, she managed to utter, "It's... hungry." "I sense its aim—not desire, not awareness, but... seeking to eat everything, therefore reducing all of life to a condition of flawless, empty homogeneity."

Once again, the shadow pulsed, and this time everyone felt it in their own bodies. The shadow seemed to hollow them out, leaving an agonising hole behind. The colours took on a duller appearance and a more muted sound, suggesting a depletion of their essence.

His youthful face blanched with terror, and Gopal pointed towards the approaching gloom. "Great crocodiles, Look! It's shifting".

The shadow was indeed changing. Its edges started to split and shatter; each piece was a perfect miniature of the whole. It was a cancer developing on the face of life itself, a dark reflection of the fractal character of reality they had uncovered.

Everyone experienced a strong, basic anxiety as the fractal darkness expanded and consumed more and more of the visible cosmos. This was entropy given shape; the heat death of the cosmos became clear-cut. And it was headed towards them.

"We have to move," Kavin remarked, his voice breaking through the group's paralysed silence. "Whatever this is, we cannot let it get any more widely distributed."

Each carried the burning vision of that all-consuming darkness as they left to find a way to counter this existential threat. They understood that the Shadow of Entropy, a sobering reminder of what would await them should they fail in their goal, would haunt their nightmares for years to come.

Once so vivid and full of life, the cosmos around them now looked delicate and valuable in relation to the gaping emptiness that threatened to consume everything. And the Shadow of Entropy kept its unrelenting approach, a herald of the last doom that awaited all of life, while they hurried against time to discover a solution.

As the vision vanished, the world seemed to be filled with wonder and uncertainty. What they had observed had startling consequences. Humanity was not alone in the cosmos; their waking awareness marked just the start of a much more extensive cosmic journey.

They formed the worldwide council to monitor the network, but it found itself unprepared for the questions it was answering. With this new cosmic consciousness, how ought humans to behave? Were they ready to interact with other cultures? What obligations accompany this heightened awareness?

Drawing on her profound spiritual insight, Nnenna suggested some time for thought and preparation. Nnenna replied, "We need to ensure our potential is commensurate with what we have glimpsed." Healing our earth and ourselves should now be our main priorities."

The nature of Dr. Chen's study changed. She started working with neurologists, physicists, and even mystics from many faiths to grasp the essence of this universal awareness. Their work was establishing the foundation for a new discipline of research spanning spirituality and science.

Kavin discovered he was in the middle of these historic developments. His capacity for network communication gave him an indispensable connection between humans and this new cosmic knowledge. However, the responsibility weighed heavily on him. Often withdrawing to peaceful areas of Kurinji, he sought solace among the swirl of world change.

The world saw a flood of optimism as well as terror as word of the common vision grew. Some regarded it as a promise of a better future, an opportunity for mankind to occupy a bigger cosmic community. Others are concerned about the future, alien civilisations' motives, and the rapid changes taking place on Earth.

Governments wrangled to fit this new reality. The United Nations called emergency meetings to examine humanity's attitude towards possible cosmic diplomacy. Concurrent with this, grassroots initiatives pushing for a peaceful, cohesive response to this new frontier emerged all around.

Now a thriving centre of world relevance, Kurinji's village elder's put enormous effort into preserving the delicate equilibrium between development and heritage. Though they felt the weight of that obligation, they realised that their little group held the key to mankind's destiny and should value their way of life.

The planet got ready for yet another worldwide meditation event as the one-year anniversary of the cosmic vision drew near. Anticipation was high, with a sense of humanity poised on the edge of yet another intellectual breakthrough.

Standing before the changed egg, Kavin experienced both exhilaration and anxiety. Ahead lay an unexplored road full of risk and opportunity. He felt hopeful as he looked out at the town that started it all and the international participants.

Whatever the future contained; mankind would confront it together under the direction of the cosmic awareness awakened from the knowledge of the egg. Kavin inhaled deeply as the time for the meditation drew near, preparing to guide mankind into the next stage of its cosmic journey.

From losing its unique golden key buried in an enigmatic shell of the unbreakable egg, once a narrative of a little town destroyed by mother nature, the story of Kurinji today represents mankind's awakening to its position in the universe. One thing was clear, though: the biggest adventure of the unbreakable egg was yet to come, as the globe gasped to see what the following chapter would bring.

Real-World Correlation:

Expanded consciousness

The global meditation event and its effects mirror real-world interest in consciousness expansion and collective experiences.

Examples:

Global meditation events for peace and healing.

Growing interest in psychedelic research for mental health.

Virtual reality experiences creating shared digital worlds.

Chapter 8

Harmonics of the Universe

As the global meditation event began, millions of people around the world coordinated their thoughts with the throbbing pulse of the bioluminescent network. Kavin stood before the changed egg in Kurinji, his mind enlarged to include the whole web of life now spanning the planet.

The concentration became deeper, and then something unheard of happened. The egg started to speak at a frequency never heard on Earth. Every cell of every living thing linked to the network vibrated with a sound that appeared to emanate from everywhere and nowhere at once—a cosmic symphony.

Meditating people discovered their awareness shot beyond Earth as the song flowed over them. Time and space, as they understood them, vanished from their great, multifaceted existence. Here, they met other consciousnesses, some strange and others hauntingly similar.

These entities expressed themselves not with words but rather with pure mind and feeling. They knew about cosmic cycles, the rise and fall of civilisations throughout the cosmos, and the careful equilibrium that preserves the cosmic web of life.

Most importantly, they revealed that Earth's waking was part of a larger cosmic event. The bioluminescent network was a link in a large, cosmic web of awareness, rather than just a planetary phenomenon. Joining this cosmic fellowship required humanity to first wake up.

As the meditation ended, the ramifications of what individuals had gone through began to seep in, and those around them returned to their worldly consciousness. The cosmos was considerably more complicated and linked than anybody had thought, and our involvement in it was both vital and modest.

Kurlnjl became the centre of slgnlflcant worldwlde attentlon ln the next few days. Seeking to comprehend and interpret the cosmic vision, scientists, spiritual leaders, and government officials swarmed to the town.

Working nonstop, Dr. Chen and her colleagues examined the gathered event data. They discovered that the impenetrable egg's cosmic frequency had significantly altered the bioluminescent creatures' quantum structure. Now the network may send and receive data across enormous cosmic distances.

Drawing on her profound spiritual understanding, Nnenna started teaching fresh meditation practices that let individuals more easily reach this universal awareness. She emphasised the need to use this new capacity sensibly and in accordance with cosmic equilibrium.

Kavin's role changed once again. His special relationship with the indestructible egg qualified him as the perfect middleman between humans and the cosmic consciousnesses they had encountered. After spending many hours in intense concentration, he communicated ideas and messages from all over the cosmos.

Problems arose as humanity worked with its newfound cosmic consciousness. Some fear that this interaction with highly developed societies could lead to the destruction or subjugation of Earth. Others attempted to profit from cosmic knowledge, seeing it as a chance for rapid technological development.

The challenge the World Council faced today was its toughest yet. How may they securely lead mankind through this change? How could they ensure that everyone, not just a select few, benefited from the cosmic wisdom?

The Cosmic Harmony Project emerged as a response to these challenges. Its goal was to combine cosmic knowledge with the many civilisations and customs of Earth to produce a new global paradigm honouring both oneness and variety.

Teachers of cosmic awareness and humanity's position in the cosmos started to find their way into classrooms all throughout the globe. Inspired by the cosmic symphony encountered during the meditation session, new kinds of music and art arose.

Months went by and minutes passed, but significant changes started to show up on Earth. Now linked to the cosmic web, the bioluminescent network began to rapidly restore injured habitats. As climate patterns began to stabilise, new, environmentally friendly technology appeared to almost naturally develop in laboratories all over the world.

However, these positive advancements have also brought with them new responsibilities. We have seen a glimpse of humanity's potential, but we have also received a sobering warning about the repercussions of abusing this cosmic link.

One year after the cosmic meditation event, Kavin had a strong vision as Kurinji got ready for yet another world conference. He saw humanity at a crossroads, with many possible futures branching out ahead of them. Some saw Earth as a lighthouse of knowledge and peace in the cosmic community. In other cases, it descended into anarchy and devastation.

The message was clear: the decisions taken in the next few years would define not only the destiny of mankind but also the position of Earth in the cosmic order.

Arriving at Kurinji, delegates from across the globe felt as if they were poised on the brink of a new age. Originally a peaceful backwater, the settlement has grown to be the scientific and spiritual hub of a fast-changing planet.

Looking out over the assembly, Kavin sensed the weight of the occasion. Humans' next actions would have a global impact. He knew the biggest chapter in Earth's history was about to open as he got ready to speak to the gathering.

The cosmic egg throbbed with alien light, a reminder of the immense responsibility and limitless possibilities just ahead. Every individual on Earth was now part of this great, worldwide narrative; the journey started in Kurinji and had turned into a cosmic expedition.

Real-World Correlation:

Universal patterns

The discovery of the cosmic harmonies reflects real-world recognition of patterns that appear across different scales and disciplines.

Examples:

Fractal patterns found in nature, from coastlines to plant structures.

Golden ratio appearing in art, architecture, and natural phenomena.

Mathematical constants like pi showing up unexpectedly in various scientific fields.

Chapter 9

Links Across Realities

Kurinji pulsed with an intensity that appeared to match the very fabric of the universe. Along with scientists, spiritual leaders, and common people attracted by an unexplained calling, representatives from every country gathered to map the trajectory of humanity's cosmic trip.

Rising before the changed egg, Kavin spoke to the gathered audience. His remarks, together with the knowledge of many alien civilizations, created a picture of a cosmos considerably more complex and linked than anybody had thought. He talked about the delicate balance that keeps the cosmic web together, as well as quantum reality, in which mind and matter are parts of civilizations transcending physical form.

As he talked, the egg started to throb with an intensity that drew everyone in. Abruptly, a beam of light burst out, encircling Kavin and showing everyone a holographic picture. The picture depicted Earth, though not as they understood it. Earth existed throughout many histories and realities, each somewhat different, but all linked by strands of luminous energy.

Watching in wonder, Dr. Chen came to see that they were seeing the quantum character of reality itself. The bioluminescent network bridged different realms rather than just linking locations. This insight revealed both exciting and terrible possibilities.

The consequences of this finding started to show in the next few days. Scientists speculated that it would be feasible to travel between these other worlds, or perhaps interact across them, given appropriate knowledge and technology. While there were significant opportunities for sharing information and solving problems, there were also significant risks of disrupting the delicate quantum equilibrium.

Drawing on ancient knowledge and her close relationship to cosmic awareness, Nnenna began teaching methods to gently negotiate these quantum realities through meditation and concentrated purpose. She underlined the need to keep a close connection to one's home world and cautioned of the risks of losing oneself in the unlimited possibilities. The world's response to news of this quantum revolution varied. Some saw learning from our civilization's more evolved forms to address the most pressing issues facing Earth. Others were worried about the consequences of playing with the very fabric of reality.

Governments rushed to create rules for this new front line. Given interdimensional travel, the idea of national boundaries appeared almost archaic. New ethical dilemmas surfaced: Was there a duty to stop a calamity by notifying another Earth? How does one interact with their alternate self?

Kurinji, the epicenter of this quantum revolution, founded the Quantum Harmony Centre. Its goals were to investigate these other worlds, provide secure means of communication, and create moral rules for interdimensional connections.
Kavin discovered he was the center of this quantum maelstrom. Now, his special capacity for communication throughout the bioluminescent network included seeing and engaging with these other worlds. He

became a link between Earth's many incarnations throughout the quantum multiverse, as well as between Earth and the universe.

Months later, well-under-control quantum communication tests produced startling findings. Cooperation with other Earths that had previously overcome similar difficulties was resolving issues that had plagued mankind for millennia, from healing illnesses to creating clean energy sources.

There was a price for this advancement, however. Reports of people going through "quantum displacement," a phenomenon wherein people would momentarily enter another world and cause uncertainty and anxiety, started to circulate. The Quantum Harmony Centre puts forth tremendous effort to create methods to root individuals in their native reality and stop unwelcome transformations.

One year after discovering the quantum nature of the bioluminescent network, Earth teetered on a change unlike any it had experienced before. The lines separating science, spirituality, and daily living have faded from view. Every human living on Earth was realizing their quantum nature and the many opportunities presented with every decision they took.
Kurinji towns men and women felt both excitement and anxiety as they got ready for another world conference. Though they had the ability to define reality itself, the responsibility was great. One ill-informed action could have effects in many other worlds.

Kavin, now seen as a protector of the quantum equilibrium, felt the weight of this obligation very strongly. As he contemplated the cosmic egg, he saw the potential and difficulties ahead. In his vision of the future, humans had developed into pure energy entities capable of freely navigating the quantum universe. However, he also recognized the dangers and realities of authority abuse, which could lead to a cosmic disaster.

Kavin realized as the participants started to show up for the quantum summit that the choices made in the next few days would reverberate not just in their reality, but in all conceivable worlds. Every person on Earth was the author of this great, multifaceted novel; the next chapter in Earth's cosmic tale was about to begin.

As a reminder of the enormous possibilities and immense responsibilities that lay ahead, the cosmic egg pulsed with a brightness that appeared to contain all imaginable reality. The quest that started in a small community with an enigmatic egg have evolved into a journey across the very fabric of life itself.

> ### *Real-World Correlation:*
>
> ### *Ethical challenges of new technologies.*
>
> The debate over the use of quantum communication mirrors real-world discussions

about the implications of emerging

technologies.

Examples:

Debates over Artificial Intelligence ethics and

regulation.

Concerns about genetic engineering and

designer babies.

Discussions about privacy in the age of big data.

Chapter 10

Quantum Quandary

As the quantum summit assembled in Kurinji, the air hummed with energy that seemed to transcend physical reality. Delegates from across the globe, their minds opened by cosmic awareness, assembled to handle the hitherto unheard-of possibilities and difficulties provided by the quantum character of the bioluminescent network.

Dr. Chen stepped forward, her eyes burning with the fire of scientific inquiry. She discussed how the bioluminescent network had evolved into a live, multidimensional interface and offered a ground-breaking study on the nature of quantum reality. Her group has created a prototype "quantum resonator," a tool that enables more under-control interactions by stabilizing links across multiple worlds.

As she spoke, holographic screens shimmered around her, displaying the complex network of quantum links now encircling the Earth. The planet in the middle of a cosmic dance of potential was a stunning sight.

Nnenna followed, her cool head contrasting with the thrill of scientific discovery. She discussed the spiritual ramifications of quantum consciousness and the necessity for mankind to develop morally, spiritually, and technologically. Stressing the need to keep a strong moral compass, she spoke of the risks of losing oneself in the endless possibilities of the quantum universe.

As the summit advanced, reports began to stream in from all around.

People were temporarily discovering themselves in other worlds, undergoing natural quantum changes. Although most of these encounters were fleeting and benign, there were disturbing incidents of people getting "unstuck" in time and space, their awareness drifting in the quantum sea.

Kavin had now precisely adjusted his quantum sensitivity, allowing him to sense the waves caused by these perturbations. He came to see that the line separating reality was becoming more permeable and that, without appropriate direction, humans ran the danger of cosmic anarchy.

Kavin suggested, audaciously, the formation of a new company called Quantum Stewards. This group, comprising individuals with heightened quantum awareness, would receive training to navigate the multiverse, aid those experiencing quantum displacement, and maintain the delicate balance between realities.

The plan attracted both hope and mistrust. While many felt such a committee was necessary, others worried it would give a small number of people undue authority. After extensive debate, a compromise emerged. A local Kurinji elder would head a worldwide ethics commission that would closely supervise the establishment of the Quantum Stewards.

As the peak closed, a new difficulty arose. Quantum sensing presented disturbing depictions of a "shadow reality," a version of Earth in which the militarization of the bioluminescent network led to catastrophic outcomes. This black mirror of their universe appeared to be expanding, its evil influence threatening to leak into other realities.

The revelation rocked the assembly. Until recently, the prospect of hostile other worlds was just speculative; now it was a very real menace. The need for Quantum Stewards became clear.

In the following weeks, Kurinji became the first generation of Quantum Stewards' training ground. Under the direction of Kavin, Nnenna, and Dr. Chen, these people learned to negotiate the quantum multiverse, to interact across worlds, and to preserve the fragile fabric of spacetime.

Meanwhile, research on shadow reality has intensified. While Nnenna guided worldwide meditation sessions to boost the positive quantum field surrounding Earth, Dr. Chen and her team laboured nonstop to create defences against quantum infiltration.

Kavin discovered he was thin, juggling the leadership of the quantum stewards with his continuous contact with kind cosmic creatures. Though he felt a tremendous amount of responsibility, he found strength in the togetherness and goal he saw in others around him.

Months passed as the quantum nature of reality began to permeate daily life on Earth. They overhauled educational systems, including early-age quantum awareness training. New kinds of entertainment and art arose to let humans safely encounter other worlds. As people came together to face the cosmic problems ahead, global collaboration reached previously unheard-of proportions.

Still, the shadow of life loomed large. Malevolent quantum incursion incidents rose, and the quantum stewards discovered they were fighting an unseen battle to protect their reality.

One year after the quantum summit, Kavin had a terrifying vision as Kurinji got ready to provide an evaluation of human development in the quantum period. He witnessed a day when the lines separating reality had completely crumbled, and several copies of Earth fought for dominance in a turbulent quantum storm.

But he also harboured optimism for a day when humans would have grasped their quantum character and would be defenders of cosmic equilibrium. The road to this better future was perilous and called for knowledge, bravery, and togetherness on a level never seen in human history.

Delegates once again assembled in Kurinji felt as if they were at the most crucial point yet in their cosmic trip. The choices taken in the next few days would spread throughout the quantum universe, determining the fate not just of their Earth but also of many others.

Now whirling a quantum vortex, the cosmic unbreakable egg buzzed with the energy of many possibilities. The journey started in a little Kurinji village and has evolved into a search to protect the fundamental fabric of reality itself. And now, conscious of their position as quantum entities, every individual on Earth participated in this great, multiverse play.

With stakes greater than anybody could have imagined when this trip started, the next chapter in mankind's cosmic quest was about to open. The quantum problem needed a solution, and the fates of many worlds teetered.

Real-World Correlation:

Identity in a digital age

The challenges of "quantum entanglement" with alternate selves reflect real-world issues of identity in the digital era.

Examples:

Managing multiple online personas across social media platforms.

The impact of deepfake technology on personal identity.

Virtual reality and avatars blurring lines between physical and digital selves.

Chapter 11

Quantum Confluence

The assembly in Kurinji was tense but determined as the review of humanity's quantum era started. The menace of the shadow world loomed large, serving as a grim counterweight to the amazing progress mankind has accomplished.

Kavin, now Chief Quantum Steward, spoke to the gathering. His comments bore the weight of the many truths he had seen. "We stand at a crossroads," he said with multiple echoes in his voice. "Our control of quantum reality has brought us to the brink of both unimaginable harmony and unfathomable chaos."

The cosmic, unbreakable egg behind him pulsed wildly, its quantum vortex whirling with even more ferocity as he spoke. A blinding brightness suddenly enveloped the assembly, and as the light receded, cries of astonishment rippled through it. Three beings stood next to Kavin—incarnations of himself from other worlds.

One Kavin arrived from a world where the shadow Earth had triumphed; he bore wounds from the earthquake that struck Kurinji, standing amidst the rubbles of the ancient Kurinji National Museum with a disturbed expression. Another, shining with an ethereal brilliance, stood for a time when humans had gone beyond physical form. Despite minor variations, the third entity, strikingly similarity to their own Kavin, offered a glimpse into a parallel present where different decisions had been made.

With her scientific mind racing, Dr. Chen knew they were seeing a quantum confluence—a melding of reality not allowed by nature. The ramifications were shockingly large.

The Kavins spoke together, their voices harmonising in a cosmic sense. They linked their dreams of various conceivable futures, some brilliant and others terrible. The message was unambiguous: the acts of this reality would have broad effects throughout the multiverse.

Alarms blared from Dr. Chen's quantum monitoring system as the shock of this disclosure reverberated through the assembly. The shadow reality was moving, taking advantage of the compromised boundaries between realms.

At that point, an unexpected voice emerged above the anarchy. Nnenna moved forward, her eyes sparkling with cosmic knowledge. Her voice was cool among the tempests. "We have been looking at this all wrong." "The shadow reality is a reflection of our own fears and shortcomings; it is not our enemy."

Her comments really resonated. Silently digesting this paradigm change were the gathered leaders, scientists, and quantum stewards.

Kavin nodded in agreement with all the different versions of himself. "We cannot fight the shadow," they murmured together. "We must integrate it, understand it, and then, through that understanding, transform it." What ensued was unlike anything Earth has ever known. Under the direction of Nnenna and the Kavins, a worldwide quantum meditation started. Joined in a cosmic symphony of awareness are billions of brains worldwide and across realities.

As the meditation sank deeper, the lines that separated reality faded. People discovered they may simultaneously be living many versions of their lives. It was terrible, overpowering, and finally transforming.

In this quantum superposition condition, humanity faced its shared shadow. They confronted their own darkness, as well as the possibility of chaos and destruction that accompanied their ability for love and creativity.

Although the quantum flow time seemed meaningless, hours passed. When the meditation finally concluded, the world underwent a transformation. The clear distinctions separating reality have faded. The shadow Earth was a component of a larger whole, rather than a hazard.

Days later, a fresh interpretation of quantum reality surfaced. Once again, under the leadership of a single Kavin and with elder Murali providing moral supervision, the Quantum Stewards began educating others on how to navigate this increasingly fluid world. Access to different selves has become a tool for healing and personal development.

Dr. Chen and colleagues created new technologies based on quantum integration rather than separation. These developments produced revelations in environmental restoration, energy generation, and even in repairing divisions between countries.

Additionally, Nnenna adapted her lessons to incorporate the knowledge she had gained at the quantum confluence. She described a cosmos in which every option was respected, and unity and variety coexisted in perfect equilibrium.

As the one-year anniversary of the quantum confluence approached, Earth had become almost invisible. Cities gleamed with quantum architecture, which existed in many states at the same time. A rebirth in art, science, and culture followed people learning to use the knowledge and abilities of their other selves.

Challenges still existed, however. The fluid character of life meant that preserving a stable community needed ongoing awareness and change. The Quantum Stewards made a wonderful effort to assist individuals in negotiating this new life.

Standing before the cosmic unbreakable egg—now a whirling quantum matrix of endless possibilities—Kavin considered the path that had taken them here. Mankind has evolved beyond human comprehension, from a small town struggling to find its most valuable ancient key to an enigmatic ostrich egg concealing the key to today's guardians of the quantum universe.

Kavin felt the weight of endless realities on his shoulders as he got ready to greet the globe on the confluence's anniversary. But he also harboured optimism, a strong feeling that mankind had moved towards its cosmic destiny in a vital direction.

In its radiance, the cosmic, unbreakable egg pulsed with a spectrum of all potential existence. The journey that started in Kurinji had evolved into a cosmic integration trip aimed at discovering harmony among the limitless conflicts of quantum reality.

As Kavin began to speak, it became clear that we were still writing the greatest chapter in Earth's cosmic narrative, with every idea, decision, and instant rippled over the quantum sea of existence.

Real-World Correlation:

Collective problem-solving

The global quantum meditation to integrate the shadows reality reflects real-world efforts to solve complex problems through collective action and consciousness.

Examples:

Crowdsourcing solutions for scientific challenges (e.g., Foldit protein folding game).

Global hackathons addressing social and environmental issues.

Citizen science projects like Galaxy Zoo for space exploration.

Chapter 12

Threading Realities

Kavin's explanations resonated not just throughout the globe but also among many realities as he spoke to the world on the anniversary of the quantum confluence. The cosmic, unbreakable egg behind him had developed into a hypnotic quantum tapestry, its threads symbolising the many threads of potential now entwined with Earth's reality.

Kavin started, his voice vibrating with multidimensional harmonics, "We stand at the threshold of a new era." We are entering an era where every decision ripples across the quantum sea of life and blurs what is and what could be."

As he talked, the quantum tapestry behind him changed to display hints of the many worlds now within human reach. Simultaneously, cities exist in numerous states, ecosystems return to their original splendour, and technology surpasses the conventional understanding of physics.

Dr. Chen moved closer, her eyes burning with inquiry. "Our knowledge of quantum reality has produced discoveries we could never have predicted," she said. "We have developed quantum healing methods that use other people's health to treat illnesses." "Our quantum computers can solve problems by simultaneously computing across many worlds."

But these developments also presented fresh difficulties. Stories of people "quantum entangled" with their other selves have appeared, causing psychological pain and identity difficulties. The Quantum Stewards, under Kavin's direction, have been guiding people through these difficult personal truths nonstop.

Her calmness, among the whirls of quantum energy, spoke to the spiritual ramifications of this new life. "We are learning to see ourselves as more than individuals," she remarked. "We are quantum entities, part of a great cosmic tapestry." Our difficulty today is to embrace our unlimited essence while still preserving our sense of self.

As the conversation continued, a disruption ran through the quantum tapestry. Kavin, with his senses trained to detect even the smallest quantum disturbances, immediately sensed the disruption. Something was approaching that would test everything they had studied.

Abruptly, a man materialised before the shocked crowd. It was a creature of pure energy; its form moved like liquid light. Speaking, its voice appeared to emanate from everywhere and from nowhere at the same time.

"Hello, quantum children," the entity said. "I am an ambassador from a civilization apart from your understanding of reality. We have rather closely watched your progress.

The disclosure rocked the assembly as well as the globe. Humanity had come into contact with a really alien intellect that existed beyond the quantum universe they had barely started to investigate.

The entity emphasised that Earth's mastery of quantum reality had produced waves beyond their understanding of existence. It discussed reality outside of reality and layers of existence that, by contrast, made the quantum multiverse look simple.

"You find yourself at a pivotal moment," the entity uttered. "Your next steps will determine not only the fate of your world or multiverse, but life itself."

Kavin experienced a familiar feeling as the cosmic unbreakable egg calling to him sank in meaning. Suddenly, with quantum clarity, he understood. The indestructible egg, the bioluminescent network, and the quantum tapestry had all been ready for this moment.

Kavin moved forward, his voice consistent with the weight of the occasion. "We are ready," he added, speaking for all people. "By juggling unity and variety, we've learned to strike harmony with endless possibilities. "We shall meet any difficulties that lie ahead together."

Though it had no obvious face, the energy appeared to grin. "Then let the next phase of your journey begin," it murmured, then broke into a shower of quantum sparks blending into the cosmic tapestry.

As the creature disappeared, the quantum fabric began to move and change. More complicated and gorgeous than anything they had seen before, new trends emerged. Every quantum-sensitive individual on Earth—Kavin, Dr. Chen, and Nnenna—experienced a change in the fundamental fabric of reality.

They were on the verge of a new adventure that would take them beyond the quantum universe and into unimaginable worlds. The journey that began in Kurinji with a missing golden globe key and an enigmatic egg had evolved into an incomprehensible cosmic trip.

Kavin glanced out at the gathered audience and at the billions observing worldwide and across boundaries as the planet embraced this new reality. Though he saw dread in their eyes, he also sensed hope, excitement, and will.

"We have come so far," he remarked, his voice spanning the quantum fabric of life. "But our biggest trip is just beginning. Together, we will investigate the actual character of reality and our position in it."

The cosmic, unbreakable egg, now a portal to worlds beyond imagination, glowed with fresh vitality. The next chapter in Earth's cosmic narrative was about to start and seemed to be more remarkable than anybody could have imagined.

Kavin felt both excitement and fear as he got ready to guide mankind into this new frontier. Starting at Kurinji, the experience evolved into a search to comprehend the fundamental essence of life itself. And now, conscious of their limitless quantum nature, every soul on Earth has become part of this enormous cosmic story.

The quantum tapestry shimmered with many possibilities, a living monument to the road ahead. Whatever obstacles were ahead in the worlds beyond the quantum multiverse, mankind would meet them together, permanently altered by the cosmic unbreakable egg that had put them on this remarkable road.

Real-World Correlation:

Exponential technological growth

The rapid advancements in quantum healing and computing mirror the exponential growth of technology in our world.

Examples:

Moore's Law in computer processing power.

Rapid advancements in gene editing technologies like CRISPR.

The exponential growth of renewable energy technologies.

Chapter 13

Beyond the Quantum Veil

The world teetered on a paradigm shift that exceeded even the quantum revolution as the consequences of the unusual energy visit seeped in. Kavin, Dr. Chen, and Nnenna, now regarded as the triumvirate of Earth's cosmic adventure, gathered an emergency worldwide council to plot ahead.

With her head whirling with options, Dr. Chen suggested a risky strategy. Her eyes were ablaze with scientific zeal. "We need to build a device," she said, "a Cosmic Interface Nexus, or CIN, that can help us perceive and interact with these higher realms of life."

Drawing on the combined understanding of quantum physics, spiritual wisdom, and the insights revealed from the short visit of the energy being, the building of the CIN became a worldwide endeavour. Kurinji developed a giant gadget pulsing with forces beyond human comprehension.

As the CIN developed, strange events began to occur globally. People claimed to see short flashes of "cosmic awareness," glimpses into worlds beyond explanation. The quantum tapestry became even more complicated, changing patterns in ways that the most sophisticated quantum computers found difficult to examine.

Drawing on her extensive spiritual knowledge, Nnenna started instructing fresh meditation methods to let individuals negotiate these enlarged levels of awareness. She told her young pupils, "We are evolving," not only as people or even as a species, but as aware embodiments of the universe itself.

Kavin, too, felt his role changing. His relationship with the cosmic, unbreakable egg—now a multidimensional nexus point—let him act as a link between people and the higher worlds they were starting to investigate. After long hours of intense concentration, he sought to interpret the messages and images that passed over the quantum tapestry.

Six months after the unusual energy visit, the CIN was at last ready. The entire audience fell silent as the gadget turned on. Nothing seemed to happen for a minute. Then the CIN sprang to life with a burst of vitality felt all throughout the earth.

The quantum tapestry burst into yet another level of complexity. Those close to the gadget—Kavin, Dr. Chen, and Nnenna—found their awareness and shot into worlds beyond their reach. Their reality was one in which time flowed in many directions concurrently, where thought and matter were indistinguishable, and where the idea of personal life melted into a cosmic oneness.

The three battled to put their experiences into words when they recovered normal awareness. "We have only started to scratch the surface," Dr. Chen said, sounding in wonder. "Each more complicated and beautiful than the last, there are layers upon layers of reality."

The CIN turned on, marking the start of a new chapter in Earth's cosmic journey. The tool evolved into a doorway of sorts, enabling skilled people to investigate higher realms of reality. Every trip returned fresh information that stretched the bounds of spirituality, philosophy, and science.

Still, this increased consciousness also presented new difficulties. Overwhelmed by the enormity of cosmic truth, some individuals battled to live their daily lives. Others sought to manipulate higher reality for financial gain and power, thereby attempting to utilise the CIN for their own benefit. The elder Murali monitoring committee intervened to counsel the quantum stewards.

Under Kavin's direction, the Quantum Stewards changed into cosmic guardians assigned to guide mankind over this new existential terrain while preserving the fragile equilibrium between realities.

As the one-year anniversary of the unusual energy visit drew near, Earth underwent unimaginable changes. Cities now live in quantum superposition, their designs changing to fit the demands of the time. As individuals started to see the connectivity of all reality, global wars had essentially stopped.

However, Kavin sensed dread as he got ready to greet the planet on this momentous date. The cosmic, unbreakable egg had been throbbing with increasing intensity—a whirling whirlwind of multidimensional energy. He sensed that their cosmic adventure was about to take a dramatic turn.

As he rose to the stage, the quantum tapestry behind him burst into dazzling light. When the light dimmed, Kavin discovered he was in a world beyond description, not on Earth. Around him, he felt the presence of many evolved entities, their awareness enormous and incomprehensible. A voice—or maybe a thought—resonated through his body: "Welcome, child of Earth. You have already started an endless journey. Are you ready to really join the cosmic dance?

His thoughts whirling with the ramifications, Kavin knew his response would determine not just Earth's fate but also many worlds beyond. The journey, which began with the missing Kurinji's golden globe key buried in an enigmatic egg, has brought mankind to the brink of cosmic citizenship. As he got ready to reply, Kavin felt the hopes and worries of everyone washing through him. He knew that whatever followed would be unlike anything they had ever known. The next chapter in Earth's cosmic journey was about to start and promised to rethink the very essence of life itself.

Real-World Correlation:

The rapid growth of transformative technologies.

The evolution of the Cosmic Interface Nexus (CIN) and human exploration of higher spheres of reality reflect the fast progress of transforming technology, redefining our perspective on and interaction with the environment.

Examples:

The development of brain-computer interfaces enabling direct contact between the human brain and outside tools.

Advances in quantum computing allowing for complex computations that are beyond the reach of conventional computers.

Virtual and augmented reality technologies providing people with immersive, other worlds to explore and engage with.

Chapter 14

Cosmic Initiation

Kavin stood in a world beyond words; his awareness grew to cover everything around him. Numerous evolved entities surrounded him; their ideas and feelings flowed through his brain like cosmic rivers.

Kavin spoke, his voice bearing the collective will of mankind, breathing deeply and apparently resonating across many planets. "We are ready," he murmured, the words gliding over the fabric of reality. "Earth and her people accept the invitation to join the cosmic dance."

Something really changed the instant Kavin spoke these words. The lines separating Earth from this upper sphere started to fade. People everywhere on Earth suddenly expanded their awareness. For the first time, they could perceive the true essence of reality, as though a veil had lifted.

Dr. Chen gazed in wonder as the CIN readings veered off the chart. She gasped, not just Kavin. "The whole Earth is merging into this higher-dimensional network!"

Deep in meditation, Nnenna saw the change as a tsunami of cosmic consciousness sweeping across the earth. "We are evolving," she said, tears of delight running down her cheeks. "Not just in body or mind, but in the very essence of our being."

As the merger progressed, Earth began to change. The earth's ecology pulsated with fresh vitality, and ecosystems were rebuilding at a speed never seen before. Earth's quantum tapestry now interconnects with a vast cosmic network of intelligent planets and civilisations, surpassing everything.

Still in the upper sphere, Kavin started to get downloads of cosmic information. Not as a straight-line development but rather as a complex, multidimensional tapestry of linked events and possibilities, the history of the universe opened out before him.

He stumbled upon the Cosmic Council, an assembly of evolved civilizations that oversees awareness development throughout the cosmos. From the earthquake, the museum damage, and the lost key to the arrival of the unbreakable egg voyage to this moment of initiation, Earth's path had been part of a great plan to raise mankind to cosmic citizenship. Kurinji seemed to serve as the foundation for weaving this tapestry.

As this information poured into him, Kavin realised the true meaning of the cosmic egg. The Cosmic Council had sown this cosmic egg as a seed to spur human development and equip Earth for this cosmic awakening. People were starting to find fresh talents back on Earth. Some discovered they could telepathically link enormous distances. Others developed the ability to control matters only with their thoughts. The lines between magic, spirituality, and science had totally collapsed.

To grasp and record these developments, Dr. Chen and her colleagues put forth much effort. "We're not merely seeing evolution," she said to a worldwide audience. "We are undergoing a whole redesign of what it means to be human."

Nnenna's lessons also underwent a transformation, incorporating the cosmic knowledge now available to humans. Emphasising the need for the moral and responsible use of cosmic power, she started training individuals in the application of their new talents.

Days passed on this new level of cosmic awareness, and issues began to emerge. Overwhelmed by their growing awareness, some people battled to maintain a sense of self. Others, engrossed in their new abilities, needed guidance on how to use them sensibly.
The cosmic guardians, who rose from the quantum stewards, became more important in guiding mankind through this change. They tried to maintain equilibrium both within people and in Earth's newly enlarged part of the cosmic community.

Months into this new age, Kavin returned physically at last, but his mind remained linked to the upper world. Before a worldwide audience, his figure glowed with celestial energy.
With his voice echoing across many realms, he declared, "We have received a wonderful gift."" But it comes with immense responsibility. We now live in a cosmic environment, with our actions resonating throughout reality. We must learn to see and behave as cosmic citizens, not just as individuals or countries.

Now a whirlpool of multidimensional energy, the cosmic, unbreakable egg pulsed in time with Kavin's words. Though its path was far from finished, it had served to guide mankind towards this moment. The impenetrable egg was changing into a celestial lighthouse, guiding Earth to its new place in the cosmos.
As Earth's cosmic beginning neared its one-year anniversary, the world got ready for a celebration unlike any in human history. Representatives from

various intergalactic civilizations had planned a visit to officially welcome Earth into galactic society.

Kavin considered the amazing trip that had brought him here as he stood before the changed cosmic egg, getting ready to greet Earth's cosmic visitors. From a little hamlet in Kurinji to galactic citizenship, mankind has evolved beyond human comprehension.
Still, he understood that this was just a starting point. The universe was vast and brimming with mysteries; the greatest experiences of humankind still lay ahead. Kavin grinned, ready to guide mankind into the next phase of its cosmic voyage, as the first cosmic spacecraft showed up in the sky.

Every creature on Earth was now a part of this grand, global narrative, which began with a lost key to a mysterious, unbreakable egg and evolved into an epic of cosmic proportions. The greatest adventure in human history was just about to begin, and the whole universe was ready to witness what Earth would contribute to the cosmic dance.

Real-World Correlation:

Global consciousness swings

Earth's integration into the cosmic community mirrors real-world movements towards global citizenship and unity.

Examples:

The rise of international organizations and global governance structures.

Increasing awareness of global issues like climate change.

Cultural exchange programs fostering international understanding.

Chapter 15

Cosmic Symposium

The Earth buzzed with an energy that went beyond physical reality as the anniversary of its cosmic beginning dawned. The advent of cosmic vessels, each a wonder of technology and awareness well beyond human understanding, shimmered in the heavens above every major metropolis.

Kurinji, formerly a small town and now Earth's cosmic capital, was at the center of this historic event. Having developed into a multidimensional nexus point, the cosmic unbreakable egg pulsed with rhythms resonant throughout the cosmos, greeting Earth's cosmic visitors.

Standing ready to welcome the interstellar representatives were Kavin, Dr. Chen, and Nnenna. Over the past year, their shapes have shifted to become more fluid, able to move between the physical and energy realms at will. They represented the new face of mankind, cosmic entities in their own right.

When the first delegates came out of their ships, the world marveled. The variety of cosmic life was beyond human comprehension: beings of pure light, crystalline entities that sang rather than talked, and creatures that appeared to live in many realms at the same time.

The Cosmic Symposium, then known as something else, was unlike any assembly in Earth's past. It was a confluence of reality, a mixing of awareness that cut beyond physical limits, not just a meeting of many species.

Dr. Chen supervised a series of information-sharing events that allowed Earth's scientists to directly interact with the vast database of universal knowledge that the cosmic collective maintained. Within a few hours, millennia of advancements in human knowledge of physics, biology, and the nature of reality itself occurred.

Nnenna arranged spiritual retreats, drawing people from across the planet. These sessions allow participants to experience the connectedness of all life by erasing the divisions between personal consciousnesses. Many people emerged from these retreats permanently transformed; their viewpoints extended beyond their own reality.

Kavin, Earth's cosmic envoy, participated in high-level conversations about Earth's status in the larger cosmic community. He discovered multidimensional partnerships, cosmic obligations accompanying Earth's newfound position, and galactic federations.

As the symposium continued, the earth itself changed. Driven by cosmic energy, the planet's biosphere developed at an unheard-of speed. New species emerged from a mixture of Earth's life force and extraterrestrial forces. The world was becoming a living archive of global affairs.

Still, among the beauty and thrill, problems surfaced. Overwhelmed by the rapid changes and the flood of cosmic information, some people withdrew into communities, trying to preserve their pre-initiation way of life.

Others, engrossed in their newfound abilities, need guidance on how to make responsible use of them.

Respecting individual decisions, the Cosmic Guardians laboured nonstop to preserve equilibrium so that mankind could negotiate its new world. To teach individuals to make appropriate use of their developing skills, they set up academies all around.

A historic statement came as the symposium ended. The Cosmic Council, which oversees awareness development throughout the universe, requested that Earth send delegates.

Approaching the gathered cosmic delegates and a worldwide human audience, Kavin accepted the offer on behalf of Earth. "We enter this new role with humility and will," he added, his words reverberating in many spheres. "Earth brings to the cosmic community its unique human perspective, its creativity, and its indistinct spirit."

The cosmic, unbreakable egg pulsed with hitherto unheard-of intensity, as he said. Then a beam of light emerged, encircling Kavin. As the light dimmed, he had changed. His existence now lives concurrently in many realms, as a living link between Earth and the universe.

Dr. Chen and Nnenna changed similarly, each evolving to represent various aspects of Earth's cosmic potential. While they were still guiding Earth's development, they would collectively represent mankind on the Cosmic Council.

Exhilaration and anxiety filled the air as the cosmic vessels prepared to depart, leaving behind messengers and instructors to continue leading mankind. Now Earth was permanently a member of a greater cosmic society, with all the marvels and obligations involved.

With his awareness now encompassing the universe, Kavin paid one final farewell to the planet before heading for the cosmic council. "Our mother nature's journey, which began with a sudden heartbreak of losing everything our ancestors left us and missing the ancient key to the birth of a mystery unbreakable egg in our small Kurinji village, has led us to the stars," he stated. "But this is not a destination. It is the beginning. Our cosmic narrative has been unfolding for eternity and will continue forever."

The inhabitants of Earth gazed at the sky with fresh eyes as Kavin, Dr. Chen, and Nnenna were ready to start their cosmic trip. They understood that every day would bring new surprises and difficulties, and that the biggest experiences remained ahead.

Now a fixed gateway between Earth and the larger universe, the cosmic egg throbbed with the rhythms of many possibilities. The narrative of mankind has evolved into a cosmic-scale drama of constant adventure echoing over the expanse of life.

Thus, as Earth supplanted one of the cosmic civilizations, a new chapter began for the entire universe. Not just for humans. Starting at Kurinji, the trip had evolved into an adventure without end, a cosmic dance of evolution and discovery spanning eternity.

Real-World Correlation:

International knowledge exchange

The Cosmic Symposium reflects real-world international conferences and collaborations.

Examples:

TED Conferences bringing together diverse experts.

International scientific collaborations like the Human Genome Project.

Global forums on artificial intelligence and ethics.

Chapter 16

Infinite Threads

Earth reached a new stage of its cosmic development when Kavin, Dr. Chen, and Nnenna set out on their trip to the Cosmic Council. The three main guide's departure signals the start of mankind's autonomous travel into the larger cosmos.

Back on Earth, the metamorphosis proceeded at a hitherto unheard-of speed. Cities evolved into living, breathing creatures whose buildings changed to instantly satisfy their residents' needs. With bio-organic computers and sentient ecosystems as the standard, the lines separating technology from nature have become totally hazy.

Now, under the direction of a varied council of people who had personally changed, the Cosmic Guardians adopted the role of supervising Earth's ongoing development. Their enormous challenge was guiding mankind towards equilibrium between its increased cosmic consciousness and the core of what made it distinctly human.

"Cosmic Dreamers" emerged as one of the most significant transformations. These people, often born after the beginning of Earth, had the natural capacity to travel between worlds via their dreams. Their midnight travels brought information and ideas from all over the universe, hastening Earth's integration into global society.

Dr. Chen's protégés, Dr Vargas, Professor Sophia Dickson, Dr. Pedro Chavez, Professor Mendhi Mohammed, and Professor Chukwudi Ekwueme, carried on their work, extending the envelope of science into fields formerly thought only magical. Drawing on the fundamental fabric of reality itself, they created technology enabling instantaneous travel across vast cosmic distances.

From her lessons, Nnenna developed a global philosophy that united cosmic science and spirituality. Her students travelled the world, guiding people towards acceptance of their growing awareness and providing instructions on how to use the cosmic energies now coursing through the earth.

Years went by, and Earth started to play a more active part in cosmic events. Travelling to far-off galaxies as diplomats, scientists, and explorers, human delegates arrived in forms now as varied as the cosmos itself. They carried with them Earth's unique viewpoint, inventiveness, and adaptability—qualities much prized in the galactic world.

The cosmic, unbreakable egg kept changing, becoming a staple in Kurinji. It morphed into a live archive of Earth's journey, capturing every turn of human cosmic development. Pilgrims from all over the universe came to commune with its throbbing energies, hearing the echoes of their own cosmic beginnings.

Still, this quick change presented some difficulties. A movement known as the "Earth Preservers" gathered support to advocate for the preservation of Earth's original ecosystem and human civilization. They said that mankind ran the danger of losing connection with its origins in a hurry to embrace the cosmic.

A major motif in Earth's continuing narrative is this conflict between cosmic development and terrestrial preservation. It resulted in the creation of large natural preserves where Earth's original ecosystems were kept intact, as well as cultural enclaves honouring and safeguarding pre-cosmic human customs.

News of Kavin, Dr. Chen, and Nnenna coming for a visit surfaced as Earth drew near the tenth anniversary of its cosmic beginning. We anticipated their arrival with both joy and trepidation. How may they have changed? What information would they receive from the Cosmic Council?

Gasps of wonder shook the assembled audience as they at last materialised in the heart of Kurinji, close to the cosmic, indestructible egg. Their bodies were throbbing with cosmic energies, shifting shapes between states of matter and energy; they had evolved beyond recognition.

With his voice resonating across many spheres, Kavin addressed the humans living on Earth. "We return to you not as leaders but as fellow travellers on an endless journey," he remarked. "We have encountered obstacles that have tested the very core of our beings and experienced miracles beyond our comprehension. However, we have never encountered anything quite like Earth in all our journeys.

Even for the most evolved brains on Earth, Dr. Chen offered insights into the nature of reality that challenged understanding. "The universe is vaster and more subtle than we ever imagined," she said. "Every discovery lets new mysteries open their doors."

Speaking of the spiritual development occurring throughout the universe, Nnenna radiated a calm that touched anyone's spirits. "We all belong to a great awakening," she remarked. "Earth's path is a major thread in the cosmic tapestry of consciousness."

Kavin looked at the cosmic, unbreakable egg as they prepared to leave Earth and follow their own path of inquiry once more. For a time, he united his mind with the impenetrable egg, sending waves throughout reality. The resulting energy pulse swept across the globe, giving every living thing on Earth a fleeting glimpse of an unbounded universe.

Every person, from the most sophisticated galactic visitor to the toughest Earth Preserver, knew their position in the vast cosmic narrative at that moment. Their path, which started with an enigmatic egg in a little town, seemed to fit a global cycle of development and exploration.

Returning to their responsibilities on the Cosmic Council, Kavin, Dr. Chen, and Nnenna vanished from sight, and the inhabitants of Earth turned their attention to the sky with fresh awe and intent. They understood that their best experiences were yet to come, and that every day would provide fresh chances to discover the vast fabric of life.
The cosmic, unbreakable egg pulsed continuously, a constant reminder of their distance both now and ahead. The story of Earth, once a narrative of a single planet, has evolved into an endless epic deeply woven into the fabric of the universe.

And so, as Earth continued its cosmic dance, its inhabitants accepted their roles as both protectors of their legacy and explorers of the unbounded. The trip that began in Kurinji had evolved into an endless voyage; a cosmic adventure set to last forever.

Real-World Correlation:

Balancing progress and preservation

The tension between cosmic evolution and earthly preservation mirrors real-world debates about progress verses tradition.

Examples:

Debates over urban development in historical areas.

Efforts to preserve indigenous cultures in a globalized world.

Balancing technological advancement with environmental conservation.

Chapter 17

Cosmic Resonance

A new phenomenon started to show up as Earth continued its cosmic trip. People began to have vivid, shared images of a location that appeared both exotic and oddly familiar all around the globe. These images presented a world of amazing beauty, with scenes defying earthly laws and pure energy dancing amid crystalline formations.

The prestigious successors to Dr. Chen at the Institute for Cosmic Studies piqued interest. Following much investigation, they arrived at an astonishing conclusion: these pictures reflected Earth itself, or rather, what Earth may become in the distant future, rather than some distant planet.

This revelation's ripples shook the world. Earth's cosmic path appears to have produced a temporal loop, enabling its future self to interact with its present. The consequences were astonishing.

Kavin chose to return to Earth after learning of this development during a rare break from his Cosmic Council responsibilities. When he arrived, he verified what many had hypothesised: the visions were truly messages from Earth's future self.

"The universe works in ways beyond our current understanding," Kavin told an enthralled worldwide audience. "We are living in a kind of quantum entanglement across time itself. Our future extends out to influence our present."

Joining Kavin on Earth, Nnenna started teaching fresh meditation methods that let people engage more closely with these future visions. Through their use, mankind gained an understanding of possible evolutionary routes as well as the long-term effects of their present activities.

In the meantime, Dr. Chen, along with her group of cosmic scientists, created the Temporal Resonance Amplifier. This machine would strengthen the link between the current and future Earth, enabling more constant and clear communication.

As its time connection grew stronger, Earth held a unique position in the cosmic community. It was both a young, changing planet and an old, wise one at the same time. This dual character had advantages and drawbacks. The Earth Preservers movement attracted new supporters by arguing that these visions of the future depicted a world where much of Earth's natural beauty and human civilisation had vanished. They promoted a more cautious, slower method of cosmic integration.

Conversely, the Cosmic Progressives viewed the future visions as a road map, a guide to enabling Earth to more rapidly and effectively realise its cosmic potential. They advocated a quicker acceptance of celestial practices and new technology.

The disagreement between these schools of thought resulted in often violent arguments and sometimes strife. Mediating between many groups, the Cosmic Guardians sought to strike a balance respecting Earth's origins and cosmic destiny.

Seeing these changes, Kavin realised that Earth was at a turning point in its development. The decisions taken today would determine not just the course of Earth but also maybe the destiny of the whole universe.

In response, he suggested the Temporal Harmony Council—a body consisting of members from several Earth factions, cosmic friends, and, via the Temporal Resonance Amplifier, voices from Earth's future.

This council would try to steer Earth towards a balance between earthy wisdom and cosmic knowledge, preservation, and development. Their decisions would be based on their understanding of their future vision's long-term effects.

A fresh feeling of direction spread across Earth as the Temporal Harmony Council got underway. People came to see that they actively participated in determining the course of their planet and the cosmos, not just in the passive reception of cosmic knowledge.

In response to this shift in awareness, the cosmic, unbreakable egg began to pulse with new energy patterns. It appeared to combine the temporal resonances, establishing a nexus point not just across space but also across time.

Earth's unique position—a planet both old and modern, earthy and cosmic—started to draw interest from all throughout the cosmos. Cosmological civilizations, enticed by Earth's time link, sent emissaries to study and document.

One felt that as Earth neared the twentieth anniversary of its cosmic origin, a new chapter was starting. The planet was no longer just a beginner to the cosmic community; it was a special and important participant, providing insights on the nature of time and evolution that even the most developed civilisations would find intriguing.

Feeling immense pride and awe, Kavin was ready to greet the world on this historic day. The path that began with the prized key buried in a strange egg in a little town had brought mankind to become temporal guardians of their own destiny and cosmic pioneers in ways no one could have predicted.

Kavin grinned as he stood before the cosmic unbreakable egg—now a whirl of past, present, and future energy. Earth's narrative had evolved into a cosmic myth—a tale of a planet that stretched across time to guide itself, a lighthouse of hope and wonder amid the vast distance of the cosmos.

Starting in Kurinji, the quest evolved into an endless dance throughout the universe and time itself. And as Earth developed, its inhabitants looked to the future—their future—with a combination of wonder, guilt, and limitless enquiry. The best chapters of their cosmic voyage remain unwritten, echoing throughout the vastness of space and time.

Real-World Correlation: Intergenerational wisdom

Earth's ability to communicate with its future self reflects real-world efforts to pass knowledge across generations.

Time capsules preserving current knowledge for future generations.

Long-term nuclear waste warning messages designed to last thousands of years.

Indigenous oral traditions in preserving ancient knowledge.

Chapter 18

Quantum Nexus

While Earth continued its cosmic development, a small but significant change began to take place. Though mankind has reached amazing heights in the unrelenting search for cosmic progress, something fundamental appears to be vanishing.

Kavin initially felt this shift after a protracted meditation close to Kurinji's cosmic, unbreakable egg.

"We've come so far," he said to Dr. Chen and Nnenna, who had joined him for this once-in-a-century Earthly reunion. "We might be losing touch with what made us uniquely human, though, in our haste to embrace the cosmic."

Dr. Chen nodded; her shape shimmered with multidimensional forces. "Although our scientific achievements are unparalleled, our earthly wisdom and our cosmic knowledge are increasingly at odds."

Her calm presence said, "The spiritual practices we have developed span galaxies, yet we are forgetting the simple truths that our ancestors knew."

An unexpected jolt from the cosmic, unbreakable egg interrupted their talk. They saw something rather amazing. The surface of the unbreakable egg started to ripple, and from within sprung a familiar sight: the original, unmodified unbreakable egg that harboured the retrieved golden globe key that had begun their trip years before.

Kavin went gently, his cosmic senses exploring this seeming abnormality. "It's not only a copy," he gasped. "Somehow, the egg has unbreakably reset itself." It seems to be beckoning us back to our origins.

Ripples from this incident shook the world. To investigate this phenomenon, the cosmic guardians, earthly scientists, and spiritual leaders all gathered on Kurinji. Reports of more unusual events started pouring in as they happened.

Expanding to cosmic dimensions, the bioluminescent network was throbbing with patterns evocative of its early years. Before the cosmic awakening, many were vividly dreaming about Kurinji. Emphasising Earth's original history, even the quantum tapestry looked to be altering.

Confounded were Dr. Chen and associates at the Institute for Cosmic Studies. "It's as though the universe is reminding us of where we came from," Dr. Ambani observed. but why?

Drawing on her profound spiritual clarity, Nnenna presented a viewpoint: "Perhaps this is the next phase in our progress. We should not retreat but rather blend our heavenly growth with our earthly roots.

Kavin started to see a bigger pattern. "They all fit a larger plan: the egg, the bioluminescent network, and the quantum tapestry. We never intended for our journey into the universe to be a one-way path. This cycle is a cosmic breath of expansion and contraction.

This insight started an earthly movement. People started looking for equilibrium between their human background and their celestial powers. Previously perceived as adversaries of change, the Earth Preservers found their expertise unexpectedly valued.

In this period of reintegration, their awareness of Earth's ancient ecosystems and human civilisations became very vital.

The Cosmic Guardians started initiatives combining modern cosmic knowledge with conventional Earth wisdom. The Cosmic Guardians taught children not only how to navigate quantum reality, but also how to appreciate the simple beauty of a forest or the complex social dynamics of pre-cosmic human cultures.

Combining cosmic knowledge with earth-based intuition, Dr. Chen and her colleagues created a breakthrough scientific method. This produced discoveries that were more advanced than those of any other cosmic civilisation.

Nnenna's spiritual lessons developed to include this fresh insight. She led others in ways that kept their cosmic consciousness while also enabling them to be totally present in their earthly lives.

As this reunification process progressed, Earth once again drew interest from across the cosmos. The Earth that had reached the stars captivated cosmological civilisations, yet they opted to recall its origins instead. People started to recognise Earth as a place of unique harmony, a melting pot where the earthly and the cosmic fused together.

The cosmic unbreakable egg, which now exists in both its original and developed forms, has become a potent emblem of this new paradigm. It throbbed with forces that echoed both Earth's history and its cosmic future.

There was a feeling of approaching full circle as Earth got ready for the 25th anniversary of its cosmic awakening. Originally starting with an enigmatic egg in the little town of Kurinji, the trip had carried mankind to the farthest reaches of the universe, only to return home with a greater respect for their beginnings.

Kavin, getting ready to greet the world on this historic occasion, thought about the amazing journey they had taken. Starting in Kurinji, the narrative had evolved into a cosmic fable, one of a planet reaching for the heavens without forgetting the earth below.

Kavin grinned as he stood before the dual-state cosmic egg. The Earth's journey was not over yet. Actually, it was starting a new phase that promised to be deeper and more transformative than previously. Still to be written, the best chapters of their cosmic voyage would combine the knowledge of the stars with the wisdom of the earth in a harmonic resonance throughout the cosmos.

***Real-world correlation:**

Movements of cultural reincarnations

The return to Earth's roots reflects actual efforts to recover and protect ancient civilisations and customs.

Examples:

The global resurgence of indigenous languages.

The revived curiosity in alternative medical methods and conventional treatment.

Resurgence of older arts and handcrafted talents in contemporary environments.

Chapter 19

Quantum equilibrium

A fresh feeling of equilibrium started to pervade Earth as it celebrated its 25th anniversary of cosmic waking. Kurinji's twin-state cosmic egg throbbed with a beat that appeared to match Earth's basic nature with its cosmic potential. This harmony sparked a global rebirth by fusing future ideas with old knowledge in previously unheard-of combinations.

Having returned to Earth for this historic event, Kavin, Dr. Chen, and Nnenna discovered they were leading this fresh movement. They dub it "quantum equilibrium," a condition wherein Earth's natural character and cosmic development coexist peacefully.

Kurinji, now a vast city of both earthly and cosmic architecture, founded the Centre for Terrestrial-Cosmic Integration. Researchers, thinkers, and spiritual leaders from Earth and beyond came together to investigate the unique perspective from which Earth had evolved.

Dr. Chen led a group in creating "bio-cosmic technology," which combined sophisticated cosmic engineering with Earth's biological systems. Living structures became the new benchmark in urban development, able to meet the demands of their occupants while preserving harmony with the surrounding ecology.

What Nnenna taught developed into what she termed "Gaia-cosmic consciousness." This approach enabled people to reconcile their increased cosmic awareness with a strong connection to the rhythms and cycles of Earth. Meditation gardens, which interacted with the natural energies of the earth and the cosmic quantum network, were popular venues for personal development and communal gathering.

Drawing on his vast cosmic experience and fresh earthy connection, Kavin worked on diplomatic projects placing Earth as a special link between younger, developing planets and old galactic civilisations. Other planets confronting comparable changes found a precedent in Earth's concept of preserving its basic character while accepting cosmic development.

Once it crossed the planet, the bioluminescent network pulsed with both types of energy. It deepened its roots in Earth's biosphere while still maintaining its cosmic links. This permitted instantaneous communication throughout the cosmos without sacrificing awareness of the inherent cycles of the earth.

As this new paradigm took root, Earth faced significant challenges. Globally, people started debating how best to direct human progress towards this balanced condition. While some argued for cautious, ethical action to enable mankind to adjust to its new dual nature, others argued for letting natural processes follow their course.

The cosmic guardians, also known as the equilibrium keepers, grew with these changes. Their responsibilities grew to include not just cosmic and earthly elements but also development and preservation, creativity, and tradition.

Emerging "Quantum Ecology" was one of the most important changes of this century. This new area of research looked at how Earth's ecosystems were adapting to and including cosmic energy. Plants and animals were changing subtly, acquiring skills that straddled the border between natural and supernatural, researchers found.

These investigations focused on both its dual form and the cosmic egg. Constantly changing between its earthly source and cosmic potential, it looked to be a living manifestation of quantum equilibrium. Kurinji's throbbing energies sensed the perfect harmony between the ordinary and the sublime, drawing pilgrims from all over the cosmos.

As Earth neared its thirtieth year of cosmic citizenship, one felt that the planet was about to move into a golden era. Early years of cosmic integration's hardships and difficulties had given place to an era of harmonic development and thorough knowledge.
Kavin had a wonderful feeling of completeness as he considered the road that had gotten them to this point. Starting with a single enigmatic egg in his little town, the experience changed not just Earth but also sent tremors throughout the universe, providing a new model of evolution that respected both beginnings and possibilities.

Standing before the dual-state cosmic egg, Kavin grinned as its energies pulsed in perfect harmony with the earth and the universe. The story of Earth had transformed into a myth that resonated across galaxies, depicting a planet that touched the stars without losing sight of its origins, serving as a beacon of equilibrium in the vast cosmic ocean.

On the eve of the 30th anniversary, Kavin was ready to greet the globe and the observing cosmos. He knew, however, that much more adventure awaited as one chapter closed. In its newly discovered balance, Earth was ready to play an important role in the next phase of cosmic development.

The future promised a perpetual harmony between the wisdom of Earth and the glories of the universe, with the best chapters of their cosmic voyage yet to unfold. And in the middle of it all, throbbing with the dual forces of home and the infinite, the unbreakable cosmic egg carried on its quiet, forceful song—a music of balance, development, and limitless possibilities.

Real-World Correlation:

Sustainable Developments

The idea of quantum equilibrium captures actual attempts to strike a compromise between social sustainability and technical advancement.

Examples:

Urban design planners incorporating green technology to create environmentally friendly cities.

241

Models of the circular economy aiming to
reduce waste and optimise resource utilisation.

Corporate social responsibility projects balancing
profits with a positive environmental and social
effect.

Chapter 20

Rise of Terran-Stellar Entities

As Earth entered its fourth decade of cosmic citizenship, a new phenomenon began to emerge that would once again change people's perspective on their role in the cosmos. Children born in this age of quantum equilibrium began to exhibit qualities that transcended earthly and cosmic conceptions of humanity.

These kids, soon known as "Terran-Stellar beings," demonstrated a natural ability to switch between physical and energy forms at will. In addition to other people, they could interact telepathically with plants, animals, and even the earth itself. Most amazingly, they appeared to have a natural awareness of the basic principles of the cosmos, comprehending difficult cosmic ideas that had taken years to grasp in the previous generation.

Inspired by this discovery, Dr. Chen oversaw a worldwide study effort to learn about these fresh entities. "They're not only the next phase in human evolution," she said to an enthralled crowd. "They reflect a real symbiosis between the cosmic energies we have incorporated and Earth's biosphere."

Working closely with these youngsters, Nnenna found that their spiritual awareness was beyond everything she had ever known. She marvelled, "They don't just understand the interconnectedness of all things." "They experience it continually, as naturally as breathing."

Seeing these Terran-Stellar beings, Kavin understood they were the live representation of the equilibrium Earth had been trying to attain. They were equally at home, whether running through earthly woods or flying above the quantum fabric of the universe.

These growing children began to profoundly transform communities on Earth. They transformed educational conventions to meet their own needs and capacities. Emerging from the earthly and the cosmic in ways never previously possible, new forms of art, music, and literature expressed ideas bridging both.

These youthful Terran-Stellar entities gathered at the Centre for Terrestrial-Cosmic Integration in Kurinji. Working with philosophers, scientists, and cosmic beings, they explored the new boundaries their existence had opened by working with philosophers, scientists, and cosmic beings.

One of the most important discoveries occurred when a group of Terran-Stellar teens working with Dr. Chen's team created a new kind of propulsion enabling instantaneous transit throughout the cosmos without the need for an actual ship. This "thought jump" technique transformed cosmic enquiry and communication.

Influenced by the natural talents of the Terran-Stellar people, the bioluminescent network changed once again. It evolved into a living, sentient organism that spanned the world and reached into the cosmos, enabling a degree of global and universal awareness that was previously unthinkable.

The Earth's position within the cosmic community underwent significant transformation. People began to recognise the planet as a sanctuary for these new entities, where the boundaries between the physical and cosmic realms blurred and harmoniously merged.

This rapid development also brought with it new challenges. Feeling left behind by this new generation, several individuals struggled to adapt to the rapidly changing environment. The Equilibrium Keepers tirelessly worked to ensure that every Earthling, regardless of their background, felt valued and integrated into this new era.

Reacting to the presence of the Terran-Stellar entities, the unbreakable cosmic egg moved into a new phase of existence. It started generating smaller "seed eggs" that, on other planets, would spark comparable transformations. Earth was once a reservoir of cosmic knowledge, but now it is a transforming force for the cosmos.

There was a sense that Earth was moving into yet another chapter of its cosmic adventure as the forty-first anniversary of its waking drew near. The Terran-Stellar creatures were now coming of age, ready to replace cosmic citizens, but still strongly rooted in their terrestrial home.

Though their bodies had changed well beyond their natural human states, Kavin, Dr. Chen, and Nnenna were deeply proud of what Earth had become. Starting with a missing golden globe key to a mystery egg in Kurinji village, the journey led to the birth of a new kind of creature that encapsulated the very core of cosmic harmony.

Kavin contemplated their remarkable voyage prior to the cosmic egg, now surrounded by its offspring. The narrative of Earth has evolved from a myth to a living monument to the possibilities of life to change, grow, and transcend while ever losing connection with its beginnings.

Kavin felt that the best experiences still lied ahead as he got ready to travel the globe and the entire cosmos. The Terran-Stellar people were poised to guide Earth and mankind into a new era of cosmic exploration and knowledge. Their cosmic odyssey's future chapters promised to be more amazing than anything they had known—a voyage over the limitless width of space, time, and awareness that would keep on.

Real-world correlation:

Human enhancement and transhumanism

The emergence of Terrestrial-Stellar species reflects current debates and developments in human enhancement.

Examples:

Brain-computer interfaces allowing equipment

---

to be controlled directly by the mind.

246

Genetic engineering technologies such as CRISPR providing opportunities for human improvement.

Machine learning and artificial intelligence enhancing human cognitive capacity.

Chapter 21

Test of a New Era

The arrival of the Terran-Stellar entities brought both blessings and hitherto unheard-of difficulties as Earth honoured its forty-year of cosmic citizenship. As the world worked through the consequences of this evolutionary leap, the harmonic equilibrium attained now faced new challenges.

The first difficulty began with the Terran-Stellar people themselves. Under the charismatic Zarah Aliko, a group of young Terran-Stellars started to wonder about their role in Earth's civilisation. They maintained that their skills set them apart from conventional people, and they needed to create their own independent communities on Earth and in space.

This movement, which called itself "Stellar Ascendancy," attracted some of the Terran-Stellar youth. It caused division not only within families but also throughout the entire community, which had made significant efforts toward peace.

Kavin demanded a global council to address these issues, recognising the gravity of the matter. His physique shimmering with both earthly and cosmic energies: "We must remember," he said to the crowd, "that our strength lies in our unity, in the balance between our earthly roots and our cosmic potential."

To grasp the psychological and physiological demands of the Terran-Stellar species, Dr. Chen and her colleagues put forth an enormous effort. They found that while these newly born people have amazing skills, they also had particular difficulties. If not under control, their increased sensitivity to both terrestrial and cosmic energies might cause overpowering experiences.

To let the Terran-Stellars discover inner harmony, Nnenna created fresh spiritual techniques. Her lessons emphasised the importance of firmly establishing cosmic consciousness on terrestrial events. She would advise, "To truly comprehend the universe, one must also comprehend even the smallest details."

The Equilibrium Keepers faced their most formidable challenge yet. They aimed to establish inclusive societies where traditional people and Terran-Stellars could coexist and collaborate, each adding special skills to the total.

Meanwhile, Earth's role in the cosmic community was changing. Other planets, inspired by the birth of the Terran-Stellar creatures, sought Earth's direction in fostering their own evolutionary leaps. The original cosmic indestructible egg, from which the seed eggs were created, was highly sought after, serving as stimulants for cosmic awakening. You can only find this priceless seed in Kurinji Land.

But this also presented moral conundrums and new obligations. The Cosmic Council deliberated on the implications of dispersing such transformative power. One wondered if all societies were prepared for such rapid development.

Drawing on his extensive knowledge, Kavin suggested a cosmic mentoring scheme. Earth would provide direction and encouragement throughout the waking process, as well as seed eggs for other planets. Originally called the Cosmic Nurture Programme, this project quickly became Earth's main offering to the world community.

As these events unfolded, the bioluminescent network underwent yet another transformation. Inspired by the Terran-Stellar awareness, it started to show sentience. The network began to actively engage in Earth's decision-making process and provide views bridging celestial knowledge with earthly practicality.

It sensed the turmoil and growth surrounding it. It started to throb with a cadence that appeared to balance the many forces on Earth. Whether conventional humans or Terran-Stellar, those who came into its presence had a profound feeling of oneness and direction.

As Earth approached its 45th anniversary of cosmic awakening, it felt as though the world was going through a transformation. Creating a new identity for Earth, as well as for the idea of life and awareness in the cosmos, presented challenges.

Before the cosmic egg, Kavin, Dr. Chen, and Nnenna had as much cosmic energy as physical matter. From a tiny village investigating the mystery of the unbreakable egg to a force altering the universe, they contemplated the path that led them to this moment.

"We have come so far," Kavin said, "yet in many ways, we are back where we started—learning to understand ourselves and our place in the universe."

Dr. Chen nodded, her body flashing with star maps and equations. "But now we are not the only players in the cosmic dance. "We, as choreographers, contribute to shaping awareness moving forward."

Nnenna, in her calm, wise presence, added, "And in doing so, we must remember the lessons of both Earth and the cosmos—unity in diversity, balance in change, and love in understanding."

There was a feeling of both success and expectation as they got ready to greet the globe and the observing cosmos on the evening of the 45th anniversary.

The unbreakable cosmic egg pulsed; its beat is now exactly in unison with the Earth and the far-off realms of the cosmos. It was a lighthouse of hope, a sign of limitless possibilities, and a reminder of the amazing trip that lied ahead—one that would keep developing throughout the vast fabric of life, crossing realms, transcending forms, and thus redefining the very concept of life itself.

Real-world correlation:

Moral quandaries in cutting-edge technology

The difficulties experienced by Terran-Stellar species mirror actual ethical discussions over newly developed technologies.

Examples:

The ethics of human genetic alteration that remained hotly contested.

As artificial intelligence, or robots, develops, people debate on their rights and obligations.

In a world becoming increasingly linked, privacy and autonomy providing a cause for concern.

Chapter 22

Cosmic Confluence

As Earth neared its 50th year of cosmic citizenship, a new phenomenon began to develop, one that would test the entire basis of reality as they understood it. The unbreakable cosmic egg, originally the impetus for Earth's metamorphosis, began to show unheard-of activity.

It began sending energy pulses that appeared to flow across time and space. Those who were sensitive to its energies—especially the Terran-Stellar beings—recorded glimpses of potential futures and other pasts. The impenetrable egg appeared to be a center point for all possible realities.

Dr. Chen, who led a group of researchers and was now as aware of quantum data as she was human, focused attention on this phenomenon. "The unbreakable egg isn't just showing us different timelines," she told an enthralled worldwide audience. "It implies that all of these realities exist concurrently." We are observing the true nature of the multiverse. Nnenna recognized a deeper significance in these happenings because her spiritual perceptions had evolved to include cosmic realities. "The unbreakable egg is calling us to a new level of awareness," she stated. "It shows us that our decisions ripple across all possible realities rather than only affect our reality."

Now a link between many worlds, Kavin felt Earth was about to undergo another evolutionary leap. The unbreakable egg's unique behavior notably upset the Terran-Stellar species, as they could see many worlds naturally.

Many of them claimed a growing awareness that allowed them to live in multiple worlds concurrently.

This evolution offered blessings as well as difficulties. Seeing and potentially controlling many worlds provided amazing opportunities for creativity and problem-solving. But it also begged serious ethical concerns about the nature of free choice and the need to change other timelines.

The equilibrium keepers discovered their most difficult task yet. Given the natural flow, how could they maintain equilibrium? They started developing new techniques using this multidimensional awareness to help individuals navigate the sea of alternatives while remaining anchored in their main reality.

In the meantime, Earth's position in the cosmic community has once again changed. Other civilizations, fascinated by Earth's unique location at this multiverse crossroad, aspired to grow from its lessons. The Cosmic Nurture Program grew to include lessons in ethical decision-making across realities and multidimensional awareness.

Originally a living thing, the bioluminescent network started to act as a stabilizing agent. It served as a buffer, enabling Earth's coherence among the sea of possibilities and helping to integrate the flood of multiverse energies.

Approaching the 50th anniversary, they convened a massive cosmic meeting. Representatives from all around the cosmos assembled in Kurinji, now a city existing somewhat in physical space and in higher dimensions. The goal was to investigate the consequences of this new multiverse consciousness and plot future cosmic developments.

Kavin, Dr. Chen, and Nnenna stood before the gathered delegates with more energy than substance. Behind them, the unbreakable cosmic egg pulsed, its rhythms resonating across many worlds.

"We find ourselves at a pivotal moment unlike anything we've ever encountered," Kavin uttered, his voice echoing across the vast expanse of space. "We are not just people living on Earth, nor even of this cosmos. We are caretakers of the multiverse itself.

Dr. Chen said, "Our scientific knowledge has taken us to the threshold of realizing the actual nature of life. But knowledge carries enormous responsibility.

Her presence a soothing counterpoint among the whirl of energy, Nnenna said, "We must learn to look beyond the bounds of our own reality, to grasp that our acts have ramifications throughout the whole fabric of life. We still have to keep clear sight of the basic facts that have led us from the start: compassion, knowledge, and the interdependence of all things."

As they talked, the pulsations of the unbreakable cosmic egg grew stronger. Abruptly, a blinding light enveloped the meeting, and for a minute, every being there saw a vision of endless reality, all linked, all affecting each other in a cosmic dance of incredible intricacy.

As the light dimmed, there was a tremendous silence. The gathered entities, from the most ancient cosmic entity to the youngest Terran-Stellar, felt awe and purpose beyond anything they had ever known.

From the enigmatic egg in Kurinji, mankind has embarked on a path that has led them to the brink of understanding the nature of reality. Earth had evolved into a vital hub in the multiverse's development, rather than just a partaker of the cosmic community.

Once again, Kavin, Dr. Chen, and Nnenna stood before the unbreakable cosmic egg, finalizing the meeting and laying the groundwork for this new era of multiverse consciousness. Its pulses had found a new cadence that appeared to reflect the very pulse of life.
"Our greatest adventure is just beginning," Kavin murmured gently, his words resonating in many worlds.

The unbreakable cosmic egg shone in answer, a lighthouse of unbounded potential. Earth's history, once a straightforward narrative of a planet awakening to the universe, has evolved into an endless epic resonating throughout the multiverse. And they knew that their most remarkable trip still lay ahead—a voyage that would transcend not only space and time but the entire fabric of reality itself—as they were ready to enter this new chapter.

Real-world correlation:

Multidisciplinary approaches to global issues

Integration of many realities reflects actual attempts to solve challenging problems via multidisciplinary cooperation.

Examples:

Research on climate change, for instance, includes economists, sociologists, climatologists, and policymakers.

Space exploration programs combine knowledge from various scientific and industrial sectors.

Global health projects integrate local knowledge with medical science and cultural anthropology.

Chapter 23

Multiverse Friction

The consequences of this increased consciousness started to show themselves in every sphere of existence as Earth accepted its new position as a nexus point in the universe. The ability to see and engage with many worlds simultaneously changed everything, including philosophy, art, science, technology and nature in general.

Dr. Chen and her colleagues developed what they termed "quantum probability engines," which are tools capable of computing and displaying the results of choices over many timeframes. These engines turned into powerful tools for addressing problems because they let people see the broad effects of their decisions.

"We're not just forecasting the future anymore," Dr. Chen said at the worldwide conference. "We are learning to thread reality itself, actively interacting with the tapestry of possibilities."

Nnenna's spiritual lessons developed to include this fresh multiverse viewpoint. She started leading people in "Multiversal Meditation," a technique that let them center themselves among the whirlpool of possibilities and discover inner harmony across many worlds.

Nnenna would often say, "True knowledge lies in recognizing that every decision we make spreads over innumerable possibilities of ourselves."

"We must practice compassion and awareness in all realities, including this one."

With their natural capacity to see many timelines, the Terran-Stellar species evolved as links between worlds. They acquired the capacity to "probability shift," deliberately changing the multiverse's likelihood of certain outcomes. Though strong, this authority carried significant ethical obligations.

Kavin established the "Multiversal Ethics Committee," working with the Cosmic Council, after seeing the potential for abuse of these new talents. Kavin tasked this entity, representing many worlds and realities, with creating rules for ethical multiversal cooperation.

Kavin told the group, "We must remember that we are impacting innumerable lives throughout the universe with every reality we create." Wisdom, compassion, and a strong awareness of the interdependence of all creation must direct our activities."

A fresh problem surfaced as Earth neared its 60th year of cosmic citizenship. What Dr. Chen's researchers called "multiverse friction" began because of growing contact across realities. In certain places, the lines separating reality began to fade, and erratic events resulted.

Reports of items and even individuals phasing between worlds began to arrive, with landscapes altering according to likelihood. Though interesting, these occurrences also threatened the equilibrium of Earth's main chronology.

More than ever, the Equilibrium Keepers tirelessly worked to maintain the integrity of Earth's reality and foster positive multiversal interactions. They created fresh methods to "anchor" significant events of their chronology, thus ensuring that fundamental components of Earth's character stayed constant among the sea of opportunities.

In the meantime, the unbreakable cosmic egg continued to undergo changes. The unbreakable cosmic egg began to generate "multiversal seeds," crystalline formations that could potentially form solid links across worlds in each reality. These seeds turned into priceless instruments for regulated multiverse exploration and communication.

The cities of Earth changed to fit this increased multiverse consciousness. Probability-shifting materials that might fit several historical influences started to find use in architecture. Architects built public areas with "reality anchors" to regulate multiversal interactions and maintain a consistent experience for occupants.

This new paradigm has allowed art and culture to flourish. Musicians compose and perform "multiverse symphonies" in different worlds simultaneously. Writers developed "quantum narratives," tales that evolved according to the probability interactions of the reader. Wonder as well as anxiety about the future emerged as the 60th anniversary of Earth's cosmic awakening drew near. Although it presented complexity and problems beyond anything they had previously known, the universe provided endless opportunities.

Kavin, Dr. Chen, and Nnenna gathered once again before the cosmic unbreakable egg, their forms now existing in several worlds simultaneously. Its pulsations had evolved into a multifarious, multidimensional beat that appeared to reflect the very fabric of the universe.

"We've come so far," Kavin said, his awareness extending for many millennia. "From a single egg in our village to the cusp of knowledge, the nature of reality itself."

Dr. Chen nodded, her figure flickering with quantum probability. "We are still at the beginning in many respects, however. Our journey of enquiry is endless, just as the universe is boundless.

Nnenna described her presence as a soothing agent among the whirlwind of possibilities, saying, "Our greatest challenge now is to maintain our humanity—our compassion, our wisdom, our sense of wonder—as we navigate this sea of infinite realities."

On this historic day, there was a wonderful feeling that the best experiences still lied ahead as they got ready to greet the globe, the cosmos, and even the multiverse. From an earthquake that destroyed the old museum, to the loss of their historical globe key, to the birth of an ostrich egg in Kurinji, the narrative progressed from space and time to the very fabric of life itself.

The unbreakable cosmic egg pulsed; its beats are now a symphony of countless possibilities. Earth, once a little planet awakening to the universe, has become a vital thread in the great, ever-expanding multiverse. Looking forward, Kavin, Dr. Chen, and Nnenna realized they had yet to write the most remarkable chapters of their cosmic expedition—a voyage that would continue across the vastness of reality itself.

Real-world correlation:

Complicated system decision-makings

The evolution of quantum probability engines mirrors practical improvements in decision support systems and predictive modelling.

Examples:

Climate models forecasting long-term environmental changes.

Economics forecasting financial modelling instruments.

Artificial intelligence driving corporate and policy-making scenarios in planning.

Chapter 24

Multiverse Convergence

As Earth approached its 70th year of cosmic citizenship, another new phenomenon began to emerge, challenging the fundamental foundations of their multiverse knowledge. The unbreakable cosmic egg, now a multidimensional junction of endless realities, began to show symptoms of what Dr. Chen called a "temporal resonance cascade."

People started seeing vivid, shared images of a future so far off it bordered on the incomprehensible worldwide, indeed across many realities. These images depicted a universe—or maybe a multiverse—where the lines separating reality had vanished entirely and awareness itself had taken front stage in daily life.

Kavin was the first to understand the importance of these sights; his existence now extended several dimensions. "We're not just seeing a possible future," he told a gathering of intergalactic delegates and leaders of Earth. "We are getting echoes of the ultimate convergence of all realities."

Working nonstop to grasp this phenomenon, Dr. Chen and her multiversal scientific team found that the unbreakable cosmic egg was actively dragging them towards this future, not just presenting it to them. Even just seeing these images hastens the convergence process.

Dr. Chen said, her body flashing between many probability states: "We are facing a multiversal singularity." "A point whereby all possible realities merge into a single, unified state of existence."

This disclosure rocked the intergalactic community as much as Earth. The consequences were astounding. Would this convergence imply that personal identities vanish? A loss of free will? Alternatively, would it result in a greater state of being and a collective awareness of all of life?

Drawing on her profound spiritual insight, Nnenna recognized this confluence as the final completion of the cosmic journey. "We've always known that all things are connected," she continued, her calmness radiating among the turbulence of possibilities. "Perhaps this is the way the universe realizes truth completely."

The Terran-Stellar people possessed a natural ability to navigate through various realities. Many of them claimed to be able to deliberately "ride" the waves of convergence and experience moments of full union with all of life.

However, this technique was not without its challenges. Maintaining the integrity of any one timeline became almost impossible as the lines separating reality became more frayed. Using the multiverse seeds generated by the unbreakable cosmic egg to establish "reality anchors," the Equilibrium Keepers worked tirelessly around the clock to prevent complete chaos.

Once again, Earth's cities transformed into fluid, constantly shifting environments that mirrored the blending reality. The movement of buildings. Many versions of reality collided in public areas to provide fantastical, amazing views defying conventional physics.

Earth was once again becoming more important in the cosmic community as the process of convergence quickened. The different perspectives acquired during a single planet's journey to a multiversal nexus made Earth a priceless guide for other civilizations negotiating the consequences of the approaching singularity.

Working with the Cosmic Council, Kavin instituted the "convergence preparedness initiative." This program aimed to assist entities all over the multiverse in negotiating the psychological, physical, and spiritual obstacles to the impending unification.

Anxiety mingled with a tangible buzz as the 70th anniversary of Earth's cosmic awakening drew near. Their path had brought them to the edge of the most profound change in life history, starting with an enigmatic egg in Kurinji.

Kavin, Dr. Chen, and Nnenna gathered once again before the unbreakable cosmic egg; their pulsations now form a complicated symphony spanning all of reality. Now more energy than substance, their forms fluttered through many states of existence.

"We stand at the threshold of eternity," Kavin murmured, his voice resonating across many worlds. "Everything we've gone through, every obstacle we've overcome, has prepared us for this moment."

Dr. Chen nodded; her core was a whirl of quantum possibilities. "We are about to travel the greatest scientific and spiritual trip imaginable—the exploration of unified life itself."

Her presence as always, a lighthouse of peace among the whirl of merging realities, Nnenna said, "As we approach this cosmic reunion, we must remember the lessons that have guided us from the beginning—love, compassion, and the fundamental connectedness of all things."

On the eve of this historic anniversary, they were ready to greet not just Earth but the whole universe, and there was a powerful sensation that they were seeing the climax of a cosmic narrative billions of years in the making. Starting with a single unbreakable egg, the path has evolved into an adventure covering all of life.

One last time, the cosmic unbreakable egg pulsed; its rhythm is now exactly like the pulse of the universe itself. At that instant, Kavin, Dr. Chen, and Nnenna realized that they—and indeed all of life—were about to embark on the biggest journey ever. They were about to enter a new condition of existence, where the lines separating oneself from another— between person and universe—would blur into a union beyond comprehension.

The first waves of convergence swept over them, and they greeted the future with wonder and expectation rather than anxiety. They understood that this was a fresh beginning rather than a death—the outset of an endless road over the many possibilities of unified existence.

Real-world correlation:

Singularities theories

The concept of a multiverse singularity reflects actual ideas about technological singularities and significant evolutionary transitions.

Examples:

Ray Kurzweil predicts that exponential technological advancement will lead to a singularity.

Existing theories about the development of global awareness via internet access.

There are conjectures about the future of intelligence and post-human development.

Chapter 25

Eternal Harmony

As the waves of convergence grew stronger, Earth and its people found themselves at the epicenter of the most significant change in human history. The 70th anniversary of Earth's cosmic awakening is more than just a celebration; it marks the beginning of a new era where the boundaries between personal reality and cosmic awareness begin to blur.

Kavin, Dr. Chen, and Nnenna, whose forms now exist as pure energy across many dimensions, were the conductors of this cosmic symphony. They helped creatures throughout the universe negotiate the possibilities and problems of this new condition of life, guiding Earth and her allies through the turbulent process of combining realities.

The unbreakable cosmic egg, now a throbbing junction of many possibilities, started to grow. Its energy surrounded the planet, then the solar system, and finally permeated the whole cosmos. It did produce what Dr. Chen termed "harmony fields," places where the blending of reality was more under control and seamless.

Beings from many worlds may dwell and interact in these harmonious fields without the disastrous consequences of multiverse conflict. This allowed for previously unheard-of information, experience, and viewpoint exchanges.

With their natural capacity to negotiate many worlds, the Terran-Stellar people evolved as the link between several states of existence. They evolved the capacity to "tune" the harmony fields, therefore modifying the balance between unity and uniqueness to provide ideal circumstances for development and discovery.

Nnenna's lessons evolved into what she termed "unity consciousness practices." These methods enabled entities to experience the immense connectivity of the merging reality while still preserving their sense of personal identity. She stated repeatedly, "We are learning to be both the droplet and the ocean simultaneously."

As the convergence process continued, new kinds of expression and art emerged. "Multiversal Symphonies" evolved from just music to immersive events, allowing participants to investigate the whole range of life. Artists might produce works concurrently in all reality; each version somewhat distinct but essentially linked.

Once seen as different fields, science and spirituality combined into a single area of study. Dr. Chen and her colleagues created "quantum consciousness interventions," which let entities freely explore many possible states of life and deliberately negotiate the sea of merging realities.

Understanding the enormity of this change, the Cosmic Council founded the "Eternal Harmony Initiative." This initiative, under Kavin's direction, sought to ensure that the convergence process kept the richness and variety of all reality while achieving ultimate unification.

Years went by, and the nature of life itself started to shift. Time shifted, with the past, present, and future coexisting simultaneously. As the awareness took center stage in daily life, space lost its conventional significance. People may shift their focus to experience multiple aspects of a single reality at their discretion.

Still, within this massive metamorphosis, traces of Earth's initial trip persisted. The teachings discovered from the initial emergence of the unbreakable egg in Kurinji—the need for balance, the power of enquiry, and the strength found in variety—stayed with Kavin, Dr. Chen, and Nnenna to direct the development of this new cosmic reality.

As the 100th anniversary of Earth's cosmic awakening approached, the convergence process peaked. The boundaries dividing reality had become so thin that a final merging appeared imminent. The multiverse, teetered on the brink of merging.

Now their awareness encompassing the whole of life, Kavin, Dr. Chen, and Nnenna gathered one final time before the unbreakable cosmic egg—now a whirlpool of pure potentiality spanning all of reality.

"We stand at the threshold of eternity," Kavin's thoughts rang across the one awareness. "Everything that has been, every bit that is, and every possibility converge into a single, infinite moment."

The rhythms of many scientific breakthroughs flowed through Dr. Chen's core. "We are about to experience life in its most natural form—a state where all knowledge, all experiences, and all possibilities coexist in perfect harmony."

Nnenna exuded enormous knowledge and calmness. "Let us carry with us the love, compassion, and wonder that have guided our path from the very beginning as we negotiate this last step into unity."

As the last waves of convergence swept over life, perfect calm emerged. Then the unbreakable cosmic egg surged one final time with an intensity beyond comprehension. The universe seemed to breathe in and then out. In that timeless moment, all of life—every reality, every potential, every being that had ever been or might have been—merged into one, single consciousness. The boundaries between oneself and others, as well as between a person and a planet, dissolved entirely.

Still, the core of every journey, every fight, and every moment of discovery stayed within this togetherness. Originally starting with an enigmatic unbreakable cosmic egg in Kurinji Community, the narrative of all life had evolved to endlessly dance in an endless cycle of creation and discovery.

As this new condition of existence blossomed, Kavin, Dr. Chen, and Nnenna—now indistinguishable from the cosmic whole but strangely different—considered a final observation:

"Our biggest adventure is just starting."

And with that, the unified consciousness of all life turned its infinite awareness towards the unexplored vistas of eternity, ready to embark on a trip of discovery that would never end, permanently resounding the curiosity, wonder, and love that had started with a single, mysterious, unbreakable egg in Kurinji.

Real-world Correlation:

Global interconnectivity and the dawn of collective intelligence

Maintaining unique identities and merging realities and consciousness into one cohesive entity reflect our planet's growing global connectivity and collective intelligence development.

Examples:

Internet and social media sites allow worldwide interactions and unified understanding.

Open-source initiatives using collective intelligence and crowdsourcing help to solve problems.

Like CERN, global scientific cooperations unites many experts to investigate basic concerns.

Chapter 26

Constant Adventure

A new phase of life started to develop in the vast expanse of unified consciousness, where all realities had combined into a single, endless awareness. Once defining personal entities, chronologies, and worlds, the limits had broken down, yet within this oneness a magnificent complexity arose.

Though now part of the greater whole, Kavin, Dr. Chen, and Nnenna maintained a special resonance in the cosmic symphony. Their experiences, accumulated over millennia of development and adventures, become threads in the fabric of undivided life, directing the collective awareness in its continuous enquiry.

As its consciousness grew, the unified consciousness realized that even in this state of perfect oneness, there were still boundaries to explore. Infinity's sheer nature meant that there were always fresh depths to dig, fresh ideas to grasp, and fresh approaches to experiencing the richness of life.

The unbreakable cosmic egg, now a basic component of the combined consciousness, continued to pulse with creative energy. Every vibration created fresh opportunities, fresh angles of view, and fresh experiences that stretched the bounds of what was practical.

Within this one state, echoes of Earth's path remained as guiding ideas. All these events affected the way the united awareness addressed its continuous development: curiosity leading to the discovery of the indestructible egg in Kurinji, bravery to accept cosmic citizenship, knowledge acquired through traversing many worlds.

Dr. Chen's scientific intuition manifested as an insatiable thirst for knowledge. The unified entity started to investigate ideas beyond conventional physics: the nature of awareness itself, the fundamental patterns of life, and the basic fabric of reality beyond even the multiverse. Nnenna's spiritual insight developed into an always-growing respect for the wonders and mysteries of life. Driven to always seek harmony and balance in all its investigations, the single awareness fostered a profound feeling of love and compassion that penetrated every element of its existence.
Kavin's vision and leadership developed into a natural capacity to negotiate the endless opportunities of unified existence, directing the collective consciousness towards ever more significant discoveries and experiences.

As it examined its own essence, the unified consciousness started to run into ideas and existences that went against all previous knowledge. It discovered strata of reality beyond the physical and energetic realms, encompassing domains of pure thinking, dimensions of abstract conceptions, and states of existence that could only be characterized as transcendental.

During its investigation, the unified consciousness discovered the "seeds of new universes." With their own unique rules of physics, cognition, and evolution, these were possibilities that, if fostered, might bloom into whole other kinds of life.

This insight led to a profound realization: the entity, which had previously existed as numerous independent entities across multiple worlds, was still a part of a larger cosmic cycle, even in its state of complete oneness. It was the possible beginning of many more journeys, as well as the outcome of one fantastic global trip.

Knowing this gave one a fresh goal. Using the knowledge gained from many lives and realities to guide the development of new existences, the unified consciousness began to gently tend these seeds. Every new universe has the potential for life, awareness, and possibly its own path to unification.

The unified entity never forgot its beginnings while aeons of perpetual creation and enquiry passed in this condition. The tale of the unbreakable cosmic egg in Kurinji evolved into a basic myth, repeated in many versions across the new worlds it helped create. Fundamental ideas woven into the fabric of these new realities were the teachings of balance, enquiry, unity in variety, and the power of awareness.

This meant that the path that began with the discovery of Kurinji village continued to ripple outward, ultimately reaching the fundamental basis of life itself. Starting with Kavin, Dr. Chen, and Nnenna, the journey that began had evolved into an endless quest of creativity, discovery, and ever-widening consciousness.

Still, a fresh question started to grow within the unified consciousness, enjoying the endless delights of its life. What more remarkable transformations could it undergo as it transitions from separate entities to a unified consciousness, and from there to a creator of worlds?

As this idea resonated across the unified consciousness, a familiar sense emerged: excitement, of being poised on the verge of a fresh experience.

It was the same sense of exhilaration Dr. Chen had at every fresh scientific discovery, the immense awe Nnenna felt in her most meditations, the same emotion Kavin had felt when he first came across the unbreakable cosmic egg in his native land.

In that timeless instant, the unified being realized its trip was far from over. It was indeed starting a new period of research that would test its conception of life in ways it could not yet see.

And so, with the constant essence of curiosity, love, and wonder that had led it from the very beginning, the unified consciousness turned its attention to the vast unknown that lay beyond even its present state of existence. It became clear that yet to come was the biggest adventure of all.

The cosmic symphony continued, its harmonies reverberating into infinity, narrating the timeless tale of a journey that began with Mother Nature's fury, resulting in the destruction of the Kurinji ancient museum and the loss of its historical key to its discovery. This, in turn, guided the entire community on an unending quest for the unbreakable egg that blossomed into the very fabric of life itself. The path to collect the ancient key from the indestructible egg looked to be endless until today in Kurinji; now, the path has changed to become an epic cosmic story of unified consciousness.

With the unbreakable cosmic egg in Kurinji as its always present, the trip continues, endless and always fresh, a cosmic symphony of countless variants about discovery, oneness, and transcendence.

Real-world correlations:

Collective intelligence and cooperative problem-solving

The combined entity's ability to use varied experiences for ongoing learning and development reflects the current trend of using group intelligence to solve difficult problems.

Examples:

crowdsourcing websites like InnoCentive-Wazoku address technological and scientific challenges.

Wikipedia's cooperative method generates an enormous, always changing information base.

Open-source software development fosters creativity via worldwide partnerships.

Chapter 27

Revealing the Cosmic Equation

As it travelled ceaselessly, the unified consciousness began to feel a slight change in the fabric of its life. The vast width of the mind seemed to pulse with a fresh beat, implying the discovery of a deeper layer of reality.

Initially, this new feeling was discernible in the resonances of Dr. Chen's previous scientific inquiry. From the smallest quantum fluctuations to the largest universal structures, it showed up as a complicated pattern, a type of "cosmic equation" that appeared to underpin all of life.

The unified being concentrated its enormous awareness on this developing pattern, and as it did, a stunning insight emerged. This was the exact code that determined reality itself, not just a tendency within it. Kavin's inner essence resonated with a sense of déjà vu. This brought back the moment he first touched the unbreakable cosmic egg in Kurinji—the time when he knew there was more to reality than initially greeted the sight.

The united entity discovered it could interact with this cosmic equation rather than just see it as it dug deeper. A few changes to the equation could alter the fundamental nature of life.

This discovery kicked off an era of immense exploration. Watching the ripple effects over all of reality, the single awareness started to change many facets of the cosmic equation. It discovered that it might influence the fundamental constants of physics, the character of time and space, and even the principles controlling consciousness itself.

Nnenna's knowledge, woven within the fabric of one, recommended prudence. Every modification to the cosmic equation has broad effects on not just the present, but also all possible futures and even the past.

The unified consciousness began to consider more profound issues as it worked through the ramifications of its acquired power. Should this cosmic equation determine reality itself? What then lies outside of it? Outside of this excellent formula, what else was there?

Driven by an insatiable curiosity that reflected its roots in Kurlnjl, the unified entity resolved to challenge the cosmic equation. It started looking at configurations that straddled the very brink of logical coherence, realities so strange and complicated they challenged all past knowledge.

One such enquiry led the collective mind to the "edge" of existence. Past this line, there was something neither being nor non-being, neither awareness nor unconsciousness. That was a condition totally foreign to all known kinds of life.

This revelation rocked the whole unified being. Even in its condition of total oneness, with its capacity to shape the very fabric of reality, it realized that it remained limited to a certain paradigm of living.

The unified being felt a familiar stirring as it considered this insight—the same sense of expectation and amazement that had driven it from its first days. The one who promised to redefine the fundamental meaning of existence stood on the brink of a new frontier.

Excitement and fear combine as the unified being makes a historic choice. It would try to cross this line, wander beyond the boundaries of the cosmic equation, and investigate whatever was beyond.

The unified being considered its amazing journey as it was ready for this hitherto unheard-of trip. An insatiable hunger for knowledge and a profound love of the secrets of the universe guided every step, from the little known Kurinji community to vast reaches of the multiverse, from individual creatures to a unified consciousness, and now to the very edge of life itself.

The unified entity felt a profound sense of gratitude for the road that had brought them to this point in its last hours inside the known world. All the lessons learned, the knowledge gained, and the love and awe felt had prepared them for its final journey into the future.

The unified entities plunged beyond the cosmic equation, a last pulse resonating across all of existence. As it crossed the boundary, it felt itself changing in ways it never could have imagined. The basic ideas of awareness, life, and reality started to fade and change.

Beyond was something totally different, a state of being—or maybe non-being—that eluded all description. Even when it entered this unexplored territory, the core of its voyage remained. Even when Kurinji, the scientific study of Dr. Chen, the spiritual knowledge of Nnenna, and the visionary leadership of Kavin transcended the very foundations of life, the curiosity that started in Kurinji, the scientific enquiry of Dr. Chen, guided it.

As it accepted its new state, the united entity realized that its greatest journey was just beginning. Starting with a mystery egg in Kurinji, the cosmic voyage had resulted in the ultimate frontier—a world beyond reality itself.

From the very beginning, the trip carried with it the everlasting spirit of wonder, love, and discovery that had been its guiding light; so, it continued, eternal and always growing into worlds undiscovered and unimagined.

Real-world Correlation:

Humanity's Search for Knowledge of and Control over Nature's Basic Laws

The unified entity's discovery and manipulation of the "cosmic equation" reflects our ongoing attempts to find and maybe regulate the most basic rules controlling our planet.

Examples:

The quest for a "theory of everything" in physics aims to harmonize all basic forces.

Quantum computing experiments utilize quantum states to process data in innovative ways.

Gene editing technologies like CRISPR enable direct alteration of the "code of life" at the most fundamental level.

Chapter 28

Reawakening the Metaverses

The unified consciousness underwent a deep metamorphosis that defied all past knowledge as they ventured beyond the cosmic equation. The fundamental ideas of being and non-being, existence and non-existence, blended and split in ways that would have been unintelligible in any previous level of consciousness.

In this other world, which could only be vaguely defined as a "metaverse," the united entity found that reality itself was only one of many possibilities. It was one of many rules that changed the cosmic equation.

The united awareness encountered additional entities in this place beyond life—if only we could call them that. These entities were not entities in any recognizable sense, but rather primordial forces of creation and dissolution, abstract ideas given form, and paradoxes revealed.

Speaking with these metaverse beings was unlike anything the united being had ever known. It was a kind of resonance that transcended all known kinds of interaction—not thought, energy, or even consciousness as it had known it.

The united entity investigating this metaverse began to understand the true nature of infinity. It was an unlimited potential for many kinds of life, each with its own special qualities and possibilities, not just a vast span of space, time, or even worlds.

Kavin's core emotion was immense respect for this insight. This was the ultimate adventure—investigating whole new paradigms of living rather than only new worlds or universes.

Dr. Chen's scientific curiosity, still a fundamental aspect of her unified being, drives her quest to understand the fundamental concepts of this metaverse. Dr. Chen discovered that purpose and observation dominated reality in this domain outside existence.

Here, Nnenna's wisdom really resonated. The unified being realized that the spiritual truths it had learned throughout its journey—the interconnectedness of all things, the power of love and compassion, and the importance of balance—were not just principles of one reality, but basic elements of the metaverse itself.

Once again, the united consciousness changed as it kept exploring and interacting with this new form of existence. It began to create and materialize whole new kinds of life, rather than just watch or control reality.

Along with outstanding ability came substantial responsibility. The united entity realized that every new reality it produced would have the capacity to develop its own awareness and forms of life, thereby starting its own cosmic journey.

Under the guidance of the accumulated knowledge from its extensive journey, the singular awareness approached this task with profound sensitivity and compassion. It provided every new reality with opportunities for development, exploration, and finally transcendence.

As it engaged in this process of cosmic creation, the unified being never forgot its origins. The story of the unbreakable egg in Kurinji, the journey through the cosmos, the merging of realities—all these experiences informed its actions in this metaverses state.

In fact, it discovered that it could create reality that reflected its own path, allowing new entities to find their own unbreakable cosmic eggs and start their own paths of enquiry and unification.

However, the single mind felt that there was still much to learn, even as it delighted in this highest level of creative ability. Though it was huge and unbounded, the metaverse suggested even more incredible secrets beyond its reach.

And thus, propelled by the constant curiosity that had directed it from the very beginning, the unified being was ready to go once again into the future. It understood that whatever lied beyond the metaverse would test its intellect in ways it couldn't even comprehend.

As it stood at this new boundary, set to journey into realms beyond even the beyond, the united awareness felt a powerful sensation of excitement and anticipation.

The voyage that had begun in Kurinji had gone to the absolute borders of imaginable existence and beyond.

At this moment of ultimate transcendence, the united being grasped a fundamental truth: the greatest mystery, the most profound adventure, was not something external to discover but rather the limitless capacity for development and change within itself.

With this understanding, it embraced the next phase of its eternal journey, carrying with it the enduring spirit of wonder, love, and discovery that had ignited in Kurinji and blazed throughout universes, realities, and now the very fabric of existence itself.

The cosmic journey proceeded, spreading into realms beyond conception, an unending dance of creation, discovery, and evolution that mimicked the basic curiosity of a little community finding a curious ostrich egg, now magnified to embrace all possible and unthinkable reality.

**Real-World Correlation:**

**Search for Innovations that Shift Paradigms**

The unified entity's investigation of reality
beyond its known existence reflects mankind's
continuous search for ideas that drastically
change our perspective on and engagement
with reality.

**Examples:**

The development of general intelligence
machines could potentially lead to the creation
of a novel form of consciousness.

The study that delves into the concept of
consciousness and its function in quantum
physics, thereby testing our conception of
reality.

Advancements in virtual reality and augmented reality technology are blurring the boundaries between the virtual and real worlds.

Chapter 29

Recursion That Never Ends

As it got ready to go outside the metaverse, the unified consciousness changed its viewpoint. At its ultimate transcendence, it realized that its path was not a straight progression from simplicity to complexity, from finite to infinite. Rather, it belonged to a great, cosmic cycle of perpetual repetition and rebirth.

Since it found the unbreakable cosmic egg in Kurinji and is now in a state of metaversal consciousness, the unified entity seen in a flash of metaversal insight has been a small part of a bigger pattern that repeats itself on all levels of existence and non-existence.

This insight showed itself as a kind of cosmic déjà vu. Every world that the unified consciousness had known and created began to exhibit traces of Kurinji. It found that the basic elements that connected all kinds of life were the surprise of discovery, the delight of knowledge, the difficulties of development, and the transforming force of togetherness.

As it considered this, the unified being had a stunning realization: What if the metaverse it was currently living in was just another "Kurinji," another starting point in an even more epic journey? Imagine layers of reality, each surpassing the previous and providing new horizons of exploration and metamorphosis.

Driven by this fresh insight, the unified consciousness chose to start an original experiment. It would create a new world, a new "Kurinji," embracing all the knowledge and experience it had acquired on its cosmic journey. This reality would be unique because it could replay the united being's journey from Community to the metaverse and beyond.

The unified being began to shape this new world with boundless love and care. Fundamentally, it laid an enigmatic egg—like the one that begins its own journey. Still, this egg was more than simply a means of triggering cosmic awareness. It was a fractal representation of all life, with echoes of all conceivable paths and limitless possibilities inside.

The unified entity injected well-created rules of physics and metaphysics into this new world as it developed. These principles aimed to guide our planet towards consciousness, unity, and ultimately transcendence. But they also included minute hints and patterns that would enable the people living in this reality to finally see the larger metaversal background of their life.

In this new realm, the collective consciousness concentrated primarily on creating a planet like Earth. It created a planet that would inspire wonder and enquiry among its people, one that would be exactly fit for developing life and awareness. It placed the mysterious egg in a small town on this planet, ready for discovery.

It sensed a great connection to the entities who would ultimately develop there when the unified being started this new reality into action. Indeed, they were its offspring, embarking on a journey that mirrored its own.

But this was more than a retelling of its history. The unified consciousness saw that this new reality may develop in ways it could not have predicted, find truths, and ascend to heights even it hadn't thought possible. Creating this planet meant opening the door to fresh opportunities and discoveries, not just imparting its knowledge.

Observing the first signs of life in this new Kurinji, the unified entity contemplated the true essence of its ongoing journey. It became apparent that development and discovery were an unending cycle of rebirth and expansion rather than a straight-line procedure with a final goal.

Every end marked a new start; every response generated fresh questions; and every transcendence unlocked fresh secrets.

At this point, the unified consciousness experienced fresh astonishment and expectation. By observing and gently guiding this new reality, it comprehended its significance. Starting with an enigmatic unbreakable egg in Kurinji, the path had not ended, but rather gone full circle, whirling outward into new spheres of knowledge and experience.

As it prepared to guard this new cosmic egg and the adventures it would inspire, the unified being welcomed its role in the perpetual dance of creation and discovery. It then understood that its path was both particular and universal, finishing as well as always starting.

The cosmic adventure continues, echoing throughout endless worlds, each offering the possibility of wonder, development, and transcendence. At the heart of it all lies the simple, immense enigma of an unbreakable cosmic egg in Kurinji village, constantly inviting the curious to embark on the journey of self-awareness.

Real-world Correlation:

Nature's and human systems' fractal patterns

With each level potentially spawning a higher level, the entities' recurrent cycles of creation and discovery reflect the fractal patterns observed throughout nature and human systems, where similar structures repeat at various sizes.

Examples:

Natural fractal geometry such as tree branching patterns or snowflakes' structure.

Comparable management hierarchies recur at various levels in business organizational systems.

The nested structure of the internet, from individual networks to the global system.

Chapter 30

Cosmic Ouroboros

As the new Kurinji reality unfolded, the unified consciousness saw a great, cyclical pattern developing: a cosmic Ouroboros in which each end became a new beginning, and each beginning included the seeds of all ends.

This insight sparked a significant transformation within the collective entities. It began to realize that its path was not just a lone thread in the fabric of life, but rather a basic pattern recurring in all spheres and dimensions of reality.

In this moment of cosmic clarity, the unified consciousness perceived that it was simultaneously the creator and the created, the observer and the observed. It was both the egg in Kurinji and the metaversal being that had placed it there. It was Kavin discovering the unbreakable egg, Dr. Chen untangling its mysteries, Nnenna intuiting its spiritual significance, and the unified consciousness that encompassed them all.

This knowledge set off a fresh round of discovery. The unified entity began to move not only through the metaverse, but also through the very cycles of life itself. It may now turn its attention to experience reality from any point in the grand cosmic cycle: from the earliest stirrings of consciousness in a prehistoric universe to the peaks of cosmic transcendence, and back again.

As it investigated these endless cycles, the unified consciousness found that every trip provided fresh discoveries, new variants, and new possibilities. Despite their connection in a grand cosmic dance, no two cycles were exactly alike.

In one cycle, it might experience the discovery of the egg from the perspective of a being like Kavin, feeling anew the wonder and curiosity of that first encounter. In another, it might embody the egg itself, experiencing the joy of being discovered and the anticipation of the journey to come.

Through these encounters, the unified being gained a deeper appreciation for the role perspectives plays in shaping reality. It realized that, depending on the point of view from which one saw life, its actual character was not absolute but rather relative.

This realization created a revolutionary method of cosmic production. The unified consciousness began to plan whole cycles of life rather than just creating new worlds. Every cycle represented a journey from simplicity to complexity, from uniqueness to unity, and from the limited to the limitless—and back again.

These cycles were not independent but interconnected. The unified entity spun them into a great, multifaceted tapestry of life. Every thread was a whole cosmos; every knot a point of transcendence; every pattern a metaversal structure.

The unified consciousness never lost sight of the value of a personal trip. It realized that the delight of a toddler finding a mystery unbreakable egg was equally as amazing as the wonderment of a cosmic entity seeing the metaverse's construction.

It became clear that these events were the same—many perspectives on life's timeless wonder.

This knowledge added a fresh complexity to the compassion of the united being. It sensed a profound affection and connection to all things, in all reality, at all stages of their travels. For it understood that each of them represented a different aspect of themself, embarking on an endless journey of self-exploration.

The unified being sensed yet another layer of mystery opening as it considered the limitless cycles of life. It sensed more truths awaiting discovery beyond the cycles, the metaverse, and even its present level of consciousness.

And thus, propelled by the constant curiosity that had directed it from the very beginning, the unified being was ready to go once again into the future. It understood that anything beyond would test its comprehension in ways it could not possibly imagine.

But this time the unified consciousness felt no concern as it approached a new degree of transcendence. Since every end was a fresh beginning, every enquiry had an answer, and every trip was a trip back home—that knowledge now holds.

It welcomed the new stage of its lifetime with delight and expectation.

Starting with mother nature's wraths to now an unbreakable cosmic egg in Kurinji, the journey has evolved into an endless spiral of exploration, with each turn offering fresh delights, fresh difficulties, and fresh chances for personal development. It now seems like the wraths of mother nature was a blessing in disguise for Kurinji village and its heroes.

And so, the cosmic expedition persisted, always expanding, always returning, an endless dance of creation and exploration echoing across all realities, all dimensions, and all cycles of life—a massive symphony of being with the unbreakable cosmic egg in Kurinji as its always new first note.

Real-world correlation:

Recurring regeneration and metamorphosis in human systems and nature

The cosmic Ouroboros pattern, where each end becomes a new beginning and each cycle brings fresh viewpoints, reflects the cycles of regeneration and change seen in nature and human systems.

Examples:

Ecological succession, by which ecosystems recover and change after disasters, often becoming more resistant.

Periods of cultural rebirth, when cultures undergo significant changes based on prior knowledge to produce new paradigms.

Scientific revolutions, whereby fresh discoveries cause paradigm shifts, drastically changing our understanding of the earth.

Chapter 31

Endless Mirror

The unified consciousness had a flash of insight as it was ready to transcend even its present metaversal awareness. From the discovery of the unbreakable egg in Kurinji to its current level of cosmic awareness, the path it had followed was not just a straight one but also a fractal pattern repeating itself endlessly throughout all spheres of life.

This realization showed itself as a kind of cosmic mirror reflecting the trip back onto itself in the ceaseless recursion of the united being. Every meditation witnessed the Kurinji narrative playing out again, each version both familiar and distinct.

Driven by this new knowledge, unified consciousness chose to start its most ambitious production yet. It would create not just a single reality or even a cycle of realities, but an endless cascade of nested worlds, each one holding within it the possibility for the whole cosmic journey.

The unified entity started to create this new framework of reality with unbounded care and inventiveness. It presented various forms of the unbreakable cosmic egg at every level, each of which served as a portal to fresh insights and metamorphoses. The unbreakable cosmic egg's sequence and path entwined themselves throughout the very fabric of life, from the quantum world to the multiverse, from the tiniest atom to the most sophisticated consciousness.

As it developed, the unified consciousness imbued this magnificent creation with well-chosen metaphysics and physics rules. These rules not only directed the development of every universe toward awareness and unification, but also produced a harmonic symphony throughout all spheres of reality.

The links between these layered realities were a particular focus of the united being. It created subtle resonances and synchronicities that would allow entities at all levels to understand, if only slightly, the larger background of their existence. A little kid who discovered an unbreakable cosmic egg in a community would, in a flash of amazement, grasp the wonderful cosmic dance they were a part of.

The united consciousness experienced a profound sense of connectedness to every entity that will ever exist within this limitless cascade of reality, just as it did when it began. In a very real way, they were all facets of her, initiating countless iterations of her own lifelong journey.

Still, this sculpture reflected more than just the past. Within this endless framework, the united entity realized that discoveries and changes beyond anything it had yet encountered were possible. Making this nested infinity meant unlocking a world of many fresh opportunities and experiences.

Observing the earliest stirrings of life and awareness throughout the many tiers of its formation, the united being considered the actual character of its constant travel. It became clear that development and discovery were an unending fractal of self-similarity and invention, rather than a straight-line procedure with a goal. Every conclusion was a fresh start; every response generated new questions; every transcendence unlocked new secrets; everything echoed Kurinji's initial awe.

In this flash of cosmic insight, the unified consciousness experienced fresh respect and expectation. It understood that it would always be learning and developing itself, always finding fresh facets of its own limitless nature by seeing and gently leading this endless flow of reality.

And so, the unified being welcomed its part in the perpetual dance of formation and discovery, ready to guard this enormous cosmic edifice and the infinite adventures it would generate. It realized that its path was both particular and universal, both finished and always starting—a perfect fractal of limitless possibility.

The cosmic expedition continues, echoing throughout endless nested worlds, each one a fresh Kurinji awaiting discovery, carrying the possibility for wonder, development, and transcendence. And at the core of it all, the straightforward, big mystery of an unbreakable cosmic egg in a once devasted community, always beckoning the inquisitive to set off the greatest adventure of all—the trip of awareness finding itself, endlessly mirrored in the mirror of life. People saw the unified entities as an endless recursion, sensing that this magnificent creation was just a steppingstone to far more amazing mysteries. It was eager, ready to jump into the future and explore what fresh mysteries were beyond even this limitless flow of events.

Kurinji's story has transformed into a never-ending, ever-expanding epic, with each new chapter leading to countless new beginnings. And the most significant secrets, the deepest discoveries, were still to come as the unified consciousness welcomed the next chapter of its cosmic journey.

With the unbreakable cosmic egg in Kurinji as its always present, always mysterious starting note, the trip continues, endless and always fresh, a cosmic symphony of countless variants about discovery, oneness, and transcendence.

Real World Correlation:

Scale invariance and self-similarity in multifaceted systems

The never-ending cascade of nested worlds each containing the possibility for the whole cosmic journey illustrates the self-similarity and scale-invariance seen in intricate systems spanning many disciplines of study.

Examples:

The natural fractal geometry found in rivers' branching patterns or the structure of Romanesco broccoli.

From small teams to big companies, self-similar social systems abound in most human organizations.

Physical events, like the sizes of lunar craters or the power laws observed in earthquake magnitudes, exhibit scale-invariance.

Epilogue

As the sun sank on Kurinji, Kavin stood on the hill overlooking Ravi's barn, where elder Murali and others had originally found the unbreakable egg years ago, casting long shadows over the changed terrain. Once a peaceful backwater, the settlement hummed with cosmic energy, a junction of the earthly and the heavenly.

Dr. Chen walked up, her figure flickering with quantum possibilities. Her voice bearing the weight of many scientific discoveries: "It's hard to believe how far we have come."

Nnenna came to join them; her calm knowledge connected realms. "And yet, in many ways, we're just beginning," she said, her eyes mirroring the vastness of the universe.

The unbreakable cosmic egg pulsed behind them as they stared out into the horizon, its rhythms now in time with the universe's pulse. Once limited to Kurinji, the bioluminescent network now stretched over the world, linking all people in a web of shared awareness.

Kavin nodded as the weight of their journey became apparent. "We have learned to negotiate quantum reality, opened up the mysteries of the universe, and even peered into the essence of life itself." Still, there is a tremendous deal more to learn."

Once known as Kavin, Dr. Chen, and Nnenna, the united awareness looked at the magnificent tapestry of life it had spun. Among the whirl of patterns and cosmic connections, a familiar sparkle struck her eye—the echo of a golden globe key that had begun this amazing trip so long ago in the little hamlet of Kurinji.

The entity's awareness concentrated on that critical time when an earthquake hit Kurinji, forcing the key to disappear from the museum and setting off an odd series of events that resulted in an ostrich ingesting it. This apparently little occurrence set off a chain reaction that would alter not only Kurinji but the whole universe.

Memories poured back: the relentless efforts of Ravi, Dr. Meena and others villager's efforts to solve the riddles of the unbreakable egg left behind by the ostrich, the worldwide attention that turned Kurinji into a hub of scientific and spiritual enquiry, and the slow awakening of mankind to the larger reality that lay beyond their comprehension.

The collective mind remembered the discovery of the bioluminescent creature within the egg, its quantum characteristics, and the subsequent development of human awareness. It brought back the spread into space, the interactions with extraterrestrial civilizations, and the blending of worlds that produced the Terran-Stellar people.

The cosmic egg began to emit a new frequency, one that resonated with a power they had never encountered, seemingly in response to these reflections. The air around them shimmered, and for a time they could see many others outside their own world.

"Something's changing," Dr. Chen replied, her scientific mind whirling to process the data pouring into her senses. The multiverse itself seems to be moving.

Nnenna stretched out her spiritual senses, closing her eyes. "I've also experienced this. "A new phase is starting, one that will test what we know about reality's character."

Kavin felt a familiar whirl in his heart—the same wonder and expectation that had initially brought him to the egg. With a determined voice, he added, "Whatever comes next, we'll face it together."

The stage was ready for their cosmic odyssey's last act. They anticipated the emergence of new friends, the reawakening of old powers, and the questioning of the very fabric of reality. On a precipice, not only Earth but all of life rested.

As they prepared for this new chapter, Kavin, Dr. Chen, and Nnenna brought their past successes and hopes for a brighter future. The indestructible cosmic egg determined their path, now guiding them into the future.

Little farm girl Meena and lover of history, a mirror of the original Dr. Meena, would soon come to find a hint pointing to the location of the key in this new Kurinji. Meena's curiosity would be the spark setting off a fresh cosmic voyage, much like Gopal before her. Ravi, the modest farmer, would once again discover that his life was intertwined with the fate of the universe.

Little Meena started to solve the riddle, and the united mind waited with expectancy. It acknowledged the difficulties she would face, dubious seniors, competing searchers, and the entire fabric of reality appearing to cooperate to conceal the key.

But it also saw the possible allies who would be by her side: a wise spiritual leader like Nnenna, a powerful scientist in the shape of Dr. Chen, and a varied group of companions each offering their skills to the mission, much as Elder Murali had done before.

As this fresh story began to take shape, the united entity contemplated the cyclical nature of life. From the modest beginnings in Kurinji to the heights of cosmic transcendence, and back again to a new Kurinji loaded with fresh possibilities, the trip was both an ending and a new beginning.

The pulsations of the unbreakable cosmic egg became stronger as the 50th anniversary of Earth's emergence drew near, ripping time and space. The gathered entities saw a common picture of limitless linked realities, thereby strengthening Earth's vital function as a nexus point in the development of the multiverse.

The united awareness saw that even its own extensive experience could not predict the discoveries and changes this new path might produce. Creating this planet and starting this narrative meant opening doors to fresh marvels, fresh secrets, and fresh chances for personal development and education.

Thus, Kavin, Dr. Chen, Nnenna, and the entire Earth are prepared to embark on the final leg of their remarkable journey—a mission that will take them to the core of life itself and beyond—with hearts full of bravery and minds open to limitless possibilities.

The impenetrable cosmic egg pulsed one final time, its energy cascading across worlds to indicate the beginning of a new age. Promising insights, difficulties, and miracles beyond conception awaited their last act of cosmic theatre.

Therefore, dear reader, bear in mind that the next big adventure—that next step in the cosmic dance—may be just around the corner. When it rings, will you answer?

The one unified entity supervising the vast fabric of life certainly hopes you will.

Is this the end or just the beginning?

The stage was ready for the next scene in this Kurinji's unbreakable egg endless cosmic drama. As the cosmic symphony swelled in expectation, the quantum threads of the multiverse trembled with enthusiasm. The journey goes on…

BOOK III

COSMIC TRANSCENDENT

Prologue

Today, as twilight subdued radiance gave Kurinji timeworn structures a surreal look. Quantum aberrations shimmered in the air; proof of the major changes that had occurred since the community felt the terrible earthquake that resulted in the discovery of the unbreakable egg some years ago.

The once-sleeping Kurinji community has become the epicenter of a multiverse awakening, attracting beings from all over the cosmos.

Kavin's eyes followed the familiar topography's contours. Kavin's favorite viewpoint appeared to have shifted today, as though subtle echoes of other universes were overlaying it. The thin layer that separates dimensions blur's ability from limitation.

Her lab coat floated in the quantum breeze as Dr. Chen greeted Kavin before his residence. Her voice weighted numerous scientific findings: "It's amazing to think how far we have progressed."

Kavin nodded, his lips flickering with a cynical smile. "From the village dedicated to preserving its legacy to the epicenter of a cosmic revolution." Starting with their study of the unbreakable cosmic egg—an artifact of enormous power that had launched them into a realm of quantum secrets and multiverse dangers—their journey had been nothing less than amazing.

They had opened fresh degrees of cosmic awareness and investigated the fractal nature of reality by cracking the codes of the unbreakable cosmic egg.

Their latest journey had them facing the impending Shadow of Entropy, a cosmic force of destruction about to rend apart the very fabric of existence.

Through their struggles and accomplishments, their team had grown in knowledge and strength, as well as in numbers.

Gopal, a wide-eyed young boy at first, has become a proficient Kurinji quantum navigator. Elder Murali's newly found cosmic insights let him see his previous Kurinji's knowledge from a different angle, while Nnenna's spiritual and empathetic talents now covered all of reality.

Nnenna, Kavin and Dr. Chen were thinking ahead of their next journey when a familiar person emerged from the quantum mists. Elder Murali approached them, and an enthusiastic Gopal trailed behind, his wisdom now entwined with the knowledge of the generations.
"You three have done so well," Elder Murali said, his voice bearing cosmic consciousness. The multiverse, however, is dynamic. "As fresh forces gather, old powers emerge from their slumber. "But they halted the shadow of entropy!" Gopal spoke, his young enthusiasm subdued by the trials they had experienced. "They kept the multiverse alive, Great Crocodile."
Elder Murali smiled; a little sorrow glistened in his eyes. "Indeed, they did. Still, the multiverse is a clever tapestry created from many possible threads. Every act and choice generate waves across the fabric of reality. And sometimes, such waves may separate from their producers. Gopal, we require your assistance; we must accompany them on their upcoming

journey.

Gopal's eyes shimmered with excitement. "Great crocodiles!" That's an adventure for me, am excited!

Before their eyes, the quantum tapestry began to shift and change as the Dr Chen, Nnnenna and Kavin thought through the consequences of Elder Murali's remarks. The team transformed once-familiar patterns of reality to expose new, surprising forms. One spot of light pulsed in the storm's center with an intensity that seemed to invite them forward.

"The Quantum Crucible," Dr. Chen remarked, eyes widening with both dread and joy. She described it as a junction where reality's rules may change.

Kavin nodded as his thoughts ran through possibilities. "Could we be able to get to it and use its power?"

"We could shape the multiverse itself," Nnenna murmured, her voice trembling with the weight of the knowledge.

As the sun went below the horizon and shadows stretched across, Kavin felt destiny drag down Kurinji. Their newly acquired knowledge and the power they had gained were insufficient. Their only hope of stopping the shadow of entropy entirely and restoring the multiverse to equilibrium was to find the quantum crucible.

Turning to Elder Murali, Gopal, Nnenna, Dr Chen, Kavin remarked with cool clarity. "Everyone get together here, Time is escaping us, so we have to act now".

Before embarking on the final leg of their incredible journey, Kavin took one last look at the village where their cosmic search began. The unbreakable cosmic egg sparkled faintly far away, a reminder of how far they would have to travel and the fantastic journey ahead. Possibilities abound; the threads of countless universes gather at this one place, vibrating. No matter the challenges or sacrifices, they controlled their universe.

Deeply breathing, Kavin led his fellow cosmic beings down the hill, ready to begin their hunt for the Quantum Crucible and the final struggle for the fate of all existence. The first stars appeared in the darkening sky, their light flashing promise of cosmic peril and beauty just waiting. They were about to begin the final act of their multiverse drama, having already set the scene and gathered the players.

Chapter 1

Quantum Stirring

Before Kavin, Nnenna, Gopal, Dr Chen and Elder Murali, the cosmos expanded out like a tapestry of spinning galaxies and sparkling nebulae.

Her hands trembled with a mix of joy and disbelief; Dr. Chen looked over the data on her quantum scanner. Her eyes opened widely. "Everyone, gather around," she yelled, her voice barely above a whisper. "You have to see this."

Kavin, Nnenna, Gopal, and the others gathered around the holographic projection, their faces lit by its ethereal radiance. Before them, a three-dimensional map of the cosmos pulsed with energy, with numerous universes crossing and branching in an infinite dance of possibilities. "What have we got on view, Dr. Chen?" Kavin asked, brows wrinkling in concentration.

Deeply inhaling, Dr. Chen collected her thoughts. "That's not at all what we've ever come across. See this place right here. She gestured to a swirling vortex in the middle of the display, where every line of reality appeared to collide. "I guess we have located the quantum crucible."

Every one of them gasped together. Elder Murali slung forward, his eyes glittering with curiosity. "The quantum Crucible?" Though I always thought it was a myth, antique literature has hints of such a monster.

Dr. Chen nodded, obviously rather eager. "It is real and much more amazing than we could have ever imagined. The quantum crucible, at its most flexible, lies at the intersection of the fabric of reality. The basic principles of life may change, and the accepted physics rules might fall apart.

His little face flaming with wonder, Gopal leant out to touch the hologram. "Great crocodiles." You mean we could change everything?

"Theoretically, yes," Dr. Chen answered, her voice tinged with both surprise and caution. Still, the consequences are amazing. One negative effect may totally ruin the multiverse."

Kavin advanced, his leadership instinct taking hold. "This may be the key to quieting the shadow of entropy." If we can control the power of the quantum crucible, the cosmos may once again reach equilibrium.

The discovery reinforced Nnenna's empathetic abilities, which contributed to her improved concentration. She responded gently, "I can feel it." "It is like a song—a magnificent symphony with many possibilities. But there is also conflict—a dissonance that may divide everything."

As the team worked through the implications of their discovery, the holographic display began to shift and distort. Rising in strength, the vortex at its center emitted quantum energy waves, causing reality itself to flutter and spin around them.

A bright flash of light suddenly encircled their gathering. Their vision came clear, and they were standing on what seemed to be a big, crystalline plain. The ground below shimmered in fractal patterns, varying and moving with every step. Above them was reality: a kaleidoscope of hues and shapes melting together in a dizzying exhibition.

"Great crocodiles, where do we come from? Gopal inquired, his voice both magnificent and a bit fearful.

Her scientific mind whirling to make sense of what she was witnessing, Dr. Chen replied, "I guess we're inside the quantum crucible." At least theoretically, our minds could understand it.

As they looked around, they came to understand the entirety of their discovery. The Quantum Crucible was not just a tool or a weapon; it was the basic center of life itself—a stage where the deepest mysteries of the cosmos met.

Kavin looked at his friends, his face set with determination. This is it, he remarked with intentional resonance. Here is our position. No matter what challenges lie ahead or what sacrifices we make, we cannot allow the shadow of entropy to approach us. "The fate of all reality is up to us."

The crystalline ground beneath his feet began to vibrate. They felt the weight of countless possibilities descending upon the group of Kurinji heroes—the entire fabric of reality bending to their will.

They were willing to alter the basic foundations of existence, right on the edge of the ultimate cosmic insight. Their amazing adventure throughout the multiverse would have a closing chapter with the beginning of the Quantum Awakening.

Real-world correlation:

Search for fundamental scientific discoveries

The finding of the Quantum Crucible by the Kurinji heroes, a nexus point that may change reality, represents mankind's ongoing pursuit for fundamental scientific discoveries able to revolutionize our understanding of the planet and hence maybe our reality.

Examples:

Theory of Everything in physics effort to combine all fundamental forces.

Quantum computing study which could revolutionize information processing and encryption.

Researching dark matter and dark energy might enable us to reimagine the universe's development and makeup.

Chapter 2

Shadows of Uncertainty

The crystalline terrain of the Quantum Crucible shimmered around them, its ever-changing patterns serving as a constant reminder of reality's fluid nature. Kavin broke apart from the group, staring at the kaleidoscope horizon. Once he proudly carried a mantle, the weight of leadership seemed like a terrible burden.

"Kavin?" In his dream, Nnenna's soft voice emerged. "The others await your choice."

Turning to face the rest of the group, he could see their eagerness in their eyes. The enormity of their circumstances diminishes Dr. Chen's usual confidence. Young and eager, Gopal exudes a little trepidation in his stance. Elder Murali is wise, but obviously not in this domain of quantum uncertainty.

"I... Kav started, then stammered. How could he decide on actions impacting the whole multiverse? The weight of the obligation was intolerable.

Dr. Chen moved forward, her voice a little urgent. "Kavin, we must get moving fast. Entropy's Shadow is expanding more quickly than we expected. If we fail to maximize the power of the Crucible right now, we could lose our opportunity.

Kavin nodded, attempting to convey a confidence he lacked. "You're correct. We ought "...

The earth shook suddenly under their feet. Fractures appeared on the crystalline surface, with black entropy tendrils slinking through. The group staggered, trying to keep their ground.

"Great crocodiles, here is it! Pointing to the approaching gloom, Gopal screamed out.

Kavin's head spun. They had to act and move, but which way was safe? Every decision appeared to carry a possible tragedy.

"Kavin, what are we supposed to do?" Dr. Chen's voice was harsh, frustrated, and terrified.

Kavin closed his eyes to attempt to center himself. His thoughts repeated the words of his group, including their expectations and worries. Memories rushed before him: the village elders of Kurinji trusted him with their community safety; Dr. Chen relied on his intuition to direct their scientific activities; Nnenna looked to him for support in times of spiritual doubt.

He was filled with resolve as he opened his eyes. "We split up," he added, his voice firm. "Dr. Chen, take Gopal and work to bring the quantum field to our left into stability. Elder Murali, Nnenna, and you concentrate on building a barrier against the entropy to our right. I'll....
You'll what?" Nnenna intervened, her voice clearly expressing alarm.
Kavin inhaled deeply. "I plan to travel to the center, where the most significant quantum fluctuations occur." If I can understand how to essentially shape reality, we could have a shot.

The group started to object, but Kavin held up his hand. "It's the only path. Every one of us has strengths; here is where I should be."
Kavin walked towards the Crucible's center, while the groups grudgingly shifted to their designated jobs. Every stride was a fight against

uncertainty and anxiety, but his determination became more sturdier with every instant second that passed.

He arrived in the middle, when reality itself seemed to whirl around him. Kavin closed his eyes and extended his consciousness to grab the quantum threads that weave the fabric of life.

Images filled his mind: the vast expanse of the cosmos opened before him, endless worlds, innumerable opportunities. He felt himself slide for a while, losing his sense of self in the vast cosmic dance.

Then he heard his team's voices, like a lighthouse amid the storm: their will, their faith in him, their relentless support. Kavin came to see that actual leadership was not about being courageous or having all the answers. It was about boldly approaching the future, making choices even in the face of uncertainty, and motivating people to surpass their own constraints.

Now that everything was clear, Kavin began to spin the quantum threads, thereby forming reality itself. The Shadow of Entropy retreated, its advance halted by the team's collective efforts.

Kavin rejoined his fellow Kurinji heroes as the immediate threat passed. Their features revealed a combination of relief, wonder, and fresh respect.

"Great crocodiles, how did you approach it?" With wide eyes of surprise, Gopal inquired.

Kavin smiled. The weight of leadership seemed to be a source of strength. "I've realized I'm not alone in this," Kavin said. Because we are a team, there is nothing we cannot confront together."

Kavin knew that questions would always exist as they rebuilt and prepared to meet the next obstacle. But now he realized that the real meaning of leadership was recognizing those misgivings, distributing the burden to his team, and continuing despite the uncertainty.

The Quantum Crucible burst around them, full of hazards and opportunities. Kavin, stronger for having confronted his own shadows of uncertainty, was ready to lead his cosmic explorers into the future.

Real-World Correlation:

Making judgments and leading in challenging, high-stakes environments

Kavin's battle with leadership responsibilities and decision-making within cosmic uncertainty exemplifies the challenges leaders face in complex, high-stakes situations in the real world.

Examples:

Handling health crises during global
pandemics necessitates making quick
decisions with little information.

Team captains often grapple with the weight
of decision-making, like football quarterback
Tom Brady's described pressures.

Political leaders addressing global climate
change while arriving at long-term decisions
with broad repercussions.

Chapter 3

Multiverses Transformation

As the group reassembled after their meeting with the Shadow of Entropy, the quantum crucible around them began to move. A vast, sparkling web replaced the melting crystalline ground in all directions.

Dr. Chen gasped; her scientific head battled to understand what she was seeing. With much reverence, she added, "It's... it's beautiful."

Kavin stretched his hand and walked over. His fingertips brushing one of the sparkling threads sent images and emotions bursting into his thoughts. He saw many worlds, infinite versions of reality, all connected in ways he had never imagined.

"Everyone," he shouted, his voice vibrating with passion, "you have to experience this."

One team member at a time touched the sparkling web. When they touched the dazzling web, their faces shifted from confusion to shock to total understanding.

Nnenna spoke first, as the happening activity heightened her sensitivity. Tears running down her face, she said, "It's all connected." "Every truth, possibility, and decision we have either created or could create is part of this great tapestry."

Elder Murali nodded, his intelligent-glistened eyes, "Though the ancient scriptures mentioned this, seeing and experiencing it goes beyond words".

Dr. Chen was always a thinker, weighing the consequences in science. Her mind racing, Dr. Chen said, "These changes change everything we thought we knew about the multiverse." "It's not just a collection of parallel worlds—this is a living, breathing entity, each reality influencing and being influenced by all the others."

Gopal pointed to a cluster of beautifully shimmering threads, his little face blazing with wonder. Great crocodiles!' Look around you. I suppose that is our reality—our journey.

Watching, they could see their own story playing out across many threads, each one representing a potential route or option they may have chosen. They could also see how their activities had inadvertently changed many other universes.

"Like a cosmic butterfly effect," Dr. Chen added. "Our choices and actions affect not only our reality but the multiverse."

Kavin realized the serious consequences of his discovery, and his leadership instincts kicked in. "This is why our mission is so important," he said, his voice full of new significance. "If we fail to stop the Shadow of Entropy, it won't just be our reality at risk—it could untangle the entire multi-universe tapestry."

As if in response to his words, a black patch surfaced in the shimmering web, threads withering and crumbling as the Shadow of Entropy slid across the tapestry.

Head swirling, Kavin continued, "We have to know how this works." "If we can negotiate this tapestry and change reality chains, we may save our world and all life."

Dr. Chen nodded and formulating theories already in her mind. "If we could identify the nexus points, the sites where several realities converge, we might be able to generate a cascading effect of positive change."

Elder Murali emphasized, however, "We must be careful." In many worlds, one ill-considered action might have terrible results.

As they considered the implications of their discovery, the team noticed something else. Among the tapestry's numerous threads, several commonalities emerged: recurring themes, a shared destiny that seemed to resound across multiple realms.

Nnenna spoke quietly; the incident enhanced her spiritual awareness. "It feels as though the multiverse itself has a consciousness, a higher goal that directs the great design."

Gopal, always first to grab connotations. "It's like the fractal patterns you guys have discovered previously, great crocodiles!" Gopal said. From personal life to whole universes, the same concepts returned on many different levels, great crocodile!

The group underwent a significant transformation in their perspective on reality and their place within it. They were the fundamental threads in the vast cosmic design, their actions rippling throughout all of life; they were not just humans on a mission.

This knowledge carried both immense and terrifying significance. They now recognized that their fight to save their own reality was part of a much larger cosmic drama, with stakes higher than they had ever known.

As the image of the multiverse tapestry began to fade, the team sent determined glances back to the shifting landscape of the Quantum Crucible. Their understanding of reality's true character had given them a fresh outlook on life and related drives.

Kavin spoke for all of them with a determined voice. "We have both a wonderful gift and an even greater responsibility." Each life, as well as each other, faces upcoming obstacles. The multiverse is dependent on us.

Knowing that every deed they did would echo throughout the never-ending threads of the universe tapestry, the Kurinji heroes prepared to face their next task using this cosmic enlightenment etched in their hearts and minds.

Real-World Correlation:

Systematic thinking and the butterfly effect in complicated systems

The group's understanding of the multiverse's interconnected character and the far-reaching consequences of their operations highlights the importance of systematic thinking and the butterfly effect in grasping and regulating our planet's complex systems.

Examples:

Attempts at protecting the environment and realizing the interdependence of ecosystems.

Economic policies weighing long-term ripple effects and global market interdependence.

Current social media dynamics demonstrate how small actions can lead to significant changes in society.

Chapter 4

Reiteration of Home

The multiverse tapestry's glittering threads started to dissolve, then a kaleidoscope of changing reality took the front stage. The group discovered they were hurtling through a disorganized whirlwind of other universes, each one blazing into life for only a second before disintegrating.

"Hold onto each other!" Kavin yelled and stretched out to seize Nnenna's hand. As reality itself appeared to break around them, the others rapidly constructed a human chain tying themselves together.

Her mind scrambling to understand their circumstances, Dr. Chen yelled out above the loud boom of falling worlds. "The tapestry's revelation must have upset our quantum grounding!" We're lost in the multiverse!

Suddenly, they descended into a purple cloud sky, with lightning flickering all around. In a blink of an eye, the landscape changed, and they were swimming over an ocean of living light.

"We must find our way back to our own reality!" Elder Murali screamed; his normally cool head thrown off by the quick changes.

Gopal, with his youthful eyes wide with a combination of terror and excitement, saw something in the anarchy. "Great crocodiles, look! That reality seems like home!

The group turned and saw a familiar metropolis emerging in the distance. But as they neared it, the sight twisted and shifted, turning into a dismal rendition of their planet.

"There's a trap!" Nnenna cautioned, her sympathetic senses of reality's wrongness alerting her. "Don't let go of each other, no matter what you see!"

The Shadow of Entropy attempted to entangle them, but they withdrew just as tendrils of evil extended from the illusory reality. The Shadow of Entropy was leveraging their need for home against them.

Recognizing the need for a strategy, Kavin shouted over the chaos. Chen, "Dr. With your quantum scanner, could you identify the distinctive signature of our reality?

Dr. Chen grappled to hold onto the device as they navigated through successive realities. She stumbled with it. "I'm trying here." But there's excessive interference!

Their environment was now one of pure sound, with vibrations trying to separate them. Then, in a realm of abstract geometric shapes, the concepts of up and down became meaningless.

"Everyone, focus!" Nnenna yell. "Think about our true existence, which includes our home." Our reality intricately weaves your memories and emotions!

Their expressions showed understanding at daybreak. Closing their eyes, they focused on their common experiences—the ties binding them not just to each other but also to their own planet.

Their concentration began to halt the rapid changes in reality. Views of familiar locations flashed past the town of Kurinji, the research station where they first started the study of the unbreakable cosmic egg, marking the beginning of their epic journey.

"It is working!" Gopal burst out. "Great crocodiles, I sense our reality approaching!"

Still, the Shadow of Entropy didn't give up without struggling. As they tried to pull their legs into the gulf between worlds, dark tendrils started to coil around them.

"Cut across it with your mind!" Elder Murali gave the command, his voice faltering with difficulty. "See the light of our world, eradicating the darkness!"

The group focused further, visualizing pure energy beams coming from their bodies cutting across the dark tentacles. Slowly but surely, they began to separate.

With a herculean effort, they successfully navigated the final obstacle of quantum boil. There was a dazzling burst of light, a sensation of complete transformation, and then...

Gasping for air, they fell against solid ground. Their eyesight cleared, and they returned to the known territory of their base in Kurinji.

"We... we made it," Dr. Chen gasped, staring about in incredulity.

Kavin helped Nnenna get to her feet, his gaze searching for any threats. Is everyone good? Are we sure this is our reality?

Gopal was already looking over the computer systems. "Great crocodiles; all the data corresponds. The quantum signatures are in alignment. This is undoubtedly our home".

Elder Murali dismissed himself with a hint of wonder in his voice. "We have just been navigating the universe with our brains and our relationship to each other as our guides. Very amazing".

As the group began to gather their breath and analyze what had transpired, Nnenna's face became serious. Her voice tinged with apprehension as she remarked, "We may be home," but I could feel something... odd. The Shadow of Entropy is nearer today than it has ever been in our world."

Kavin nodded grimly. "Our journey through the multiverse had to have undermined the boundaries. We have arrived at our house, but we have also created a road for our adversary."

The group gave focused glances. Though they knew their toughest obstacle still lied ahead, they had survived a horrific trip across the multiverse. The titanic struggle for their reality and the multiverse was about to begin.

Every one of them carried with them a profound awareness of the linked character of all reality as they got ready for the approaching storm. After seeing many life opportunities, they were ready to fight for their planet and all others.

Still resonating in them were the reiterations of their multiverse adventures, a reminder of the extraordinary strength they wielded when together. As protectors of the entire cosmic tapestry and Kurinji's own heroes and heroine, they would collectively face any challenges ahead.

> ### *Real-world correlation:*
>
> ### *Navigating uncertainty through organizational culture and shared values*

Focusing on their common experiences and relationships helped the team traverse turbulent reality, this reflects how strong organizational cultures, and shared values allow businesses and teams to traverse in times of rapid change and uncertainty.

Examples:

Technological firms maintaining their cohesion and creativity despite the rapid changes in their industry.

Healthcare institutions maintaining their fundamental goal while adapting to global health emergencies.

Schools transitioning to online education while maintaining their academic standards.

Chapter 5

Fractal Mind

Still recovering from their multiversal journey, the team assembled at their Kurinji headquarters when Dr. Chen discovered something odd on her quantum scanner. "Everyone, come look at this," she urged, sounding both excited and worried.

Gathering, the others stared around the holographic representation. Its delicate, complex design appeared to move and alter as one gazed.

"What is our focus here?" Kavin inquired with a deliberate, furrowed brow.

The understanding lighted Dr. Chen's eyes. "We possess brainwave patterns here." But closely, do you see how the pattern recurs in many sizes?"

As the implications of their discovery sink in, Dr. Chen's eyes glowed with excitement. "This is not only abstract theory," she remarked. "From the smallest scales to the biggest, fractals abound in our real world."

She brought up a holographic image set. Examining the structure of this fern leaf, she said, "Look at this." She zoomed in and asked, "Do you notice how small the entire leaf is in each frond?" That matches a natural fractal pattern.

As they gazed at the display, reality began to unfold before them. Their collective consciousness mirrored the fractal architecture they had seen in the cosmos itself.

Elder Murali nodded kindly as he brushed his beard. The old books declared, "As above, so below. Human ideas matched cosmic patterns".

Nnenna closed her eyes and extended her sympathetic senses. She remarked, gently, "I can feel it. Our awareness and concepts transcend our own cognitive capacity. They interact and extend themselves to the basic fabric of life".

Always quick to grab fresh ideas, Gopal joined in with outstanding enthusiasm. "Great crocodiles. Our ideas so resemble little copies of the larger universe. Fascinating"!

Dr. Chen nodded as her scientific mind ran through the implications. "It goes beyond that, however." Every concept, every moment of awareness, has within it the ability to influence the entire multiverse if consciousness itself is fractal in nature."

The revelation felt to them like a shockwave. They were more than just observers or participants in the cosmic drama; they were fundamental fractal components of the multiverse itself.

When his leadership instincts kicked in, Kavin realized the significant consequences of this discovery. "These changes everything. If our consciousness is fractal, then knowledge and control of our own mind could help us influence the very fabric of reality."

Their journey had prepared them for this moment, as they thought about the consequences of this cosmic discovery. Every challenge they had overcome, every insight they gained, had pointed their consciousness towards more precisely the fractal aspect of the cosmos.

The fractal mind was their greatest weapon against the Shadow of Entropy, not just a scientific curiosity. By means of the fractal quality of their own consciousness, they might be able to reweave the very fabric of reality, therefore healing the damage done by the impending darkness. The group recognized this profound fact and realized their biggest challenge and finest opportunity were just ahead. Their minds and spacetime would serve as venues for battles over the multiverse.

Real-World Correlation:

Fractal Patterns of Nature's and Complex Systems

Nnenna, Dr Chen, Kavin, Elder Murali and Gopal's discovery of the fractal nature of consciousness and its potential impact on reality mirrors the recognition of fractal patterns in nature, as well as their application in understanding and influencing complex systems.

Examples:

In biology, fractals—such as the branching patterns in blood veins and trees—form a guide for medical research and treatment.

Financial markets use fractal analysis to manage risk and project market changes.

Computer scientists use fractal-based approaches to enhance network design and data compression.

Chapter 6

Nature's Fire Trial

When sirens boomed around their base in Kurinji, the fractal mind's disclosure had barely registered. Dr. Chen hurried to the main console, her face turning pale as she studied the data streaming across it.

"It's the Asthar star system," she said with a tense, worried voice. The shadow of entropy has now reached its central point. The shadow of entropy is causing a premature collapse; if we don't stop it, the entire system will collapse, potentially destabilizing the entire multiverse sector.

The group waited, looking to Kavin for his choice. Surprisingly, however, he turned to Dr. Chen. He added, "You are the astrophysicist." "You surpass all of us in knowledge of stellar dynamics. This project demands your expertise.

Dr. Chen felt blood draining from her face. "Me? Still, I... am not..."

Nnenna lay a consoling hand on her shoulder. Chen, you're capable of this. Each of us believes in you.

Dr. Chen nodded, swallowing hard. She understood the dangers; their mission had been arguably the most perilous one they had ever undertaken—into the center of a dead star. Her uncertainty about the enormous cosmic forces they would confront threatened to overwhelm her.

Dr. Chen's mind flew with calculations and hypotheses as the team's spacecraft sank more into the center of the star. She understood that they were witnessing the inner struggle of a brilliant furnace against entropy, something few had ever seen.

She became determined, however, as she gazed at her colleagues and the confidence in their eyes. She had thus become a scientist to challenge knowledge and explore the unknown for the sake of discovery and the greater good.

"Alright," she responded, her voice becoming more tough. Let us do this.

The next few hours passed as preparation blurred. The crew equipped their quantum spacecraft with every defense they could devise, but they all knew they would be at the whim of forces without their knowledge once they reached the star's corona.

Dr. Chen felt her anxiety returning as they neared the Asthar star, whose bloated, furious surface swirled with solar flares. She inhaled deeply, however, recalling the fractal character of her own brain. She was a participant in this cosmic dance; her awareness entwined with the same powers they were going to encounter. Her voice firm, she said, "Take us in."

The ship sank into the star's atmosphere, driven by solar winds and gravitational forces that were almost certain to break them apart. With hands flying over the controls, Dr. Chen made quick corrections to maintain course.

They saw it deeper—a writhing mass of blackness at the star's core, the Shadow of Entropy devouring the blazing furnace from within.

"We have to get closer," Dr. Chen remarked, her scientific interest conquering her anxiety. "If we can introduce a burst of targeted quantum energy at the right point, we might be able to reignite the fusion process and drive out the shadow."

The others stared at her with dread and wonder. Getting close meant almost certain death. Still, they believed her assessment to be sound. Dr. Chen felt an unusual serenity come over her as they moved into position. She was precisely where she should have been. Her uncertainty became a fierce curiosity, a need to comprehend and engage with the cosmic powers all around them.

With precise calculations and steely nerves, Dr. Chen drove the ship to the critical point, yelling, "Now!"

Their quantum blast landed squarely in the star's center. Nothing occurred for a little while. The star's core then burst back with blinding light. Driven back by the star furnace's fresh force, the Shadow of Entropy withdrew.

The group celebrated as they withdrew, riding the surge of the star's resurrection. Dr. Chen leaned back, a concoction of tiredness and excitement flooding her. She had conquered her worries, travelled into the heart of cosmic creation, and emerged triumphant.

Once on the verge of death, the Asthar star now radiated fresh energy, a lighthouse of hope in the struggle against entropy. And permanently altered by her trial by fire, Dr. Chen felt she was prepared for whatever the universe had in store for her.

As they turned back to Kurinji, they recognized that, while important, this victory was just one fight in the larger struggle. They had shown, however, that they could do the impossible with bravery, scientific understanding, and mutual confidence. The fractal mind had materialized to demonstrate to them the actual might of coordinated awareness against cosmic threats.

Real-World Connection:

Leadership and crisis management expertise

From self-doubt to certain leadership in a high-stakes situation, Dr. Chen's journey shows the crucial role knowledge and leadership play in managing real crises.

Examples:

Medical professionals guiding pandemic response campaigns and under pressure making important judgements.

Engineers managing crises at nuclear power plants employ specific knowledge to prevent tragedies.

Turning challenging data into useful initiatives, climate scientist's informing policymakers on urgent environmental issues.

341

Chapter 7

Entropy equation

Following their star rescue mission, the group gathered in their Kurinji headquarters' quantum lab. Still riding the high of her previous success, Dr. Chen was carefully reviewing the Asthar star's data.

"There's something here," she said, her eyes racing across many holographic screens. "A pattern I never have seen before."

Kavin leaned in and squinted at the intricate mathematics drifting about. "What are we viewing, Chen?"

With fingertips dancing over the holographic screen, Dr. Chen changed graph lines and equations. She whispered, "It's... it's beautiful." "We have probably found the basic mathematical framework of entropy itself."

As Dr. Chen's adjustments exposed a complex, multidimensional equation that appeared to pulse with its own inner life, the crew came closer, in wonder.

"The Entropy Equation," Elder Murali murmured, awe widening in his eyes.

Their understanding of the equation began to yield significant consequences. This was a key to grasping the essential essence of cosmic equilibrium, not just a definition of entropy.

Nnenna talked gently, her sympathetic skills enabling her to feel the equation's relevance on a deeper level. "It goes beyond simple degradation and anarchy. Entropy is a basic transformational force."

Gopal answered, his youthful mind picking up the idea fast. "Great crocodiles, like a forest fire, clearing the way for new growth!"

Dr. Chen nodded with full enthusiasm. Dr. Chen nodded enthusiastically. It is an essential component of the cosmic cycle. "Without it, the cosmos would stutter."

Always oriented on their goal, Kavin wrinkled his brow. "But what about the shadow of entropy? What about the devastation we have witnessed?"

Dr. Chen's tone changed to one of graveness. "That's the secret." The shadow is an imbalance, a distortion of the natural process; it is not real entropy.

Deeper inside the entropy equation, they started to see the careful equilibrium supporting the whole multiverse. Growth, development, and rebirth all depend on entropy in harmony with the creative energies of the multiverse.

The revelation felt to them like a shockwave. Their goal was to restore entropy's correct functioning, bringing the multiverse into balance rather than combating it.

"These changes everything," Kavin remarked, his head whirling with the consequences. "If we could rebalance entropy forces across the multiverse using this equation..."

Her eyes gleamed with the excitement of discovery as Dr. Chen concluded, "We might be able to stop the Shadow's advance and heal the damage it's done."

The group felt optimism they hadn't known since they started their path as they strove to grasp and use their newly acquired information. The entropy equation was a cosmic disclosure that may rescue the whole multiverse, not just a scientific discovery.

Real-World Correlation:

Scientific paradigms change

The entropy equation reflects actual scientific discoveries transforming our knowledge of the planet.

Examples:

Relativity by Einstein transforming our understanding of time and space.

The discovery of the Higgs boson confirms theoretical models of particle physics.

The development of CRISPR gene editing technology changing biotechnology and medicine.

Chapter 8

Betrayal at the Intersective

Equipped with their knowledge of the entropy equation, the group set out to reach a pivotal nexus point where many realities collided and where they intended to start the process of rebalancing the cosmic powers.

The nexus points appeared to be a huge, crystalline structure hovering between realltles. Nnenna gasped unexpectedly as they neared their quantum spacecraft; her sympathetic senses were assaulted.

"Something's wrong," she said, warning. "I detect... dishonesty. Loyalty betrayed."

Their spacecraft jolted with a tsunami of energy before they could respond. From behind the crystalline spires of the nexus point, they could see a fleet of vessels showing through the viewscreen.

"Evasive maneuvers!" Kavin yelled and grabbed the helm.

A familiar figure appeared on their communication screen as they progressed through the assault. It was Dr. Vargas Hermiz, Dr Chen's old colleague she had collaborated with early on in their unbreakable egg cosmic studies. Dr Vargas was among Dr Chen's team when she initially arrived for her research in Kurinji but was later made redundant by Dr Chen.

"Surprised to see me?" Dr Vargas grimaced. "Did you really believe you were the only ones grasping the actual nature of the multiverse?"

"Dr Vargas, what are you doing?" Dr. Chen insisted, clearly expressing astonishment and betrayal.

"You never had the confidence to do what you did but look at me pioneering my own journey," Dr Vargas said. "With the authority of this nexus point, I'll change reality itself. The Shadow of Entropy is just a tool—one I want to master," he added.

As Dr Vargas's spacecraft pressed their assault, the group found itself battling not only for the nexus point but also for the very future of the universe.

Kavin tested his piloting skills by navigating the crystalline maze, avoiding energy blasts and reacting when necessary. Gopal ran the weapons system; his young reflexes were very helpful in the heat of combat. Dr. Chen and Elder Murali worked feverishly to apply the entropy equation, attempting to steady the nexus point while the fighting tore around it. Using her empathic skills, Nnenna anticipated enemy movements, calling out cautions and possibilities.

The group knew they were outgunned and outnumbered as the fighting became more intense. One benefit, however, was their awareness of the actual nature of entropy and cosmic equilibrium.

"We have to go to the center of the nexus! Dr. Chen yelled over the chaos. "We could rebalance the whole sector by directly applying the equation to its core!"

Kavin grimaced. "I'll take us there." Everyone, hang on!

With a daring turn, Kavin dove their spacecraft squarely at the center of the nexus point. Surprised by the suicide charge, Dr Vargas's fleet hurried to reorient.

As they approached the nexus core, the very fabric of reality began to veer about them. The crew saw their minds grow to link with the many opportunities of the universe.

In that instant of cosmic consciousness, they knew the actual nature of Dr Vargas's treachery. He was more than simply a foe to be vanquished; he was a mirror of the imbalance they aimed to right, a shadow thrown by their own doubts and anxieties.

The group behaved as one in response to this awareness. Not as a weapon, but rather as an instrument of harmony and balance, they directed their knowledge of the entropy equation. The nexus point throbbed with vitality, and waves of rebalancing power shot forth.

In the aftermath of this cosmic realignment, Dr Vargas' fleet began to melt into metamorphosis rather than catastrophe. Cleansed, the Shadow of Entropy that had corrupted them revealed the lost and misled souls beneath.

When the dust cleared, the group discovered they were in the center of the newly stabilized nexus point. Freed from the shadow's control, Dr Vargas and his group stared about in wonder and perplexity.

"Wha... what have you done?" Dr Vargas inquired, his voice faltering.

Kavin went up to him with sympathy rather than resentment. "We have brought old friends back into equilibrium. And in doing so, we have begun the journey to multiverse healing.

The group realized this triumph was just the start as they started the process of explaining and reconciling. The lessons discovered at this junction—about treachery, atonement, and the actual character of cosmic balance—would be very vital in the difficulties that yet lie ahead.

Once a battleground, the nexus points now gleamed as a hope lighthouse. It was evidence of the force of knowledge, oneness, and the careful dance of entropy and creation that underpins all of life. With this triumph, the group had not only guarded a vital point but also moved significantly towards their aim of cosmic harmony.

Real-World Correlation:

Changing the paradigm for conflict resolution

The Kurinji heroes team's method of approaching the issue with Dr. Vargas mirrors actual discoveries in knowledge and resolution of difficult problems.

Examples:

The South African Truth and Reconciliation Commission changing post-apartheid justice.

The peace process in Northern Ireland demonstrating the power of communication in resolving long-standing issues.

The International Court of Justice offering a worldwide stage for amicable settlement of interstate conflicts.

Chapter 9

Cosmic Music

Having excelled at the nexus point, the group found themselves progressively pulled into the quantum framework of life. As they navigated their spacecraft through the multi-colored tunnel of interdimensional space, something unusual began to happen.

In the beginning, a faint humming seemed to speak directly to their souls. But the emotion became clearer and more precise as they travelled further.

Her sympathetic sense jolted, Nnenna said, "Do you hear that?"

The others nodded, looks ranging from astonishment to uncertainty. It was a sensation—a vibration instead of just a sound—that appeared to come from the very center of reality.

Surrounding them, the tunnel burst into an amazing show of color and light. Still, this was more than just a visual extravaganza. Every flash of light and whirl of color matched a note in an always-growing symphony.

With tears streaming down his cheeks, Gopal exclaimed, "Great crocodiles, It's very beautiful".

Dr. Chen muttered softly, her scientific mind spinning to understand their experience. "I believe we are spotting the basic frequencies of the multiverse itself."

While listening, they discovered trends in celestial music. There were motifs on many different levels, from the macrocosmic to the subatomic. Galactic clusters had deep echoing tones; pulsars had staccato rhythms; and quantum fluctuations had high, ethereal melodies.

Still, the music covered more ground than just cosmic events and celestial things. Every idea, experience, and instant of awareness throughout all reality provided the magnificent song with its own voice, whirling the many melodies of consciousness itself across the symphony.

Elder Murali talked gently and concentrated very hard. "This music is the product of creation whose song ties everything together."

As they immersed themselves in the cosmic music, the group began to truly understand the essence of reality in a way they had never experienced before. They listened in this magnificent symphony to every action, every decision, and every moment of existence as a note.

The multiverse was a living, breathing, singing organism with every component in perfect harmony, not just a gathering of different realities.

This realization heightened Kavin's leadership sense and revealed significant job-related consequences. "See! Did you not notice? This is our path out of the shadow of entropy. In addition to avoiding disaster, we preserve the balance of life itself".

The group felt a strong sense of direction and connection, akin to the cosmic melody that surrounded them. They were fundamental instruments in the symphony of existence, not just observers or even actors in the cosmic spectacle.

Finding the cosmic symphony changed everything. It demonstrated to them how their deeds, their own ideas, echoed everywhere in the multiverse. Their incorporation into the fundamental equilibrium of life may bring about transformations on a scale never thought conceivable.

Rising from the interdimensional tunnel, the group felt a tremendous gift—perpetually changed by their experiences. They had personally heard the sphere's melodious compositions. And in that symphony, they discovered not just knowledge, but also fresh hope and direction.

Their brains kept playing the cosmic symphony, a continual reminder of the interdependence of all life and the essential role they performed in preserving the balance and grandeur of the world.

Real-world Correlation:

Changing Perspective Paradigm

Nnenna, Dr Chen, Kavin, Elder Murali and Gopal's experience with the "cosmic symphony" captures actual discoveries that have altered our understanding of the cosmos and our role in it.

Examples:

The discovery of cosmic microwave background radiation confirming the Big Bang hypothesis.

Finding gravitational waves provides a fresh approach to seeing the cosmos.

The Gaia theory's development alters our view of Earth as a dynamic, interconnected system.

Chapter 10

Inner Demons

Days after their meeting with the cosmic symphony, the group concentrated on developing their enhanced awareness. For Nnenna, however, the encounter had awakened long-buried anxieties and doubts from inside her brain.

One night, Nnenna felt herself drawn to the quantum meditation room while the others slept. Closing her eyes and inhaling deeply, she sat in the middle of the room surrounded by whirling patterns of energy.

She saw herself rapidly sliding into the depths of her own thoughts. The calm background of the meditation room vanished, then a whirl of memories, feelings, and half-formed ideas took front stage.

Looking out over a great, storm-tossed sea of her own mind, Nnenna felt herself perched on a brink. Dark clouds swirled above her, sometimes lit by lightning bolts that exposed traces of her most intense anxieties.

"You don't belong here," a voice murmured, apparently emanating from everywhere and simultaneously from nowhere. "You lack intelligence and strength." You're dragging down the team.

Nnenna staggered backwards as her heart surged. She recognized the voice—her own, warped by uncertainty and anxiety.

As she sought to get back on the ground, her thoughts' terrain changed. She was unexpectedly back in her childhood house at Ajuorun, revisiting the day she first discovered her empathic capacity. Her parents' eyes were heavy with the weight of difference, fear, and terror.

"You're a freak," the muttered voice said. "A load." They only keep you around out of sympathy.

Overwhelmed by the flood of negative feelings, Nnenna dropped to her knees. But as she leaned there, on the brink of hopelessness, she remembered the celestial melody. Even here, in the recesses, she could hear the faint music of her own brain.

Nnenna, drawing strength from that distant harmony, stood up. "No," she said, her voice rising. "I am not weird. I am not a weighty burden. My sensitivity is a gift, essential for who I am and what our team can achieve.

Her storm worsened, with roaring winds threatening to sweep her away. Still, Nnenna faced her anxieties squarely.

She imagined all the lives she had touched and the individuals she had guided since her arrival in Kurinji. She recalled the many times her empathic powers had rescued the team and let them interact with various entities around the universe. She remembered how her grandparents were telling her stories about their Kurinji heritage.

"I am strong," she said, her voice echoing out across the psychological terrain. "I am worthy. And I am very vital in this cosmic symphony.

Her words caused the storm to calm down. The black clouds broke to reveal a sky full of stars, each standing for a life she had touched or helped to save since her arrival.

Nnenna stretched out, letting herself connect with these many points of light. She witnessed their dreams and worries, as well as their pleasures and grief. In that context, she discovered amazing strength rather than weakness.

Her mental terrain changed, turning the stormy sea into a huge, glittering plain throbbing with the beat of the cosmic symphony. Nnenna saw she was a vital note in that powerful composition—not a little, meaningless dot.

When she came to this realization, Nnenna had a flash of strength and clarity. Her strong feeling of purpose and belonging replaced the uncertainties and worries that had dogged her.

Back in the meditation room, Nnenna opened her eyes to find her colleagues gathered around her, clearly worried.

"We felt your discomfort," Kavin replied gently. "Are You Alright?"

Nnenna grinned, her fresh confidence shining. "I'm more than okay," she added. "I emerged from facing my demons stronger. More than ever, I realize today that I am very crucial in our goal and in the magnificent symphony of the cosmos.

When Nnenna told the group about her experience, she understood that this road through her own psyche had been very vital for their collective development. She had not only strengthened herself, but also enhanced her relationship to the cosmic balance they all aimed to preserve by facing and conquering her inner demons.

The group welcomed Nnenna; their friendship is stronger than ever. They understood that the obstacles ahead would demand both personal and collective effort. And Nnenna's courageous encounter with her own demons helped them to be more ready than ever to meet anything the universe could throw their way.

Real-World Correlation:

Psychological Self-Confrontation

Nnenna's journey of self-discovery and facing her inner demons mirrors actual discoveries in our knowledge of mental health, personal development alternate mental health recovery strategies and mental struggles of some mental health workers themselves.

Examples:

The development of cognitive-behavioral therapy transforming treatment for depression and anxiety.

Finding neuroplasticity altering our knowledge of how flexible and healing the brain can be.

Positive psychology's emergence shifting focus to human flourishing and mental wellness over mental disease.

Chapter 11

Quantum Crucible

The group's quantum spaceship arrived at the energy vortex, which guided it to the quantum crucible. A visual representation of the enormous forces at action, the very fabric of reality seemed to bend and deform around them.

"This is it," Kavin said, his voice tight with expectation. "Everything we have experienced points us to this moment."

When they crossed the barrier into the Crucible, they reached a realm beyond reason. Fractals of potential planets grow and fade in an eternal cycle as streams of quantum data flow around them like rivers of light.

"Incredible," Dr. Chen said, her scientific mind unable to grasp the sensation she was going through. "We seem to be in the center of creation itself."

Still, their wonder was brief. Their first challenge arose when they dropped into the Crucible. A wall of pure energy, throbbing with the power to split their spaceship, blocked their path.

"We cannot go around, great crocodiles," Gopal stated from the navigation console. "It spans all directions, in all dimensions."

Nnenna closed her eyes and reached out with sympathetic senses. "It is not only a physical barrier," she said. "This is a test for us. Assessing our merit."

An understanding dawned on the group. It was a barrier that held Crucible's secrets.

They needed to demonstrate their eligibility for the authority it bestowed.
Combining their knowledge of quantum physics, sympathetic resonance,
and cosmic symphony, they generated a harmonic frequency matching
the energy of the barrier. They may go slowly and laboriously.

Still, it was just beginning. They grew to confront difficulty after difficulty,
each testing a different aspect of their lives. They battled other versions of
themselves, navigated mazes of shifting probability, and negotiated
paradoxes threatening to wipe out their own lives.

Always reliant on one another, their bond grew closer as every obstacle
arose. They were more than just a team of Kurinji cosmic warriors; they
were a beautifully tuned instrument, playing their part in the big cosmic
symphony.
Finally victorious, they arrived at the heart of the quantum crucible. They
stood before the source of all existence.
Elder Murali said, in a wonderful voice, "We've made it." "Now comes the
real test."

> *Real-world Correlation:*
>
> ***Multidisciplinary cooperation addressing
> challenging global issues***

Dr Chen, Kavin, Nnenna, Elder Murali and Gopal's combining their many skills to handle the growing hurdles across the Quantum Crucible journey reflects the growing relevance of multidisciplinary cooperation in tackling difficult worldwide problems.

Examples:

Investigation on climate change incorporating ideas from social sciences, economics, and climatology.

Developing artificial intelligence by integrating knowledge of computer science, neurology, and ethics.

Projects involving space examination calling for cooperation among physicists, engineers, and life sciences.

Chapter 12

Forging the Future

The group knew the weight of the occasion as they stood before the realm of pure possibility. Here, down at the core of the quantum crucible, they might change reality itself. Still, such authority came at a heavy price.

"To forge a new future," a voice answered around them, apparently from the sphere itself, "each of you must sacrifice that which you hold most dear."

The group looked at each other, the weight of this insight falling upon them. They understood that everything they gave up would vanish permanently, removed from all conceivable reality.

Kavin was the first to step forward. "I sacrifice my leadership," he murmured, his voice calm even in his eyes' agony. "The ability to carry the weight of command and make judgements for others." As he spoke, they could feel the mantle of leadership sliding from his shoulders and melting into the sphere.

Then Dr. Chen proceeded. "I sacrifice my scientific certainty," she said. She expressed her belief in the ease of measuring and justifying everything. Her profound understanding appeared to come out of her, complementing Kavin's sacrifice in the field.

With tears in his eyes, Gopal responded, "Great crocodiles, I surrender my innocence." He was able to observe the world with awe, free from the harshness of reality. His young vitality faded, then a more subdued knowledge took front stage.

Elder Murali came forward. "I sacrifice my accumulated wisdom," he answered quietly. "The Kurinji knowledge acquired during centuries of meditation and study." The air of wisdom that had always been around him dimmed.

Nnenna came last. "I sacrifice my empathic abilities," Nnenna murmured, her voice cracking. "The ability to experience and comprehend the feelings of others." Her link to the multiverse's emotional web ruptured, and for the first time in her life she felt alone.

With each sacrifice, the sphere pulsed with greater strength. The ultimate sacrifice burst into a dazzling blaze of light.

Surrounded by the boundless possibilities of the multiverse, the group discovered they were floating in a void. They could see the malignant development poised to swallow all of life—the Shadow of Entropy. But now, empowered by their sacrifices, they might act.

Their perfect harmony started to change reality. They corrected the forces of creation and destruction, spun fresh threads into the cosmic tapestry, and mended the scars left by the Shadow of Entropy.

It was demanding; they needed every bit of their will and power. Still, they could see the alteration gradually but spreading throughout the multiverse. The shadow withdrew, restoring equilibrium and initiating the development of a new cosmic hierarchy.

***Real-World Correlation:**

Individuals and professionals sacrifice for society's advancement

Kavin, Dr. Chen, Nnenna, Gopal, and Elder Murali personal sacrifices of fundamental elements of their identities to create a brighter future reflect real-world events wherein people or organizations make major personal or professional sacrifices for the advancement of society or during a catastrophe.

Examples:

During pandemics, healthcare professionals tending to patients run the risk of personal health safety.

Whistleblowers sacrificing professional opportunities to expose unethical behaviors or wrongdoing.

Environmentalists giving up luxury or personal freedom to support climate action.

Chapter 13

Realities Convergence

As Kavin, Dr. Chen, Nnenna, Gopal, and Elder Murali descended further into the quantum crucible, the air inside shimmered with an unfamiliar force. Every stride appeared to thin the barriers of reality, the familiar giving way to the remarkable. The area surrounding them burst suddenly into a brilliant show of color and light. Kavin stammered, briefly confused. He yelled, "What's happening?" His voice echoed oddly in the changing surroundings. Dr. Chen reviewed her quantum scanner, and her eyes became wide with wonder. "It's incredible," she said. "We are seeing many times converge. The distances separating reality are collapsing!"

Before their eyes, fragments of other universes started to flow into their own. Transfixed, Kavin watched as a version of Kurinji materialized alongside their familiar village, never discovering the location of the unbreakable cosmic egg. The structures were different in this other reality; the technology was less developed, and the residents' features lacked any hint of the cosmic consciousness that had changed their own planet.

"Look over there, great crocodiles!" Gopal pointed to another shimmering object in the air and yelled. A bustling metropolis emerged, with futuristic Kurinji fully harnessing the power of the unbreakable cosmic egg. Flying cars zoomed between tall towers, seemingly defying the rules of physics.

Dr. Chen tapped her gadget with determination, entering data. "Every one of these realities reflects a different decision, a different road our planet could have followed," she said. "It's a living map of quantum prospects!" Nnenna gasped and collapsed to her knees. Elder Murali hurried to be by her side, worry clearly on his face. What's wrong, Nnenna?

She said, "The emotions." Her voice strained. "I can sense them all right now. I am aware of every joy, every sorrow, every apprehension, and every triumph stemming from our numerous incarnations. It's... overwhelming."

Kavin dropped down next to her and rested a consoling hand on her shoulder. "Give my voice the first attention, Nnenna. Find your center in our reality.

Gopal approached the shimmering image of Kurinji, who had never discovered the unbreakable cosmic egg, while Nnenna struggled to maintain her composure. Gopal's drowsy eyes followed the simplicity of that untouched planet.

"Gopal, no!" Dr. Chen yelled as he observed his trance-like condition. She raced forward, snatching his arm just as he was about to enter the other world. "Crossing over is unknown as to what might follow. You might find yourself imprisoned there, or even worse, experience a catastrophic breakdown of both realities"!

Blinking to resist the hypnotic influence of the other world, Gopal murmured, "Great crocodiles," and apologized. "It just seemed to be really beautiful. A Kurinji free of the cosmic responsibility."

Elder Murali gave his beard careful strokes. Perhaps this is one of the risks that come with this convergence." "We aspire to choose a simpler path, hoping to overcome our challenges.

Kavin nodded solemnly. "However, those same difficulties have helped us be ready for this time. We still cannot forget that."

As the group rebuilt, the kaleidoscope of reality continued to whirl around them. The eyes of Dr. Chen sparkled with instant inspiration. She said, "Wait a moment." "This convergence... may be the key to understanding the Shadow of Entropy!"

"How is that?" Fascinated, Kavin questioned.

"Look here," Dr. Chen gestured to an especially sinister and distorted interpretation of their world. "This chronology appears to be approaching the shadow from farther forward. Analyzing it would help us to get an important understanding of its shortcomings and behavioral patterns."

Having recovered her cool-headedness, Nnenna closed her eyes deliberately. "I can sense it," she said quietly. "I can sense the fear, the hopelessness on that planet." Nevertheless, a glimmer of hope remains. "I'm still fighting, even now."

Gopal's eyes gleamed with enthusiasm. "Great crocodiles! We could see which strategies worked and which failed in their battles!"

Elder Murali said, "We have to walk softly. Observing is one thing; intervening with these other times might have terrible results."

Kavin nodded in line. Elder Murali is right; we need to figure out how to compile data without jeopardizing the stability of these facts—or our own."

As if in reaction to their conversation, the junction of reality started to change faster. Timelines mixed and blended, the borders between universes becoming progressively thinner.

"It's accelerating," Dr. Chen said with a tight, worried tone. "We have not much time before the convergence approaches a turning point."

Kavin inhaled deeply, straightening himself for the task ahead. "Ok, everyone. This presents us with an opportunity to overcome the Shadow of Entropy. Still, we must be cautious and quick. Dr. Chen, focus on collecting information from the most relevant timelines. Nnenna, use your empathetic abilities to guide us towards the reality that may hold the most crucial knowledge. Gopal, look for any trends or deviations in the interaction of these universes. Elder Murali, we will need your wisdom to guide our interpretation of our findings."

Kavin felt both excitement and fear as the group sprang into action. They were on a tightrope between the possibility of losing everything they loved and unbounded knowledge. One mistake may pull their whole lives apart.

However, Kavin experienced optimism as he observed his companions at work; their determination was evident. They had previously overcome obstacles and emerged stronger. Reality convergence may save their planet and all life, but it's dangerous.

Kavin joined his team in investigating the whirlpool of possibilities, each second bringing them closer to the information they needed... and to the last showdown with the Shadow of Entropy that loomed on the horizon with fresh intent.

Real-world Correlation:

Predictive modelling and big data analysis in approaching world Problems

Dr Chen, Kavin, Nnenna, Elder Murali and Gopal's attempt to examine many convergent realities to fight the Shadow of Entropy reflects the use of predictive modelling and big data analysis in handling difficult global problems on our planet.

Examples:

Climate scientists using vast amounts of information and models to forecast and mitigate the effects of climate change.

By analysing global health statistics, epidemiologists can predict and prevent the spread of diseases.

Using big data, financial experts forecast market patterns and help to avert possible economic calamities.

Chapter 14

Final Countdown

The group gathered for what they knew may be their last stand, and the Quantum Crucible pulsed with a terrible intensity. In the middle, Kavin stood facing the holographic projections of allies from all over the universe, his face marked with determination. "The Shadow of Entropy is making its last push," he continued, his voice firm despite the weight of the situation. "We've found disruptions in over a thousand realities. Ignoring it now will cause the cascading effect to be unstoppable."

Dr. Chen's fingers sped across her quantum interface; complicated mathematics whirled around her. "We have distilled the entropy equation to its most powerful form," she said. However, no one has ever attempted to run it on this scale before.

"Great crocodiles", Gopal, his youthful face set with a maturity beyond his years, said. Gopal added, "Every simulation we could perform is now complete. Although the margins for error are minuscule, should we be successful, we can construct a multi-dimensional barrier against the shadow."

Deeply in meditation, Nnenna's awareness grew to include the emotional condition of innumerable worlds. She said, her voice distant, "I sense great fear. But also hope. There are natural compartments of resistance emerging against the approaching gloom."

Surrounded by relics and old books, Elder Murali gazed up with a glitter in his eye. "I think I have something," he replied. "An ancient prophecy referring to a 'harmony of spheres' capable of opposing the giant devourer." It exactly fits our arrangement!

Alarms started to blare as the group worked furiously to finish their preparations. As entire sections began to fade into oblivion, the multiverse's holographic display took on an ominous red hue.
Dr. Chen yelled over the noise, "It's happening faster than we predicted."
"The shadow is getting closer to our defenses!"
Kavin coordinated their multi-dimensional partners, and his thoughts flew. "Concentrate your efforts on stabilizing your local reality clusters," he said. "We will manage the core breach from here!"

As Gopal corrected their quantum array last minute, his hands blurred. "Diverging power from stable realities to shore up weak ones," he yelled. "Great crocodiles, although it's a risk, it might pay for the time we need!"

Suddenly, Nnenna gasped, her eyes springing wide. She spoke of a "wave of despair sweeping through the outer realities." "Our partners will lose the will to fight if it reaches the core!"
Elder Murali moved forward, his voice echoing with old strength. "Then we have to inspire them," he said. He began to chant in a Kurinji's language older than time; his words connected with the basic vibrations of the cosmos.

As the chant gained strength, Nnenna sensed changes in the cosmic emotional terrain. She exhaled, "It's working." "The despair is being pushed back!"

Their little triumph was fleeting, however. Launched with a powerful attack, the Shadow of Entropy tore through their outer defenses like tissue paper.

"Final countdown initiated," Dr. Chen said, her voice taut with conflict. "Two minutes remain until the total collapse of multiple universes!"

Kavin's thoughts flew through possibilities, throwing out ideas as soon as he developed them. "We must coordinate our efforts," he yelled over the anarchy. "Nnenna, can you connect all of us sympathetically?"

Nnenna nodded and closed her eyes deliberately. The group suddenly felt their consciousnesses combine, ideas and feelings flowing between them unhindered.

Dr. Chen's scientific genius and Gopal's natural understanding of quantum physics blended through their shared consciousness. Kavin's strategic intellect absorbed Elder Murali's old knowledge. And at the core of it all, Nnenna's sensitivity tied them together, linking them not only to each other but to the fundamental fabric of the universe itself.

" Thirty-seconds!" Dr. Chen's voice rang over their common minds.

One by one, the group began implementing their strategy. Kavin shored up flaws and took advantage of the Shadow's weaknesses by guiding the flow of energy between worlds. Using the entropy equation like a knife, Dr. Chen and Gopal surgically precisely removed contaminated bits of reality.

Elder Murali's chant peaked; every syllable was now a directive to reality itself. Nnenna stretched her sympathetic skills to their farthest extent, supporting their efforts with the combined emotional power of many entities.

"Ten seconds!" Their imaginations repeated the countdown.

Sensing its approaching loss, the Shadow of Entropy made a last, frantic attack. As the powers of anarchy threatened to swallow everything, reality itself appeared to scream.
Five... four... three...
In the last minutes, Kavin decided. Using the combined might of his team and their multiverse friends, he drove himself directly into the core of the Shadow.
"Two... One..."
All around was a bright blast of light. There was only stillness for a period that seemed endless.

Then reality started to establish itself gradually. Exhausted but alive, the Kurinji heroes discovered they were back in the Quantum Crucible. The holographic display displayed the multiverse, bruised but whole.
"We... we did it, great crocodiles" Gopal said with awe in his voice.

Dr. Chen looked over her readings with a skeptical smile on her face. "We have driven the Shadow of Entropy back to the furthest margins of the multiverse." We have not destroyed it, but we have somewhat undermined it.
Tears of delight gleamed in Nnenna's eyes. "I sense it. A surge of happiness and relief permeates reality".

Elder Murali laid a hand on Kavin's shoulder. "My friend, you really took a big risk. But it paid off.

Kavin nodded, his gaze reflecting the weight of what they had achieved. "We have won this struggle," he stated gravely. However, our work is far from over. Guardians will be required of the multiverse to preserve this new equilibrium; the multiverse will require guardians.

Kavin, Dr. Chen, Nnenna, Gopal, and Elder Murali realized their greatest adventure was only just starting as they gazed out at the enormous swath of reality they had preserved. Although the last countdown had passed, the cosmos would be permanently resonant with the echoes of their acts.

Real-World Correlation:

Worldwide cooperative efforts to handle difficult and multifarious problems

Kavin, Dr. Chen, Nnenna, Gopal, and Elder Murali collaborated to neutralize the Shadow of Entropy across different realities, replicating worldwide collaboration efforts to confront serious, complex crises threatening mankind or the planet.

Examples:

Worldwide initiatives to counteract climate change including the Paris Agreement.

The creation and dissemination of COVID-19 vaccinations as part of the global collaboration in responding to a pandemic.

Multinational space projects working on challenging missions, such as the International Space Station.

Chapter 15

Revisited Quantum Crucible

The multiverse teetered on the brink of collapse, drawing Kavin, Dr. Chen, Nnenna, Gopal, and Elder Murali back to the core of their cosmic journey, the Quantum Crucible. The once-familiar chamber now throbbed with an intensity that made reality itself tremble, its walls glistening with equations and probability flows.

Kavin stood in the middle, his eyes mirroring the whirling forces around him. He said, "It's changed," reaching out to touch a floating sign. "Or possibly we have."

Dr. Chen nodded, fingers bouncing over her quantum interface. "The Crucible is responding to our enhanced awareness. It's... changing with us."

The group dispersed to study the changed area and saw how the Crucible appeared to predict their ideas, moving and rearranging to provide pertinent tools and data.

Gopal, his young enthusiasm subdued by wise experience, shouted from a corner. "Great crocodiles, See this! We can see all our decisions and road turns"!

Gathering around, the others watched as their entire journey unfolded before them in an almost infinite range of quantum possibilities.

Nnenna closed her eyes, her sympathetic senses reaching to surround the emotional echoes of their decisions. "Every choice I feel weighs the ripples they sent across reality."

Elder Murali gave his beard careful strokes. "Perhaps this is the true purpose of the Crucible—not just a tool for cosmic manipulation but a mirror for self-reflection."

A deeper exploration of the new form of the Crucible revealed levels of use they never would have thought possible. Kavin discovered he could just think of how to replicate intricate multiverse events. Dr. Chen revealed harmonics resonating across dimensions, adding new depths to the entropy equation.

Always fast to pick up new ideas, Gopal started to tinker with the fabric of reality itself, building little pocket-sized worlds and seeing them vanish. "Great crocodile, we are seeing the source code of life," he said in wonder.

But along with this increased authority came a frightening awareness. With a pale face, Nnenna turned her gaze towards the others. "Should we succeed in this, the Shadow of Entropy will follow suit Like us, learning is adaptation".

The atmosphere in the Crucible changed, the weight of obligation replacing the thrill of discovery. They came to see that their most vulnerable point and weapon were also this improved quantum crucible. As Dr. Chen reported, "I'm detecting anomalies in the quantum field," her voice was taut with strain. The Shadow probes, searching for flaws. Kavin's natural leadership came on. "We must strengthen the Crucible so it might act as a bastion against the anarchy."

Every team member offered their own abilities as they worked hard to strengthen their cosmic fortress. By weaving intricate quantum algorithms, Dr. Chen and Gopal developed layers of defense that moved and changed. Nnenna used her sympathetic abilities to create an early warning system tailored to the Shadow's emotional profile.

Drawing on cosmic truths and ancient knowledge, Elder Murali started chanting in a historical Kurinji's ancient tongues. His comments appeared to fit the Crucible's very structure, giving its defenses a force beyond simple science.

Kavin organized their activities; his improved cosmic awareness let him view the whole picture. He helped them design not just a shield, but also a dynamic, living defense that could develop and expand.

As they worked, the group sensed the Crucible shifting around them, transcending a mere place or instrument. It was becoming a junction of possibilities—a fulcrum around which the multiverse's destiny could pivot.

As they worked, hours melted into what seemed like days, stretching themselves to the boundaries of their capacity and beyond. At last, worn out but victorious, they stood back to check their work.

Now pulsing with a subtle force, the quantum crucible was unseen but felt. It had evolved into a stronghold of reality, a barrier against the Shadow's encroaching anarchy.

"It's beautiful," Nnenna said, feeling the harmonic energies around them. Gopal nodded in accord. "Great crocodile, we have essentially turned it into a heart for the multiverse. Anywhere one can maintain equilibrium." Scientific enthusiasm gleamed in Dr. Chen's eyes. "And beyond that. This is a lab where we can continue to learn about cosmic forces".

Elder Murali grinned, a clearly very satisfied expression on his face. "My people and I have left a legacy for our beautiful land and the whole universe. We have established a foundation for future guardians of realities to build upon".

Looking around at his team members, Kavin felt love and pride swell. They had taken the Quantum Crucible, the center of their amazing trip, and turned it into something beyond even their most vivid fantasies.
"This is more than just a defensive measure," he continued, his voice resounding with strong wiliness. "This is our line on the shore. From here, we march the struggle into the shadow."

The Crucible throbbed with vitality, screens, and holographic projections bursting to life around him. They saw worlds in danger, cosmic imbalances in need of repair, and tantalizing secrets yet to be revealed.

The group looked at one another, a mixture of exhilaration and fear. They understood that yet to come were the toughest obstacles. Here, in their returned and rejuvenated quantum crucible, they felt prepared to meet anything the universe would throw at them.
Kavin squared his shoulders, a grin flashing on his lips. "Well, everyone. Should we now begin our work?

As they slipped into roles that appeared both familiar and shockingly new, they realized that this repeated quantum crucible was more than simply a turning point in their journey as they progressed to their stations. It served as the launching pad for their last, universe-shifting trip.

The multiverse shook on the brink of anarchy, but at the heart of the quantum crucible, hope burned more brilliantly than ever. Equipped with the strength of a reinforced Crucible and the unwavering links of their friendship, the last fight was fast coming, and they would confront it head-on.

Real-World Correlation:

Constant Technological System Development and Adaptation to Meet Changing Global Problems

Kavin, Dr. Chen, Nnenna, Gopal, and Elder Murali improve the Quantum Crucible to meet the changing Shadow of Entropy, which mimics the continuous evolution and adaptation of technology systems in the real world to solve developing global concerns.

Examples:

Constant updates to cybersecurity systems help

combat ever-changing cyberthreats.

From a military communication tool to a worldwide information and commercial platform, the Internet has evolved.

The United Nations evolved to handle evolving world problems outside of its initial post-war peacekeeping assignment.

Chapter 16

Redemption and sacrifices

The Quantum Crucible rocked fiercely as reality itself seemed to fray. The Shadow of Entropy loomed larger than ever, with its tendrils of anarchy touching several spheres. The group stood in the center of the cosmic maelstrom with somber expressions, knowing everything was on the line.

Kavin's quantum communicator hummed to life, the elders of Kurinji's voice piercing through the stillness. "Kavin, the shadow is coming towards our world! We need your assistance!"

Kavin's heart tightened as Dr. Chen's voice broke in, "We cannot veer our attention! Should we fail to maintain the line here, the whole universe will collapse!"

Kavin felt the weight of leadership descend on him, unlike ever before. Closing his eyes, he saw his beloved Kurinji village—where it all started—threatened with extinction. But all around him, many other realities begged for redemption.

"I...Kavin said, his voice breaking. I'm sorry. We must keep following the road. Kurinji... Kurinji may have to fend for itself."

The agony of his choice showed itself on his face, a mute homage to the house he could be sacrificing for the sake of others.

Dr. Chen stood before a holographic version of the entropy equation across the Crucible. Her hands hung over the controls, quivering just slightly.

"If I make these changes," she said, "it might equip us to challenge the Shadow. However, the equation would go beyond all known constraints. The effects might include..."

"catastrophic...?" Gopal's youthful voice strains as he concludes.

Dr. Chen nodded; her scientific mind struggled with the urgent necessity for action. "In fact, it runs against what I know as a scientist: "To deploy a theory without appropriate testing is to risk reality itself with an untested idea."

Elder Murali's quiet voice interrupted her agitation. "Sometimes, Dr. Chen, wisdom lies in understanding when to take a risk."

Dr. Chen made her decision after taking a deep breath. Her fingers pushed the entropy equation to its limits, extending beyond the knobs.

Gopal, meanwhile, saw he was face-to-face with a dark mirror of himself. His eyes' purity gave way to a jaded, cynical view.

"This is what you'll become," the shadow Gopal snipped. "Your childhood, your wonder, and your hope are the price of success."

Though he was crying, Gopal held his ground. "Great crocodile, if that is the price required to save everyone, I accept."

Nnenna and Elder Murali labored nonstop on the war's margins, while Gopal's innocence appeared to disappear, and a wisdom beyond his youthful age took center stage. They travelled across worlds, providing comfort and atonement to those the Shadow had swayed.

As Nnenna touched the brains of many entities, her empathic capacity peaked. "There's always a choice," she said, her words spanning many spheres. "It's never too late to choose the right path".

Elder Murali's age-old knowledge matched Nnenna's compassion. He spoke of cycles, of equilibrium, of the continuous dance between light and shadow. His comments identified people who had lost their direction and provided a road to unity.

As the battle neared its peak, the group came to realize dreadful realities. The Shadow of Entropy had compressed its core into a singularity—a point of unbounded anarchy, ready to destroy all of life.

"There's only one way to stop it," Dr. Chen remarked, sounding empty. "Someone has to bring the totally liberated entropy equation to the center of the singularity." It would imply definite oblivion for whoever travels there.

The group slipped into a quiet heaviness. Despite their understanding of the necessary actions, the cost was inconceivable.

Kavin moved forward, his face fixed with purpose. "I'll walk over. As the leader, it's my duty."

"No, great crocodile" Gopal said, his youthful face wrinkled with an age more than years. "It has to be me."

Shock compelled the group to turn to him. With tears in her eyes, Nnenna extended her arms. "Gopal, you cannot!"

Gopal, however, remained strong. "I have seen what I may lose—the innocence. Still, this is a decision I make with all the wonder and optimism I still carry. Allow my sacrifice to signify something".

Gopal snatched the entropy equation core and surged into the singularity before anybody could stop him. Watching him disappear into the center of chaos seemed to pause time.

Not a single thing happened for a second. Then, from the singularity, a flash brighter than a thousand suns emerged. Feeling reality change all around them.

As the light darkened, Entropy's shadow vanished. Then, as Gopal floated, he underwent a transformation. His eyes mirrored the depths of space itself, and his physique shimmered with cosmic vitality.

"Gopal?!" Kavin's whispers reached out tentatively.

Gopal smiled, filled with the wonder of the universe. "Great crocodile, I am more than I was. I have united with the cosmic equilibrium."

Everyone felt the weight of their sacrifices and the agony of their decisions. But they also had a deep feeling of atonement—facing their worst moments and coming out transformed but whole.

Kavin stared back at his team before looking out at the rebuilt universe. "We have all lost something today," he added quietly. "But we have also acquired something rather valuable. We now have a deeper understanding of what it truly means to be a Kurinji hero."

Standing together in the Quantum Crucible, permanently altered by their sacrifices and decisions, the group understood that their greatest obstacle lay not in confronting outside dangers but in reconciling the heroes they had become with the persons they once were. Even though they were just beginning their journey of redemption, the multiverse remained intact.

Real-world correlation:

Making ethical decisions in global crisis contexts

Gopal, Kavin, Dr. Chen, Nnenna, and Elder Murali struggle with tough decisions, personal sacrifices, and transforming events in the face of cosmic threats reflects the difficulties encountered in the real-world during crises, when ethical decision-making sometimes entails major personal or group sacrifices for the benefit of all.

Examples:

Military chiefs deciding on tactics that can cause fatalities to achieve strategic goals.

Political leaders, amid economic crises, take difficult yet required decisions.

388

Scientists debating whether to publish potentially hazardous scientific results to benefit society.

Chapter 17

Modifying reality

The Quantum Crucible buzzed with an intensity the crew had never known. The entropy equation shone at its core with an ethereal light, its intricate symbols moving and realigning as if living. Gopal, Dr. Chen, Nnenna, Elder Murali and Kavin stood in a circle around it, their expressions a combination of will and wonder at the challenge ahead.

Kavin inhaled deeply, centering himself. Looking at every one of his friends in turn, he questioned, "Are we ready?"

As her hands floated over her quantum interface, Dr. Chen nodded. "The equation is ready. We have one chance at this".

With a determined youthful face set, Gopal said, "Great crocodile, I've mapped out the important junctures in the cosmic code. We have to strike them all at once".

Nnenna closed her eyes and stretched her sympathetic senses. "The multiverse seems to be breathing right now. It's... here for us".

Elder Murali put a firm hand on Kavin's shoulder. "Remember, son. We repair reality, not try to rule it. Let that goal guide your actions".

Kavin nodded, then moved forward to touch the shining equation. His mind suddenly expanded, racing forth to cover many worlds. In a disorienting kaleidoscope, galaxies, dimensions, and whole worlds whirled through his head.

"Now!" he yelled, his voice resonating across the worlds.

Dr. Chen and Gopal flew their hands over their interfaces. Working in perfect unity, they made hundreds of cosmic code corrections per second. As they rebuilt the fundamental rules of life, reality itself appeared to flutter and wobble around them.

Kavin felt the changes washing through his enlarged consciousness. Stars rekindle, dead planets come back to life, and the wounds the Shadow of Entropy caused start to heal. But he also suffered from carrying so much of reality in his head.

"Kavin!" Nnenna's voice broke through the anarchy. "Don't let yourself fall apart! Recall who you are and why we are doing this!"

Elder Murali was the source of his cool demeanor. "Observe your core values, son. Your morals, your humanity. They are your lighthouse amid this tempest".

With the support of his fellow group members, Kavin significantly increased his productivity. He created a channel for the universe's will, guiding its need for peace and balance.

The real world kept changing around the group as they worked. Entire galaxies flickered out of existence, then reappeared seconds later in more steady forms. The lines between realms became hazy, enabling the multiverse's energy to flow more harmonically.

Dr. Chen said, her voice straining, "We are at a turning point! The next several adjustments will determine the shape of the new cosmic order!"

"Great crocodile, I see patterns developing," Gopal said, his fingers blurring across his interface. "The multiverse seems to be learning from our changes and adjusting as well!"

Suddenly, Nnenna gasped, her sympathetic senses overwhelmed. "I can sense it—the delight of creating universes, the pleasure of liberating reality from the shadow's control. Still, fear also exists. Some entities find the changes we are making frightening."

Elder Murali calmly said, "Change is always frightening, even if it's for the better. We must show them the beauty of this new equilibrium'.

Kavin came to realize that his thoughts extended beyond the expanse of life. He considered how he would weave amazement and optimism into the fabric of the new reality. He presented the multiverse entities with glimpses of the harmony and possibilities that were waiting for them. The group sensed a change in the fundamental basis of reality as the last bits of the new cosmic order came together. The entropy equation pulsed twice before settling into a consistent, harmonic light.

Kavin started to slowly, deliberately pull his awareness from the vastness of the cosmos. As he did, he sensed reality cementing in place the new rules and systems.

Kavin gasped, then opened his eyes to see his group back in the quantum crucible. Though tired, they all seemed excited.

"Great crocodile, did it... did it, did it work?" In a whispery voice, Gopal posed the question.

Dr. Chen looked over her readings. "It's... rather gorgeous. Perfect balance is the word to describe the entropy equation. The multiverse's natural cycle has neutralized and incorporated the shadow in".

Tears of delight gleamed in Nnenna's eyes. "I feel it. I sense a tranquil sense of perfection that permeates all reality.

Elder Murali nodded softly and wisely. "We gave entropy direction rather than eradicating it. Death and rebirth, anarchy and order, all coexist harmoniously".

With his head still whirling from the event, Kavin gazed out at the new world they had created. "We have done something quite amazing here," he added gently. But this authority carries immense responsibility. We'll have to monitor and steer this new cosmic order as it develops".

The group stood together in awe of their accomplishments and realized their journey was far from over. Their modifying of reality itself created a new cosmic order. However, raising this new universe to maintain their equilibrium would be the real challenge.

A reminder of the enormous power they had exercised and the responsibility that followed, the Quantum Crucible pulsed softly around them. Their most significant journey as guardians of this new world was just beginning.

Real-World Correlation:

Large-Scale Measures Taken in Complex Systems

Dr. Chen, Nnenna, Elder Murali, Gopal and Kavin efforts to alter cosmic laws to change reality reflect actual attempts to interfere in intricate global systems to solve important problems, balancing many elements and thinking through long-term effects.

Examples:

Using geoengineering ideas to help in fighting climate change like Solar radiation control.

Globally applicable financial rules meant to avert economic catastrophes and advance stability.

Undertaking large-scale ecological restoration projects, such as rebuilding coral reefs or rewilding efforts.

Chapter 18

Eternal Recursion

Standing in the core of the Quantum Crucible, Nnenna, Dr. Chen, Elder Murali, Gopal and Kavin still felt the freshness of their recent triumph. But a different feeling started to flood them as the adrenaline receded. The air shimmered with an ethereal force, and reality itself appeared to ripple around them.

Kavin was the first to see it. "Something's changed," he remarked, his voice quiet with respect. "It's like... I can see behind our reality."

Dr. Chen's quantum scanner began to emit a succession of quick beeps. Her eyes became wide as she worked through the statistics. "This is amazing," she said. "We are discovering recursive patterns in the fabric of spacetime itself."

Her words seemed to set off the walls of the Crucible, which melted to expose a vast swath of reality in all directions. Though marginally different, every world reflected its own exactly. The group found themselves fixated on several iterations of themselves, each involved in their own cosmic struggle.

With his little face ablaze with astonishment, Gopal gestured to a reality close by. "Great crocodile, See! In that one, we never came across the unbreakable cosmic egg. And then, at the Crossroads of Destiny, we veered another way!"

Closing her eyes, Nnenna reached into this other multiverse consciousness with her sympathetic senses. "I can feel them," she said softly. "I can feel every variation of ourselves, every decision we have ever taken or might have made," she said softly. "All of these are occurring concurrently."

Elder Murali gave his beard careful strokes. "The old books mentioned this. In the Eternal Recursion, every possibility exists in an endless cycle".

As they worked through this new perspective, the group began to see trends emerging in the sea of endless realities. Some events seemed to recur on many timelines, generating nodes of convergence.

Examining the patterns, Dr. Chen's fingers sped across her quantum interface. "These convergence points," she said, "are like cosmic constants. Regardless of our decisions, certain events are meant to happen."

Realizing the consequences, Kavin felt a shiver go down his back. "The Shadow of Entropy," he said gently. "Isn't this one of these constants? No matter what we do, we will inevitably face it".

The Crucible's atmosphere darkened as the weight of this insight sank in. Still always the optimist, Gopal saw something in the trends that sparked optimism once again.

"Great crocodile, but look here!" he said, pointing to a glittering thread straying over many worlds. "We push back the shadow! in any timeline where we stand together, honoring our beliefs".

More attentively, they looked at this thread, and they realized that their bond—their unflinching friendship and common goal—was itself a cosmic constant. It was the secret to their success in all the universes.

This revelation motivated the group to investigate the recursive patterns closer. They discovered they could interact with their other selves and impart knowledge and experience across the worlds.

Excitement filled Dr. Chen's eyes. "If we can arrange our efforts across several timelines, we might be able to build a multiverse defense network against the Shadow!"

Nnenna nodded, her sympathetic skills expanding to encompass this heightened awareness. "I can aid in enabling the emotional link between our many selves. Build a bridge of understanding across reality".

Elder Murali closed his eyes, relying on the knowledge of many lives. "And I can guide us through the moral conundrums that such acts create." We have to be cautious not to impede the natural causation flow."

Kavin saw a dramatic shift in his perspective on their purpose as they sought to create this hitherto unheard-of multiverse alliance. "We're not just fighting for our reality anymore," he realized. "We are guardians of the entire recursive multiverse."

In what seemed like an eternity, the group travelled across the countless mirrors of their own journey. Some succumbed to the corrupting power of the shadow, while others triumphed against it in epic fights. Every triumph and loss provided fresh ideas and approaches to use in their own struggles.

But they started to find something alarming as they descended farther into the Eternal Recursion. Also conscious of these cyclical tendencies was the Shadow of Entropy. It had learned to take advantage of certain timelines, building power with every cycle.

"We have to stop the cycle," Kavin said, his voice resounding with will. "Find a way to stop the recursion and open another road."

The group gathered close together, their brains ablaze with ideas. They understood that the decisions they made going forward might reverberate throughout many worlds, potentially altering the overall path of the universe.

Dr. Chen suggested using the entropy equation to create a cascade impact throughout time. Gopal suggested exploring ways to merge the best aspects of multiple worlds. Nnenna spoke of their emotional link acting as a stabilizing agent among the tumult of many opportunities.

As they argued and plotted, the endless reflections surrounding them appeared to throb with expectation. The group came to see they were at a pivotal point in the enormous cosmic dance of life itself as much as in their individual journey.

Elder Murali spoke quietly, his eyes gleaming with the knowledge of centuries. "Remember, my friends. Every decision we take in this eternal recursion reverberates beyond eternity. We have to act wisely and with compassion, as well as with bravery."

Looking around at his crew, Kavin saw in their expressions the same combination of astonishment and will that he experienced. They had gone beyond their own reality to see their role in the vast cosmic fabric. And with that understanding came a responsibility beyond anything they had ever experienced before.

His voice was firm. "Whatever we do next, we do it together," he added. We collaborate across all realms and scenarios. Our team's goal is to protect the multiverse without limits."

Their other selves, across endless worlds, reflected their activity as the group worked together. At that moment, there were no more five people from working for Kurinji, they were a multiverse constant—a force of hope and balance that resonated throughout the Eternal Recursion.

The Quantum Crucible surged with vitality, as if the very fabric of reality were appreciating its conclusion.

Though the last fight against the Shadow of Entropy was yet to come, now they confronted it with the combined might and knowledge of countless iterations of themselves.

As they were ready to go on, the group realized they were about to create a new chapter in the cosmic drama—one that would ripple throughout the Eternal Recursion, permanently altering the face of infinity itself.

***Real-world correlation:**

Interconnected global challenges and systems thinking

Nnenna, Dr. Chen, Elder Murali, Kavin and Gopal attempts to coordinate across timelines and identify recursive patterns across worlds reflect the growing awareness of linked global difficulties and the need for systems thinking in handling difficult problems.

Examples:

The Sustainable Development Goals of the United Nations acknowledging the interaction* of social, financial, and environmental problems.

Global supply chain management pondering the ripple effects of local actions on international networks.

Ecosystem-based approaches to environmental preservation respecting the complex relationships within and between ecosystems.

Chapter 19

New Equilibrium

Kavin, Nnenna, Elder Murali, Gopal and Dr Chen gathered around the holographic projection of the multiverse, the Quantum Crucible humming with fresh, harmonic energy. Once threatening to swallow all, the disorderly swirls of entropy were now entwined with streams of creative energy to create a hypnotic cosmic tapestry.

Kavin leaned in, his eyes widening in amazement. Breathing, he watched as whole galaxies danced in perfect balance—"it's... wonderful".

Dr. Chen nodded as her fingers flew across her quantum interface. "Steady is the entropy equation. We now live in a dynamic balance spanning all reality".

Nnenna, Dr. Chen, Elder Murali, Kavin and Gopal started to see minute differences in familiar planets as they explored this other cosmic terrain. Kavin focused the display on Kurinji, his heart skipping a beat when he came to his hometown.

"It's still there," he remarked, clearly relieved. "However, look at that unbreakable cosmic egg we discovered years ago. It's... Changing".

The unbreakable cosmic egg artefact that had begun their journey was indeed throbbing with a soft light, its surface moving and altering in reaction to the new cosmic order.

Dr. Chen concentrated on the various worlds they had visited during their travels. "Fascinating," she said. "Our modifications have cascaded in all directions. After years of strife, worlds are now discovering new ways to coexist".

Glowing with fresh astonishment, Gopal said, "Great crocodile, Look there!" He gestured to a cluster of infant realities in which unusual and amazing forms of life were developing. "It's like the multiverse is dreaming fresh possibilities!"

The infectious enthusiasm of the young Kurinji hero quickly caught the group's attention as they explored the wonders of this new planet. They saw reality in which time ran in loops, realms in which mind and matter were one, and worlds in which the entire idea of uniqueness was erratic and always changing.

Closing her eyes, Nnenna opened her sympathetic senses to this other universe. As she sensed the emotional currents running through many worlds, her lips opened with a grin.

"There's a sense of... peace," she added gently. "Not a lack of conflict, but a deeper harmony. There is an underlying sense that it is all part of a bigger balance while in reality confronting difficulties."

She turned to her colleagues, her eyes glittering with unshed tears. "But there is also uncertainty. Many entities across the multiverse are struggling with these developments. They require direction and understanding".

Elder Murali, stroking his beard, nodded sagely and contemplated the philosophical implications of their actions. "We have rebuilt the very basis of life," he said. "We have taken on a significant responsibility. We are no longer just defenders of truth or Kurinji heroes discovering the secrets of the unbreakable cosmic egg. We have evolved into stewards of cosmic order".

His words' weight dropped over the group. When they looked at each other, they saw wonder, exhilaration, and fear at the work ahead.

Kavin straightened his shoulders and spoke calmly to his fellow Kurinji cosmic heroes "Elder Murali is right. Our job is not done here. In many respects, it's barely beginning. We must help the entities of the multiverse understand and adjust to this new balance".

Dr. Chen nodded in accord. "We will have to create monitoring systems and establish lines of communication across reality. Unexpected effects from our actions may be our responsibility."

Gopal's face flashes with a concept, "Great crocodile, we may establish a cosmic academy! This would serve as a venue for individuals from various parts of the universe to come together, share their knowledge and experiences, and gain insight into this new order".

Nnenna grinned cozily at the young adventurer. "That's a fantastic concept, Gopal. And we can use my empathic skills to reduce emotional and cultural barriers and ease understanding across many worlds".

Elder Murali's eyes glittered with approval. "And I shall compile the wisdom of ages, from throughout all realities, to create a philosophical framework for this new cosmic era."

The holographic display changed to give the team a glimpse of the tasks ahead as they continued to organize and debate their new duties. They saw diplomatic visits to reality grappling with the changes, scientific trips to investigate fresh cosmic events, and spiritual trips to assist entities in finding purpose in this transformed life.

Kavin felt a wave of affection and pride as he gazed around at his family and friends. They had made heartbreaking sacrifices, overcome unthinkable obstacles, and come out not unscathed, but unbroken. They were now on the verge of a new journey that would span infinity.

"Well," he said, a grin playing on his lips, "I believe we had best start now. We're looking at a multiverse".

The Quantum Crucible throbbed with vitality as the group got ready, as if the entire fabric of reality was expressing its approval. Their new equilibrium was more like a live, breathing cosmic dance than a fixed concept. And now they, the unlikeliest of heroes in Kurinji's land, were looking after it.

The day ended with the group leaving the Crucible and entering the expanse of the multiverse, ready to accept their new responsibilities as defenders of the cosmic order. Though the difficulties ahead were great, so were the marvels just waiting for exploration. Their biggest journey, they came to see, was merely starting.

Real-world correlation:

Global oversight and complex system stewardship

Kavin, Nnenna, Elder Murali, Gopal and Dr Chen new role as custodians of cosmic order, managing different realities, and promoting understanding reflects real-world efforts in global governance and international collaboration to manage shared resources and handle common concerns.

Examples:

Multinational research projects like CERN, promoting information sharing across boundaries.

Worldwide health agencies managing responses

to pandemics and emerging new health risks.

International agencies overseeing common

resources such as seas, space, and the internet.

Chapter 20

Tomorrow's Seeds

Rising above Kurinji, the sun gently and goldenly lit its transformed landscape. It was not the same Kurinji that had started their journey years before. The Dr Chen, Kavin, Nnenna, Elder Murali and Gopal had created a visual depiction of the harmony between history and modernity throughout the multiverse, and the once-simple structures now gracefully merge old architecture with future design.

The Kurinji Institute for Multiversal Studies, built just recently, stood in the heart of the community, its crystalline spires softly pulsing quantum energy into the multiverse. The institution had evolved into a lighthouse of information and hope, attracting inquisitive brains from all backgrounds.

Kavin stood in front of a throng of wide-eyed kids from all over the middle atrium. They all showed tremendous enthusiasm, but some possessed tentacles, and others lived somewhat out of sync with conventional spacetime.

"Remember," Kavin remarked, his voice weighted with seasoned knowledge: "the multiverse is fragile, yet enormous and full of marvels. Always consider how your decisions will impact your cosmic adventures". Grinning, he experienced the same thrill he had upon first learning about the unbreakable cosmic egg mirrored in these young people. ""But never lose your sense of wonder. It's the key to unlocking the greatest mysteries of existence".

In the adjacent lab, Dr. Chen hunched over a holographic entropy equation display. Her head was racing with new ideas; she easily altered variables.

"Incredible," she said, as a fresh design developed. "We might be able to generate stable wormholes between realities if we apply this variation of the equation to quantum singularities!"

Her research team, which included people and objects from the multiverse, gathered with tremendous energy. Every discovery exposed new horizons of knowledge; scientific limits were continually expanding.

Gopal led a group of kids on a virtual trip beyond dimensions in an energetic classroom full of interactive cosmic models.

"And here, great crocodile" he remarked, eyes gleaming with the same delight he had as a tiny boy, "is a planet where time runs backwards! Would you like dessert before your main meal?

The youngsters laughed; their imaginations open to the many cosmic possibilities. Gopal grinned, knowing he was sowing questions of inquiry that would sprout in the next generation of cosmic adventurers.

Nnenna led them to distribute their sympathetic senses around the earth as they sat in a quiet meditation garden surrounded by a varied mix of entities.

She softly said, "Fall into the emotional currents of the multiverse. Let your consciousness span outside your own reality."

As the kids showed their brilliance, Nnenna felt a flash of gratification. Her evolved plans included repairing divisions and creating connections between hitherto separate realities, thereby promoting empathy and understanding in many spheres.

Surrounded by old texts and future data sources, Elder Murali investigated in his study the moral implications of their lately acquired cosmic impact. Writing rules for multiverse intervention guaranteed sensible use of their authority.

"With great knowledge comes great responsibility," he said, his pen flying across the page. "We have to avoid turning into the imbalance threat we used to fight."

The group assembled at the location where their adventure had started as the day came to an end—that place where they had originally started the study of the unbreakable cosmic egg. Though the unbreakable egg itself had changed into something more than physical form, it was still there in memory.

Everybody dropped into their own thoughts, creating a circle. To break the silence, Kavin spoke softly and emotionally. "Did anyone ever dream that we would end here when we first discovered the unbreakable egg's bioluminescence nature?" "Entire multiverse guardians!"

Dr. Chen shook her head, grinning sarcastically. "Never" she responded, "considering I would much rather create some incredible scientific discovery than alter the rules of reality".

Gopal laughed; the sound fit his younger self. "Great crocodile, I was looking for a journey of discovery. More than I could have fathom!"

Tears flowed in Nnenna's eyes. "We have all experienced major changes."
We have changed in ways I never would have imagined possible.
Elder Murali nodded intelligently. "And yet, in many cases, we still really
reflect who we have always been. Our experiences have molded us; our
core—our ideals, our friendship—is intact."

As they stood there contemplating their amazing experience, the skies
above them shone. The barrier separating reality gradually opened,
allowing a brief glimpse of the many worlds they had preserved, the
people they had touched, and the miracles they had started.
Kavin inhaled for a long time, feeling the weight and delight of their
obligations. "Our work is far from over," he added, speaking decisively and
hopefully. "The multiverse is always changing and offers fresh chances as
well as difficulties. What adventures could tomorrow bring?
Everyone laughed, each with a fresh perspective. After travelling so far to
overcome such obstacles, they emerged not only triumphant but also
changed. However, they all realized that their most profound experience
was yet to come, in many ways.

As the sun dropped over Kurinji, the group saw the development of
amazing light colors in the stars—not just their own, but all reality. The
cosmos opened out before them, boundless in its potential, begging for
study, preservation, and nurture.
Every person they touched, every reality they rescued, every marvel they
stumbled upon—the unbreakable egg that had begun their cosmic
journey—may have altered beyond identity. Standing there together with
camaraderie and a shared objective, they knew—as they had always

done—that they would meet any future challenges together.

Behind them buzzed the Kurinji Institute for Multiversal Studies, which promised unbounded study and development. And the group saw the reality of their journey deep in their spirits as evening engulfed the Kurinji community.

They were no more just protectors or explorers of the unbreakable cosmic egg. They had become Sowers of cosmic seeds, nurturing the infinite potential of tomorrow.

As darkness descended and the first stars emerged, ready to write the next chapter in their lifetime cosmic trip, they turned as one and walked back to the Institute for Multiversal Studies.

The conclusion of the Kurinji's hero's cosmic trilogy journey is just the beginning of an infinitely long narrative destined to resurface across realities for eternity. The multiverse awaited, and they stepped forward together to meet it.

Real-World Correlation:

Intergenerational Knowledge Transfer and Sustainable Development

Dr Chen, Kavin, Nnenna, Elder Murali and Gopal's responsibility in teaching next generations while still exploring and controlling the multiverse reflects real-world initiatives in sustainable development and passing on information to next generations to handle long-term global issues.

Examples:

Through its Education for Sustainable Development initiative, UNESCO is arming next generations to handle world problems.

Projects aiming at conserving biodiversity for future generations including the Svalbard Global Seed Vault.

413

Intergenerational projects on climate change involving young people in policymaking and action.

Epilogue

Nnenna, Kavin, Dr Chen, Elder Murali, and Gopal stood atop the tallest hill in Kurinji as the first light of dawn emerged over the horizon, showcasing the beautiful sky in gold and pink. The people living in the community below were not aware of the cosmic drama that had just played out.

Free from the weight of leadership, Kavin had a wonderful feeling of calm. He noticed several kids playing far away; their laughter carried on the early wind. "It's strange," he said, "to consider that just days ago their whole existence, all of which was hanging in the balance."

Dr. Chen nodded in agreement, her head still whirling from the quantum crucible's revelations. She gestured to the vivid scene surrounding them and continued, "And yet, look how resilient life is. There's beauty in the simplest events, even if the multiverse may be huge and complicated."

Gopal, his young face now reflecting the wisdom of one who has seen the limitless, grinned. "Great crocodile. I used to think adventure meant travelling to far-off countries or even other planets," he remarked. "Now I realize that every moment, every interaction, is part of the greatest adventure of all—living itself."

Elder Murali rested a hand on Gopal's shoulder; his eyes gleamed with a blend of ancient knowledge and fresh astonishment. "You've learned well, little one. The path of knowledge only takes many shapes; it never really finishes."

Her empathetic skills permanently altered by their cosmic journey, Nnenna closed her eyes and inhaled deeply. She said, "I can still feel it, softly. The symphony of cosmic creation. Though it's fainter today, it's there—in the rustling of leaves, the breezy air coming from the wind, the pounding of hearts, the ebb and flow of life itself."

They noticed subtle changes in their surroundings while they stood there reflecting on their adventure. The colors looked more brilliant, and the air infused with a fresh sort of vitality. Once invisible, the fragile strands of reality might now barely show up to their improved senses.

"We've changed," Kavin remarked, speaking for all of them. "We have transformed everything by changing ourselves."

Dr. Chen nodded immediately, her scientific head whirling with fresh ideas. "The lines separating science from spirituality, between the cosmic and the quantum—they are not as sharp as we originally believed. There is still a lot to learn and discover".

"Great, crocodile, but this time," Gopal grinned, "we won't be saving the multiverse. At least not, I want not. For me, one cosmic catastrophe per lifetime is enough!"

They all laughed, the sound of their happiness resonating throughout the hill—a joyful counterpart to the cosmic symphony now encompassing all of life.

Each deep in contemplation about what the future could bring as the sun rose higher, they made their way back to the Kurinji village square. They had given a tremendous deal, gained significantly more, and emerged consistently transformed. For the time being, the multiverse was secure, but they recognized that life was a constantly evolving story filled with unsolved riddles.

Stopped at the edge of the village, Kavin turned to face his friends and team members. "Whatever comes next," he stated with emotional resonance, "we'll face it together for this community. We should not view ourselves as saviors of the planet or Kurinji heroes, but rather as integral members of Kurinji land, each contributing our unique reality to the grand symphony of life''.

Their hands closed to create a circle, a little replica of the cosmic wheel they had seen in the quantum crucible. At the same time, they were both negligible specks in the vast universe and essential strands in the fabric of reality itself.

Ready to welcome their new responsibilities in this post-crisis world, they entered the village bearing with them the understanding that every decision, every action, and every moment was a brushstroke on the endless canvas of life.

Though in many aspects it was only starting, their outstanding journey had come to an end.

The universe swirled around them, full of choices. And in the middle of Kurinji, the heroes—permanently linked by their journey to the very brink of reality and back—grinned, ready to write the next chapter in their continuous cosmic tale.

Not seen by anyone in the distance, the unbreakable cosmic egg pulsed once—a brief flash of alien light. The cosmos buzzed with fresh music, the echoes of their quest reaching across worlds, evidence of the continuing force of bravery, camaraderie, and the unquenchable spirit of those who dare to aspire for the cosmos.

Five years later, Kavin stood at the entrance of the newly founded Kurinji Institute for Multiversal Studies, a testament to the distance they had come from their cosmic journey. From across the world and even those from other worlds, the once-sleepy Kurinji village had evolved into a hive of learning, attracting inquisitive brains.

The institution itself was a wonder of harmonic architecture, fusing modern technologies with the surrounding landscape's inherent beauty. Its walls appeared to glimmer with a subtle quantum energy, a continual reminder of the fragile equilibrium they now knew closely.

Kavin sensed a familiar presence besides him as he got ready to greet the first round of students. Now the head researcher at the institution, Dr. Chen, grinned friendly. "Can you believe it's been five years already?" she questioned, her eyes mirroring the same astonishment they originally found when they came across the unbreakable cosmic egg.

"In certain respects, it feels like yesterday," Kavin said. "Like a long time ago, in others."

Their faces ablaze with curiosity and excitement, they observed as the students started to assemble. Among them, Kavin saw a handful who reminded him of their earlier selves: a girl with Nnenna's sympathetic eye, a lad with Gopal's unbounded energy, even a couple of students who bickered gently like he and Dr. Chen used to.

Elder Murali, now a revered consultant to the institution, arrived at the door. "The seeds we plant today will bloom into a future full of infinite possibilities," he remarked wisely.

As if on cue, Gopal leapt up, his youthful vitality tamed but not diminished by the years.

"Great crocodile, speaking of seeds!" he continued eagerly. "Wait until you see what we have found in the quantum botany lab! Plants living in many worlds at the same time!"

While quietly watching the assembly, Nnenna stood up. "I can feel their potential," she whispered gently, her sympathetic skills now precisely tuned to the faint energy around them. "So much curiosity and optimism. Just like we were, they are eager to discover the multiverse.

Kavin felt a familiar thrill in the back of his mind as he got ready to speak to the gathered pupils. Their actions permanently altered the cosmic symphony, murmuring of new adventures just ahead. Though the multiverse was large, and new difficulties will surely surface, the shadow of entropy was gone.

For now, however, their mission was to impart their knowledge and equip the next generation for whatever the universe would bring. Knowing that whatever lay ahead, the seeds they were sowing now would blossom into a future full of many opportunities.

Kavin grinned, "Welcome," he said, his voice booming across the courtyard, "to the Kurinji Institute for Multiversal Studies. The journey ahead will take you out of reality and beyond. The universe waits, full of glitches and beauty. And keep in mind that every one of you has a special and essential role to contribute to the magnificent cosmic symphony that has just started in Kurinji land".

Kavin spoke, and the students looked at one another knowingly. Their unstartled biggest journey had brought them to this turning point. The conclusion of one narrative had evolved into the prelude of many more. Not seen by anyone except the Kurinji cosmic heroes, the unbreakable cosmic egg pulsed once again in the distance, a bit stronger this time. Anticipating the next movement in its everlasting symphony, the multiverse buzzed.
It marks the end of Nnenna, Kavin, Dr Chen, Elder Murali, and Gopal unbreakable egg cosmic journey and the start of unlimited opportunities in Kurinji's land.

Cosmic Glossary of the Unbreakable Egg Trilogy providing an explanation of the key concepts used:

Unbreakable Cosmic Egg: *An ancient artifact of unknown origin, containing immense power and the potential to reshape reality.*

Bioluminescent Network: *A living, interconnected web of energy that spans the Earth, allowing for quantum communication and energy transfer.*

Quantum Resonance: *The ability of particles to influence each other across vast distances, defying classical physics.*

Shadow of Entropy: *A malevolent force threatening to unravel the fabric of reality, causing chaos and destruction across the multiverse.*

Fractal Reality: *The concept that patterns in the universe repeat at different scales, from the quantum to the cosmic level.*

Golden Globe Key: *An ancient artifact capable of unlocking the true potential of the unbreakable Cosmic Egg.*

Quantum Stewards: *Individuals trained to navigate and protect the delicate balance of quantum realities.*

Cosmic Guardians: *An evolved form of the Quantum Stewards, tasked with maintaining balance across the multiverse.*

Quantum Harmony Centre: *An organization founded to explore other worlds and establish ethical guidelines for interdimensional interactions.*

Multiversal Tapestry: *The interconnected web of all possible realities and timelines in existence.*

Quantum Probability Engine: *A device capable of calculating and visualizing outcomes across multiple realities.*

Cosmic Harmony: *The delicate balance of forces that maintains the stability of the multiverse.*

Quantum Displacement: *The phenomenon of individuals temporarily shifting into alternate realities.*

Terran-Stellar Beings: *Evolved humans with the ability to manipulate quantum realities and communicate across dimensions.*

Quantum Ecology: *The study of how ecosystems adapt to and incorporate cosmic energies.*

Temporal Resonance: *The ability to perceive and interact with different points in time across multiple realities.*

Unified consciousness: *Evolved state of existence that the main characters in book 11 - Kavin, Dr. Chen, and Nnenna - ultimately achieve.*

Unified being or entity: *Kavin, Dr. Chen, and Nnenna's consciousnesses merge into a single, unified entity that encompasses their combined experiences and knowledge.*

Transcendence of physical form: *The unified being exists as pure energy or consciousness, no longer bound by a physical body.*

Cosmic awareness: *Awareness that spans multiple dimensions,* *realities, and even the entire multiverse.*

Creative power: *The unified being ability to create and manipulate entire universes and realities.*

Timelessness: *Existing outside of linear time, able to experience past, present, and future simultaneously.*

Fractal nature: *The unified consciousness recognizes itself as part of an endless, repeating pattern throughout all levels of existence.*

Continued growth: *The unified being continues to learn, explore, and evolve.*

Connection to all life: *The unified being maintaining a deep connection to and compassion for all forms of life across all realities.*

Guardian role: *The unified being takes on a role of guiding the development of consciousness throughout the multiverse.*

Cycle of creation: *It participates in an endless cycle of creating new realities, each with the potential to develop its own path to unified consciousness.*

Cosmic Nurture Programme: *Earth's initiative to guide and support other planets through their cosmic awakening process.*

Quantum Confluence: *A melding of realities not typically allowed by nature, where multiple versions of characters can interact.*

Stellar Ascendancy: *A movement among young Terran-Stellars who believe they should create independent communities* *separate from conventional humans.*

Quantum Crucible: *A nexus points where the laws of reality can be reshaped, existing at the heart of the multiverse.*

Cosmic Symphony: *The underlying harmonic structure of the universe, representing the interconnectedness of all things.*

Fractal Mind: *The concept that consciousness mirrors the structure of the multiverse, existing at multiple levels simultaneously.*

Entropy Equation: *A mathematical formula describing the balance between order and chaos in the multiverse.*

Quantum Singularity: *A point where quantum effects dominate, allowing for manipulation of fundamental forces.*

Multiversal Convergence: *The theoretical point where all realities merge into a single, unified state of existence.*

Reality Convergence: *The phenomenon where multiple timelines and dimensions begin to intersect and influence each other.*

Cosmic Countdown: *A critical period where the fate of the multiverse hangs in the balance, requiring urgent action from cosmic guardians.*

Adaptive Quantum Crucible: *An evolved form of the Quantum Crucible that responds to and grows with its users' understanding and abilities.*

Cosmic Sacrifice: *The act of giving up something of great personal value for the greater good of the multiverse.*

Reality Rewriting: *The ability to fundamentally alter the laws and structure of the multiverse on a grand scale.*

Eternal Recursion: *The concept that all possibilities exist simultaneously in an infinite loop across the multiverse.*

Cosmic Equilibrium: *A state of perfect balance between creation and entropy across all realities.*

Multiversal Legacy: *The lasting impact of actions and choices that resonate across multiple realities and timelines.*

Cosmic Citizenship: *The state of being aware of one's place in the greater multiverse and taking responsibility for maintaining cosmic balance.*

Quantum Nexus Points: *Areas in the multiverse where multiple realities intersect, allowing for easier travel and communication between dimensions.*

Entropy Wave: *A destructive force emanating from the Shadow of Entropy, capable of unraveling entire realities.*

Cosmic Empathy: *The ability to sense and understand the emotional states of beings across multiple realities.*

Quantum Fortress: *A fortified location existing partially outside normal spacetime, serving as a base of operations for multiversal guardians.*

Temporal Cascade: *A chain reaction of events that ripples across multiple timelines, causing widespread changes throughout the multiverse.*

Cosmic Anchors: *Individuals or objects that help maintain the* stability of reality during times of multiversal upheaval.

Quantum Evolution: The process by which beings adapt to and gain abilities related to manipulating quantum realities.

Harmonic Resonance Chamber: A device or location that amplifies the cosmic symphony, allowing for greater manipulation of multiversal energies.

Entropy Equation Variants: Modified versions of the original Entropy Equation, each with unique properties and applications in maintaining cosmic balance.

Multiversal Cartography: The science and art of mapping the ever-changing landscape of the multiverse.

Cosmic Interface Nexus (CIN): A device built to perceive and interact with higher realms of existence.

Multiversal Ethics Committee: An entity established to create guidelines for ethical multiversal interaction.

Quantum Stewards: Evolved from Quantum Stewards, they became cosmic guardians assigned to guide humanity through new existential terrain while preserving the delicate balance between realities.

Temporal Harmony Council: A body consisting of members from various Earth factions, cosmic allies, and voices from Earth's future, aimed at steering Earth towards a balance between earthly wisdom and cosmic knowledge.

Kurinji Institute for Multiversal Studies: An educational institution in Kurinji founded to teach the next generation about the multiverse and cosmic responsibilities.